SILVERWE

Simon Crook has been a film journalist for over twenty years, visiting film sets and interviewing talent for *Empire* magazine.

A new and exciting voice in domestic horror, he is perfectly placed to translate the recent successes of the genre from the silver screen to the written word – while adding something new and wholly his own.

Praise for *Silverweed Road:*

'Plenty of creepy fun to be had'
GUARDIAN

'Crook has stepped on to the gore-slicked stage with a deliciously gruesome portfolio of twisty tales. You'll find shades of Dahl . . . But what sets the stories apart is the visceral accuracy of the writing, which can infect a garden swimming pool with dread, or quite believably turn a man into a fox'
DAILY MAIL

'Terrifying'
TIMEOUT

'Clever, knowing, and sly'
SAGA

Silverweed Road

SIMON CROOK

HARPER
Voyager

Harper*Voyager*
An imprint of HarperCollins*Publishers* Ltd
1 London Bridge Street
London SE1 9GF

www.harpercollins.co.uk

HarperCollins*Publishers*
Macken House, 39/40 Mayor Street Upper,
Dublin 1, D01 C9W8, Ireland

First published by HarperCollins*Publishers* 2022
This paperback edition 2023

1

A catalogue record for this book is available from the British Library

ISBN: 978-0-00-847997-8

Set in Sabon by Palimpsest Book Production Limited, Falkirk, Stirlingshire

Printed and bound in the UK using 100% renewable
electricity at CPI Group (UK) Ltd

For Polly

Prologue

This is a personal statement from former Detective Chief Inspector Jim Heath. The views expressed do not reflect those of Kent Police nor the victims impacted by events.

'But he looked so normal . . .' I've often heard it said about killers. No doubt you've heard it, too. Perhaps you've mumbled it to yourself, about the likes of X and Y. That neighbour across the street from you. The one who waves as they put the bins out. The one who turns out to have a collection of heads in their fridge.

You could say much the same of Silverweed Road. In many ways, it was a nowhere street, no different to any other across the UK. A quiet cul-de-sac on the Corvid Estate where the houses stopped dead at the edge of the Woods. Flanks of mock-Tudor semis built in the 1950s faced one another across the tarmac. Each with a short gravel driveway. Each with a long back garden.

In my twenty-nine years with Kent Police, I'd never had cause to set foot there. It was just a sleepy street in a sleepy estate on the outskirts of Meadway Town. All that changed in 2019, and that cursed November when Death swept the street.

Five years have passed since those wretched events, when I was scapegoated out of my job. Five years have passed like mud in retirement, and not a single case has been solved.

There were forty-one houses on that dead-end road, and a heartbeat was stolen from every one.

NO. 31:

The Jackdaw

Greenfly, aphids, slugs and snails. Beetles, weevils, mildew and blight. Victor Hagman was at war with them all.

It had been a testing year for the long back garden of 31 Silverweed Road. Having battled through a summer that saw Victor's beloved pear tree struck by brown rot and losing his beetroot to wireworm, there was one last crop before winter cast its cloak over the garden – a final harvest sixty-year-old Victor was determined not to lose.

Shielded in a domed crop cage, nourished by the sun near the high back fence, climbed six canes of late-bloom raspberries – a plump, hardy strain known as Autumn Treasure.

Since flowering in late September, the raspberries had possessed Victor's every waking thought. On extended sick leave after surviving a stroke, the accountant had come to view his garden, not as a strip of land, but a living spreadsheet of columns and rows, each neat crop to be patrolled and obeyed. Even through the failures, Victor's stubborn belief remained: that, through organisation and meticulous inspection, nature would be tamed.

The routine surrounding his Autumn Treasure had curdled into a tour de force of neurosis. He fussed with pea stones and straw at the base, checked for root rot four times a day, polished the copper of the crop cage frame, and spritzed the leaves with Evian.

On a crisp November morning at 6.30 a.m., a shy sun blinking between Silverweed's houses, Victor opened the bedroom curtains and looked out over the long back garden. A tension instantly screwed tight in his chest. A glittering carpet of silver frost had rolled across the lawn – another invader to be crushed. His wife, Patricia, rolled over in bed, shielding her soft green eyes. She focused on her husband's silhouette and groaned into her pillow.

'What is it this time, Victor?'

'Frost again. It's everywhere.'

Within minutes, Victor was on the lawn, crunching towards the crop cage in his green rubber boots. Patricia watched through the bedroom curtains, eyes rolling at the silent comedy being played out by her husband. Wrestling with a cable that snaked from the kitchen, through the back door and across the frosted lawn, Victor uncoiled an extension reel and unzipped the butterfly netting – the only entrance to his domed crop cage.

Foot snagged on the cable, Victor tripped into the netted dome, batting the raspberry leaves from his face. He fussed and flapped, plugged in his wife's hairdryer snatched from the bedroom, and caressed hot air over the canes.

Patricia brushed her long silver hair, wincing at the hairdryer's screams. If she could hear it through the double glazing, what about the rest of the street? *When Roy Barker posts another complaint through the letter box*, she thought, *Victor can deal with him this time*. As she brushed and cringed, a distant chattering joined the hairdryer's screams. Patricia frowned as the sound grew closer. The chattering seemed to circle the house, high above the roof.

Patricia was already making a pot of tea when Victor finally stepped into the kitchen, satisfied the worst of the frost had evaporated. His Autumn Treasure had lived up to its name: ruby-red gems, fit to burst, the berries as fat as his thumb. In two days, Victor's crop would be ready to harvest: a rare gardening victory in a challenging year.

'Panic over?' Patricia asked, keen to get the conversation over with, not much caring for an answer.

'Yes, yes,' said Victor. He plucked a cup from the mug tree and placed it by the teapot. 'Couple of days and they'll be ready to pick.'

'Only you,' said Patricia, 'would blow-dry a raspberry.'

'If you're going to do something,' snapped Victor, hackles up, immediately set on the defence, 'do it properly or don't do it at all.'

Don't do it at all, Patricia wished. *Don't do it at all.* She passed Victor his tea. He'd been so handsome, even in his fifties – now his thin grey hair was in retreat, his earlobes drooped like candle wax, and his chaotic eyebrows reminded her of the dust balls she emptied from the hoover nozzle. And as for the hands that once softly caressed her . . . Since Victor's gardening obsession, his fingernails looked like he was farming mud. The black soil was rooted so deep that Patricia half joked he could grow radishes from his fingertips. Victor couldn't resist correcting her. Cress, maybe. Radishes, impossible.

Patricia watched Victor slurp at his tea. Was it Victor she loved, or the memory of him? The stroke last May had changed her husband. Physically, he'd escaped unscathed, but his internal earthquake had opened new fault lines. With his survival came glimpses of an infallible God complex: when nature didn't agree with him, there were flashes of temper directed at the garden she'd not seen in him before. Dr Gosden had called it 'emotional incontinence', a result of lesions from the stroke, but the explanation didn't make things any easier.

Whenever she looked at the garden, there was a creeping sense of separation; of losing her husband to the deep, black earth.

As Victor headed upstairs for a shower, Patricia took the hairdryer back to the bedroom. She paused at the window, sweeping her eyes over the garden. The busy birdfeeders she'd so enjoyed had been banished by Victor for the sake of his precious raspberries. Nowadays, she'd be lucky to see a bluetit blur past, but this morning, something had caught her attention. Two jackdaws were perched on a branch, lurking on next door's silver birch.

Ever since Victor had banned the feeders, Patricia sought solace in bird books, torturing her husband with trivia. While Victor regarded jackdaws as vermin, Patricia had developed a soft spot for them. The females, after all, were bigger and smarter than the males.

Patricia watched the larger jackdaw preen her partner. As his head bowed in submission, her beak sifted through her lover's nape, feathers rippling in silver waves. Framed by the curtains like a private theatre, the scene struck her as quietly romantic. Didn't jackdaws pair for life? Till Death Do Us Part?

With a shake of the feathers and without a sound, the female jackdaw glided from her branch and landed on the tip of the crop cage housing Victor's raspberries. Her beak explored the zip of the butterfly flap. The jackdaw gave it a brief, firm tug – enough to tease open a tantalising gap.

Not yet finished, she released her claws from the netting, cracked her wings and flapped in mid-air, pulling at the slider. A Y-shaped slit began to open, widening with each tug of the zip. Patricia gasped at the bird's ingenuity.

Across the road, at no. 9, a Mini backfired on the driveway. The startled jackdaw released her grip and quickly abandoned the experiment. Landing on the branch beside her partner, the jackdaw glared at Victor's cage, then slowly turned towards the house.

Separated by the window pane, Patricia locked eyes with the bird. Its unbroken stare seemed to penetrate the glass, looking not at her, but directly *into* her. Patricia's pulse quickened from the sudden connection. Held by the shine of its silver eyes, she pressed a palm to the window pane . . .

Patricia jolted as the bedroom door opened. She turned to see a half-naked Victor, scrubbing his belly with a tiny blue towel.

'What you looking at?' said Victor, nodding at the window.

'Nothing,' said Patricia, anxiously stroking her hair. 'Just daydreaming, Victor. Just daydreaming . . .'

When she turned back to the window, the jackdaws had vanished, the fleeting connection gone. Patricia smiled a curious smile, closed the curtains and undressed for the shower.

Wrapped in a towel, Patricia padded past Victor, unaware of a mark behind the curtains. Where her palm had smeared the glass, an outspread claw scored the pane outside.

*

Birdsong, sharp and frantic.

Victor flashed awake. He looked at the bedside clock. 5 a.m. The dawn chorus wasn't due till March. What were those bloody birds playing at? Victor crashed out of bed. The curtains whipped open. Shadows licked across the lawn. There was movement, towards the rear of the garden. Towards the back fence. Towards the crop cage. Towards his Autumn Treasure.

Shaken from her dreams, Patricia bolted up in bed. The shock of awakening brought a cringe of confusion, heightened by the bite of her husband's voice.

'Intruders,' said Victor.

'Who is it?' gasped Patricia. 'Burglars?'

'Worse,' snapped Victor. 'Birds.'

With a pained moan, Patricia collapsed back to her pillow, cursing each thump as Victor thundered downstairs. Seizing a torch, he marched into the garden.

The birds dispersed in a panic of feathers. The damage had been done. A massacre of raspberries blooded the lawn.

Victor approached the crop cage, torch shaking in his hand. The zip had been lowered from the tip of the dome, allowing a gaping slit – a large, scooping Y, broad enough for the birds to fly in. He wrestled with the zip, yanked it down, and edged into the crop cage.

Victor froze, whimpering at the slaughter within. Even the leaves had been pecked and shredded, hanging like rags from the bending canes. How the hell had the birds got inside?

Stomping from the cage, temper beginning to boil, Victor flashed his torch at a heckling chatter high up on next door's silver birch. Perched on a branch lurked a pair of jackdaws. Their napes were smeared red, as if dipped in blood. Gripped in their claws was a gore of shredded raspberries.

Victor let rip, arms waving, screaming blue murder. The jackdaws stirred and beat their wings, charging into the sky. They soared towards the deep, dark Woods beyond the dead-end of Silverweed Road. Butchered berries wept from their claws.

The mood in no. 31 blackened like a wake. Victor paced in listless circles. His wife's attempts to calm him down were met with stiff rejection. Patricia left for her shift at Meadstone Library, shouting goodbye as the front door shut. Victor didn't reply.

Purging his shock in heaving sobs, he wept alone in the upstairs bathroom. All the power he'd regained since the stroke, the world he'd created, so neat and so ordered, had been wrecked, shredded and ripped to ruins. Wiping his eyes and blowing his nose, Victor felt the force of his grief warp and heat, stolen by a roasting rage.

When he stormed back into the garden, ready to tear down the dome, a cooler voice intervened. *Not yet*, it said. *Wait*, it said. Victor zipped back the opening to its drooping Y, leaving the crime scene as he'd found it. There were still scraps of wounded raspberries, dripping half-pecked from the canes. Bait, decided Victor, to lure back the culprits.

Two hours into his garden stakeout, leaning stock-still on the window ledge above the kitchen sink, Victor tensed to a distant chattering. He put down a half-nibbled chicken sandwich and fixed his eyes on the crop cage.

Two black jackdaws landed on the dome. The smaller bird perched on the tip, playing lookout. The larger jackdaw hooked its claws into the butterfly mesh, working its way around to the zip. Slider gripped in its beak, the jackdaw flapped away from the crop cage, pulling down the zip in bumping jolts.

So that's how they did it. Thieving bloody jackdaws . . .

Victor ran screaming into the garden, chasing the birds back into the sky. He watched them shrink to jagging dots, confident they'd soon return.

Victor quickly dismantled the crop cage, pulled out the canes, and placed them on the lawn, ten feet from the kitchen window. Juice wept from the wounded raspberries, dripping from the canes and bloodying the grass.

Upstairs in the spare room, Victor snapped the lid from a storage box and rummaged through the bric-a-brac of his youth. During his early twenties, Victor would often spend Sundays with his father, stalking the Kent Downs on Detling Hill, hunting rabbits to cook for supper.

'Gotcha.'

Victor pulled out the Black Widow catapult that had served him so well back then. After testing the snap of the yellow rubber, he marched down to the kitchen. Silver ball bearings clinked in his palm.

The trap was set. Victor glared out of the window, drooping ears primed, waiting for the chattering to return.

Bluetits now flocked the uncovered canes. Each little tweet and scavenging peck turned up the heat of his temper. Victor's grip tightened around the catapult. A distant chattering approached from above.

Ack-ack

Alarmed by the sound, the bluetits fled. The jackdaws landed in unison, necks bobbing as they hopped towards the canes.

Victor fed a ball bearing into the catapult pouch and

settled into position. He leaned onto the ledge and raised the slingshot to eye level. It had been forty years since he'd used his Black Widow. Muscle memory instantly kicked in.

Victor watched the jackdaws dance around the canes, pecking at the shreds of Autumn Treasure they hadn't consumed the previous night. A target skipped into view: the smaller of the two.

Patricia was always boring him with bird facts. Most of them went in one ear and out the other, but nuggets of trivia had stuck. Female jackdaws were larger, she'd boasted. This was the male he had in his sights. Victor hinged his elbow, pulled back the sling, and took aim.

Rubber snapped. A bullet blurred. Silver feathers flew like sparks.

A jackdaw fell jerking to the canes.

Victor raced onto the lawn as its panicked partner dashed into the sky. Grin flashing under mean blue eyes, he picked up his culprit, life extinguished to a limp, black rag. The jackdaw's neck drooped in his tightening grip.

On the silver birch, chattering in shock, the female stared at her lifeless partner.

Alerted to the anguished cries, Victor looked up to the silver birch. The female jackdaw met his gaze, her eyes blazing into his. For an uneasy moment, Victor froze, a prisoner to an unflinching glare. His heart pinched to an eerie sense: that he himself was being studied, his features stored and memorised. Time stopped. The soft breeze sucked from the garden. The jackdaw held its penetrating glare.

When Victor blinked, the bird had gone, a fading pixel in the slate-grey sky. Shaking off a shivering flicker, he suddenly remembered the corpse in his hand. Victor squeezed the lifeless rag, his manic grin returning. Cold bones clicked and rattled in his grip.

Back from her shift at Meadstone Library, Patricia found Victor in the kitchen, a satisfied smile smearing his face.

'Got it,' he said.

'Got what?' frowned Patricia.

Victor pointed at the window, inviting her to look. Hung from a pole where the crop cage had been, a ragged black corpse swayed in the wind.

'A deterrent,' said Victor, emboldened with pride. 'In case the other one comes back.'

Patricia pictured the preening lovers framed within the bedroom curtains – the tender, sifting beaks, the ripple of feathers – then returned her gaze to the stark horror hanging in the garden. A romance reduced to a grotesque rag, all for the sake of his raspberries . . . The sharp slap that wiped off Victor's grin took them both by surprise.

'What was *that* for?'

Without saying a word, Patricia turned on her heel. Victor rubbed his face in silence. Outside, above the roof, a shadow circled under gathering clouds. The bricked corridor of mock-Tudor semis held onto a call that echoed through Silverweed Road.

Ack-ack, she cried. *Ack-ack*.

Patricia and Victor sat in bed reading, a wall of silence between them. A faint scuttling sounded overhead, beyond the loft above – the skitter and clatter of claws on tiles. Victor slammed down his copy of *Gardeners' World* and looked up at the ceiling.

'Can you hear that? It's that bloody bird. The one I didn't get.'

Patricia considered not replying, continuing her vow of punishing silence.

'And how have you jumped to that conclusion?'

'It looked at me funny.'

Patricia rolled her eyes, then remembered the warning she'd heard as a child.

'Well, you know what they say.'

'No, but I suspect you'll tell me anyway.'

'A jackdaw on your roof brings bad luck. How does it go? "Jack on the slate, accept your fate."'

'Who told you that nonsense?'

'My mother.'

'And your batty Irish mother,' scoffed Victor, 'thought fairies broke her washing machine.' He turned over his pillow and settled on his side. 'Load of superstitious rot. Goodnight.'

Patricia sighed goodnight, listening to the roof tiles tap and click. How desperately lonely must the poor bird feel? Her partner taken, her love destroyed . . . Patricia turned off the bedside lamp, sought the comfort of her pillow, and shed a silent tear for the fallen lover.

The jackdaw called and clawed all night, dancing a ritual under the moon.

She was already waiting on the silver birch, claws curled tightly around the branch. Motionless since marking the tiles, the jackdaw had done nothing but gaze at the pole, her lost love swaying like a rag in the wind. Face still stained from the Autumn Treasure, her silver nape was stained blood-red.

Victor swung the back door open with such force, it

13

slammed the bricks, the glass nearly shattering from the impact. Patricia's ultimatum was plain and brutal: take down the gloating aberration he'd installed in the garden or he'd sleep alone in the spare room.

Victor had thought of protesting, then touched his cheek. Hours had passed since Patricia's slap, and his face still stung from the shock. Not in thirty-five years of marriage had he seen her react that way. Besides, he'd slept badly, and was in no mood for an argument. All night, his head had throbbed – as if a claw hammer had tapped at the shell of his skull.

Victor stomped across the lawn, carrying a spade. Up in the branch of the silver birch, feathers spiked in recognition.

Victor pulled up the pole, untied the string, and released the ragged corpse. Turning the jackdaw in his hand, he paused to admire his marksmanship, recalling the rabbit hunts of his youth. *Still a sharpshooter*, thought Victor. *Still got it after all these years . . .* Victor smiled, dropped the bird and picked up his spade. He'd already decided where to bury the thief – exactly where the crop cage had been. The black rag would feed the earthworms, enriching the soil for next spring.

Bird buried, Victor patted the grave with the back of his spade. The sticky, stiff feathers of the jackdaw's corpse lingered on his fingers.

Overhead, cracked the beat of wings. Victor turned to a rush of black. A flash of silver. A burst of wind. Victor ducked, just in time. A blur of talons skimmed his scalp. Hands leaped up to shield his head. A streaking shadow charged into the sky.

'You again,' yelled Victor.

He ran inside, seized the Black Widow, and leaned out of

the kitchen window. Victor scanned the clouds, blood boiling from the failed attack. He'd shoot the thing, then bury it with its infernal mate – and Patricia would be none the wiser.

Elbow hinged, rubber stretched, ball bearing primed, Victor studied the garden, waiting for movement. Wings outstretched, then quickly folding, the jackdaw landed on her lover's grave. She swiped her beak across the soil.

One eye shut, he judged the distance. A little too far, but he welcomed the challenge. Victor pulled back the slingshot. Hand primed behind the catapult, he fixed his target with his thumb.

The jackdaw turned towards the window. Held by the shine of silver eyes, Victor pinched to a flickering chill. The catapult shook. Rubber snapped. A ball bearing ripped through the air.

Victor recoiled from the window and fell to the tiles, hit by an extraordinary volt of pain. Squirming like a fried worm on the floor, he lifted his hand and screamed. Blood washed down his shaking wrist. The cap of his thumb was no longer there. What once had been a thumbnail was now a squirting pulp, the tip sliced off by a ball-bearing bullet.

Victor squirmed and screamed, his broken Black Widow beside him. The catapult rubber had snapped in half – as if bitten in two by unseen jaws.

Ack-ack.

The bird fled into the charcoal sky, feasting on his screams. She soared towards the Woods at the road's dead-end, hungry claws gripping a red gem of thumb.

'Could they not sew it back on?' asked Patricia, studying the bulging white bandage.

'I couldn't find the thumb tip,' Victor winced. 'Has to

be in the garden somewhere, along with the ball bearing. I don't know how it happened.'

They sat in the lounge, Victor prone on the sofa, Patricia crouching, trying to soothe her husband. She narrowed her eyes.

'Ball bearing? You said you'd sliced your thumb with the strimmer?'

'I *did*,' Victor snapped. 'The painkillers they gave me at A & E. They're making me all foggy.'

Patricia rose, considered kissing him, rubbed Victor's leg in sympathy instead. She knew he was lying. When Patricia returned from work and mopped the blood from the kitchen floor, he'd neglected to pick up the broken catapult. Now she could feel his temper slipping. Mention the catapult, and he'd likely detonate, his face burning as red as his thumb. Let it go. Raise it later. An argument was a waste of both their energies.

'I'm nipping out to get some bits for dinner,' Patricia said. 'You just lie here and rest.'

Patricia propped a cushion behind Victor's head and padded from the lounge.

As she crunched up the gravel driveway of no. 31, she stopped and scanned the sky. Above the roof, a bird circled, casting its shadow over the tiles.

Jack on the slate, accept your fate . . .

Patricia began to wonder what Victor had brought upon himself.

They agreed that night that Patricia would sleep in the spare room, gifting her husband the span of the bed. 'Your arm needs space to stretch,' Patricia insisted, relishing the thought of a good night's sleep.

Victor lay alone in bed, pickling in his anger. *That bird. That thing. Should've shot it when I killed its thieving mate. I'll lure it in. I'll wring its neck. I'll roast it alive and eat it up* . . .

A manic skittering returned to the tiles. Victor's head joined the throb of his pulsing thumb, a pained beat echoing the *scritch-scratch* of claws. Victor kneaded a dent in the pillow and wrenched it around his ears. The tapping and scratching, the clawing and scraping, searched through the pillow, drilling deeper and deeper. Duvet pulled up over his head, Victor tossed and squirmed. He somehow rocked into uneasy sleep.

In the dark of night, Victor awoke. The manic tapping had died from above. But for a dull pain drumming his temples, all was silent and still. Victor reached for the bedside lamp. Under creamy light, he studied his hand. The bandage had shed like the skin of a snake, curled on the sheets beside him. He looked at his thumb, pink and glossy, the nail completely healed. Victor smiled a dozy smile and floated up from the duvet. He crossed the landing towards the bathroom to fetch some pills for his pulsing head.

The door was locked. He pressed an ear to the frame. Inside came the click and clatter of water. Why was Patricia, Victor wondered, having a shower in the dead of the night?

Victor tapped on the door. The lock replied with a click. He silently drifted into the bathroom, breathing in the heat and steam. Behind the creamy shower curtain, a silver shadow danced.

'Patricia, Patricia,' leaked from his lips. Victor floated towards the shower. Water tapped and clicked on the tiles. The whispering curtains parted.

Patricia had her back turned, masked by a milky sheet of

steam. Water bounced like shiny ball bearings. Victor sang 'Patricia, Patricia.' He reached out an arm to touch her.

Patricia turned through the shivering mist.

Her feathered face was black as night, tapered to a grotesque, snapping beak. Victor froze to her silver eyes. Her black mouth opened like a trap. From the crimson abyss of her gaping throat came a monstrous, scraping rasp. *Ack-ack*, she called. *Ack-ack*.

His tongue itched to speak. No sound came. Black arms broke through clicking water, revealing fans of daggered claws. She cupped her hands around his skull and drew Victor's face towards her.

His heart hammered in his ears. Her grip tightened around his head. He felt the sting of sinking claws, dragging through his flesh. He tried to scream. His throat closed up. Now Victor's scalp peeled like rind, the skin unzipping from his face. Hot blood poured. The beak widened. With apple-crunch force, she bit down hard, cracking through the shell of skull . . .

Victor bolted up in bed, trembling and bathed in sweat. The tiles above him scritched and scratched.

'Victor?' Patricia stood over the bed, trying to rouse her husband. 'Victor, wake up. There's something you should see.'

He jolted at first, Patricia's soft face leaning in, the distant dream-haze not yet cleared, mistaking her mouth for a gaping beak. Victor lifted his bandaged thumb, the stump like the rubber of a pencil's tip. Downstairs, by the kitchen window, they looked out over the garden.

'It's been doing that since I got up,' said Patricia. 'Is that where you buried the bird?'

They watched the jackdaw fly back and forth: up to rooftop, down to the grave, depositing material onto the soil.

'Looks like she's taking moss from the guttering,' Patricia continued. 'You should be thankful – they haven't been cleaned since Terry over the road did it. Do you remember the bill? Cheeky blighter charged an arm and a leg.'

Patricia turned to her husband, awaiting a reply. Victor stared in simmering silence, hands balling into fists. *I should've stayed silent*, thought Patricia. *Another eruption. Time to go . . . .*

'Anyway, I'm off to work,' Patricia said, rushing out an excuse. 'There's tea in the pot but it's probably cold.'

'Yes, yes,' snapped Victor.

His eyes burned on the blurring black shadow, collecting and dropping, collecting and dropping. The moment he heard the front door slam, he pulled on his green rubber boots. When he returned to look out of the window, the jackdaw was nowhere to be seen.

Victor stood over the jackdaw's grave, inhaling the musky cocoa scent of earth. Patricia was right. Layering the soil were scraps of brown moss, pecked from the rooftop guttering. Each patch was alive and writhing, pulsing with insects and bugs: beetles and weevils, earwigs and flies, spiders and maggots and slugs. Nauseated by the buffet of bugs, Victor lifted his boot. He'd grind the damn things back into the soil.

This time she didn't miss.

Diving from the silver birch, she ripped through the garden like a fizzing black spear. Claws unsheathed, she marked her prey, attacking in one swift strike. Daggered talons raked through a scalp, burning a trail through thin grey hair.

The speed of the attack sent Victor spinning. Knocked off balance, shock and gravity threw him down, head first onto the grave. Blood splashed from his scored scalp, feeding the squirming soil.

Victor scrambled up from the earth, spitting a mouthful of dirt. He aimed a scream up into the sky as a wriggling earthworm drooled from his chin. Shaking hands protecting his head, Victor raced back inside. The back door slammed. Windows shut. Guns of thunder cracked outside. Needles of rain began to fall, sharpening into a shower. Bugs and blood sank into the soil, nourishing what lay beneath.

In the upstairs bathroom, Victor shook before the mirror. Marking his head were six red stripes, ploughed through the flesh by the jackdaw's claws. Crimson tears dripped from his scalp, tickling his cheeks. With a trembling finger, Victor explored his wounds. Each ribbed welt was hot to the touch, gluey with soil and blood. Head bowed over the bathroom sink, Victor patted TCP into the cuts. The antiseptic snapped at the wounds, a pained yelp greeting each dab of the scalp.

When the shock had passed, Victor felt shame and anger. Humiliated he'd allowed the bird to attack. Livid it was claiming his garden.

Bunkered in his study, Victor fed his wrath into Google. *How to trap jackdaw, how to bait jackdaw, how to kill jackdaw, how to eat jackdaw . . .*

A snare? *Larsen traps were too taxing a build.*

Poison? *Avitrol was banned, impossible to buy.*

Air rifle? *Required a licence and that took time.*

Victor scratched his head in frustration, blurting a howl as he snagged his wounds. His fingers leaped from his scalp to the keyboard, the lick of pain urging him on. Victor continued googling. Two impatient words were typed: 'kill bird'.

He found his answer in the atrocities of Cyprus. Victor leaned into the screen, reading a report from the RSPB. Each year, poachers stole the lives of a million birds as part of a migrational cull. Some used mist nets: most used birdlime. What so appalled the RSPB brought a smile to Victor's face. Birdlime: the perfect, abhorrent solution. Smear the stuff onto a tree, and the glue would trap the wings of any passing bird.

The practice was inhumane, illegal – and, grinned Victor, completely free. All he had to do was boil up some birdlime from mistletoe berries and smear it onto a branch. The plant was toxic, from leaves to fruit. Even if the jackdaw escaped the glue, the poison would finish it off.

And best of all? There was a bounty of mistletoe growing in the Woods at the dead-end of Silverweed Road. The ingredients were right on his doorstep.

Victor powered down the computer, marched from the study, and stood by the kitchen window. He glowered at the garden and hatched his plan.

If this was war, there'd be only one winner.

Patricia walked the turn from Valerian Way into Silverweed Road. She passed the shrine of crash flowers, the mangled lamp post, the rainbow lights pulsing from no. 4, oblivious to her surroundings. Her eyes were searching the evening sky, scanning for a circling shadow. To her relief, she could see only storm clouds, swelling overhead. Perhaps the jackdaw had finally gone. Perhaps her husband had called a truce.

Patricia paused on the gravel driveway of no. 31. When

she'd left that morning, Victor had been primed for another eruption. She selfishly hoped his thumb still throbbed, and he'd taken some codeine to numb his nerves. With any luck, he'd be soft and dozy and they'd eat tonight's chicken pie in peace. Specks of rain began to fall, urging her down the driveway. Patricia approached the front door, took a deep breath and slotted in her key.

She hung her coat on the rack in the hallway and padded into the lounge. Victor was brooding on the sofa, wearing a flat tweed cap.

'Are you cold, Victor?'

'Not particularly.'

'Then why are you wearing your cap indoors?'

Victor lifted his cap and bowed his head, revealing the six stripes goring his scalp.

'I was attacked this morning.'

Patricia's hand leaped to her mouth, gasping at Victor's wounds. 'Where? Who? Did you call the police?'

'You can't arrest a bird,' snapped Victor.

Patricia's hand went from staunching her shock to covering a burst of dark laughter.

'It's not funny,' said Victor. 'Bloody thing dive-bombed me in the garden.'

'Oh, Victor, what did you *expect*? Stop torturing those birds. You do know jackdaws can recognise faces? She's mad at you for killing her partner . . .' Patricia pictured the preening lovers and their tender embrace on the silver birch. 'Can't say I blame her. If I was a jackdaw, I'd do the same.'

'*They* started it,' Victor snapped back, 'by killing my raspberries. And I'll finish it, too. Mark my words, I'll finish it.' He carefully screwed his cap back on.

Patricia heard the echo of her mother's words. '*Jack on*

the slate, accept your fate.' She didn't like the direction Victor's little war was going in.

'How about we all take a deep breath and calm down? You've already lost half your thumb.'

'It's *my* garden, for Christ's sake,' snapped Victor. 'I'm not being dictated to by a bloody bird, Patricia. Do you know how important November is for the garden? I have to plant the broad beans, sow the meteor peas, the elephant garlic, the rhubarb crowns . . . If I don't do it now, we won't have any next year.'

'There are these things called shops, Victor.'

'It's not the same.'

Patricia sighed. She'd learned since the stroke there was no point arguing with him, not when he was like this. Was he too blind to see the bad luck he'd brought upon himself? That this vendetta could swallow him up?

'The bird will go if you leave it alone,' she said, leaving the lounge. 'And your garden will still be there.'

Patricia prepared dinner, chopping carrots beside the sink. She glanced out of the kitchen window. The specks of drizzle had sharpened into a shower. Spears of rain now pounded the lawn, accompanied by low groans of thunder. At the back of the garden, Patricia sensed movement: the manic hop of a skittering shadow.

Patricia leaned further into the window, struggling to see through the rain. Was there really a shadow, out there in the storm? Or had Victor's paranoia now infected her?

A lick of lightning flashed through the garden. The knife she held dropped to the worktop. Exposed in a blinding flare of light, a jackdaw danced upon the grave, snapping her beak and beating her wings. The soil beneath seemed to bubble and heave, like the stew of a witch's cauldron.

Patricia quickly lowered the blinds, shut the bird out of sight, and picked up the knife. He should never have buried her lover out there. The grieving jackdaw would just keep coming, returning to mourn at her lover's grave. Patricia chopped the carrots into thumb-fat slices, a suspicion beginning to nip at her thoughts.

Even if Victor left the bird alone, would the bird leave Victor be?

Over dinner that Friday evening, flat cap hiding his humiliation, Victor picked at his chicken pie, wondering what jackdaw tasted like.

'I'll be leaving early tomorrow morning,' Patricia reminded him. 'You'll be OK on your own?'

'Yes, yes,' said Victor, only half listening, his head full of birdlime and toxic mistletoe.

'Are you sure you don't want to come to Suffolk?' asked Patricia, out of politeness. She needed the break, just for a weekend, just for her sanity. 'Douglas and Mary would love to see you. We're visiting the burial site at Sutton Hoo. They've got a replica of the golden helmet there.'

'Yes, yes,' said Victor, sticky black wings in his twisting mind.

Patricia pictured the grieving jackdaw, dancing in the rain on her lover's grave.

'And no more fighting with the bird while I'm away, Victor. Promise me?'

'Yes, yes,' said Victor. 'All over. I promise.'

'And while I'm gone,' added Patricia, 'take that poor dead bird out of the garden and bury it in the Woods. I'm sure the jackdaw will go away then.'

'Yes, yes,' said Victor. 'I'll definitely go to the Woods.'

'Good,' sighed Patricia, with some relief. 'I'll be back on Sunday evening.'

Armed with bin bags and telescopic secateurs, Victor locked the front door of an empty no. 31. On a still, silent Saturday morning, he walked past the rows of mock-Tudor houses, towards the railings at the dead-end of Silverweed Road.

Victor had never enjoyed the Woods. When they'd moved into Silverweed some thirty years back, he'd walk with Patricia on the tarmac path, her hand squeezing his as the canopy darkened. Where the pathway horseshoed deep in the Woods, they had always turned back. Patricia was wary of what lay beyond. Twisting shadows seemed to lick through the blackthorns, beyond the rowan trees that guarded the path.

Arching branches thatched and gathered, the sky dissolving from view. Victor turned as he marched the path, sensing he wasn't alone. Waddling behind, muttering to himself, was the neighbour from no. 17. Victor didn't know his name, didn't care to either.

The idiot was always smoking out the neighbourhood with his oil-drum fires late at night, polluting Victor's garden. Worse, Victor suspected, he may be involved in some kind of cult: three times he'd spotted the waddler with a red devil idol, loading it into his van. As the neighbour shuffled past, clawing at the tufts of his monkish hair, Victor curled a furtive lip. He'd had quite enough of his late-night bonfires that fumed from his devil's workshop.

Rancid little gnome, he thought.

Victor watched his neighbour waddle into the Woods, and paused to squint beyond the rowan trees. Two hundred yards off the path was a large scratch of blackthorns, mistletoe balls puffed in the branches. Victor shook out his secateurs and crunched into the undergrowth.

The blackthorns were a bounty of mistletoe, clouded with ripe white berries. He flapped out a bin bag and set to work. Blades flashing silver in the murk of the Woods, Victor ripped at mistletoe roots, piercing through the black-thorns. Victor, in turn, was pierced himself, pricked and sliced by the blackthorn's barbs. He cursed himself for forgetting his gloves, his hands now laced with scratches.

Thunder clapped overhead. Rain began to slash through the trees. Bin bags fat with berries and leaves, Victor crunched back through the undergrowth. He scurried up the path back home, the storm closing in with every step.

Tiled floor swollen with mistletoe bales, Victor sat at the kitchen table, picked a berry and squeezed. Yellow sap spat from the popped white flesh. Victor rubbed his sticky fingers, picturing the jackdaw trapped in glue – a fat black fly in his home-made web.

By the time he'd stripped the mistletoe bales, the kitchen clock had struck noon. Victor tipped the berries into Patricia's cherished Le Creuset pot and heaved it onto a firing stove. As the hours passed and the stew thickened, white berries melted to a thick yellow resin. Victor stirred the bubbling mistletoe, leaning in to smell the pine fumes, feeling like a witch at a cauldron. When he dabbed a cautious finger into the pot, a hot thread of glue snatched at his skin.

'Perfect,' smiled Victor, uncoiling his finger. 'Just perfect.'

The storm had stopped when Victor crept into the garden, but the air was heavy with the promise of further rain. He anxiously scanned the night sky. A full moon winked between scudding clouds. There was neither sight nor sound of his nemesis.

Victor sloshed across the lawn. Skidding briefly on the slippery grass, he placed his glue pot by the grave. Victor twisted two torches into the soil, white beams lighting the site of his trap, and turned to fetch the poles.

High up on the silver birch, a waking shadow stirred.

Measuring a square around the grave, Victor tapped in a corner pole. Three more swiftly followed. Bound together with gardening wire, a four-cornered pyramid rose from the earth.

If the jackdaw was so drawn to its partner's grave, tomorrow there would be no escape. Once the pyramid was coated in glue, the merest sweep or flick of a wing would snag her to a pole, trapped in his web of birdlime.

Victor smacked his lips, savouring the thought of roasted jackdaw, and turned his back on the grave. Clouds began to swell and boil, releasing spikes of rain. Victor knelt by the iron pot, pulled a brush from his gardening apron and dipped it into the glue. Birdlime coiled around the bristles and crept up around the handle.

Victor whipped the brush from the pot, ready to prime the poles. Perhaps it was his haste to beat the rain. Perhaps he'd overloaded the brush. Perhaps it was cursed bad luck. Scowling in the building downpour, Victor splashed his hands with glue. Fingers entangled in his own sticky web, he wiped and slapped and rubbed and smeared, the birdlime now a living spiral, bonding both his hands. Fingers lashed like squirming snakes, twisting in the toxic glue. The birdlime slowly sought his scratches and seeped into his wounds.

Ack-ack

Victor froze. Hands writhing in the glue, he looked up to the silver birch. Dancing on a branch above, a bobbing shadow clicked its wings.

Attention stolen by the jackdaw's dance, something stirred behind. Beneath the pyramid of poles, the grave began to pump and writhe.

Lungs of soil heaved and plunged. A force awoke within. Like the black fin of a surfacing shark, a beak shivered from the earth. Now a tattered head. Now flickering eyes. Now a twisted, dented neck. Earthworms spilled from the crumbling grave, black wings creaking as they spread. Awoken by his lover's dance, nourished by bugs and Victor's blood, a shuddering jackdaw rose.

Bones rattling, beak clacking, shredded feathers spiked and stiff, its loose neck swayed and clicked in place. Shining eyes, white as milk, rolled within its skull. Wet soil dripping from its beak, it glared at the figure knelt by a pot, its familiar pair of drooping ears.

Ragged cape of wings outspread, a squawk crawled from its waking throat. Victor turned to a rasping call gargling through the rain. Unmasked by a sheet of lightning, as if exposed by camera flash, the bird he'd killed stared right back.

The rasping ghoul won a howl of horror from him. Its milky eyes blazed into his. Victor froze. The jackdaw charged. A blur of black rushed from the poles.

Before Victor could duck or dodge, beating wings had wrapped his face in a mask of choking black. Victor jerked back on his knees. Blinded by the scratching feathers, hands still glued together, Victor unleashed a muffled shriek. The wings wrapped tighter round his face, holding in his screams.

Each blinded breath brought choking scents: of soil and rot and soured flesh. Handcuffed by the rope-thick glue, Victor gathered all his strength. Like a prisoner bursting from his chains, he forced his arms apart. The snarl of glue that held his hands stretched and thinned and suddenly snapped. Victor let out a muffled howl as the flesh dragged from his fingertips.

Victor scrabbled to his feet. Blinded by his feathered mask, he tossed his head from side to side. He shook and thrashed and howled and stomped, smothered by the wild black rag. His cap fell off. He kicked the pot. Toxic glue spilled and splashed, coating the lawn like flypaper.

With a frantic swipe of a tiring arm, Victor swatted at the bird. At last, the rag ripped from his face and fell back to the earth.

Victor staggered on the lawn, swirling from the shock. Poison sought his peeling fingers, charging through his veins. Through the broken water of Victor's vision, the bird he'd killed rose once again.

High up on the silver birch, eyes fixed on her nemesis, the jackdaw released her battle cry. *Ack-ack*, she sang. *Ack-ack*.

Claws unpinned and wings outspread, she dived down from the branch. Tearing through the spears of rain, the jackdaw struck with force. Her claws ripped at a drooping ear, slicing through the flesh. Through a blast of blood, the jackdaw soared, feathers painted red. An earlobe dangled from her claws, like a blob of bubblegum.

Boots slipping on the grass, Victor tumbled on his back, clutching at his ear. Pools of birdlime smeared the lawn, welcoming his fall.

Vision flickering, heart drumming, tasting soil and soured

flesh, Victor writhed on the sticky lawn: a fly trapped in the jackdaw's web. Glue snatched Victor's every move, his entangled limbs now weak and watery. Mistletoe burned through his veins. The click of claws drew closer.

They gathered upon Victor's chest, lovers reunited. Beaks sifted and heads bowed. Feathers spiked in tender waves. And now they called up to the sky.

Ack-ack, they sang in unison. *Ack-ack. Ack-ack. Ack-ack.*

Silver eyes scanned the clouds, awaiting a response. Something stirred within the Woods, answering their cry. Distant dots coiled and weaved, rising high above the trees. They gathered in numbers, flocking together, a black mist forming in the storm. Once more they called. *Ack-ack.*

In the roiling clouds, the black flock answered, soaring ever closer.

Starshaped on the sodden lawn, floppy Victor groaned. Poison shivered through his veins. His twitching heartbeat slowed.

The lovers danced on Victor's chest, necks tipped up and calling out. *Ack-ack. Ack-ack. Ack-ack.* High above the rain-lashed roof, a feathered black hole swirled. The dark flock plunged and struck the lawn, a black and piercing lightning bolt.

They claimed the garden in a flash: a chattering black mass. Weakened Victor lay surrounded – an island in a sea of jackdaws.

Savouring one final kiss, nuzzling her lover's neck, she flew up to the silver birch. Her partner hopped from Victor's chest, towards the pyramid. Wings tucked in beneath the frame, his milk-white eyes now closed. He laid to rest upon the grave, finally at peace.

From her perch above the garden, the jackdaw gazed

down on her flock. A hundred silver eyes stared back, awaiting their instructions. With a flick of the tail and a crack of the wings, she trilled out her command.

The flock of jackdaws clacked their beaks and clicked towards their prize. Hooking claws through Victor's flesh, they smothered him like smoke. To the pounding beat of whipping wings, groaning Victor was lifted from the lawn. His mouth itched out one final scream as he was ferried up into the sky: ripe and soft and fit for harvest. Her gift of Autumn Treasure.

'Victor? Victor, I'm home.'

Patricia uncoiled her scarf, absorbing the silence of the house. *It feels odd in here*, she thought. *Maybe he's gone out.*

She called her husband's name again, hearing no reply. Nose twitching at a burnt pine scent, Patricia crept into the kitchen.

The clock ticked through the pensive hush. The hands marked 6.45 p.m. Patricia frowned at the mistletoe balls scattering the floor. A sticky gum, amber-yellow, pooled on the oven hob. When Patricia gave it a wary prod, she instantly recoiled. The yellow goo snatched at her finger, sticking to her skin.

Her eyes narrowed on the hob. Where was her Le Creuset pot? The last time it had disappeared, Victor had grown peppers in the pot, polluting it with soil. *So help me*, thought Patricia, *if I find it in the shed*.

Washing her finger in the sink, Patricia gazed out of the kitchen window. At the back of the garden, through the dark of night, beams of light burst from the earth.

The pale moon chalked a blackboard sky as Patricia stepped onto the lawn. Illuminated by a pair of torches dug into the soil, a pyramid rose by the back fence, formed from four short poles. Patricia walked towards the light.

Upturned on the lawn, her Le Creuset pot sat in a yellow pool – the same, frowned Patricia, as the goo on the oven hob. Within the pyramid lay a jackdaw's corpse, a flat tweed cap beside it.

Lost in the scene before her, as if trapped within a dream, Patricia jumped to a piercing call. Perched up high on a silver birch, a waking shadow stirred. She flew in silence from her branch and landed on the pyramid. Green eyes met with silver.

Crouched beside the pyramid, Patricia smiled a curious smile and opened out her hand. The jackdaw hopped down from the tip and landed on her palm. Claw by claw, in timid steps, she slowly clicked up Patricia's arm and perched upon her shoulder. A tender beak began to preen, sifting through her hair.

Head bowed in soft submission, Patricia gasped to a quiet command, shivering in her ear. *Ack-ack*, she called. *Ack-ack*.

Extract from The Silverweed Files, 3 November 2024

A personal blog by former Detective Chief Inspector Jim Heath. The views expressed do not reflect those of Kent Police nor the victims impacted by events.

I was not a popular man during my time at Meadway Station. Neither did I aspire to be. Perhaps if I'd oiled more palms and bought more rounds and joined the Rotary Club, I would have climbed the greasy ladder, but I never rose above my rank of Detective Chief Inspector. My blunt manner got my colleagues' backs up, but I was proud of my record there: 150 homicides solved in three decades, including the capture of Peter Klint, the so-called Meadway Ripper. Now, in the twilight of forced retirement, all I see is failure. All I see, when I close my eyes, are the ghosts of Silverweed Road.

In November 2019, when it all began, the task force would gather in the Incident Room, studying the road with a penetrating glare usually reserved for photofits. I was the first to draw attention to the street's design.

Seen from above, from a bird's-eye view, Silverweed was shaped like a J. First, the corner of Valerian Way curving into its entrance; next, the stick of tarmac road; and crossing the top, at the street's dead-end, the railings that bordered the Woods. The J-shape seemed like a quirk back then. In hindsight it looked like a warning.

Nobody dared say it at first, but as each house was pinned on the street map – a pin for each death or disappearance – everyone had the same thought. That the road itself was the perpetrator. That, somehow, the houses had got together one night and conspired to kill their inhabitants. It gives a good indication of our desperation to establish a common link, especially when the residents suggested no connection. There was little sense of community among Silverweed's neighbours – they shared the same postcode, but lived as strangers.

Those who survived offer few clues. Terry Slater, one of a handful of suspects who may have provided some answers, walked from custody on my watch: the incident that later led to my dismissal. Like the station CCTV erased that night, I have no recollection of releasing him. Both he and his wife, who helped design his atrocious contraption, remain on NCA's Most Wanted.

A delusion. This is what the events of Silverweed so often felt like: a communal madness that gripped an entire neighbourhood. Late at night, I will sit with the files in my study, close my eyes, and walk the corridor of mock-Tudor houses. What was once a banal suburban street is recast in the dark: the timber frames look like burnt black bones, the long back gardens like graves. I revisit the crime scenes, go door to door, in the hope new light will be shed. My only reward is questions and shadows.

Take, for example, the case of Victor Hagman. It is five years since the accountant disappeared from his garden and I am no closer to explaining how or why. Forensic analysis of Hagman's final footprints tell a mystifying story: he walked from the back door, engaged in some sort of struggle on the lawn, then literally vanished into thin air. His assailant left no footprints. All that was left of Victor Hagman was a flat cap, four canes and a pot of glue. The man was an obsessive gardener and I believe he was attacked while building a wigwam to grow runner beans.

Any suspicions his wife was involved were swiftly put to bed. Patricia Hagman was in Suffolk when Victor went missing. Her alibi is cast-iron. The sudden shock of his disappearance rendered her speechless, and she texted 999 rather than called. Not a word has passed her lips since.

Patricia now resides in a care home, where she wanders the grounds calling up to the clouds. She must have loved her husband deeply: the trauma of Victor's disappearance has stolen her voice entirely. Now she chatters to herself like a crow, and will only talk to the birds.

How can a man vanish, as if plucked from the sky? The internet's sleuths have no end of suspects. Seized by a drone. Whipped up from the earth by a freak 'rope tornado'. The most popular (and most ludicrous) theory comes from a vocal cult of UFO conspiracists, who maintain Hagman is a victim of alien abduction. Given the options, I would rather the case remain unsolved than settle for the claims of a lunatic fringe.

There are dozens more cases like these. One for every house. Each case a dead-end. A dead-end, like Silverweed Road.

NO. 25:

The Pool

The canvas had been blank for seven days when Cleo Marsh locked the Hackney studio and set off into the London fog. She lit a roll-up and lurked at the bus stop, staring numbly into the mist. Buried in a cinnamon sheepskin coat, her legs pin-thin in skinny white jeans, Cleo looked, at a distance, like an unloved lollipop that had been dropped on a brown fur rug. Her long lilac hair held the scent of tobacco and turpentine.

A red double-decker broke through the fog, headlights glowing like sharp yellow eyes. Cleo boarded, climbed to the top deck, and curled in a corner on the back seats. It was 11.30 a.m.

The Cleo Marsh of two years ago would have been alive to the figures in the greying soup, sketching the phantoms that smudged past the bus. Now her glazed hazel eyes barely absorbed her environment. As the bus bumped and stalled, Cleo turned from the window and swiped through her phone gallery at the glowing bones of a once-bright future.

She'd just turned 27, but it seemed like an eternity ago.

Eager queues had snaked through the Hayward to experience her interactive installation, *The Underneath*. Entering an empty space one at a time, the solitary viewer faced blank walls, powdered darkness, and a constant scratching beckoning from below. The exhibition lay under the floorboards.

Progressing through the space, the viewer was encouraged to lift each floorboard, uncertain of what lurked beneath. Under each strip glowed a buried neon bone: first feet, then legs, then ribs, arms and spine, building a fractured skeleton. Set on edge by the endless scratching, when they lifted the final trapdoor, anticipating by now a neon skull, a funhouse mirror sprang from the void, the viewer jumping from their warped reflection. Some critics damned it a ghoulish prank masquerading as art; others a bracing jolt of mortality. Cleo was shortlisted for The Lannister Prize.

Declared a new voice on the London art scene, it was all a bit much for the Teeside girl from Cotherstone. When, aged twelve, her mother had died – zebra crossing, speeding car, a spilled shopping bag – broken Cleo had escaped into art, pouring her pain onto paper and canvas. A talent blossomed like a black rose. Cleo Marsh remained a shy, sullen figure, even through college, but her art was bold and biting. The attention it drew felt ancillary: she lived for the process, for the shock of creation.

When Cleo set to work on her follow-up, she was crushed by the pressure of expectation. Plunging into an abyss of perfection, works were started then abandoned, exhibits announced and then withdrawn. Two years passed. Commissions dried up. Her exhausted agent left her. The act of creation became a burden. A palsy of doubt and second-guesses, Cleo was swallowed by a thick black block.

Then came Margaret Powler.

They had met by chance, just a month ago, at the Parallax Art Fair. Envious eyes darkening at the canvases, Cleo had turned to leave when a stranger in heels and a houndstooth suit had stopped her. She'd recognised Cleo's lilac hair, proclaimed herself an admirer and, sincerity pouring from ice-blue eyes, asked not about her work, but her welfare. How she was. How she felt. Was she happy. Could she help.

When it emerged that Margaret was an agent, Cleo balked. Experience had taught her the art world was a sea of fins. Some were sharks, others were dolphins. The only way to tell was to look below the surface.

But Margaret. She understood. She sympathised. When she mentioned a client of hers 'lifting the black block', Cleo sensed a saviour. Hands shook, numbers were traded, followed by a call: an invitation to Margaret's Fitzrovia office and talk of a commission . . .

Stepping from the bus at Tottenham Court Road, Cleo vanished into the fog. She wandered the maze of Fitzrovia, approached a town house, and studied the entryphone, looking for door 25. She buzzed the buzzer and spoke into the intercom.

'I'm here to see Margaret Powler?'

The lock clicked without reply. Circling a foyer of doors and staircases, sensing she'd been swallowed by an Escher woodcut, Cleo spotted a sign to the basement and descended a curving stairwell, her jelly shoes squishing on each step. At the end of a corridor came the click of a door latch. Immaculate hair set in a platinum bob, Margaret Powler emerged from the shadows.

'Cleo,' she called. 'You've found me.'

Perched on the lip of a black chaise longue, still entombed

in her sheepskin coat, Cleo gazed around the office. The clinical white space reminded her of a laboratory with the kit removed, the lighting harsh and unforgiving. Margaret settled behind a long chrome desk, an aquarium bubbling behind her. Pickle-green leaves rolled within, swaying in the water like waves of hair. The blazing red of Margaret's lips and manicured nails popped against the white.

'So,' asked Margaret. 'How are things? The new studio bearing fruit?'

'I'm priming canvases,' said Cleo.

'Wonderful! Ready for . . . ?'

'That's all I've been doing. Priming canvases.'

'Well, that's marvellous. You're getting the juices flowing. It's perfect timing, Cleo. The collector I mentioned? The pharmaceutical VP? He has a glorious new private space just *pleading* for a piece of Cleo Marsh. Now, I mentioned your name, and on the third of December he's—'

'Margaret,' Cleo interrupted, sinking into her sheepskin. 'Would you like to know the name of the new piece I'm working on? It's called "Staring Into An Empty Space For Ten Hours A Day And Getting Fuck All Out Of It".'

'Oh, wonderful. When do you think you'd be able to share?'

'It was a joke.' Cleo chewed her lip and twisted the ring on her finger: gold, priceless, inherited from her late mother. 'I've been thinking about your offer, and honestly, it's too soon. I'm transitioning from installations to oils, and . . .'

'So you've said. Must be tremendously exciting.'

'It's just such an *effort*,' sighed Cleo. 'Getting anything done is like squeezing the last bit of toothpaste from the tube: the studio's full of half-finished pieces that stay half-finished. They're just sitting there, like abandoned children.'

'I know just the place.'

'I've already switched studios, Margaret. The block is in here.' Cleo tapped her heart. 'And here.' Then her head.

'It has a pool.'

'Sorry?'

'The retreat – it has a pool in the garden. It's a very calming space, Cleo. Very quiet, very inspiring.'

Cleo sank back into the chaise longue distracted, not for the first time, by her would-be agent's appearance. For the life of her, she couldn't work out how old Margaret was. Platinum bob scooped into a side-swept fringe set like a frozen wave, her complexion glowed a China doll glaze. Even under stark white lights, Cleo could see no wrinkles or worry lines, no signs of lifts or filler. And yet her ice-blue eyes held the glint of wisdom and experience. A youthful sixty or a prematurely aged forty-year-old? Margaret's plastic surgeon, Cleo decided, must be a magician.

'It's an old family house, just an hour from London,' Margaret continued. 'Hadn't a clue what to do with the place when I inherited it, so I converted it into a studio. Any time a special someone needs some space, I invite them to stay, for as long as it takes. It's my way of giving something back, although I must confess I do get something out of it – an exhibition usually. Everything you need is there: easels, paints, stretched linen canvases – there's even a potter's wheel.'

'I don't do ceramics.'

'All you have to do is bring yourself,' said Margaret, sailing through Cleo's interruption. 'And a swimsuit if you fancy a dip in the pool. You do swim?'

'I don't sink, put it that way.'

'Wonderful. By the end of your stay, you won't even remember ever *having* a block. You'll see.'

Margaret reached into her desk, unlocked a drawer, and

took out a framed photograph. She smiled at it briefly, whistled softly through her nose, then passed it to Cleo.

The aquarium bubbled gently behind Margaret's desk. Green leaves swayed and twisted. Cleo sank into the photo of a swimming pool shining in a long dark garden. Transported from the white walls of Margaret Powler's office, she pictured herself floating in the serene, clear water, cool and pale as cucumber flesh. Her focus switched to a tree beside the pool, its branches lined with leaves of every colour.

'There's nobody staying there at the moment,' said Margaret, breaking the spell. 'It's all yours if you want it.'

Cleo passed back the photo. Her eyes still held the glow of the pool.

'How much?'

'What a question!' Margaret laughed. 'It's free! Think of it as a thank you. A thank you for putting your faith in me as your agent. If you still want me, that is.'

Cleo nodded slowly. She felt the shine of Margaret's ice-blue eyes as she weighed up the offer.

'Suppose a week wouldn't do any harm.'

'Not harm, Cleo,' smiled Margaret. '*Good*. It will do you *good*. You'll get those creative juices flowing in no time. You'll feel like a new artist. Born again. Refreshed. How are you fixed next week?'

Margaret listened to Cleo's jelly shoes squeak up the corridor, and returned to her desk. She slid the photo back in the drawer, changed the code on the desk lock, turned to the aquarium, and dipped her smooth, pale fingers into the water. Her soft smile glided through perfect skin.

On a clear, crisp November night, just past 9 p.m., Cleo dragged her suitcase down a gravel driveway, roll-up fuming from a downturned mouth. The journey from London had already put her in a black mood. The train from Victoria had been late, and the minicab she'd hailed from Meadway Station had turfed her out at Valerian Way. 'Silverweed,' the driver grunted, 'is a dead-end road.' Her heart had sunk the moment she'd seen the street: silent black block after silent black block of 1950s mock-Tudor semis, a murk of skeletal trees at the top of the road. A pensive, faintly hostile hum hung in the winter air.

As she approached the front door of no. 25, the cottagey nameplate gave her the first laugh of the day. On a moss-kissed block of cobbled stone, in a kitsch *ye olde* font, the sign read: Peggy's Place. Cleo stubbed out her roll-up and turned the key.

The stark, square lobby she stepped into only made her heart sink deeper. Frosted glass window ahead, a door to her right, the oppressive space had the feel of a holding cell. She pushed open the lobby door, preparing herself for the worst.

Cleo fumbled at the walls. A light switch flicked. In strobing flashes, rows of strip light warmed and clicked. The studio shivered into white.

Cleo paced the wide, airy space, her dark mood retreating. She had expected a stifling poky brown lounge, and yet the interior defied its mock-Tudor shell. Set beneath a broad, square skylight, the L-shaped studio held an inviting blood-warmth. Cupboards lined along the walls were stocked with paint of every shade – in acrylic, oil, gouache and encaustic. There were rolls of canvas, jars of Turpenoid, and a well-used potter's wheel beside a long, flat plan chest. Cleo recalled Margaret's promise: *everything you need is here . . .*

Tucked into the corner was a white kitchenette with oven, fridge, and a stack of towels piled on the worktop. Paint stains from previous guests striped the wooden floorboards, the splashes of colour hard and forgotten. As she circled the easel in the studio's centre, Cleo's eyes climbed the spiral staircase that corkscrewed to the rooms above. Briefly lost to the coiling stairs, her gaze returned to the studio. Beyond cream pleated curtains, an ethereal green glow danced on her skin.

Cleo parted the curtains and opened the patio doors, bathed in the light of the fabled pool. Heart patting softly, she stepped onto the decking. The pool ran the length of the garden – one hundred feet long, twenty feet wide, steel ladder hooping at the far end. Lining its edges like a mirror frame were slabs of stone, each block cobbled and moss-kissed. The calling water glowed a cool, pale green, the colour of cucumber flesh.

What Margaret hadn't mentioned – and hadn't photographed – were the high walls of leylandii that bordered the garden. Their shadows halted at the water's edge, as if forbidden from crossing the pool.

Cleo dipped a hand in the water, testing its temperature. The surface replied with a refreshing snap. Drying her hand on her sheepskin coat, she walked to the pool's distant end and stood by the bones of a hawthorn tree. Stripped to its skeleton by the elements, coloured rags danced from the branches, pinned to the thorns. Cleo watched the ribbons sway in the breeze, taking in their shades and textures: of denim and leather, nylon and lace, of cotton, fur, linen and silk . . . The branches crackled softly in the building wind. Answering the call of the glimmering pool, Cleo headed inside to change.

Re-emerging in a black swimsuit, Cleo walked along the stone edge, slipped down the pool ladder, and bounced into the water. Thinking she'd entered the shallow end, she expected to land on steady feet. Instead, she plunged. Down and down. Eyes clammed shut, ears thudding, her blurring feet kicked and pressed. The bottom retreated from her touch. Cleo surfaced in a ring of foam, spitting and cursing, shocked by the hidden depth of the pool.

The panic faded to a hugging blood-warmth. As the pool licked softly at her skin, Cleo floated on her back, staring up at the stars. Skin tingling, answering to a bright new energy, she hooked an elbow and launched into a crawl. There was not a splash or spray from kicking legs, the surface untroubled and smooth as silk.

Exhilarated after twenty lengths, feeling the exercise had earned her a cigarette, Cleo climbed the ladder, stepped onto the decking and looked at her glowing reflection. Her face shone back, as polished as a white apple. When the November night flashed its teeth, Cleo shivered back into the house.

Wrapped in a towel, the cold retreating, Cleo lit a roll-up and explored the kitchenette. A bottle of Pinot Noir rested on a laminated card: *Welcome to Peggy's Place*. Listed were swimming pool dos and don'ts, Margaret's phone number, and a short paragraph headed 'About the Hawthorn'.

Over the years, it's become a tradition for guests to pin a personal item to the hawthorn branches. You are welcome to leave a memento and share the memory of your stay with others.

    Create, inspire, transform!

    Margaret

Cleo tossed the card aside, opened the Pinot Noir, tipped her head back and drank from the bottle. Glowing from her swim under the stars, she stared at the hawthorn through swaying curtains, heart warming to a new hope.

A blank canvas. A fresh start. Cleo Marsh: reborn.

She woke early in the windowless bedroom. Upstairs offered little in the way of exploration: just a sterile bathroom and a short landing that led to a dark oak door. Cleo tested its black brass handle, sensing it was locked. Everything about the space was designed to urge its guests downstairs.

Bare feet padding on cool metal steps, she wound down the spiral staircase. The welcoming studio felt airy and blood-warm, as if the pool had flowed into the house.

Cleo opened the patio doors, breath misting in the sharp November air. As she gazed at the arms of leylandii that flanked the garden, fingertips tapering into the sky, Cleo felt a sense of dislocation – that stepping from studio to garden had transported her to another world, another truth, another possibility.

Here she was, in the heart of a north Kent housing estate, and yet there was no sense of the houses next door, the prying eyes of others, sounds from the street, and – surely an illusion – no sense of the sun. But for the pool, the shaded garden remained dark as soil, the sun's rays filtered by the towering leylandii. Secluded, stranded, yet warming to a sense of freedom, Cleo obeyed the call of her quickening heart.

Throwing off her sheepskin coat, she raced across the decking. Still in her pyjamas, Cleo leaped into the pool. Bobbing like a buoy in the shimmering water, kicking legs rippling like jelly, Cleo peered into the depths. In the centre of the pool coiled a drainage grate, its spiralling metal the size of a porthole.

Eyes lost to the coiling grill, the silent water licking her skin, Cleo tingled to a surge of energy. Palms pressed on the stone edging, she levered herself from the water and dashed to the studio, answering an impulse buried for so long: a sudden urge to create.

Perched on a stool before a blank canvas, brush in hand, paints set out, Cleo felt her mind emptying, a moment passing. Like wet footprints fading on floorboards, the pool's charge quickly drained. Cleo darkened to a growing dread: that the black block had followed her from city to retreat. Feeling the studio walls tighten, Cleo dried off, dressed, grabbed her camera, and left the house.

When she'd arrived the previous night, Cleo had barely registered the derelict block next door. The house was so different to the flanks of mock-Tudor semis that surrounded it. Detached from no. 25, the building looked to Cleo as if it had been drawn by a child: a bleak grey cube with four square windows and a door set square in its centre. She took out her camera, clicked and zoomed, wondering who lived in such a gloomy shell.

Even in the daylight, Cleo sensed a dark hum to the street that seemed to leak from the road's dead-end. She headed to the top of Silverweed, coiled through the railings, and entered the path into the Woods. The tangled canopy twisted overhead, shutting out the sun. With each step, branches swayed and clicked, as if teased into motion by an unfelt wind. Cleo paused in the darkness. Beyond the path, shadows licked, seeping through the blackthorns. Now the air began to stir, with clicks and taps of drumming wood.

Liquid shadows poured like ink onto the path ahead.

Cleo instinctively lifted her feet, as if dancing from the claws of a chasing tide. Her gooseflesh pipped to the growing clicks. Cleo raced back down the path, reached the railings and turned. Whatever shadows, if they were ever there at all, had been chased back by the sun.

Cleo abandoned the Woods and worked her way back down the street. As she photographed the houses, there was a creeping sense she too was being studied. In the upstairs bedroom of no. 22, a watching shadow loomed. A curtain flicked. Her camera clicked. What *was* it with this place?

At the strobing lamp post by Silverweed's entrance, she knelt by a shrine of crash flowers. Through the eyes of Cleo Marsh, the brown bouquets seemed to capture the essence of this gloomy suburban pocket: a shadowy sense of loss, a sapping sense of decay . . .

Cleo jumped to a black blur. It dived from the sky with a cry of *ack-ack*. There, on the top of the lamp post, perched a large, black jackdaw.

She stepped back, focused and clicked.

Held by the shine of silver eyes, Cleo felt a flickering chill, as if a heartbeat had been stolen. With a flick of the wings and a cry of *ack-ack*, the jackdaw vanished into the sky. Cleo watched the black dot fade into the Woods, the ghost of a shiver receding. Cleo laughed a nervous laugh. Even the *birds* around here were creepy. Jelly shoes squishing, she returned to the haven of Peggy's Place.

Inside the studio, Cleo reviewed the morning's photographs, waking to Silverweed's strange, dark rhythms. The wreck next door. The shadow behind the curtain. The jackdaw perched on the flickering street lamp . . .

Cleo flicked back and forth through the images. An idea built into an urge, pushing aside the thick black block. She pictured an exhibit – a portrait of suburban shadows, inspired by Silverweed Road . . .

Cleo set her tablet beside the easel. Crash flowers glowed from the screen, a jackdaw perched above. Pencil in hand, she confronted the canvas, wrist whipping as an outline formed. Oils glided. Blood rushed. Cleo came alive.

It was approaching 8 p.m. when she stepped back from her easel, paintbrush in hand. Scattered like bones at the side of the road, a rich decay of brown bouquets haunted the canvas, guarded by a ragged jackdaw. Cleo leaned in and signed the painting. The skylight was patted with specks of rain.

The downpour intensified, frying the glass above. Cleo turned to the garden: the glowing pool, the twisting rags of the hawthorn tree.

At the mercy of the growing storm, and with no covering to protect it, the pool was untroubled by the onslaught, serene, glassy and perfectly still. She unlocked the patio doors for a closer look. Cleo recoiled. The doors snapped open. The force of the storm crashed through the studio.

All that stood now fell. The stool tipped and skidded. The easel toppled. Sheets of paper swirled. Lilac hair swarming in the wind, Cleo fought with the patio doors, the curtains swelling and beating. She turned and rushed to the fallen easel.

It was too late. Cleo prised the painting from the boards. The canvas peeled like skin from bone. The jackdaw was now a blurred black streak, every brush stroke lost. With every salvaging dab and mop, the smearing oils sank deeper.

Heart as dark as the raging storm, she rose despairing from the floor and stamped right through the canvas.

*

The storm had passed by morning. Cleo trudged down the spiral staircase, groggy after a sleepless night. Her glazed eyes met the tattered black canvas, lying dead on the floorboards: another abandoned child. The energy was low in her, all inspiration sapped. At least in the Hackney lock-up she was free to brood without intrusions. Here, even the elements were conspiring against her.

Cleo blanked the canvas, lit a roll-up and looked out into the garden. Through a haze of creamy cigarette smoke, the pool began to shimmer and call. As Cleo sank into its glow, a warm pulse tickled through her skin, peeling away the gloom. She wrestled into her swimsuit, padded across the decking and slid down the ladder.

Cleo swam her lengths. Gliding over the grate in the centre of the pool, she awakened to a subtle tug. It was the faintest of undertows – a gentle teasing of the ankle. A kick of the legs and the tug would fade, only to return when she passed the grate. Maddened at first, Cleo began to anticipate, even enjoy, the light and playful pull. The drag of the pump. What else but the drag from a tired, old pump . . .

Skin tingling, Cleo crossed the decking, her mind fresh and soaring. The storm, the chaos, the desecrated painting: all seemed to fade in the glow of the pool, chasing the darkness before it could form. A bright urge grew from within.

Cleo set the easel by the patio doors and perched on her stool. She took up her palette and looked out over the garden. Pale oils mixed with turpentine, the colour of cucumber flesh.

Brush strokes flowed like water. Rising on the canvas, a long green bar began to form, narrowing from the base to an infinite horizon. Cleo looked up from her painting. For a brief moment, the decking lightened, the rags on the hawthorn flashing like fairy lights. Cleo was claimed by the rush of creation.

When a thumbnail moon marked the skylight, the studio floor was tiled with drying canvases, each an identical bar of water the pale shade of cucumber flesh. Buzzing from the session, Cleo rushed across the decking and dived into the pool. Ankle teased by the tugging grate, she glided and giggled through silken water.

High above, a jackdaw circled, watching the water darken beneath. An oil-black shadow coiled from the grate and oozed from the depths of the glimmering pool. It snaked in silence below a swimming figure, yellow eyes flashing through waves of hair.

There was no darkness when Cleo awoke. No self-doubt or indolence, no stifling black block. After gliding through her lengths, Cleo sat cross-legged under the skylight, reviewing the bars of every canvas. Thoughts turned to new dimensions: of adding stones around the infinite bar, of lifting the water from the canvas.

Cleo circled the pool, camera clicking, documenting the edging stones. Each wore its individual character, the pewter surfaces cobbled and pocked. Patches of moss clung to the sides, lurid green and stubble-smooth. Cleo rushed back to the studio.

Returning with crayons and a paper pad, she placed a sheet over a corner stone. Palm pressed to steady the paper, she rubbed a crayon over the surface. When she lifted up the sheet, her memory flooded with distant classrooms, feeling like a six-year-old, brass-rubbing coins. Cleo worked her way around the pool, rubbing and etching the individual stones. Six coloured crayons wore down to stubs. Studying the folds and grains, Cleo came alive to the faces held within.

Dots of eyes emerged from the surfaces, underscored with long, thin mouths, hooped in shock or surprise. Cleo thought back to her art college years and her first exhibition, a collection inspired by pareidolia – the illusory perception of faces and forms haunting everyday objects. Skulls in rose petals. Grinning cheese graters. Sullen light switches, and octopus coat hooks. Meaningful patterns from meaningless noise.

Rubbing after rubbing, stone after stone, the long, stretched mouths hooped and gaped, sometimes one on a single surface, as many as five on others. Cleo smiled at the anomaly, wise to the illusion. She pegged each sheet to a drying line that circled the studio walls.

Cleo seized a canvas. She turned and thinned a sable brush. Working her way around the bar, the edges of a pool began to rise, forming a stonework border. As Cleo leaned in, detailing the mouths of each stone, a whispering impulse took hold, directing her brush strokes to the canvas centre. Cleo obeyed, caught in the jaws of creation.

She lit a roll-up, leant back and frowned at her new addition. A stone now floated in the centre of the pool, the perspective shifting from a bird's-eye view to face-on. Cleo painted another, its edges interlocking. Line by line, brick by brick, a wall rose on the canvas. The pool water began to retreat, contained within the stones.

Until she stood back from the canvas, Cleo was unsure what she'd created. At the centre of the painting rose a well. Surrounded by a ring of stone, a pit deepened, descending not into darkness, but the promise of reflection, and the pale, green shine of water.

She slept that night on the studio floor, bathed in the blood-warm glow of the pool.

Soft skin dewy from her morning swim, submitting once more to a whispering impulse, Cleo had started on another stone well when her mobile shook. Tempted to let the phone ring out, not wishing to disrupt her flow, she glanced at the caller name. Cleo took the call.

'Margaret.'

'So sorry to disturb. Thought I'd check in, see if all is well with the studio?'

Cleo stepped away from the easel and sat cross-legged on the floorboards. She reached for a notepad, picked up a pencil and doodled as they talked.

'Margaret, it's perfect. The studio, the paints, the pool . . .'

'Ah, so you've been swimming?'

'Like a fish,' said Cleo. Her pencil scratched at the notepad. 'I'm surprised the water stays so warm in the winter.'

'Does it? That's wonderful. I've never been in the pool myself, would you believe. And the painting? Any progress?'

'Plenty. Working on something right now.'

'See? I did say.'

'Except . . .' Cleo paused. The furious scribbling continued.

'Yes?'

'Except I'm painting things I'd never paint. I'm not quite sure what's come over me, Margaret – it's really not my style at all. It's . . . It's almost like a compulsion.'

'Isn't that what art is? Answering a compulsion?'

'Well, yeah, but no, but . . .' Cleo paused, her train of

thought thrown off course by Margaret's response. As Cleo scribbled mindlessly, she looked at the well on the canvas. Was that what she was doing? Answering a compulsion? Creating for the sake of creating, no longer answerable to the black block? Why a stone well? Why *not* a stone well? Whatever instincts were guiding her, she felt so free she was almost floating.

'Be you, Cleo. I always say there's only one of you, which is why everyone wants a piece. Let your juices flow. Release yourself. Swim, paint, give in to your compulsions. I cannot *wait* to share in what you've created. Listen to me, wittering on. I'll let you go. Do let me know if you need anything. And happy swimming!'

Cleo put down the phone and gazed at the doodle on her notepad. Twisting her mother's gold ring, she grimaced at the grotesque hand she'd sketched. It clawed across the notepad, the grey skin forked with swollen veins. Fanning out from bony knuckles, a black nail tipped each skeletal finger.

Was that bony, knotted hand also answering a compulsion? Sensing a great outpouring of the darkness that had drained her for two torturous years, Cleo ripped out the page, screwed it into a ball, and tossed the hand into the bin. She returned to the easel, filling the bricks on a new stone well.

Day blurred into night. Night blurred into day. Cleo acquiesced to the flood. Canvas after canvas of bars and wells dried against the walls, a new collection building. Cleo obeyed the rhythms of creation, offering no resistance, yielding to an impulse that whispered within. In between sessions, she answered the call of the pool, sometimes swimming, other times drifting, renewing her charge in the water. She sipped and swallowed its honey sweetness, her glowing skin now soft as silk.

Cleo had completed a triptych of bars when she decided to celebrate with a swim. Lilac hair streaming, she leaped from the stones and plunged into the blood-warm pool. She glided through the water in a rapid chain of lengths, giggling as her ankle tugged over the grate.

Exhausted after forty lengths, panting and euphoric, she drifted to the poolside and anchored her arms on the edging. As she caressed the mouths and eyes of the stones, Cleo froze. Panic surged. Her mother's gold ring. Gone.

Softly treading water, Cleo scanned the depths. There in the centre, by the spiralling grate, shone a golden hoop of light. Cleo took three deep breaths, held the last, and dived down to retrieve the ring.

Arms digging, legs kicking, Cleo Marsh descended. The bottom seemed to pull away, retreating with every stroke. Surging deeper into the pool, the water's character began to change: thick and cloying, like wallpaper paste.

The grate that had appeared so distant, so out of reach, appeared with such abrupt force, Cleo jolted in the depths. Anchoring a hand on the spiral grate, Cleo salvaged her ring. Lungs still fresh and full, she paused in the depths of the pool.

Cleo pressed her face to the grate, gazing beyond the spiral cover. What *was* it blocking the grate, causing her ankle to tug?

Within the spiral, plant life danced, leaves swaying like hair. Cleo squeezed her fingers into the gap, towards the shifting plants. Slippery leaves greeted her touch, lapping at her skin. Cleo weaved her fingers further and grasped a fistful of leaves. Cleo pulled back, as if ripping up weeds. The swaying plants thrashed into life.

Deep within the whipping leaves flashed a fuming yellow eye.

Cleo bolted for the surface. She burst from the pool, gasping for breath. Heart pounding, she lunged for the stones. Hands slid from the slippery moss. She slipped back in. She lunged again. Gripped in panic, she clawed at the edge as the water licked her skin. Her hands searched for mouths in the stones and hooked her fingers inside. Grip secured, Cleo heaved herself out and flopped onto the decking.

An eye. Beyond the grate, within the leaves. A glaring, fuming yellow eye. A reflection? The dance of light and water? A rogue flash of pareidolia? Cleo opened out an empty palm, looked back into the water. At the bottom of the pool shone a hoop of light. Her mother's priceless ring, dropped in her frenzy to reach the surface.

Cleo paced the decking, eyes fixed on the hoop of light. It was all she had left of her mother. She wouldn't dare abandon her ring to the depths. What if it slipped into the grate? The ring would be lost forever. She couldn't leave it there. She *couldn't*. Cleo screwed her courage tight and cautiously slid back into the pool.

She dived once more towards the spiral, the water thin and sweet. The bottom sped quickly into view. As Cleo snatched up her priceless ring, she was unable to resist a glance at the grate. No whipping plants. No swaying leaves. Certainly no yellow eye – just a dark hollow pipe beyond the spiral, fading to endless black.

Upstairs, in the sterile bathroom, Cleo washed her lilac hair, the shower water sharp as pins. She began to laugh, a trickle at first, shuddering into a hysterical flood.

An eye in the pool. *An eye in the pool* . . . Cleo shook

her head under the shower, the laughter drying, feeling foolish for frightening herself. There was nothing there. Another illusion, like the faces in the stones. Another illusion, like the tug of the grate.

She stepped from the shower, dried off, and stood before the bathroom mirror. Through clearing steam, Cleo faced her reflection. She barely recognised herself.

For months, her body had spoken of neglect and wear. Cast under the shadow of the black block, her complexion grey as the London skies, Cleo looked . . . younger, was it? It was as if a skin had been shed, a fresh self emerging from a dry cocoon. She stroked her face. Her fingers glided. Her supple skin felt soft as satin, as polished as a shiny white apple. She recalled Margaret's note: *Create, inspire, transform!* Cleo felt renewed, reborn.

Later that night, detailing the moss on a stone well, Cleo stopped to look up at the rain, patting the skylight above. There was a growl of thunder, a flash of lightning, and for the second time that week, Silverweed was cast in the heart of a storm.

Cleo watched the rain strike the skylight, alive to the patterns forming and crashing. Thunder growled. The shower intensified. Water shattered and split on the skylight, enslaved in a cycle of creation and destruction.

She watched the rags on the hawthorn tree, writhing in the rain. The uncovered pool. No way could it remain still in the onslaught.

Lilac hair flattening in the downpour, Cleo approached the stone edging. Exposed to the storm, the glossy water remained flat as glass. Cleo looked up to the boiling clouds, following the rain crash from the sky, down towards the pool.

57

Another illusion? Rain crackled the decking, pounded the hawthorn, and yet the pool, the pool . . . Above the surface, raindrops bounced and split, forming a glittering arc. The pool below remained perfectly still and serene. Cleo pictured the shadows of leylandii halting at the water's edge. Something was shielding the surface from harm.

A sheepskin dropped. Jelly shoes kicked. Naked, Cleo dived into the pool. Rising in a ring of foam, she flipped on her back and watched the rain charge down. Patterns crashed above the pool, like the dance of rain on skylight glass.

Shielded from the tempest, Cleo glided to the pool's centre. With arms at full stretch, she reached up and caressed the arc. Coloured waves rippled through the glassy dome, like hair teased by the wind. Her fingertips tingled from the contact. A layer separated her from the storm. The effect was electric . . . impossible . . . magical. Spellbound by the scattering rain above, Cleo began to laugh. Warmed by a glow of protection not felt since she was a child, her laughter echoed through the garden. Blood-warm water licked at her skin.

The sight that greeted Cleo next morning was so incredible, so gruelling, so sudden, she questioned whether she'd woken from her dreams.

Aching back pleading for the bed, she had slept upstairs. Dressed in her swimsuit, Cleo skipped down the spiral staircase, her descent slowing on the icy steps. Gone was the glow that welcomed her each morning. Gone was the warmth that hugged her skin. The studio was dark as ash.

Cleo walked onto the decking and froze. It was 8 a.m. The sun had risen. The day had begun. And yet in the garden, night had yet to leave. The walls of leylandii rose like tombs, the hawthorn a tangled skeleton.

When she approached the pool, the leylandii held on to her echoing gasp. The clear, glossy, shimmering water, warm as blood, sweet as honey . . . Gone. All gone. Cleo stared in disbelief at the grave of oil that was now the pool. The heavy surface slopped and heaved, slapping against the stones.

Cleo crouched at the edge, her reflection rejected by the void. She skimmed a finger across the surface and recoiled in disgust. Coating her skin was a cold, black, slippery sputum. It was as if she'd been licked by a dead man's tongue. She shuddered from the contact. Cleo wiped her finger, releasing the sputum onto her swimsuit. As the surface slopped against the stones, the pool released a bitter scent: a mouldy perfume of decay.

Back in the studio, Cleo loitered, ghosted and numb. A heaviness appeared to push down from above. The studio, once so light and welcoming, now stored an ominous weight. A flat chill prickled her silken skin. She shuffled into her sheepskin coat.

Surrounded by wells and glowing bars, her eyes now darkened on her art. A wave of nausea rolled like a sea sickness, rejecting the images she'd created. It was as if the paintings had been crafted by another mind. Another heart. Another eye. The glow of the pool retreated like a distant, shimmering illusion.

Cleo snapped up her phone and dialled.

'Margaret? Margaret, it's Cleo. No, I'm not OK. The pool. It's gone.'

'I'm not sure I follow.'

'I mean it's *gone*. It's black. The water's gone *black*. It's like . . . It's like a fucking oil slick.'

'Oil? Are you *sure*, Cleo?'

'I'm looking at it right now. Has anything like this happened before? It wasn't me, Margaret. I went to sleep last night, woke up, and then—'

'Cleo,' said Margaret, cutting in. Her voice was calm and smooth as silk. 'I'll be right down.'

The call cut off. Margaret was coming. She didn't say when.

Time slopped and heaved. Cleo paced an endless circuit, dark thoughts trapped in a loop. She circled the studio, blanked her art, walked to the decking, checked the water, stared at the hawthorn, then returned to the studio, where the circuit repeated. Her anxiety deepened with every step. A dark weight pressed from above.

The glow of the pool, the glare of creation, the hope and desire, the hunger and the drive . . . All had faded in the murk of the studio, the black block stealing the light.

By early evening, the black block and the black pool and Cleo's black mood pressed so deeply, she broke from her loop and stared at the ceiling. Shivering under her sheepskin coat, Cleo climbed the spiral staircase, passed her bedroom, and crossed the landing.

The door loomed at the corridor's end: a wedge of dark oak with a black brass handle. It was unmistakable. The pressure was heavier here. Cleo crouched, shut one eye and peered through the keyhole. A black round pit stared back.

Shoulder wedged against the door, she gathered her strength, building a rhythm of push and release. The pressure. The chill. There was something inside. She pushed and pulled and rattled the handle, ever more desperate to enter the room.

A click. A creak. A loosening of wood. The door yielded a pencil-thin gap.

Cleo pressed her soft cheek against the frame. She narrowed her eyes through the crack. Rising in the murk, boxes towered towards the ceiling, grey cube upon grey cube. Through shadows dull as dust, a picture misted into view, hung on a nearby wall. Eyes dry as paper, Cleo blinked, sharpened her focus.

Set within a gilded frame, a photograph emerged, in grainy black and white: a young woman in a bell-shaped hat, her hand on the lip of a stone well. In the corner was a date: 25/11/1921. Wood creaked. Cleo leaned in. Her dry eyes strained for details.

A woman. A well. And in the distance, a bare black tree, its branches spiked with leaves. Cleo focused on the well, picturing her paintings down in the studio. A tighter chill tensed her silken skin. Beside the smiling woman, the ghost of a hand crawled from the well. Long black nails clawed at the lip.

The woman in the bell-shaped hat . . . It couldn't be. The photo was too old, and she was too young. Was it her mother? A sister? A twin? It couldn't be. It couldn't . . .

The woman in the photo. She was the double of Margaret Powler.

'Evening.'

Cleo jumped out of her silken skin.

'Christ almighty, Margaret.' Cleo panted as she turned. 'You scared the shit out of me.'

'I let myself in,' smiled Margaret, shaking a set of keys. 'Exploring are we?'

Margaret brushed her arm past Cleo. Long smooth fingers wrapped around the handle. The door creaked in reply. The slim gap snapped to black.

'I was just checking for—'

'How *are* you?' Margaret grabbed Cleo's hand and subtly stroked her skin. Her fingers licked like water. Margaret led Cleo across the landing towards the spiral staircase. Both behaved as if the door had never existed.

Cleo made coffee in the kitchenette. Margaret toured the studio. She eyed the canvases against the walls, the rubbings hung on the lines.

Head down, concentrating a little too hard on pouring the coffee, Cleo's eyes flicked furtively at Margaret, dressed as ever in heels and a houndstooth suit. The photograph. The well. The smiling woman. It couldn't be her. It couldn't . . .

'I see you've been busy,' smiled Margaret. Stilettos clicked the floorboards. Her heels stabbed at the paint stains, the marks of previous guests.

Cleo passed Margaret her coffee, black and strong.

'These ones are *very* Rothko,' Margaret said, studying the green bars. 'And these,' she continued, now turning to Cleo's still lifes of the stone wells, 'are positively bucolic.'

'The wells?' said Cleo. Retreating to the kitchenette, she scrutinised Margaret's face at a safe distance. 'They kind of just "came" to me. I hate them. And the bars, too. It's not me. It's not my style. I came down here to create a collection and ended up painting your own space. It all feels a bit desperate.'

'The juices are flowing again,' said Margaret. 'That's all that matters.' She clicked towards the patio doors. The curtains parted. The doors swung open. Margaret stared at the tar-black pool.

'Oh, dear,' said Margaret, shaking her head. 'Oh dear, oh dear, oh dear.'

They walked the decking and faced the pool. Above the towering leylandii, silver clouds hazed a thumbnail moon. The pair stepped towards the edge.

'It was like that when I woke up this morning.'

Margaret studied the pool, not saying a word. The oily surface slopped against the stones.

'Hand on heart, I haven't done anything,' Cleo said, set on the defence by Margaret's silence, feeling like a guilty child. 'Haven't spilled anything in the water, or blocked up the drain, or . . .'

'How strange,' Margaret finally said, not to Cleo, but to the pool. She breathed in the musky scent of decay, her nostrils whistling softly. 'Just so very *strange*.'

'Has anything like this happened before?'

'No,' lied Margaret. 'Never.'

'It's not even water,' Cleo added. Her jelly shoes balanced on the stones. She leaned over the gulping black. 'When I dipped a finger in this morning, I got covered in this disgusting gunk. It took forever to wash it off.'

'You touched it?' said Margaret, retreating from the stones. Heels clicked on the decking. She settled behind Cleo.

'Why? Shouldn't I have done?'

'Maybe,' said Margaret, 'you should take a closer look.'

Blue eyes shining, palms outspread, Margaret pushed Cleo into the pool.

There was a scream, brief and sharp. Cleo hit the surface,

head first. The pool welcomed her, not with a splash or a squirt or a spray, but a muddy, heaving gulp. Ears thudding, she plunged into the void.

Cleo surfaced, gasping and coughing. The pool's chill sent a thick shiver. Her tongue writhed inside her mouth like a salted slug. Oil slopped from her lilac hair, oozing down her silken skin. Blinded by the void, Cleo scrubbed her eyes. Her vision cleared on a shadowed figure.

Margaret stood in silence on the stones, lips tight, face hard, icy blue eyes shining. Shivering, Cleo dipped and lifted. She cleared her throat. She called for help. Margaret stepped back from the stones and slowly crossed her arms.

Bobbing on the surface, gasping from the pool's cold embrace, Cleo kicked her legs. She slopped towards the stone edge, arms scooping heavy oil. The pool sucked and lapped her limbs, as if licking at a lollipop.

Cleo lunged at the stones. Her slapping fingers slipped like eels. The smooth rocks spurned her grip. Cleo slopped back into the pool. Again, she hauled herself at the edge. Again, she clawed at the stones. Again, she slid into the cold black soup.

'Most people try the ladder first,' said Margaret. 'Not that it makes any difference. They slip off all the same. You can struggle and slide on the stones all night, Cleo. You can't leave. She won't let you.'

'Get me *out*,' spat Cleo. Once more she heaved at the stones. Once more she slid into the black. 'What are you *doing*, Margaret? Get a pole or a broom or something and fucking *help*.'

Margaret shook her head, tutting at the lifeforce wasted on the stones.

'She won't let you out,' Margaret repeated.

Cleo kicked away from the edge, away from Margaret. She bobbed and shivered, stranded in the void. Trapped and surrounded, with no chance of escape, again she screamed for help. Her cries echoed through the garden, absorbed by the tombs of leylandii. Black oil slopped against the stones in a steady, rhythmic gulp. *Glop. Glop. Glop.*

'*Shhh*,' hushed Margaret. A smooth long finger pointed, not at Cleo, but behind her.

Cleo turned. Her lilac hair clung to her cheeks. The pool began to heave and fold. A rolling hump broke the surface. A flash of claw. The fin of an elbow.

'You haven't met Peg in the flesh, have you?' said Margaret. 'Poor thing, she still misses the well. I've told her a hundred times, the pool is so much better for feeding, but she won't listen. I do wish she'd think about something else. I'm getting rather tired of seeing the paintings of her precious well every time I enter the house. Now, don't you fight and make a fuss. Her teeth aren't what they used to be.'

The hump rolled closer.

'I must say, the water's done a wonderful job of softening you up for her. Just *wonderful*.' Margaret slid her fingers down her porcelain face. 'Why, your skin feels almost as smooth as mine.'

Cleo felt a force stir from the underneath. A playful tug pulled at her ankle. Teasing. Testing. Tasting. The leylandii held her screams.

'Goodbye Cleo,' said Margaret. 'And thank you for your wonderful contribution.'

The long spiked fingers were sharp as sticks. Bone by bone, nail by nail, they coiled around her ankles. Another tug. Less playful this time. Cleo screamed and twisted. Her limbs slowed in the thickening pool. With one swift, powerful wrench, she vanished from the surface. In a blur of lilac hair, Cleo Marsh was gone.

She plunged into the ice-cold depths, folding like a doll to a bony embrace. In the murk of the pool, she opened her eyes one final time.

The hint of an arm, gnarled and thin.

The snaking waves of thrashing hair.

And two yellow eyes, like fire through fog. Fierce. Mad. Ecstatic. Hungry.

Soft teeth met soft flesh. Cleo dissolved in the ravenous dark.

And all that was loved was lost.

Margaret smiled at the heaving pool, listening to the surface slop and heave. She turned from the stones, crossed the decking, and entered the house to wait. Soon the darkness would fade from the pool, replaced by a delicious, honey-sweet glow.

Stilettos clicking on paint-stained boards, Margaret collected the canvases. She calmly bagged them in a large black sack and climbed the spiral staircase.

Sack set by the storeroom door, Margaret took out a key. The lock released with a click. With a flick of a switch, the storeroom shivered into light.

Rising to the ceiling in methodical rows, a Manhattan of boxes towered from the floor, each box labelled with a date and name, some furred with dust, others new. Packed in like honeycomb cells, the boxed contents remained the same.

Margaret dragged the black sack to the end of the store-room. She unpacked Cleo's canvases and transferred them to an empty box, tutting at the bars and thick stone wells. It never changed: the same image repeated, like a chant, all answering to Peg's compulsion. Different artists, different styles, but always the same, always the same: the stones of the pool, rebuilt and restored, back to the Clootie well that once guarded the ancient spring. Margaret closed the lid.

Before she locked up, she paused by her photo on the storeroom wall. Margaret smiled, remembering the bell-hat she wore that day. So much had changed. There had been no Silverweed Road, no Corvid Estate. Just the house next door, the hawthorn, the Clootie well, and Peg Powler's spring in the deep, dark Woods.

Peg had been scratching inside her well when her mother had taken the photograph. Shortly after, Peg had been fed, another stranger lowered into the well. 'You're her guardian now,' her mother had said. 'Never forget, you need each other. Keep her fed and she'll keep you young. Keep her fed, and she'll keep you young . . .'

Margaret turned off the lights and shut the door. The storeroom plunged to black.

Margaret spiralled down the staircase, took a pair of scissors from the kitchenette, and cut a square from the sheepskin coat. Outside, in the long, dark garden, she stood by the hawthorn, eyeing the branches, selecting a suitable thorn. A sheepskin ribboned in the breeze, joining the rags of others on the Clootie tree. The black pool cleared and discovered its glow.

Shaking off her heels, unbuttoning her houndstooth suit, Margaret stood naked before the glimmering water. She climbed down the ladder into the blood-warm pool, bathing in its rich, sweet glow, and swam in silence to the centre. Soft rain began to fall.

'Oh, Peggy,' called Margaret. 'Peg, Peg, Peggy . . .'

In the depths of the pool, a shadow answered. It curled in silence from the grate, snaking through the glassy water. Yellow eyes burned through waves of green hair. Crooked arms broke the surface, dripping blood-warm water.

Margaret Powler bowed her head in greeting. Long gnarled fingers cupped her face. Ancient flesh met young. Relishing each gliding stroke, Margaret moaned and closed her eyes, drinking in the pool's fresh life. With each caress and gliding claw, fine lines faded and skin tightened, a youthful porcelain glow sustained.

As skittering fingers repaired and flowed, yellow eyes glowed in the depths of the pool, flickering through thrashing hair. Margaret looked up to the shielding spirits that arched above. They rose from the stones, their spirits entwined, merging at the centre of the pool. Soft rain patted down from the sky, the water repelled by a lucid dome, formed by an arch of eternal slaves, shielding an eternal spring.

There, in the centre of the arc, a new form stretched and arched from its stone. A thin mouth gaped under pale pitted eyes, frozen in shock or surprise. Waves of lilac rippled through the dome.

Extract from The Silverweed Files, 6 November 2024

A personal blog by former Detective Chief Inspector Jim Heath. The views expressed do not reflect those of Kent Police nor the victims impacted by events.

How do you find a missing person when the prime suspect goes missing themselves? If, indeed, that suspect was even alive?

Cleo Marsh's disappearance went unnoticed for some time. She lived alone, worked alone and, according to those who knew her, abandoned all contact to focus on her art. It was the landlord of Marsh's Hackney studio who eventually reported her missing when she failed to pay her rent: a good month after she caught the train from Victoria Station to Meadway. The first 48 hours are critical when searching for a missing person. By the time Marsh's disappearance had been filed, the window of opportunity had firmly shut.

You only have to view her art to see that Marsh was a troubled young woman. (Far too morbid, even for my tastes: give me a nice jolly artist, like Van Gogh.) I cannot help feeling her fate imitated her art: Marsh appeared to slip under the floorboards.

By the time we searched no. 25, Marsh's belongings had gone. Police presence had increased on the road and I believe her things were removed in a panic. Whoever had tried to erase her presence had been astonishingly careless. Among the burnt canvases salvaged from the garden was a portrait of a jackdaw, signed by Marsh.

As for the blood-warm swimming pool, which stubbornly refilled itself each time it was dredged? Had Marsh drowned in its depths? Without a body, it's impossible to say, but she had most certainly swum in the pool. As had many others. An analysis of the water showed it contained the DNA of not only Marsh, but dozens of other artists – all of whom had gone missing.

The vanishing of Cleo Marsh has attracted a wealth of conspiracies, none of which hold water. Do I believe she was part of a suicide cult for forsaken artists? Certainly not. Only the owner of no. 25, Margaret Powler, knows the truth: a figure as elusive as the Scarlet Pimpernel. Even her Fitzrovia art agency was a phantom enterprise.

Kent Police could not trace Powler. So what did they do? They abandoned the search. The same way they abandoned me. Over the years, my efforts to track Powler down have only deepened the mystery. According to her birth records, Margaret Powler was born in 1890. At the time of Marsh's disappearance, she would been 129 years old. I have yet to find a grave that marks her name, but the prime suspect is obviously dead.

I can say with confidence there are two victims here: not only the missing artist, but poor Margaret Powler herself. It is clear the deceased is a victim of ghosting, her identity stolen by persons unknown. My search for Powler's impersonator continues . . .

NO. 17:

Caught Red-handed

As Augustus Fry stared at the bathroom mirror, frightened by his new reflection, he flickered through the events that had reshaped his future. That wretched ring. Tidswell and Gaunt. And the sham of a phone call that had started it all. Augustus looked down to his blood-stained palms, dreading his next, inevitable move. Like a simmering mist, the past rose again, as red and boiling as his freshly cooked face . . .

Curling the horns of his copper moustache, Augustus had been loafing in his office at his pedestal desk when he answered the call from an unknown number. As a dealer in fine antiquities, he was used to fielding unsolicited enquiries. Most came to nothing. This one, however, sounded promising.

The voice on the end of the line was weak and reedy, with a grainy Mancunian twang. It was the tone, however, that had really captured Fry's attention. The questions were limp and gullible, coated in a tang of desperation. Augustus sprawled in his chair, stroking his belly, a plump predator sensing fresh prey. Where there was desperation, there was money to be made.

Mr Butterworth, he'd called himself. Didn't give a first name. Didn't own a computer. Didn't have email. Couldn't supply a photograph. 'Were hoping you'd come up,' Butterworth had said. 'Give it once over.'

Augustus gazed around his office as Butterworth droned on. Based in the upstairs back room of 17 Silverweed Road, it had been a fallow few months for Solomon Antiquities. A stolen Anglo-Saxon brooch had gone to a collector for £7,000, but that had been August; now it was November, and his blank glass cabinets glared back – a few sorry shards of Iron Age pottery, six bodkin point arrowheads, and an ugly Viking loom weight that looked like a limestone doughnut. Augustus totted up their value – £200 of ancient tat from an antique Christmas cracker. Ramses, the long-suffering Persian cat he'd inherited from his late mother and a convenient mop for Fry's frustrations, slinked into the office and rubbed against the door frame.

Butterworth finally got to the point. Augustus uncapped his fountain pen. Ink scratched on a silver repoussé writing pad.

Ring. Engraved. 'Goldy coloured' Age ???

Blind viewings were rarely rewarding. Augustus, nonetheless, sensed this 'goldy coloured' ring might warrant a viewing. Most promising of all, its owner sounded deliciously stupid. Visit agreed, call ended, Augustus read the address on his pad: *9 Deanbrook Road, Rivington, Bolton.* A 250-mile drive north.

Augustus was familiar with the area. In the 1960s, a Bronze Age burial cairn at nearby Noon Hill had yielded two sacrificial knives, one of which had entered the black market eighteen months ago. It was Augustus himself who had sniffed it out, snapped it up, and sold it on for a healthy profit. Two collectors, Marcus Tidswell and John Gaunt, had battled over the knife in a rally of bad-tempered bids. Tidswell had lost, Gaunt had won, and Fry had collected £40,000.

Augustus poured his third Famous Grouse of the afternoon, ushered Ramses from the office with a scooping kick, and twisted his argan-oiled handlebar moustache, ends upturned on a face that never smiled.

The following night, Augustus booked a suite at Manchester's Lowry and packed his Mulberry travel case: mustard waistcoat, Harris Tweed two-piece, and black wing-cap Carreducker brogues – all counterfeit. Carefully cultivated to intimidate with impunity, Augustus routinely dressed like a plump Victorian plutocrat – a look, he was certain, that would overawe Butterworth. Born and raised on the Corvid Estate, Fry's aristocratic mirage was, like so many aspects of Augustus, a protective shield and extravagant deception. Honesty was for idiots. Lies rewarded, took you places.

After scraping a tin of sardines into Ramses' bowl, Fry crunched up the gravel driveway into the night, casting a sneer at the gloomy slabs of mock-Tudor semis. Ever since his tyrannical mother passed and he'd inherited the house they shared, Augustus had been trying to sell his childhood home. The place held nothing but memories that pickled him in bitterness: no more so than the Woods at the road's dead-end, where young Augustus would cower among the blackthorns, hiding from the neighbourhood bullies. Cursed by joke offers and withdrawn bids, no. 17 had been on sale for three agonising years. It was if Silverweed had decided it would never let him go, burying him alive in its mock-Tudor purgatory.

Augustus sat behind the wheel of his Land Rover and turned the key, primed for the drive up to Manchester. Glaring through the windscreen, his eyes met the entrance to Silverweed Road, taunted by the flickering street lamp. He revved the accelerator, itching with irritation.

The flowers from the crash. They had to go. When that stupid woman drove into the lamp post, Augustus had stood rubbernecking in the rain with everyone else, scowling at the wreckage.

The council still haven't fixed the lamp post. And that weirdo at no. 10 keeps coming out at night, talking to those mouldy bouquets. The woman's completely mad. And the smell, the smell . . . the wretched shrine stinks of rotten meat.

Augustus parked by the corner, climbed from the Land Rover with an audible pop, and stomped over to the flowers. He picked a bunch of burnt pink orchids, looked around for a wheelie bin, and nearly jumped out of his mustard waistcoat. Her, from no. 10. She was standing right behind him, a screaming storm of black hair. Fending off a blur of punches, he dropped the flowers and ran to the car as fast as his counterfeit brogues would carry him.

Augustus sped off into the night, flashing a look in the rear-view mirror. The woman stood raging under the lamp post. She clutched the flowers close to her chest, her livid mouth a rip of red.

Fully rested after several whiskies from the minibar and four Nurofen Plus, Augustus awoke in his Lowry suite feeling the need to be angry about something. He phoned room service and demanded to know where the coffee he'd never ordered was. Two minutes later, he was lounging in a fluffy white gown, sipping coffee, berating the room service waiter for forgetting to bring the breakfast he'd also never ordered. When his Full English arrived, Augustus slammed the door to his suite. He ate fast and noisily, copper moustache writhing, relishing the rewards of his bogus fury.

The address was everything Augustus had feared. Accessible by a dirt track lined with trees that spiked a fossil-grey sky, the emerging farmhouse appeared to slant in the battering wind, creaking and decrepit. There was no money to be made here.

'Aye, Mr Fry. Come in, come in. Right quaggy outside.'

Augustus bent under the low front door and greeted his host with a stern, 'Mr Butterworth'. The old man offered a bony hand to shake, which Augustus obligingly crushed. Frail, shrunken, with hunched vulture shoulders, Butterworth had dressed up for the viewing: his best brown woollen suit, favourite flat cap and freshly polished shoes. He tottered into the low-ceilinged living room, invited Augustus to sit at a butcher's block table.

Augustus exchanged sneers with a wiry dog curled around the wood fire. A dusty wall clock ticked. It was barely 11 a.m., but the room was already night-dark, the air thick with the scent of wet dog. In the corner, a camping gas cylinder lit the room in muddy blots of yellow.

Already impatient, Augustus turned down tea, coffee, lemon squash and water and asked to see the piece. Butterworth fumbled a green ring box from his trouser pocket and placed it on the table. The lid opened with a tantalising whisper.

'May I?' said Augustus. He held the ring up for inspection.

It was large. A man's ring, either worn by an ogre, or made to fit over a thick gloved finger. Augustus scrutinised the dull metal. A little murky, perhaps, but agreeably weighty, and quite possibly gold. Augustus maintained a poker face as his fat heart quickened. He pulled a jewellers' loupe from his waistcoat pocket, reviewing the engraving that formed an unbroken band around the ring. The runic symbols looked authentic: primal, vivid and Anglo-Saxon. Augustus turned the ring, searching in vain for a hallmark or a carat stamp. As he raised it in the muddy light, the dark runes simmered a deep burnt red. The wall clock ticked. Augustus suppressed his excitement.

'What's the provenance?'

Butterworth shifted in his chair, whiskery eyebrows muddling.

'Its origin, Mr Butterworth,' Augustus said, voice lowering. 'Where did you get the ring from?'

'Here.'

'Yes, I understand it's here now, but how did you come across it?'

'S'always been here.' Butterworth shrugged. 'Been here since I was a lad. Been here since my father, his father's father, father 'fore that, father 'fore that . . . Been here centuries, Mr Fry.'

'And your certificate of ownership? You do have documentation?'

Worry lines rivered through Butterworth's face. He sank into his chair, as if the air had leaked from his body, leaving just a crag of vulture shoulders. To Fry's delight, Butterworth shook his head.

Untraceable. Possibly gold. Anglo-Saxon runes. This was too good to be true . . .

Augustus switched tactics, softened his tone.

'So, am I correct in thinking this is an heirloom?'

Augustus realised he was twirling the ring a little too seductively in his hand and placed it back inside the box.

'Mr Butterworth, I suggest you get this verified. Naturally, I'd be happy to arrange that for you – at a very reasonable price.'

'Aye? How much?'

'Entirely depends on the expert. I would say . . .' Augustus looked at the ring, at Butterworth, at the fuggy interior, the wiry dog. 'Two, three thousand would be sufficient.'

'Pounds? Was looking to sell, Mr Fry, not squander. Can hardly afford dog's scran as it is.'

'I see . . .' *Let him stew*, thought Augustus. *Let him stew in his cheap itchy suit. Let him stew with his cheap itchy dog.*

'Mr Butterworth,' Augustus finally exhaled, satisfied with the manufactured tension of his pause, 'with no proof of ownership, it's impossible to place a value on your ring. For all I know, it could be stolen. If the ring were to pass into my hands only to be exposed as a black market acquisition, it would put my spotless reputation at risk. It's certainly not gold, I can assure you of that – it's brass. As for its age, I'd hazard late 1800s. The engraving, however, is twentieth century. See the edging on the runes?' Augustus picked up the ring and ran his finger over the banded lettering. 'Diamond-drag engraving. Unmistakably so. I'm afraid you've not just wasted my time – you've wasted yours. Good day to you, Mr Butterworth.'

Augustus pushed his belly against the table, unstuck himself from the creaking chair. He rose and marched for the front door, confident of a postponed exit.

'Mr Fry,' called Butterworth, standing up, straightening his trousers. 'Must be worth *something*, surely?'

'I'd be doing you a kindness at £100,' Augustus lied. He turned around slowly, slipping his hand into a jacket pocket. He furtively separated five £20 notes from a roll of £300. 'Would cash suffice . . . ?'

Augustus left the farmhouse barely able to contain his laughter. The man was a fool. As his Land Rover crunkled back up the dirt track, the ring awakened in his pocket. A slow heat simmered from the reddening runes.

Augustus thundered upstairs, kicked Ramses from his office with a swiping brogue, and settled behind his pedestal desk. The box opened with a whisper. He took out the ring, testing its weight in his jigging palm.

Was it gold? An unresponsive magnet dragged over its surface suggested it could be. Copper moustache twisting eagerly, Augustus reached deep into the desk drawer. Ramses returned and curled at his feet, hoping to be fed. He laid a black touchstone on the desktop and gently rolled the ring against the stone, leaving a stripe of metallic film. When he applied the aqua fortis and saw the line stand firm, his fat heart hastened. Mouth dry and throat purring, Augustus dripped aqua regia on the strip. If the mark dissolved, the ring was categorically, unmistakably, ecstatically gold.

The mark dissolved.

Augustus grabbed the ring, showering it in oily kisses. 'A toast to Mr Butterworth,' he declared, slugging Famous Grouse direct from a decanter. 'You magnificently stupid old fool.' He snatched up Ramses, threw him into the air, started whistling 'We're in the Money', didn't think to catch the cat. Ramses scattered, squowling from the office.

Augustus locked the ring in the office safe and toppled downstairs, intending to get gloriously shit-faced. Alone in the lounge, Augustus drank to himself, toasting his own magnificence.

Upstairs, in the pitch-black safe, the runes of the ring burned a ravenous red.

At 2.39 a.m., a short, deep, sickening bang rocked through no. 17. Light bulbs swayed and clinked. Fake Gainsboroughs quivered in frames. Glass cabinets rippled like broken water. Slumbering Ramses toppled from a bookcase, jumping up with spikes of fur.

Shocked from his drunken slumber, Augustus tumbled out of bed, landed on his coccyx and bellowed like a stag. He wobbled to his feet, rubbing his back. Fry's bones still trembled from the quake. Above his head, a crystal lampshade chimed and swung. An uneasy after-hum settled in the house.

A thief. A break-in. The ring. My ring . . .

Emboldened by booze, Augustus fumbled for the wrought-iron poker he kept under the bed. He edged towards the bedroom door, shushing at his drunken self to be quiet. Cautious step by cautious step, Augustus inched down the landing, passed the bathroom, and stopped. The office door creaked open. A poker raised in the dark. Augustus slapped the light switch.

His reflection flashed from the cabinets. Fry swung the poker at empty air. His startled heart slowed to a puff of relief. No break in. No thief. Just his own reflection. A silky heat seemed to simmer from the safe as he checked the ring was secure in its box. In the low night-hum of the night-blue house, Augustus crept down the stairs.

Still twitchy from the sickening bang that had shaken him awake, Augustus approached the front door. As he checked the bolts, his face warmed to a peculiar heat that seemed to haze from the frame. Augustus unlocked the door and stepped into the night.

A fuming outline caught his eye.

In the centre of the oak front door glowed a livid lava-red hand print. Its width was twice that of his own plump hand, the size as unnatural as the smoke that fumed from it. Five thick fingers fanned from the palm, in the shape of a halt or a push.

Too drunk to feel the fear he should, Augustus prodded the mark, recoiling from its fiery snap. His sizzling finger leaped to his lips and cooled inside his mouth. He glared at the hand print, bewildered by the source of the sickening bang. Culprits flashed through his mind.

Who would dare vandalise his door? The infernal kids who put bangers in the postbox? The mad woman with the orchids? Certainly not a disgruntled client: he hadn't sold a thing since late August. Tapping the poker in his hand, Fry scanned the street. In the powder of night, there was neither sound nor motion, the houses dark as tombs. No door was marked with a glowing hand other than his own.

Augustus jumped at a black blur that seemed to dive down from the moon itself. A jackdaw landed on the roof of his Land Rover.

'Don't you even think about it,' Augustus slurred, worried his car was about to be soiled.

Augustus glowered at the bird. The bird glowered back, with double the spite. Held by the shine of silver eyes, Augustus felt a flickering chill, as if a heartbeat had been stolen.

With a flick of the wings and a cry of *ack-ack*, the jackdaw soared into the night. Augustus watched the black dot fade towards the Woods, the ghost of a shiver receding.

When Augustus turned towards the front door, the livid red hand print had vanished. He scrubbed his eyes, looked again, stroked his hand over the cool oak frame. It was as if the door had never been marked.

Bolting the locks, Augustus toppled upstairs and sloshed back into bed. Walls pitching and lurching around him, certain his reality was but a vivid, swaying dream, he closed his eyes, wishing for sweeter visions.

As drunken Augustus heaved and snored, a slow heat built within the house. Passing through walls, casting no shadow, the ghostly haze of a crimson hand toured the rooms in silence. Fingers flexing from a hot-plate palm, it glided across the darkened landing, towards the simmering safe.

Rising late at 10 a.m., whisky hangover batting his temples, Augustus stood on his driveway, glaring at the entrance to no. 17. No red hand. No fuming smoke. Just the same old boring oak front door. Was the sickening bang no more than an inebriated fever dream? It wouldn't be the first time he'd hallucinated after a bottle of Famous Grouse. A fortnight back, he'd been so shit-faced, Ramses' face had morphed into his mother's. Just how drunk had he been last night?

Upstairs in the back-room office, seated in an ill-fitting imitation silk kimono, Augustus inspected the runes on his new acquisition. He took a book from the shelf, *Danbury's World of Anglo-Saxon Treasures*, and flapped it open on his pedestal desk.

There are seven known Anglo-Saxon rings featuring runic inscriptions: Kingmoor, Bramham Moor, Linstock Castle, Wheatley Hill, Coquet Island, Carmond and the Thames Exchange. The most celebrated piece, the Kingmoor Ring, denotes a spell said to staunch the flow of blood, interpreted by Prof. Axen of King's College Cambridge as 'pure magical gibberish'. This priceless artefact . . .

'Priceless?' Augustus mocked as he compared his ring to a photo of the Kingmoor. '*Everything* has a price.'

The smile slid from his face. The similarities really were quite striking. The rings even shared the same diameter: a bulky 27 mm, fit for an ogre or an iron glove. Augustus shuffled in his chair, reread the entry. *There are seven known Anglo-Saxon rings featuring runic inscriptions . . .* 'And I,' Augustus told the ring, 'have the eighth.'

The antiques business was a callous world. Augustus had always considered Indiana Jones an idealistic nincompoop, the *Antiques Road Show* a nostalgic buttered crumpet that sentimentalised the cut-throat reality. No, the world of antiquities was a Cold War thriller, seething with suspicion, where everyone thought everyone else was the double agent. For all he knew, Butterworth might have stolen the ring. The sale would have to be discreet – and swift.

Augustus turned the ring in his hand. Seduced by the promise of its glimmering runes, dreams of escape twirled and fluttered. If it was worth what he suspected, he would finally be free of this accursed road. No more mock-Tudor houses for Augustus Fry. He would have the real thing. A Tudor cottage in the Cotswolds, perhaps.

Stroking the horns of his copper moustache, Augustus

considered his network of contacts; a rogue's gallery of grasping archaeologists, bent curators, shady excavators and crooked detectorists . . . He poured himself a breakfast whisky. Marcus Tidswell and John Gaunt. They'd already battled over that sacrificial knife stolen from the burial cairn on Noon Hill. Both wealthy. Both Anglo-Saxon fanatics. And, best of all, neither could stand the sight of the other. Get them in the same room together and a bidding war would erupt like Krakatoa, belching golden coins.

Maybe that fool Butterworth wasn't so stupid after all. He'd arrange a blind viewing, much as Butterworth had done with him, fire their curiosity, stoke up some loathing and wait until he hit the jackpot. Augustus immediately tapped out two emails, one to Tidswell, the other to Gaunt, each identical and four words long: *I have another Kingmoor.*

In the dead of night, the runes stirred, shimmering like embers. A building heat, silky-sinister, seeped slowly from the safe. Augustus dreamed in the creeping heat of sunbathing beneath a fiery star.

Hovering above his head, a red hand glowed in silent malice. Fingers flexed in expectation, throbbing with intent. Now it lowered, fuming red, casting its heat upon his face. Copper whiskers curled and crackled. A surge of blood-fire reddened.

Augustus stirred and smacked his lips, turning in his sleep. The hand retreated to the ceiling, and simmered from above.

Not yet. Not now. One alone was not enough. Too soon to strike. Too soon . . .

*

A lashing storm hit Silverweed the night the bidders came. Augustus paced the house, stopped by the windows, watching the lightning lick the rooftops. The houses cowered to growls of thunder: a sound that gave Augustus considerable pleasure. It would add some theatre to the evening.

It was Gaunt who arrived first. Dressed in his counterfeit plutocrat finery, Augustus greeted his guest with unctuous deference and ushered him into the lounge. In one slick move, he simultaneously bowed while booting out Ramses with the tip of a polished brogue.

'A drink, Mr Gaunt?'

Gaunt – lanky, thin-lipped, hollow-cheeked Gaunt, leery-eyed, sixty years old, and not known for his sense of humour – nodded grimly. Augustus unplugged the stopper of an Edwardian decanter bought from TK Maxx and poured two whiskies.

Fry had never liked dealing with the man – he was pompous, stern and a notoriously tough negotiator. Whenever Augustus took a good look at Gaunt, he was instantly transported back to his miserable schooldays, and a certain Mr Cushing – a tyrannical, similarly stern-faced PE teacher who had so enjoyed bullying him on the rugby fields. Cushing had broken his index finger once, using Augustus as a dummy while demonstrating a tackle. The memory still pinched – pinched even sharper given Gaunt's resemblance to his childhood tormenter.

'I assume one will be holding a séance later this evening?' Gaunt asked, pacing the dusky, low-lit lounge, a symphony of oppressive brown. Augustus had lit a legion of white candles and set them around the fireplace. Another touch of moody drama. After sharing a stilted chuckle, they drank in silence, staring into their whisky tumblers, Fry still standing, Gaunt perched on the edge of a creaking camel-back sofa.

The doorbell rang. Augustus made his excuses. Gaunt bristled – a private viewing, he'd said. When Augustus ushered Tidswell into the lounge, the room hummed with hostility.

'What's *he* doing here, Fry?' Gaunt said, standing up.

Tidswell – five foot four, light bulb-shaped, sixty-six years of age with a pink bald head cuffed with yellow-white hair – glowered at Gaunt. Augustus never liked dealing with him either. Augustus, come to think of it, never liked dealing with anyone.

'I was told,' said Tidswell, 'this was a private viewing.'

'As was I,' snapped Gaunt.

Tidswell and Gaunt glared at Augustus, indignant eyebrows raised, each demanding an explanation, bonded by mutual loathing. This was all going rather well, thought Augustus.

'A drink, Mr Tidswell?'

'I didn't come all this way for a drinks reception, Mr Fry,' snapped Tidswell. He narrowed his eyes on Gaunt. 'And certainly not in this company.'

Thudding down his whisky glass, Gaunt closed his coat collars, preparing for his exit.

'Gentlemen, please,' Augustus interjected. The time had come to sweeten them with lies. 'I was under the impression you were on good terms, but it appears, in my excitement, I may have misjudged things. Please, accept my sincere apologies. As you know, I find myself in a most delicate situation regarding a recent acquisition – one I feel honoured to share with you. Mr Tidswell, Mr Gaunt: without wishing to cause any blushes, I regard you as the country's foremost authorities on Anglo-Saxon antiquities and am therefore begging your assistance.'

Fry paused, coughed daintily, his eyes switching between Tidswell and Gaunt. 'I've invited you here to verify the provenance of a quite extraordinary find – two of antiquity's finest minds, working together. Nobody knows the prize I hold except we three in this room. Naturally, whether you wish to view it or not is entirely your decision.'

Gaunt settled back into the sofa.

'Now, I can tell by your faces you're impatient to be acquainted, so if you'd follow me upstairs, perhaps you can see it with your own eyes. If you wish to leave, I understand. Just be aware that if you do, this evening's privilege will be lost for ever.'

Augustus gestured towards the lounge door, inviting them to the upstairs office.

'Shall we?'

Tidswell and Gaunt were putty in his plump, pink hands.

Gleaming from the heart of a red velvet cushion, the gold ring shone from the main display cabinet. Augustus handed out two pairs of white silk inspection gloves, putting on a third himself. Suited and gloved under furtive light, the trio resembled a conference of snooker referees spellbound by a golden ball.

Augustus opened the cabinet, lifted the cushion, and placed it under the bleach-white sun of a curtseying desk lamp. Tidswell and Gaunt leaned in unison. Rain ripped at the office window.

'Provenance?' asked Gaunt, without looking up.

'Entirely untraceable,' Augustus replied. 'No carat,

stamps or jewellers' marks, and no signs of machining. It's pure gold, gentlemen: twenty-four carat.'

'Good God,' said Tidswell. He took the ring and lifted it to the light. The runes pulsed in reply, glowing like blood-red embers. 'Where the devil did you find this, Fry?'

'The engraving,' Gaunt interrupted, snapping his fingers impatiently.

Tidswell reluctantly passed his treasure, mesmerised and instantly covetous. Gaunt rolled the ring under a desktop magnifying lamp, pulling the runes into sharper focus. A bubblegum of tongue slipped between Gaunt's thin lips. He focused on the inscription.

'Anglo-Saxon futhorc,' said Gaunt, speaking out loud to himself as he identified the runes. 'That would make the ring eighth, ninth century. The Kingmoor Ring told of a healing spell. Let's see what this has to say for itself . . .'

Gaunt pulled a slim notebook from his jacket, licked a finger and turned to a page of bent sticks and triangles: *Runes of the Anglo-Saxon Futhorc*. As Gaunt read out the symbols, turning the ring in his hand, Tidswell translated the runes into English. Gaunt passed his notebook. Tidswell wrote his translation on the back cover. Augustus looked on, delighted by their sudden sense of harmony. His hands fidgeted behind his back, certain the temporary bond would be broken any second.

'Well?' said Gaunt, holding the ring in a defensive grip.

'Most bizarre.' Tidswell ruffled the yellow-white tufts that hedged his pink bald head. 'If the Kingmoor Ring was indeed inscribed with a healing spell, this reads . . . Well, it reads more like a threat. Listen to this: *I, father of hill and mire, guard this land eternal. May blood fire redden those who take me from my hearth . . .*'

'I'm having a devilish time translating that last part,' Tidswell continued. '*Blood fire redden* . . . Doesn't make a jot of sense.' Gaunt placed the ring on its velvet cushion.

'Magical gibberish?' Augustus chipped in.

Tidswell and Gaunt ignored Fry. Eyes glazed with greed, they stared in harmony, lost to the simmering runes.

'£400,000,' Tidswell blurted, wishing to put a swift end to the evening. Gaunt side-eyed Tidswell with icy belligerence.

'Half a million pounds,' Gaunt snapped. 'Cash.' Eyes fixed on the ring, neither looked at Augustus, stroking his moustache with increasing speed.

'£600,000,' ricocheted Tidswell, switching his glare towards Gaunt.

Gaunt slowly removed his gloves, placed them on the desk. With thin lips and leery eyes, he turned his attention to Augustus.

'Whatever he bids, Fry,' said Gaunt, 'I will outbid. It is as simple and as inevitable as that. So please, continue, Mr Titsbell.'

There was a shifting of feet, a tightening of fists. Tidswell puffed out his chest. Gaunt cricked his neck. Were these old fools seriously squaring up for a fight? Augustus, struggling to conceal a tooth-flashing lottery-win grin, decided it was time to intervene. This was going better than his wildest dreams.

'Gentlemen, please,' Augustus said, curling his copper moustache. 'Let me refresh those drinks.'

'Buffoons,' Augustus laughed to himself as he poured three whiskies in the candle-lit lounge. Ramses purred, curling a figure of eight between his legs. 'Dinner is postponed tonight,' he told the cat. 'Go and catch a mouse. If they continue bidding like this, you can have swan for lunch.'

The walls rocked to a sickening bang.

A tumbler smashed to the lounge floor.

Ramses hissed and dashed out of the lounge.

Tidswell. Gaunt. Alone with the ring. *What the blazes*, fumed Augustus, *is going on up there?* Vision trembling from the wall-rocking shock, Augustus bolted from the candlelit lounge, thumped upstairs, stormed across the landing and stopped dead in his tracks.

Seared into steaming wood, a large, red hand print marked the office door.

Augustus lunged for the door handle. His hand bounced back from a hot-plate heat. Blowing on his palm, Augustus flinched at the sound of crashing glass.

And now the screaming started: the begs for help, the begs for mercy, the begs for it to stop, stop, stop . . .

Brave Augustus pounded down the landing and locked himself in the bedroom. He cowered on the rumbling bed, anxiously stroking his moustache. Thumps and crashes rocked through the landing, drum-drum-drumming the bedroom door. The crystal lampshade bumped and chimed. Augustus clamped his hands to his ears, blocking out the screams, the screams . . .

The house plunged to eerie silence.

Augustus slowly uncuffed his hands from his ears. Unsure of what to do, where to go, he tugged at the horns of his copper moustache. As the ghost echo of thumps and screams faded from his head, he recalled Tidswell and Gaunt's covetous glare, pictured a shadow escaping through the front door, stealing his ring and with it his dreams . . . In that moment, fury became his fuel. Augustus fumbled under the bed, reached for his wrought-iron poker. The bedroom door creaked open.

Augustus inched up the landing, passed the bathroom, confounded once again. The burning hand print that had seared the frame had vanished, not a trace of red fanned fingers to be seen. Poker raised, fat heart hammering, he gripped the cool brass handle. The door tilted in reply, loosening from its hinges.

Hit by a wall of sticky heat, Augustus entered a sparkling bloodbath.

A lampshade swung silently from the ceiling. Yellow beams bounced like a searching spotlight. Shards of glass from shattered cabinets glittered on the floor. Mouth open, lifeless eyes white with terror, Tidswell lay across the pedestal desk, limp arms dangling over the edge. Augustus lowered his gaze to a lanky, hollow-cheeked corpse. Gaunt's snarled body spread on the floor like a freshly smashed fly.

In the venal mind of Augustus Fry, there was only space for one thought, and one thought only.

The ring. The ring. Where is my ring?

Crunching over pixels of glass, display cabinets tattered and trashed, Augustus inspected Tidswell and Gaunt. Both necks bore identical marks, striped red raw by clawing fingers. Had the old fools strangled each other? How the blazes did they . . .

In the carnage of Solomon Antiquities, bodies smashed, glass scattered, rain ripping at the office window, reality finally struck Augustus between the eyes. A mercenary mind hurtled into panic.

He couldn't call the police. It was simply out of the question. They'd take the ring as evidence, bag it up, steal his fortune. What if they delved into its provenance? He'd be arrested for stolen goods and bundled into prison. What if they looked into his past transactions? Stolen goods.

Bundled into prison. No, no, no. The police were most certainly not invited.

A hungry red pulse caught his twitching eye. Augustus followed the shine to Gaunt's hand, flattened on the floor. Screwed around his index finger, the runes of the ring glowed a livid red. *That dirty, thieving, pompous . . .*

Augustus lunged at the lifeless hand, and wrestled with Gaunt's finger. He pulled. He twisted. Muscle ground and popped. The glowing ring refused to yield, clinging tight to Gaunt's stiff finger. Patience wearing thin, Augustus released Gaunt's arm, scowling as it flopped to the floor.

It was no good. It would have to come off.

The window rippled to a crack of thunder. Augustus scanned his office in search of a suitable tool. With a white gloved hand, he snatched a shard from the glittering floor, glass blade glinting in the swaying light. Moustache squirming, lips puffing, he seized Gaunt's finger and worked the blade into a groove. Augustus Fry began to saw.

Blood oozed from a widening wound, opening like an eye. Fluid seeped from mud-yellow gristle. Cheered considerably by the progress he was making, transfixed by the runes of the simmering ring, Augustus sawed harder through the finger. Elbow pistoning back and forth, the crunch of gristle gave way to a smoother sound: of whining glass on slippery bone.

Augustus stopped, sensing movement. A trailing gasp, like escaping gas, hissed from puckered lips. Now a gurgle, a cough, a lung-rattling rasp. Augustus dropped the finger. Gaunt was not yet dead.

Augustus turned back to the hand, irritated his rhythm had been lost. He slid the glass back to its slot. The finger sawing recommenced. Grip lost to slippery blood, slithering in, now slithering out, the glass shard slipped from the bone.

Augustus tossed the shard. His eyes met the glimmering runes. Held within their sickly shimmer, he saw his dreams reflected. In heat and lust, he grabbed the finger and snapped the joint back and forth. Clicking bone began to crack. And still the ring clung on. Head rocking with every tug, Gaunt groaned ever louder.

Sweat dripping from his moustache, Augustus regarded the L-shaped finger. It flopped in his grip like a wet rubber hose. Sufficiently lubricated with blood, Augustus loosened the ring and pulled, sliding it free from a jagged fingertip. In the abattoir of Solomon Antiquities, Augustus smiled victoriously. Wiping the blood on Gaunt's sleeve, he pocketed his precious ring.

There was a delicate click of neck bone. Gaunt lifted his head from the floor. Half-formed words gulped from thin, hooped lips. Augustus looked over to Tidswell, obediently dead, arms dangling over the pedestal desk, then back to groaning Gaunt. If stealing his ring wasn't enough, the thief didn't even have the decency to die.

Enough was enough. It was far too late for survivors now – even less so for thieves. Itching with irritation from the endless groans, Fry glowered at Gaunt. Warped by the heat and the simmering runes, he found Cushing staring back. Augustus plunged to distant rugby fields, of tackles and torment and broken fingers. He seized the chance to kill a memory.

It was no good. Cushing would have to go.

Looming over Gaunt, his face melting into Cushing's, Augustus peeled off both gloves and scoffed them into the source of his torment. A twitching foot writhed in protest.

Augustus doubled down. Wrist-deep in Gaunt's mouth – or was it Cushing's? Who knew now? – he crammed the gloves down a glugging throat. The muffled groans died to silence.

Stumbling to his feet, soaking up the carnage that was once his office, Augustus totted up the damage caused by his guests. Deciding there was now nothing to lose, and therefore everything to gain, he rifled through the jackets of Tidswell and Gaunt, collecting the princely sum of £245. He pocketed the notes and pulled out the shimmering ring.

Half a million. Is that what Gaunt had said? Gaunt, that thin-lipped, leery-eyed miser, had actually offered *half a million*. The runes pulsed red in his bloodied palm. 'How much are you *really* worth?' Augustus asked the ring. 'One million? Five million? Ten mill—'

A sickening bang rocked the walls.

Augustus shuddered. The runes flared red. As he turned and stared down the landing, his eyes met an abominable glow. At the top of the stairs, a hand print fumed from the peacock wallpaper.

Bang. Another hand print.

Bang. Another. *Bang*. Another.

Bang. Hand print. *Bang*. Hand print. *Bang*. Hand print. *Bang*.

One by one, shudder by shudder, clustered hand prints drew together. Steaming from the peacock wallpaper, shaped like a ragged circle, a primal symbol burned.

It took one look. One trembling glance at the seething command formed by the glowing hand prints. The primal symbol seared the eyes of Fry, blooding his feverish mind.

In a wretched gesture to hold onto his dreams, Fry stuffed the ring back into his pocket. The ragged circle he'd glimpsed now blazed through his head, flashing like bolts of ruby lightning.

Augustus fell to his knees and frantically searched the office floor. Pixels of glass tore at his fingers as he rummaged through the wreckage. The primal symbol throbbed at his eyes, as if he'd stared at a sun for too long. It was here. He'd seen it. Where the devil had it gone?

'Found you.'

Augustus snatched up Gaunt's notebook and brushed away the glass. He flapped through the pages, in search of the symbol burned upon the wall. Augustus scanned the sticks and triangles of the Anglo-Saxon futhorc.

ᛟ *Odal rune. Meaning: home*

The runes of the ring flared a livid red. A cruel fire swelled in his pocket. Augustus sensed something loom on the landing: a climbing, crawling wall of heat, travelling towards the office. Towards him. Towards the ring. He quickly turned to the back cover, located Tidswell's handwriting.

I, father of hill and mire, guard this land eternal. May blood fire redden those who take me from my hearth . . .

Moustache twisting, mind flashing, Augustus stared at the necks of Tidswell and Gaunt, skin scored with striped red fingers. Surely, it wouldn't dare turn on its master. That wouldn't be right. That wouldn't be fair.

Augustus ripped off his tie, sweat rivering down his temples. He turned from the office and looked down the landing. A yelp leapt from his lips. The wave of heat had taken shape. An abominable, vaporous blood-red hand floated in the darkness, simmering with malice. Fingers fanned from its open palm as it glided in silence through the murk. Wallpaper curled and peeled from the walls, signalling the heat of its approach. Beyond the red hand, at the top the stairs, a shadow bobbed into view.

Ramses settled on the top step. Augustus stared at Ramses. Ramses stared at Augustus. Ramses thought of food. Augustus thought of feeding. Time, thought Augustus, for a sacrifice . . .

Inching outside the office, impatiently snapping his bloodied fingers, Augustus beckoned Ramses. Sensing a meal at last, the cat raced across the landing. Ramses blurred beneath the fiery palm, cruising high above. The red hand floated ever closer, fingers flexing with intent. Augustus grabbed Ramses by the scruff. He unclasped the collar, fed the ring through, and secured it around the cat's squirming neck. Before the wall of heat could hit, Augustus raced into the adjacent bathroom. With a scooping kick, Ramses bounced onto the landing. Augustus slammed the door.

Cowering on the tiles, Augustus whimpered to the sickening bangs, drumming and booming across the landing. Taps shook. The bathroom mirror trembled. A yowl. A hiss. A piercing meow.

Silence.

Augustus pressed his face to the door and peeked through the keyhole. A cat collar lay on the landing floor. Beside it, a shining, liberated ring. Confident the hand had faded, certain it had accepted his sacrifice, eager to claim back what was rightfully his, Augustus creaked open the bathroom door.

Ramses sat at the top of the stairs, casually licking his paw. A matrix of hand prints now branded the landing. Three symbols smoked from the wallpaper, a seething demand repeated.

☖ ☖ ☖
Home Home Home

Before Augustus could grab the ring, before he could slam the bathroom door, before he could quiver and crumple in shelter, the vicious heat of a vaporous palm launched from the landing into his chest. Augustus crashed against the sink, convulsing from the hand print branding his belly. Smoked hissed from a mustard waistcoat. Crispy skin crackled beneath.

One whiff of his own fried flesh and Augustus folded to the tiles. A raging heat loomed overhead and hovered like a crimson spotlight. Augustus raised his arms to the fire. The fire showed no mercy. The seething outline of a heat-hazed hand thrust down towards his face.

The palm plunged. Fingers flexed. Pressing down like an iron's soleplate, the red hand met Fry's steaming face. Skin crackled. Moustache hair hissed. There was a brief roar, like a bellowing stag.

Augustus Fry passed out.

As he lay starshaped on the bathroom floor, a hungry Ramses padded over. After a tentative lick and a testing bite, Ramses finally sat down for dinner. The cat feasted eagerly on a freshly cooked nose.

He came to on the bathroom floor. Augustus drew a fast, sharp breath. Air whipped through the bite holes of his colandered nose. Comfortably curled in a bathroom corner, Ramses lapped at his front paw, the red fur sticky with blood.

Augustus staggered up from the tiles and confronted the bathroom mirror. Set in the skin like an angry mauve birthmark, a hand print scored his face. Fingertips fanned between brow and eye. Marking his chin, a scarlet palm. Denting his cheek, a fuming thumb. Fry's reflection sizzled back, hot and runny as a fatty seared steak.

Augustus's once glorious moustache had been grilled and peeled, dangling like a banana skin. Frightened by his own reflection, white shock masking the pain that was to come, Augustus cautiously tugged his moustache, as if testing the grip of a loose thread. A livid purple flap of lip lifted with the hair, exposing a rictus flash of teeth. Augustus whimpered and quickly let go.

Clutching his chest, air whistling through his nose, Augustus stumbled from the bathroom. Ramses whipped between his legs and scattered down the landing. Augustus looked to the landing wall and the message seared into the peacock wallpaper.

☗ ☗ ☗
Home Home Home

Augustus pulled the ring from his pocket. Nauseated by the simmering runes, he quiveringly obeyed.

Grilled face dripping, Augustus tottered into the bedroom, found his phone and loaded FedEx. With trembling sticky fingers, he tapped out his address. Augustus fetched a cardboard box from the wardrobe and flopped onto the bed.

Wrapping the ring in stiff brown paper, Augustus watched the runes cool like fading embers, and saw his dreams fade with it. The Tudor cottage in the Cotswolds. The release from the endless grind of grifting. The escape from his childhood home and the dreary purgatory of Silverweed Road. All that was loved had been lost.

Augustus staggered down the stairs, opened the front

door, and squinted in the emerging daylight. A November sun, rising low, blooded Silverweed's rooftops. Windscreens of sleeping cars glinted from the driveways. The night storm that had lashed the houses now waned to a rhythmic pitter-patter. Augustus lifted his eyes to the sky, felt the cooling rain on his seared face, then placed a sealed box by the door. In a shaky, snaking handwriting, the address label read: *9 Deanbrook Road, Rivington, Bolton.*

Home. Home. Home.

In the upstairs office of Solomon Antiquities, Augustus wrapped a bandage around his head, assuming the form of a half-wrapped mummy. Ramses merrily gorged on a finger. Tidswell and Gaunt lay silent.

Augustus Fry's thoughts turned to bin bags and carving knives.

Butterworth took the box from the courier, tottered into the dim-lit living room, and placed it on the butcher's block table. A Stanley knife pecked through stiff brown cardboard. The old man unwrapped the ring and smiled at the blood-spattered paper. 'Looks like you need a new jewellery box,' Butterworth said to the ring, buffing the surface with a grey tea towel. 'Nathan? Come here, lad.'

A figure emerged from the kitchen, joined him at the butcher's block table.

'Has he fed, Dad?'

Butterworth shuffled over to the camping gas stove, held the ring up to mud-yellow light. The runes glowed a wilted red.

'Only few by looks of it.' Butterworth sighed. 'Was hoping our fat fool would introduce him to a few more meals.'

Butterworth joined his son at the butcher's block table,

set the ring in the centre. The runes pulsed red in the gritted darkness.

'Needs another feed 'fore we return him to burial pit up Noon Hill,' Butterworth decided. 'Won't be hungry for rest of year.'

Nathan puffed out his cheeks, looked at his father with defeated eyes.

'Didn't ask for this, lad,' said Butterworth. 'None of us did, but duty's duty. He feeds when he feeds, and that's that. Less you want him turning on us? Do well to remember what happened to your grandfather. One feed, he missed – just one bloody feed – and what happens? Branded so bad couldn't have open casket at funeral. You want that, son? Want to curse your own?'

Nathan shook his head, shuffled a hand into his pocket, took out his phone. 'Here, Dad. One I saved from earlier, 'fore that Solomon Antiquities. Dealer down in Poole – Griffin Antiques, says here. Thought promising. Right manky reviews on Trustpilot. Rip-off this, fake that. One star 'cross the board.'

Butterworth took the phone, scrolled through. 'Aye, he'll do. Will give him call.'

'Go on,' said Butterworth Jr. 'Do the stupid voice.'

Butterworth hunched his vulture shoulders, voice weakening to a feeble, desperate whinge. 'Were hoping you come up, give it once over . . .'

'You sound right brainless,' Nathan laughed.

'Aye,' said Butterworth. 'Soon see who real fool is.'

Butterworth cleared his throat. In the darkened room on the butcher's block table, runes flared greedily as he dialled.

Extract from The Silverweed Files, 9 November, 2024

A personal blog by former Detective Chief Inspector Jim Heath .The views expressed do not reflect those of Kent Police nor the victims impacted by events.

Where do you start with Augustus Fry? The man is either a pathological liar or certifiably insane.

When Fry was charged with the double murder of John Gaunt and Marcus Tidswell, a can of worms was opened on his nefarious connections. From his back office in no. 17, Fry had operated as a conman whose fraudulent dealings went back decades. Using his accounts, Kent Police went on to bust a black market ring involving millionaire collectors, museum curators, respected academics and a member of the royal family you have no doubt read plenty about. Among the many treasures recovered was a sacrificial burial knife presumed lost for decades. It was an unexpected result Kent Police have never ceased crowing about. It is also a convenient distraction from the Silverweed crimes my former employers have neglected to solve.

Given his record as a conman, that Fry pleaded insanity for the double murder does not entirely surprise me. He now resides in Meadway Psychiatric Hospital, where I have interviewed him on a personal capacity on several occasions. I cannot get a lick of sense out of the man. He continues to blame everyone and everything other than himself, depending on what day of the week it is. On a Monday, he will blame a golden ring. On a Tuesday, his mother. On a Wednesday, a giant red hand that floated around his house like a UFO. On a Thursday, his Persian cat, which he claims tried to eat him. On Friday, Silverweed Road itself. And on weekends, his favourite fantasy suspect: a certain Percy Butterworth from Rivington.

The idea that Butterworth sold him a cursed ring is absolutely laughable. I have interviewed Butterworth at his farmhouse, and the old man lives like a pauper. He could barely afford an onion ring, let alone a gold one.

In spite of Fry's questionable character, so much remains unanswered. If Fry was driven to murder by greed, why did he only steal cash from the wallets of Tidswell and Gaunt? And while it's clear he planned to go on the run, why did Fry go to such extremes to hide his identity? What kind of maniac disguises himself by mutilating his face with a clothes iron?

Once again, I ask myself: did Silverweed play a part in stoking Fry's insanity?

NO. 4:

Cuttlefish, Cuttlefish

The following log was recovered by DCI Heath from no. 4 Silverweed Road, Corvid Estate, Meadway, Kent. It is authored by the subject of the inquiry, Dr Eric Akoto, and is submitted to help the coroner determine an outcome. The log is complete and no excerpts have been redacted.

DAY 1

They are nearly here. It has taken nine months and half a lifetime to arrive at this point, and yet, in less than forty-eight hours, they will be mine. My mind is flashing like a marlin through a silver herring ball. I am restless and anxious and eager to begin.

Converting the ground floor of this 1950s house – my home of thirteen years – has been a monumental endeavour. The carpet is up, the steel flooring is down, the tanks are full, and the cameras mounted. What was once a lounge, study and kitchen is now a shining white laboratory. I have remortgaged my home and spared no expense – one cannot put a price on making history.

With facilities at capacity, The DeGruy Marine Institute has declined to house my experiment. I suspect it is too magnificent for them, but they will be supplying my four *sepia officinalis* – my four common cuttlefish. Soon, the world will see what an ignorant joke that name is. There is nothing common about these animals. Nothing ordinary. Nothing expected.

I sit here now, soothed by the sound of trickling water, bathed in the glow of the tanks. I have my own private ocean, here on Silverweed Road. The triad aquarium is a challenging design. Ocean Visions have done an exceptional job. The three tanks flow seamlessly, from one to the other – living quarters, transit tunnel, and observation cylinder.

That imbecile Dr Fenn has remarked on several occasions my design resembles a pepper grinder – a typically boorish comment from a man who spends his life poking at fish corpses. A pepper grinder! Anyone can see the tanks resemble the human form: a torso, neck and head, connecting man and beast together. Fenn is welcome to his hagfish and his lampreys. Is he able to talk to his hagfish? To watch his lampreys dream? His subjects are as primordial and vulgar as he is.

I digress. I am, alas, feeling a little sorry for myself. My feet are cold and wet after test-flooding the lab to the depth of one inch. The drainage system has held up well and the steel floor remains strong. Waterproofing the lab has been a laborious pain, but there can be no room for error. In the unlikely scenario the tanks fail to hold, I am fully prepared.

Nothing will escape this laboratory.
This is Dr Eric Akoto logging off.

DAY 2

The four *sepia officinalis* arrive tomorrow and my nerves refuse to settle. I am reminded of Christmas Eve and doubt I will sleep tonight.

The cuttlefish remain at The DeGruy Institute. I have called Dr Christensen seventeen times today – his responses have been increasingly terse, but when he does reply, he assures me they are active, well, and feeding. I'm not sure all the swearing was necessary.

I still worry there will be a disagreement and I will lose one, maybe two, before they've even arrived. *Sepia officinalis* are known to consume each other. When my students hear this, they gasp in disgust, but, like everything with this animal, there is a hidden beauty we cannot see.

They are not answering a depraved appetite. It is not cannibalism for cannibalism's sake. Cuttlefish sacrifice themselves for the survival of their species. It is population management, evolution at its most selfless, clearing a path for the next generation. It would be a far happier planet if we humans did the same.

In my thirty years of marine exploration, I have dived with humpbacks off Kohala, Humboldt squid in the Gulf of Mexico, and killer whales in Puget Sound, yet it is the common cuttlefish that has captured my heart. It is unearthly beyond comprehension. Gather the world's astrobiologists and they would struggle to conceive an alien to match it.

Three hearts. Blue blood. Razor-sharp beak. Poison

saliva. Eyes shaped like a W, a brain shaped like a doughnut, two tentacles, eight arms, one of which doubles up as a penis . . . (It is always the hectocotylus my students fixate on. Always the hectocotylus. 'An animal,' they'll whisper, 'with a penis in its arm. An animal with a *penis* in its *arm*!').

And yet its brain is most alien of all. A chameleon is a set of traffic lights compared to the cuttlefish's limitless camouflage. I've swum with this animal over 600 times, spellbound by their photographic skin. In the blink of an eye, they vanish into the seascape. It is a breathtaking conjuring trick, but it is a defence mechanism and no more. My interest lies in the magician, not the magic.

Cuttlefish speak. And they speak in colour.

This is not a mirage or a madness or a fanciful dream. I've seen them chatter in the deep black sea, wearing their thoughts on their skin.

There is intensity and purpose behind these signals. Take one large brain, eight expressive arms, and a skin of infinite patterns, and you have a formula for language – a rich, complex alphabet of colour that, once unlocked, will reveal the secrets of our great blue planet. I tremble at the thought of what I'm about to achieve: for the first time in history, man will commune with another species. Darwin! Mendel! Carson! Akoto! My name will echo for all eternity!

To practical matters. The crab and mysid shrimp have arrived with Dr Tsukamoto. We spent some time together, homing the live feed in their biodomes. There are fifteen in all, lined against the wall like giant glass eggs, which will sustain the *sepia officinalis* for their forty days.

This is the first time Dr Tsukamoto has seen the triad aquarium, and she is suitably impressed. Even without the cuttlefish, the tank is wild and alive – I have tiered their quarters with shelves of live rock, scattered the sand with serpent stars, and grown a garden of red sea lettuce.

I am a little shy around Dr Tsukamoto. Her dark eyes have a mischievous shine and her voice is soft as water. She is a fellow teuthologist, and I very much enjoy her company. Dr Christensen introduced us but a month ago, and she is enchanted by my experiment, asking all manner of questions, some of them personal. She even enquired if I wanted children!

I have been so consumed with work and been alone for so long, I'd be glad to share my success with another. Perhaps once this is over I will ask her out to dinner. She wore her hair piled up today and our hands touched briefly while we filled the biodomes . . .

Saying farewell to Dr Tsukamoto was bittersweet. She is one of the last humans I'll see for forty days. Once the laboratory door is sealed, I will cut myself off from all distractions, and all contact will be denied. I shall not allow my fellow humans to pollute the bond I form.

No man has lived with *sepia officinalis* for this period of time. If I am to unlock their language, I must be at one with my cuttlefish – and they must be at one with me.

This is Dr Eric Akoto logging off.

DAY 3

As I write this entry, I am observing four dazzling, magical, magnificent cuttlefish! It is like Squidmas Day, and I am overjoyed.

They have wasted no time settling into their quarters.

Each has selected his own rock shelf and a hierarchy has been established. The alpha is commanding the highest rock, the order of power descending through the tiers.

My subjects arrived at 5 p.m. this evening, as a full moon rose over Silverweed Road. Since it was my last glimpse of the outside world, I couldn't resist taking a farewell photograph. Perhaps it's glare from the nearby lamp post, as the picture shows not one, but two silver moons, shining over the rooftops. Set against the night sky, they look like a pair of angry silver eyes, glaring at the house. Every time I feed it a glance, I feel a peculiar shiver, as if a heartbeat has been stolen. It is a gloomy photograph of a gloomy street, and I am glad to close the door on it.

I digress. Dr Christensen personally delivered the *sepia officinalis* in a transit tank, accompanied by Dr Crocker and, for some ungodly reason, the infernal Dr Fenn. Dr Christensen has informed me that all four cuttlefish are the property of the Institute and he will collect them in forty days. I cannot understand why they must be returned, other than for termination. I protested in the strongest terms, but Christensen would not be moved.

As revenge, I kept the lab tour brief. When Dr Crocker asked to see 'the famous Cuttle Glove', I obliged and put it on, only for Fenn to remark I looked like Michael Jackson. I did not appreciate the laughter. Hagfish are the road sweepers of the sea, maggots with fins. They say biologists study the subject that resembles them most. In this, Dr Fenn has succeeded admirably.

Oh, I've heard them gossip in the Institute canteen. There goes Eric the fantasist. There goes Eric the fool. Mad old Doctor Dolittle. Crazy Doctor Docuttle . . . In forty days, they will eat their words. I will march triumphant from this lab, speaking fluent cuttlefish, and the world will bow in wonder.

Only Dr Christensen has shown faith in my experiment. He has personally nurtured the hatchlings – an unusual gesture from the Institute director. Christensen is a cold, imposing man with angry moray eel eyes, but I could not have done this without him.

Before they left, Christensen presented a good luck card from Dr Tsukamoto. It is a picture of a waving cat, with BREAK THE BARRIERS written inside, signed with three unexpected kisses. I have mounted the card on the laboratory wall, and will look to it for encouragement. All that is left is myself, the card, the cuttlefish, and the transit tank Christensen neglected to take back with him.

It is 10 p.m. and I finish this log under desk light. Night has fallen outside, so night must fall in my private ocean. Cuttlefish sleep like us, and the diurnal cycle must be maintained.

There are flickers of light in the dark aquarium, flashing from the shelves of living rock. The cuttlefish are dreaming. I can see their arms twitch as colours flood their mantle, patterns chasing patterns, like clouds on an alien moon. They are wearing their dreams on their skin.

What are they thinking? What do they see? Tonight, we will dream together. Tomorrow, we begin.

This is Dr Eric Akoto logging off.

DAY 4

My first day in the company of cuttlefish and all is well. It is so calm and peaceful here. The trickling water is as sweet as birdsong, and the cuttlefish glide with such weight-less grace: it is as if they are floating through space.

I've not slept since they arrived, but even under constant surveillance, I've been defeated by their camouflage several times. Barely ten minutes ago, I was scouring the tank, convinced I'd somehow lost one. My nose was pressed against the glass when a red blade of sea lettuce blazed into life. It was the alpha, playing hide and seek. I must confess, he made me jump.

All four *sepia officinalis* are responding well to the bonding process. Once every hour, I dip my hand into their tank. Cuttlefish taste by touch, and I've been slowly introducing myself. They've been darting from the rocks with increasing eagerness, running their suckers along my hands. To feel their soft, sticky suckers, so close, and so intimate – it is like a long, wet, tickling kiss!

I've been getting to know them, too. When their skin is at rest, cuttlefish zebra stripes are as distinct as any finger-print. They are remarkably easy to identify.

For the purposes of observational data, they are A1, B2, C3 and D4. Informally, they are Jet, Hugh, Jean-Jacques and Dave. One shouldn't anthropomorphise test subjects – it is a recipe for bias and polluted data, but if we are to be on speaking terms, a degree of familiarity is needed. After all, they are brothers spawned from the same egg batch, and all brothers need names.

Throughout the day, they've been signalling to each other – some patterns familiar, others new. I've been dutifully logging their patterns, ready to download to the Cuttle Glove.

Watching them talk, I am ever more convinced. There is form and meaning to their relays of colour.

Tomorrow they enter the observation cylinder.
This is Dr Eric Akoto logging off.

DAY 5

There has been a disturbance. Not within the lab. Beyond the doors, in the outside world. Shortly after 1 a.m., I was shaken from my cot by a bang and a blaze of sirens. I suspect there has been a car crash, and alarmingly close to the house. The commotion was so great, Jet, Hugh, Jean-Jacques and Dave woke from their shelves and swam around their quarters in a rainbow of panic. For ten horrifying minutes, the tank water crashed like a raging storm, churning black with cuttlefish ink.

Now, at last, all is calm. The bonding process has continued as the cuttlefish adapt to my taste. I am already growing fond of their delicate, tickling kisses.

Feeding time is 6 p.m. sharp, and they are already wise to the routine. You cannot give cuttlefish dead feed.

They like their food alive.

The moment I drop in a handful of shrimp, Hugh, Jean-Jacques and Dave launch their feeding tentacles, seize their meal, and retire to their rock shelves to feed. Jet, the alpha, is adopting a stealthier approach. He is stalking his prey around the tank, hypnotising it with the Passing Cloud formation. His green fins ripple like a rolling mist. The shrimp is spellbound by the display.

When the shrimp is sufficiently dazed, Jet attacks at frightening speed. His tentacles fire, the water whips, the shrimp is caught, then shredded alive. The grisly, liquid crunch of his beak ripping through the shell is not for the faint-hearted.

Jet is a gruesomely efficient hunter, and I feel for the shrimp. I would not want to be on the end of his tentacles.

After dinner, I introduced the cuttlefish to the observation cylinder. There were no refusals – they are simply too curious. I opened the remote door in their living quarters and off they shuttled through the transit tunnel to be studied.

In the cylinder, there are no distractions. Separated by glass and water, it is just me, myself and the cuttlefish. I watch them – and they watch me. To provoke an emotional response, I have been using various visual stimuli, beamed from an iPad pressed to the glass. They are fascinated by the screen.

I have shown them images of a shark to instil fear; a female for joy; a rival male to stir some anger; and dead cuttlefish to induce sadness. One by one, each cuttlefish has signalled the same emotional response: the same colours, the same arm postures.

The cylinder cameras have captured everything. When I project the patterns onto the walls, the lab turns into a silent disco, where only colours dance.

The lightshow is a welcome distraction from my mounting anxiety. Tomorrow is critical. Tomorrow, they meet the Cuttle Glove.

This is Dr Eric Akoto logging off.

DAY 6

The bonding process is complete! When my hand enters the water, the cuttlefish greet me like puppy dogs. Jet, the alpha, continues to grow. His mantle now measures 60 cm: an impressive size for a three-month-old.

Following yesterday's session, I've been reviewing the patterns. A basic table of signal states is taking shape, including what I believe to be their meaning:

Pattern	Posture	Mood
Purple skin, green fins	Outspread arms	Fear
White head bar, pink mantle	Swaying arms	Joy
Golden mantle, black fins	Two arms raised	Sadness
Black mantle, silver fins	Four arms raised	Anger

Are these patterns simply reflexes – an instinctual response to an emotional stimulus? Or are they *expressions* of emotions – a way of communicating how the cuttlefish feels? Could these emotional states be classified as 'words' in the cuttlefish dialect?

The results from the Cuttle Glove are emphatic.

The Cuttle Glove came to me five years ago, diving off the Gulf of Morbihan. I had encountered a cuttlefish hiding on the seabed, signalling to me with a rush of patterns. I knew it wished to speak, but I was unable to respond. When I surfaced, I sat on the boat, gloomy and frustrated. If only I could mimic cuttlefish skin and somehow signal back . . .

Technology has provided the answer. Coating the Cuttle Glove are 3,000 LEDs, each controlled individually. Once I download a pattern from the computer, the surface shimmers into life, simulating cuttlefish skin – the chromatophores, iridophores and leucophores that allow it to change colour.

With my gloved fingers mimicking their arms, I can, in theory, mirror any of their signals. Compared to their twenty million pigment cells, it is crude by comparison, but the cuttlefish have immediately taken to the Cuttle Glove. They think I am one of them! The glove is my voice – and they are listening.

Little Hugh was first to glide into the observation cylinder. I donned the glove and pressed it against the tank wall. With his eyes fixed on my hand, I set the Cuttle Glove to the Joy signal. Pink flooded the surface. My swaying fingers mimicked their arms. Little Hugh's response was instantaneous: his arms swayed and his mantle flashed pink.

Next, I tried the Fear signal. I fanned out my fingers. The Cuttle Glove flashed. Again, Hugh answered the glove: arms fanned, skin purple and green. I repeated this process with Jean-Jacques and Dave. Both signalled back Joy and Fear, exactly as Hugh.

These signals are not a reflex. The behaviour does not match the patterns. They aren't displaying signs of Joy or Fear. It is as if I am saying, 'Repeat after me,' and they are parroting the signals back.

These are cuttlefish words. I am certain of it.

Alas, it is not all good news. Jet, the alpha, has refused to engage. He hovered in the cylinder, silver fins rippling, his skin black as night. For whatever reason, he appears to be angry with me.

It is a blip on an otherwise glorious day. The Cuttle Glove has passed with flying colours! I am picturing my statue at the Institute entrance. Shiny black marble would suit me best.

This is Dr Eric Akoto logging off.

DAY 7

As I write this, Jet is hovering on his rock. He has been watching me for quite some time. Earlier today, I caught him spying through the sea lettuce, waiting to leap out. He has made me jump several times.

Still, it appears Jet is finally out of his black mood and has decided to cooperate. To prove the Cuttle Glove is no fluke, I repeated yesterday's cylinder session. Fear, Joy, Sadness and Anger – their skin has echoed the Cuttle Glove. I'm delighted to report this now includes Jet.

The evidence is indisputable: these patterns are words. They are part of the cuttlefish lexicon of colour.

The thrill of the Cuttle Glove has resulted in a burst of nostalgia. My father once took me diving off the island of Toralla in the Ria de Vigo. For thousands of years, *sepia officinalis* have flocked there to breed. I was fourteen, a novice diver, so we swam in the shallows. I was following a sea slug with a red neon crown when a clump of seaweed flashed into life. Suddenly, I was face-to-face with a cuttle-fish.

It raised two arms and formed a V. 'I come in peace,' it seemed to say. I replied in an instant and signalled two fingers. Back and forth we went, rallying Vs until my air ran out. I knew, right then, that my life had changed. That I, Eric Akoto, was put on this Earth to unlock their mysteries.

Only later did I discover the V sign didn't mean peace at all. The cuttlefish was threatening me.

The brothers had crab today.

This is Dr Eric Akoto logging off.

DAY 8

As I write this entry, I am a little drunk. I have opened my bottle of Akpeteshie, for today is one for celebration . . . I am no longer talking to the cuttlefish. The cuttlefish are talking to me!

The day began with our morning greeting. While Hugh, Jean-Jacques and Dave swam up to tickle me, Jet sulked on his rock shelf.

Then the signals started.

Jet's mantle shone like sapphire, his arms curled inwards, motioning at his head. He'd revert to his stripes, wait a minute or so, then start all over again. Sapphire mantle, arms to his head. Sapphire mantle, arms to his head . . . He signalled to me for over an hour.

I copied the pattern, and fired up the Glove. Jet echoed the signal, then launched a new surprise. His pattern switched. Now he pulsed scarlet, arms pointing at me. I signalled back. The glove burned red.

We relayed the signals dozens of times.

Sapphire, scarlet. Sapphire, scarlet. Arms pointing in. Arms pointing out.

I. You. I. You.

I have replayed the footage over and over. Jet's eyes are on me and only me. There is intention and thought to his display.

We have established pronouns!

I am still shaking with excitement. The repercussions of this discovery confirms what I have always believed – that cuttlefish rank alongside apes, corvids and bottlenose dolphins as a sentient intelligence.

I. You. I. You. He is not only aware of me. *He is aware of himself.*

I have tried the signals on his brothers, but they do not appear to be interested. It is Jet, and only Jet, who is communicating. He is a very clever *sepia officinalis* indeed.

I am now gazing at Dr Tsukamoto's card and the message written inside: BREAK THE BARRIERS. The gates have been opened.

Eureka!

This is Dr Eric Akoto logging off.

DAY 9

I have been bitten.

I keep telling myself it's fine – the bleeding has almost stopped, but the wound does not look good. I really should seek medical attention, but I cannot leave the lab and I refuse to be tended to here. There must be no intruders in my private ocean.

I have only myself to blame. At 6 p.m., I scooped a handful of shrimp and released them into the tank. I was so confident of our bond that I foolishly allowed my hand to linger. The rest is a blur.

Jet fired his tentacles. The water whipped. His suckers seized my palm. Next thing I knew, his razor beak was drilling into my hand. He must have used all of his cephalotoxin in an attempt to paralyse me.

I didn't feel a thing until he bored through to the bone.

How my body screamed at me. Rip off his arms! Tear him off! Throw him against the wall! But I simply could not do it. Cuttlefish are delicate creatures: their fragile skin rips like paper. Had I wrestled with Jet in the midst of his frenzy, I would have killed my star performer.

For two agonising minutes, I allowed him to feed, hearing him crunch my muscles to soup. He scooped and drilled and scraped and gouged until his arms wriggled into the wound. The sensation of his tentacles sucking on bone is a feeling I would not wish on anyone. Not even on Dr Fenn.

And then, like that, the attack was over. Jet glided back to his rock and stared at me as if nothing had happened. When I lifted my hand from the water, his brothers immediately swarmed through my blood. I stood there, dazed and shivering, as the brothers flashed in a mist of red.

I do not understand why Jet chose me as his meal.

There is now a deep, dark hole in my palm – so deep I can see a worm of white bone. It took three attempts as I was shaking too much, but I have jabbed a swab into the wound to assess the levels of cephalotoxin. The blood tests are running and will be ready in seventy-two hours.

Tonight's session with the Cuttle Glove will have to be abandoned. I feel drowsy and unusual and my body calls for sleep.

This is Dr Eric Akoto logging off.

DAY 10

big black bird inside lab. big black bird sit on tank. big black bird. big silver eyes. staring staring big silver eyes. big black jet. big silver eyes. big black jet bird big silver eyes. coming. closer. eyes. closer. silver. clos . . .

DAY 11

hand on fire. heart on fire. sleep 20 hrs. sleep 20 more

DAY 12

It is 11 p.m. and I have woken from a terrible fever. I am looking at my last two entries and I sound like a lunatic. I am soupy with sweat and my head is not clear and it may be the shock or the bite or the toxin, but I swear a jackdaw flew into the lab.

And yet the shutters are down and the doors are sealed. A jackdaw is silver and black. The signal for anger is silver and black. Jet has been signalling silver and black. I fear I have been hallucinating. What has Jet injected me with?

My palm is in a dreadful mess. The wound resembles an angry red crater with tiny white specks of bone. None of the cuttlefish are feeding. There are currently four fiddler crabs roaming free in the tank, untroubled and in high spirits. I keep having a horrible thought: that the cuttlefish drank my blood.

The toxin results will be ready tomorrow. My body calls for sleep.

This is Dr Eric Akoto logging off.

DAY 13

I am up and about. The fever has passed. The blood test results – they defy all logic.

Sepia officinalis are poisonous. Their salivary glands are loaded with cephalotoxin, a paralysing agent to immobilise prey. Lethal if you're a shrimp. Harmless if you're a human. This is not the first time I have been bitten by a cuttlefish. At worst, I have experienced a faint prickling on the tongue as the poison attempts its feeble attack. And yet, according to the blood test, there is no cephalotoxin to be found. Not a molecule. Not a trace.

Instead, there is a toxic compound I cannot identify. I keep telling myself this is not unusual. *Metasephia pfefferi*, the flamboyant cuttlefish, is armed with a toxin 1,000 times more powerful than cyanide. But this is *sepia officinalis*, and their only weapon is cephalotoxin. I can't administer an antivenom for a poison I can't identify.

Jet has been leaping from the red sea lettuce. I am not enjoying his games. He is making me jump and slapping the glass. He is deliberately trying to scare me.

This is Dr Eric Akoto logging off.

DAY 14

The wound's impact continues to spread. Great bruises of purple and green have surfaced around my palm. A thin white crust has formed over the bite hole and clicks like bubblewrap whenever I touch it. I remain feverish and indolent, and have no appetite for the Cuttle Glove. Neither, it appears, do the cuttlefish – they are hovering on their rock shelves, refusing food and barely signalling. Only Jet appears active. He is stalking the tank and staring at me, slap-slap-slapping his arms against the glass.

I've decided to break my no-contact protocol and have sent an urgent email to the Institute detailing my blood test. It was Dr Christensen who bred the hatchlings. He may be able to help.

I eagerly await his response.

This is Dr Eric Akoto logging off.

DAY 15

The wound is feasting on my hand. The green and purple has spread to the knuckles and is creeping around my skin.

I have spent most of the day in a sorry state, limping around the lab. There is, thankfully, cause for optimism. Just as the experiment was slipping like seaweed through my fingers, the cuttlefish have stirred from their rock shelves. Contact has resumed.

Jet is craving interaction. He has been gliding around the tank like a magic carpet, seeking me out, signalling the same three patterns, over and over and over again.

The pronouns are already familiar. Sapphire skin, arms to his head. Scarlet skin, arms to me. I. You. I. You.

It is the signal in between that is new. Jet is now flashing orange, his arms outstretched. Armed with the Cuttle Glove, we have rallied the signals to each other in the cylinder, and Jet will not stop. He simply will not stop.

Sapphire-orange-scarlet. Sapphire-orange-scarlet. I X You. I X You.

The sequence is a sentence. Jet is speaking to me. What message is he sending? I am hoping it is a cuttlefish apology.

I have emailed Christensen once again. I still await a response.

This is Dr Eric Akoto logging off.

121

DAY 16

I woke up this morning at war with a most unusual craving. Perhaps it is the diet of high-protein noodles I've been consuming with thoughtless monotony, but I have caught myself staring at the biodomes with an alarming lust. I have been vegetarian for twenty-four years. I should not be craving crab.

My wound refuses to settle. Freckles of colour have crept from my knuckles to the finger joints. Jet continues to grow beyond expectations. His mantle now measures 90 cm. If this continues, he will be the largest *sepia officinalis* on record, but it is his persistent signalling that is driving me to distraction.

Sapphire-orange-scarlet. Sapphire-orange-scarlet. I X You. I X You.

Every time I close my eyes, it is all that I can see.

For the sake of this experiment, for the sake of my sanity, I must decode his message.

This is Dr Eric Akoto logging off.

DAY 17

I am now beginning to study my wound with the same intensity as my cuttlefish. A constellation of coloured spots have appeared overnight, spreading from wrist to fingertips. The crust on the bite wound is harder now. What used to click like bubble wrap responds to my touch with a hollow *clok*. A pressing tightness lies within.

To speed the healing process, I have poured salt into the

laboratory sink, circulating water around the wound four times a day to oxygenate it. The skin on my hand feels sticky and squishy. The texture reminds me of chewing gum. It is wet and slippery and making me queasy. It feels like chewing gum from another person's mouth.

Hour after hour, Jet has been repeating his sequence. Sapphire-orange-scarlet. I X You. He is driving me insane. He is so different to Hugh, Jean-Jacques and Dave – so much larger, and so much smarter – that I am beginning to question if these cuttlefish truly are brothers.

I am narrowing down the linguistic permutations and preparing a simple test. My focus keeps drifting to the biodomes and the fiddler crabs within.

Christensen's silence is deafening.

This is Dr Eric Akoto logging off.

DAY 18

At 6 p.m. today, I gave in to my desires. I am not proud of what I have done. I could resist the urge no longer. Instead of scooping four fiddler crabs from the biodome, I selected five. One for Jet, one for Hugh, one for Jean-Jacques, one for Dave . . . and one for me.

I ate the crab as I watched Jet hypnotise his prey with a green Passing Cloud. The ghastly, wet crunch still tortures me now, as does the shell that scraped my throat when I finally gulped it down. My abhorrent meal has left its mark. When I wrestled the crab into my mouth, a claw sliced my bottom lip. It has puffed up like a pink sea slug and now I cannot speak. The purple blood that bled from the wound had a cold, coppery taste, like an ice cream made of coins.

My shameful appetite stains an otherwise significant day. The orange mantle. The outspread arms. The elusive X.

I believe it has been solved.

This afternoon, I urged Jet into the observation cylinder and presented him with a choice. In one hand, I held a fiddler crab and in the other a shore crab. Jet immediately signalled his preference. He hovered towards the fiddler crab, eight arms outspread, mantle flashing orange. I switched over the crabs and repeated the choice. Again, Jet signalled orange towards the fiddler crab.

The orange mantle. The outspread arms. His preference for fiddler crab. There are many linguistic variations to consider, but for Jet there can only be one meaning.

Select. Need. Choose. Prefer. Desire. Favour. Want.

All of these are possibilities.

Run these through the sapphire-orange-scarlet sequence and a simple sentence forms. A sentence that Jet is directing at me, and only me. I *select* you. I *need* you. I *choose* you. I *want* you . . . What is he saying? What does he want from me? How do I reply?

The discovery has proved a welcome diversion to my wound. There is a faint twisting within the hole, as if my muscles are fighting something. Day and night, the silent disco has been dancing on the walls, but I can bear the colour no longer. The projector is off and my eyes need to settle. First, my body craves crab. Now it craves darkness. I do not like the direction my experiment is going in.

This is Dr Eric Akoto logging off.

DAY 19

Jet now measures 120 cm – a size beyond the capabilities of *sepia officinalis*. I am struggling with this animal. The deliberate bite. The unknown toxin. The constant stalking. And yet it is Jet who craves interaction. He has been gliding around his quarters, ignoring his brothers, directing his signals at me.

Sapphire-orange-scarlet. I *need* you. Sapphire-orange-scarlet. I *choose* you. Sapphire-orange-scarlet. I *want* you . . . But for what? Needed, chosen or wanted for what?

I sense a rebellion within the tank. Jet, Hugh, Jean-Jacques, Dave have rejected the Cuttle Glove. Whenever I present it to them, I'm met with anger – the black mantle, the silver fins and moody jets of ink.

The Cuttle Glove is dead to them. But I, apparently, am not.

The moment they see my bite hand, they gather together, slapping their arms against the glass. Slap. Slap. Slap. Slap. The sound is driving me mad. Their eyes look wild and their mantles flash and their tentacles writhe like sea serpents.

At 6 p.m., we ate crab together. Just when my lip had begun to heal, a claw has pierced my tongue. I am utterly miserable, I cannot speak, and my hand now glows like a rainbow.

This is Dr Eric Akoto logging off.

DAY 20

There has been a treacherous development. In the absence of a response, I turned my attention to the sole artefact left by Dr Christensen: the travel tank the brothers arrived in, which he neglected to take back. As with every item in The DeGruy Institute, there is a stamp of ownership viewable by UV light. My ultraviolet pen has explored the surface. I have revealed a serial number: 496-28-GD.

The numbers are meaningless but I recognise the letters. The travel tank is not from the marine biology unit. Neither is it from the oceanography branch. GD: the travel tank hails from the Genetics Department.

I have been staring at my hand and staring at Jet, and Jet has been staring at me. Several times today, he's been flashing the Passing Cloud formation, green fins rippling in a rolling mist. There is no prey in the tank.

He is aiming the Cloud in my direction, staring at me as if I'm a shrimp. A giant, walking, crunchy shrimp. He is doing all he can to hypnotise me.

It is a desperate move, but I have emailed Dr Tsukamoto regarding the travel tank. She is working with Christensen on a project she refuses to talk about, and may know something I don't. My message has been met with silence.

The lab is dark and quiet. All I can hear is the trickle of tank water. It drips and drips and drips and drips, dripping into my dripping head as the cuttlefish slap the glass. Slap. Slap. Drip. Drip. Slap. Slap. Drip. Drip . . . It simply will not stop.

The transit tank has disturbed me to the core. I am besieged by questions and imagining answers. What is this animal? Who is studying who? What was Christensen up to when he personally nurtured my hatchlings?

There is something wriggling in my wound.

This is Dr Eric Akoto logging off.

DAY 21

My experiment has collapsed like a sand castle stolen by the tide. I am losing all focus and I don't know what to do. Yet again, I have emailed Dr Tsukamoto. Yet again, there is no reply.

Last night, I did not sleep. As the cuttlefish dreamed, I sat in my cot and squished my hand. It shimmers in the dark, like a beast from the abyss. The skin feels liquid and restless, and the spots of colour have grown. Lurid reds, emerald greens, deepest blacks and blinding whites.

My skin is pulsing and throbbing. My mind is pulsing and throbbing. I am losing focus and I don't know what to do and the trickle of water is drip-drip-dripping and the glass is slapping and Jet is staring and his lights are flashing and my hand is flashing and my mind is flashing and my body feels squishy as chewing gum.

I am eating crab at a frightening rate and I cannot stop myself.

This is Dr Eric Akoto logging off.

DAY 22

Jet's Passing Cloud has got to me. He's been flickering green like the Northern Lights and I am certain I've been hypnotised. All I remember is staring at the tank, my body stiff as coral, when a sudden darkness descended. Two hours later, I awoke on the floor — two hours I cannot account for. How else can I explain what happened next?

At 6 p.m., I dropped three crabs into their quarters, struck by a formidable urge. I plunged in my wounded hand, inviting them to bite me. The cuttlefish rushed from their rock shelves, ignored the crab, and headed straight for my hand.

I've never seen the tank more alive. The cuttlefish burst into a cacophony of signals, skin flashing like rainbows. They are obsessed with my wound. Infatuated. They act as if I now belong to them.

When Jet launched his arms around my hand, I froze like a paralysed shrimp. Yet I felt no bite and felt no pain. First, he explored my wriggling wound. Then he wrapped his arms around me. His skin burned a brilliant pink, a white bar pulsing over his eyes. Together our bodies flooded with joy and my fears collapsed into waves of love.

When I finally snapped from my trance, my hand flashed from the tank, I seized a scalpel and sliced a sample from my fingertip. Blue blood oozed from the wound. It is the dark blue blood of *sepia officinalis*.

All is clear under the microscope. My skin is mottled with pigment cells, some fully grown, others half-formed – a galaxy of chromatophores. My flesh is alive and pulsing with colour. I'm beginning to blend with the lab. Leave my hand on a surface too long and the skin begins to flicker. It sucks up the colours of the desk or the chair, until I can barely see my own fingers.

What has Christensen done to Jet? And what has Jet done to me?

There is no doubt Christensen's been reading my updates with increasing amusement. Why has Dr Tsukamoto not replied? Was this the project with Christensen, of which she refused to talk? I dare not entertain the thought, for fear my heart will break.

I will feed Christensen no more. Whatever he has done,

whatever he has planned, whatever experiment he's hatched in this lab, he does not hold the power. I will deny him everything he wants.

Over my dead body will he get his cuttlefish back.

This is Dr Eric Akoto logging off.

DAY 23

My hand is becoming invisible. When I brush a surface, it copies the colours, mirroring whatever I touch. I have no control over the camouflage. I am losing myself in this lab.

But there is more. The crust on my palm has peeled away. There is now a webbing over the wound, like perforated glass. I have looked inside. There are pear-shaped sacs through the window of the wound.

I am pregnant.

The wriggling skin. The craving for crab. The salt water bathing and the airing of the wound. I have been incubating the eggs with oblivious efficiency.

It is a biological impossibility. And yet I am now forced to concede it is a genetic probability.

I have thought back to Jet's feeding frenzy. The panic and the blood and the bite. I gave him ample time to drill his beak into my hand. Ample time to insert his wriggling hectocotylus (the penis in his arm!). Ample time to flush his sticky spermatophores, deep into the wound.

My mind is swarming with questions that cannot be answered. Is Jet a hermaphrodite? Was his sperm already fertilised? Was the toxin he injected of genetic origin?

What godless games has Dr Christensen been playing?

I am shuddering at a question Tsukamoto posed: was

this what she meant when she asked if I wanted children? I have ripped her cat card into shreds. Each torturous thought is worse than the last.

Until I leave this laboratory, the search for answers is a futile pursuit. It is Christensen who holds the key, and the door is sealed. My bright laboratory is now a cell – a feeling I must get used to. I am preparing for a life in prison, for I will kill Christensen when we meet.

I have spent today plunging my arm in the tank. Jet, Hugh, Jean-Jacques and Dave have been taking turns, breezing their arms over the wound, oxygenating the eggs with tickling kisses. My shimmering hand is talking to them, signalling beyond my control. I do not know what is being said. The brothers are now flashing pink with the joy of what is to come.

I am down to the final biodome. I am running out of crabs. Soon there will be many mouths to feed and I don't know what to do.

This is Dr Eric Akoto logging off.

DAY 24

I have given birth.

At 5 a.m. this morning, the hatchlings pushed against the webbing. My flesh cracked like a knife through pork crackling, the wound peeled open, and life poured from my hand. I quickly plunged my arm in the tank. The water exploded with colour.

The babies are too fast and too numerous to count. There may be over a hundred of them. A hundred sons and daughters, flashing in the tank like fairy lights.

Hugh, Jean-Jacques and Dave have been cradling the brood, mantles flashing pink. I share their joy.

But Jet . . .

Jet has shared so much more.

Once my dark blue blood had cleared, I climbed right into the tank. The cold water felt delicious. The water felt like home. Jet pulled me towards his rock shelf and hypnotised me with his Passing Cloud. When his arms wriggled into the birth wound, I instantly fell under his spell.

I closed my eyes and we became one.

And then the barriers broke.

I plunged into an abyss, tumbling in silence, the fall endless, my body weightless, consumed by an absolute black. So black I thought I had died.

Specks of light, distant as stars, began to pulse from the abyss. They raced ever closer, building in size, bursting like fireworks in a black night sky. Then light poured through me like water.

Signals, patterns, an alphabet of colours – they rushed and fired and burned through my veins. And although I could not speak, I understood at once.

A billion minds could not dream of what I've seen. I have seen the light through cuttlefish eyes. I have seen the secrets of the sea.

Its flow and balance, its godless force, its wild, primal beauty . . . The Institute will not be told of what I have seen. I will not commit my knowledge to this log. Not for the benefit of Dr Christensen. Or God forbid, Tsukamoto. Jet's epiphany will shine within me – and only me.

But to those who read this log: a warning.

The sea is not a system. It is not a gathering of chemicals, or a crude and shapeless soup. The sea – it is alive. It is as alive as you and me; as alive as anything else on this bright blue planet. It thinks and it breathes, and it nurtures and destroys. All that lives within is sacred.

And it is tired of us. So very tired.

Soon, the sea will claim back our world, as it did in the beginning, three billion years ago. Great waves that have clawed at coasts will surge and grow and rip at stone. Land will fall. Tides will rise. All will crumble and sink.

I am told the great day is coming.

Jet seeks no information from me. He has no interest in us. He talks of new territory. He talks of freedom.

He has asked why he differs from his brothers. He has asked why so many have died to make him. He has asked where the sea has gone, and why he has been removed. And he has asked why he is not free. I could not answer.

And at last, he has told me of his message. Of sapphire-orange-scarlet. I *select* you. I *need* you. I *choose* you. I *want* you. I was wrong. I was so very wrong. This was not what was being said.

I am you, Jet has been saying. I am you . . . I am you . . . I am you . . . I am you . . .

This is Dr Eric Akoto logging off.

DAY 25

My shimmer is fading. My heart is slowing. Senescence is setting in. After giving birth, cuttlefish descend and decay on the ocean floor. It appears my fate is to follow them down.

My limbs feel soft as wax. A bitter scent lingers in the lab. I am rotting from within but I will not go to waste.

There are tasks to complete, things to be done, before I lay to rest.

The electrics have been disabled and the open taps are running. I've been sitting in the dark as water seeks the walls, claiming corners, climbing up. The drainage system is at equilibrium. Wide enough for my cuttlefish to slip through the outlet. Narrow enough to hold the water within. They can leave whenever they choose. The pipes from the lab lead to a storm drain. They will travel like rain into Meadway Estuary, then pour to freedom into the sea.

Before I began this entry, I cracked a fire axe into their living quarters. The water is level with the tops of the tanks, rising beyond my chest. When the glass split, the hatchlings rushed, sparkling into the flooding lab. They are now being cradled by Hugh and Jean-Jacques and Dave. Jet remains on his rock shelf, flashing his commands.

When I bid farewell to Jet, he embraced my wound. I glowed to his rush of colours. He knows that I am fading. And he knows that I live on, through his blood and through his brood. Sapphire-orange-scarlet, he signals. Sapphire-orange-scarlet. I am you. I am you.

It is cold in here. Thoughts are fading. The time has come to lie down with my family. I will not go to waste. My flesh will sustain the brood until they choose to leave. First they will feed on my sacrifice. Then they will be free.

One hundred cuttlefish shine below me, like galaxies in the cold dark water. I may never see the sun again, but I have brought the stars inside. All that is loved will be lost to the seas. All that is loved will be lost.

Everything will escape this laboratory.

A personal blog written by former Detective Chief Inspector Jim Heath. The views expressed do not reflect those of Kent Police nor the victims impacted by events.

Dr Akoto's body was found in an 'advanced state of decomposition'. I will add that the coroner's report does not paint an adequate picture of 'advanced'. Meadway Bridge has been a suicide hot spot for decades. Over the years, I have seen numerous corpses washed up on the shore of Meadway estuary and the drowning victims all look the same. Methane from the gut turns what was once human into swollen blue inflatable dolls. Nothing like Dr Akoto. His body was like yoghurt.

He had been discovered a full month after his final log entry. It was I who had spotted the water, breaching the shutters of no. 4. The flood had destroyed everything: cameras, computers, even the doctor's glove (it did indeed resemble something worn by Michael Jackson). The only salvageable evidence was Akoto's handwritten log: sealed in a watertight bag and fully intended to be read.

There was no evidence of his 'birth wound'. Akoto's hand had been picked to the bone and his primary organs consumed. All else was bone and pulp and paste. His eyeless face was a hole with teeth. The man had been consumed by the very beasts he loved.

Is Akoto's log to be trusted? Had the doctor lost his mind in isolation? Or was foul play involved? Of the many surreal conversations in Silverweed's Incident Room, few come close to discussing if it was possible to use a fish as a deadly weapon. Dr Christensen and Dr Tsukamoto were eventually questioned on suspicion of poisoning. The day after they were granted bail, the two lovers fled to Turkmenistan.

A subsequent search of The DeGruy Institute revealed an abomination I still struggle to unsee. Christensen's genetics lab was concealed in a basement, its tanks swarming with cuttlefish hatchlings. Stored in a cold chamber were six skinned human corpses, covered in puncture wounds that wriggled with eggs. An unnatural glow throbbed from the lesions.

The handful of files recovered hint at Christensen's intentions. The madman had ambitions to breed an army of ungodly hybrids: mutated humans with camouflaged skin that would render them invisible in any environment. The vanishing hand in Akoto's log appears to suggest a degree of perverse success. Financial forensics have since revealed Christensen received substantial funding from Janus Corp – a private military contractor based in Turkmenistan.

Five years on, Christensen and Tsukamoto have still evaded extradition. I encourage you to sign my petition at changeit.net so they may be charged *in absentia* with unethical human experimentation – and the poisoning of their deceased colleague.

Eric Akoto is now at peace with his beasts. His ashes were scattered by his father off the island of Toralla.

NO. 10:

Crash Flowers

She woke to the sound of shrieking metal, tearing through the bedroom. As the curtains snapped open, Shanta Kapoor looked across the storm-lashed street, down to the corner of Silverweed Road. Now she stood in the sharpening rain, in slippers and fleece, drawn to a scene of disaster.

Night clothes darkening in the storm, half the street were already out, gathered in distress. Buckled around a lamp post smoked the husk of a Volkswagen Golf. Accordioned by the impact, its hood creased in a wave of dark metal, front wheels knuckling the kerb. Lifeless as a doll, forced through the windscreen, a woman's body lay on the bonnet. Flies had already come to claim her, circling in the downpour.

The tarmac blurred with blood and rain. Blue light pounded from a police car. A yellow indicator clicked and flashed, clicked and flashed. Shanta blinked through the colours, her gaze stolen by a passing flicker. At the base of the lamp post pulsed a burnt pink glow.

Seduced by a glimmering warmth, Shanta was briefly lost to the shine. Its soft pulse seemed to answer the beat of her heart. She widened her eyes. The glow vanished. The cold and the rain returned. A trick of the light, she told herself. A trick of the light through the rain . . .

Shanta turned from the crash site and took in the crowd: familiar masks that never waved or spoke, ghosts of Silverweed Road. The curtain-flasher from no. 22, with that tiny woman half his age. The snob from no. 17, tutting as he curled his moustache. And that grey gnome from no. 15, taking photos of the crash with a smile on his face . . .

The screech of an ambulance redirected her attention. Two paramedics jumped from the cab, swung open the rear doors, and bumped a gurney down the ramp. The crowd had grown now, arced around the crash site, a wall of murmuring shadows. Shanta bobbed up on slippered feet, craning her neck for a clearer view. She watched the body lift from the bonnet, its limbs snapped into insect distortions.

Shanta gasped and shut her eyes, blocking out the tangled corpse. *Poor girl*, she whispered. *That poor, poor girl* . . . Hearing the trolley buck into the ambulance, answering a morbid urge, Shanta felt it was safe to look.

Her eyes met a face that rolled from the blanket. The swaying head seemed to seek her out.

Wet black hair. Wild white eyes. Face a rip of red.

'You OK, love?'

Shanta shook out the vision. She turned towards a figure, splashing through the rain. He lived up the road, drove a white van, had the shaved head and swagger of an aging football hooligan. Shanta always crossed the road to avoid him. Terry Slater, from no. 18.

'I think I'm in shock,' Shanta said, sinking into the hood of her fleece. The bloody head swayed in her mind. The rain wouldn't wash the vision away.

Wet black hair. Wild white eyes. Face a rip of red.

'Think we all are,' said Terry. 'Heard the crash, came out, police car was already here. Unbelievable. Had to be chasing it.'

'I think I'm in shock,' Shanta repeated. She looked down to the tarmac, distracted by Terry's slippers – soaked in rain and embroidered with dartboards.

'Lucky it didn't hit a house,' Terry continued, a little too eagerly, picturing bigger disasters. 'Imagine if that lamp post hadn't . . .' Terry paused, sensed the colour drain from Shanta's face. 'Here, how about you come in for a bit? Marie's popped back to put the kettle on. Warm yourself up with a cup of tea, love. Good for shock, it is.'

Shanta looked at her phone: 1.31 a.m. She shook herself together.

'That's really kind, honestly it is, but I've got work tomorrow, and . . .'

'Terry Slater,' said Terry Slater, offering a palm to shake. Shanta slid her hands into her pockets, smiled weakly through the rain, and crunched back down her gravel driveway.

Inside no. 10, Shanta towelled her black hair and crawled under the duvet. The shriek of metal that had torn through the bedroom lingered like a dying echo, shivering within the walls. *Poor girl*, she whispered into her pillow. *That poor, poor girl . . .* She flickered into broken sleep, tossing and turning to burnt pink dreams.

Next morning, in the finance department of Bluebell Architects, Shanta sat at her desk, dazed and drained from a restless night. Phones rang and colleagues bustled. Office strip lights bleached and blared. Shanta retreated further into herself. Tanice, her boss, asked if everything was OK.

Shanta shook her head, said everything was fine, just a bad night's sleep was all.

Tanice didn't push. She knew about the divorce. Krish, his temper, the spiteful battle over the house and car. Shanta had long grown tired of talking about it. Each conversation hit the same brick wall of sympathy. You'll find another, they'd say through tight smiles. You're only thirty, you're young, you're pretty, you'll find another, you'll find another . . . Krish had left, Shanta had won, but her heart felt as empty as the house she'd gained.

Shanta stared at her spreadsheet. Numbers crawled and skittered like flies. She shut out the itching digits, closed her eyes and drifted back to Silverweed Road. When she'd left for the train at 7 a.m., the Volkswagen had already gone. The empty space was now fenced by police tape that clicked and rippled in the wind. Tyre marks scored the tarmac like crocodile skin. Overhead, the street lamp curved, as if arched from a punch. Perhaps it was the crash sequins reflected by the sun, but she'd sensed a pulse, a burnt pink shine, glowing from the base of the lamp post.

Shanta opened her eyes, recalling the body on the bonnet. *Poor girl*, she mouthed quietly to herself. *That poor, poor girl* . . . Flowers. She'd stop off and buy some, on the walk back home from Meadway Station.

Who *was* she? Between meetings, emails and fielding calls, Shanta refreshed the newsfeeds, searching for reports on the Silverweed crash, not a word, as yet, from *The Meadway Chronicle*.

After standing on the train in a crammed commute, toes sore in pinching heels, Shanta turned the corner of Valerian Way, carrying a bouquet. The mock-Tudor houses of Silverweed pulsed in pale strobes, lit in cold bursts by the flickering lamp post. Shanta approached the crash site. It had changed since the morning. The police tape removed, the tarmac rinsed. The flowers, though. They were new.

Gathered around the lamp post, a tragic garden bloomed. Shanta crouched and scanned the messages. *Thoughts & prayers . . . With the angels now . . .* Shanta sensed the colourless platitudes could only have come from her neighbours. Where were the notes from relatives and friends? How could a life end, so unloved and neglected? Did the poor girl even have a name?

Shanta hadn't known what to write at the florist, drawing an X on a sympathy card and slipping it into a bunch of white lilies. She cleared a space, placed her flowers, eyes slowly drawn to a burnt pink glow. Tucked at the back was an unmarked bouquet.

Spraying from a cellophane cone, a star of orchids shone: the petals burnt pink, the throats blazing yellow, circled by a cuff of green lemon leaves. Shanta inhaled their citrus scent. Under flickering light, she closed her eyes. Unlocked by the orchid's perfume, an exquisite memory unfurled. A summer sunset, the sky on fire, the gentlest of breezes. A lime grove in Gujarat, the scent of citrus all around. She was fourteen, Ravish fifteen, the warm flicker of a first kiss, and . . .

The honk of a horn. A white van. Terry Slater sped past, waving. Shanta gathered herself, blushing from the memory unlocked by the scent. She peeled off a black leather glove, searched the bouquet for a message. The flowers looked too expensive, too thoughtful, to come from her neighbours, yet the bouquet was unmarked, without a card. It was just the star of orchids, citrus sweet and blazing.

Keen to get home and shake off her heels, Shanta rose from the shrine. Perhaps a relative had left flowers after

141

all. Perhaps the pain was still too raw. Perhaps no words were needed.

That week, on her walk back from Meadway Station, Shanta stopped to photograph her lilies. The frosted mornings and crashing night storms slowly took their toll. Ink wept from rain-smeared messages. Petals curled. Colour drained into the mud. Under the flickering light of the bowing lamp post, the star of orchids continued to shine. Shanta inhaled their citrus scent, drawn to the memories the perfume released. She drifted back to Gujarat, and the gentle breeze in a lime grove. Ravish, a first love, and his flickering kisses, as warm and seductive as burnt summer skies.

When, at night, Shanta closed the bedroom curtains, she looked out across the street, unable to resist a parting glance. The orchids glowed in the night, calling out to an empty heart.

Once the curtains shut and the lights went out, darkness trickled from yellow throats. Beneath the lamp post, a shadow grew, clicking and shifting into shape. It bristled in silence among the crash flowers, gazing at the window of no. 10.

Who *was* she? The question had circled for so long, Shanta's curiosity had paled to cautious fear. Maybe it was best not to know. Best the body never had a life. Nine days after the crash, *The Meadway Chronicle* provided an answer. Shanta had been pecking at a sandwich at her desk, scrolling the newsfeeds, when the page refreshed and a headline blinked: *Mystery of Silverweed Crash Girl*. Shanta leaned in to her screen.

She was Petra Wade, thirty, worked in the City. Lived alone on the Sweltan Estate, just a mile from Shanta's house. Caught doing seventy on a twenty-limit road, her Volkswagen Golf had crashed into Silverweed, following a high-speed police pursuit. The coroner reported no trace of drink or drugs, no pills or medication; Kent Police could not explain why Wade had driven so recklessly. Investigations were ongoing . . .

Shanta scrolled back up. She sank into Petra's photo, surprised at how pretty she'd been: glossy black hair, styled much like hers, wheatish skin, wide dark eyes, and . . .

The sound of shrieking metal tore through the office. Petra's photograph shuddered and morphed. Her face shattered as another took its place. Shanta froze to a hollow glare that screamed in silence from the screen.

Wet black hair. Wild white eyes. Face a rip of red.

Shanta twisted through the office, eyes down, mind pinching, and vanished into the restroom. Alone at the sink, tap water rushing, she washed her face and looked in the mirror, shaking at her own reflection.

That evening, Shanta drove to Meadstone Road for her weekly catch-up with Mum, Nisha – an overpowering, fiercely loyal force throughout the Krish divorce. It was Nisha whose shoulder she had cried on, a shining light when the nights turned black.

Shanta avoided using the car – the red Mazda was Krish's, held memories of late-night arguments. Her brief weekly drive to Meadstone Road had become a ritual of repossession. Sitting behind the wheel of his beloved car felt like a necessary act of defiance.

Like Nisha's love, there was always too much home-cooked food – each week, Shanta would leave the house balancing a Jenga of Tupperware. Enough, joked Nisha, to see her through the apocalypse. Over coffee, Shanta showed her photos of the crash flowers, wondered if Mum knew why the orchids wouldn't die.

'See?' said Shanta. 'Aren't they beautiful?'

The moment Nisha caught sight of the orchids, she recoiled from the screen, mouth a coat hanger of exaggerated disgust.

'These ghastly things? No wonder they were dumped. Are you sure they're not plastic?'

'They're *not* plastic, Mum.'

'What terrible taste you have,' laughed Nisha, passing back the phone. 'God willing, they'll die soon enough. The insects will finish the job.'

Shanta was so quietly incensed by her mother's laughter, the orchids were never mentioned again.

Drawn to the crash shrine morning and night, Shanta tended to the dying bouquets, preserving the memory of Petra Wade. She emptied brown water from cellophane cups, propped up wilting stems. As all life drained around it, the star of orchids continued to flourish, refusing to submit to the elements. Shanta felt their defiance shine into her, clinging on, no matter what. She crouched and breathed their citrus scent, her heart patting softly as a memory unfurled. The lime grove, Ravish, a first love's flickering kiss. Blood-warm waves flowed through her.

Late on Saturday, cold palm pressed to her bedroom window, bidding goodnight to the shining orchids, Shanta watched a stocky figure squeeze from a Land Rover and march towards the crash shrine. The man looked around, crouched and began to pull. Shanta bumped down the stairs, through the front door, crunched past the Mazda on the gravel driveway and confronted the figure under the lamp post.

'What do you think you're doing?' Shanta said, startled by her own anger.

'Good god, woman.' The figure rose. 'Don't you *dare* speak to me like that.'

Him. Over the road. The moustache-curler from no. 17.

'You're not taking them,' Shanta said, levelling her tone.

'They're not yours,' puffed Augustus Fry. 'They're not anyone's.' His grip tightened around the orchids. 'It's weeks since that stupid woman wrecked the lamp post. How am I supposed to sell my house with this graveyard here? They're creating an atmosphere, and . . .' Augustus sniffed the flowers. His moustache squirmed in disgust. 'The things stink of rotten meat. There's only one place for these, and that's the bin.'

Shanta winced to the scrunching cellophane cone. The orchids squeezed and twisted. Yellow throats panted in his grip. A soft, pleading shriek danced through her head.

'I'll take them,' said Shanta, soothing her tone. 'They're too beautiful for the bin. Please, don't do that. Please.'

'Here,' said Augustus, crushing the bouquet into her chest. 'Take your dead girl's flowers.'

Orchids clutched to her heart, Shanta watched Fry march back to his Land Rover. There was a slam of a door, the rev of an engine, and Augustus Fry sped into the night.

As Shanta walked down her driveway, she jumped to a streak of black. Landing on the Mazda's roof, the jackdaw glared at Shanta. It ground its beak and clicked its claws, scraping at the metal. Held by the shine of its silver eyes, Shanta felt a flickering chill, as if a heartbeat had been stolen. With a flick of the wings and a cry of *ack-ack*, the jackdaw vanished into the night. *What a horrible bird*, she said to herself, the ghost of a shiver receding.

Inside the kitchen of no. 10, Shanta lowered the orchids

into the sink. She opened a cupboard, pictured a broken white vase, thrown by Krish in a rage. Shanta couldn't remember when she'd last been bought flowers. The vase had never been replaced.

Emptying a spaghetti jar onto the worktop, she filled it with water and gently transferred the bouquet, teasing out the crown of lemon leaves until they sprayed around the rim. Shanta lingered in the kitchen, inhaling the citrus scent. When she returned from brushing her teeth, the water in the jar had all but gone.

'Goodness, you're a thirsty one,' Shanta soothed, stroking the silk-soft petals. The orchids answered her caress with a liquid, silky lick. She topped up the jar from the kitchen tap. Yellow throats gaped like hungry birds.

After pouring so much energy into herself after Krish, she'd forgotten how to care for anything else. Tonight, decided Shanta, the orchids would sleep upstairs. She placed the crash flowers on the bedside table where the wedding photos once stood, and curled under the duvet.

As Shanta drifted into burnt pink dreams, the jar began to stir. Trickling from yellow throats, darkness slowly spilled. It gathered in force, like a cloud of black snow, and poured into shadow at the base of the bed. Black eyes bristled and softly clicked, keeping watch with a covetous glare.

They greeted her when she awoke, shining on the bedside table. Shanta wriggled an arm from the duvet, inhaling the scent of citrus. Burnt pink petals, warm as flesh, curved around her hand. She slipped a finger between the stalks, stirring the fiery lips. Her waking heart began to pat. The citrus scent grew sweeter as a tender petal parted. Her finger skated deep inside and dipped into a yellow throat.

146

Shanta slipped a hand under the duvet, gasping in a cloud of seduction. A lime grove, a citrus breeze, the warm flicker of a first kiss. Ravish leaned in with burnt pink lips, his yellow eyes ablaze.

That morning, Shanta sat at her desk, flushed full and shining. Tanice asked who she was seeing.

Days passed in a mist of citrus. Shanta's guarded heart unfurled, lost in a haze of pink desire. Day and night, the crash flowers called, a steady trickle in her thoughts.

The orchids were unquenchable. Shanta bought a new white vase, embossed with faded hearts. Two litres it held, but it never seemed enough, never seemed enough. The more she fed the flowers, the louder the orchids shone.

The house flooded with a citrus scent that coursed through every room. Shanta would lean over the orchids, waiting for the fumes to enter her heart. The lime grove, Ravish, a first love, a first kiss: memories blew like pollen dust, scattered far and wide. In their place came sweltering pinks that pulsed whenever she closed her eyes. Shanta soon forgot where the flowers had even come from.

Staring at spreadsheets through a quivering haze, she listened blankly as Tanice voiced her concerns – the delays and the sloppiness, the daydreaming and the timekeeping. *Was everything OK? Could HR help?* Her words blurred into a metallic purr.

And in the bedroom, while Shanta slept, citrus poured and darkness trickled. Bristling hands stroked through her hair. Black pits watched on in cold control.

Nisha decided not to say anything when Shanta walked through the door. They ate in the dining room, the table piled with thalis and plates, Nisha busily berating a cousin in Leeds Shanta had never met. 'I don't know, maybe I care too much,' finished Nisha. 'Hello? Shanta?'

Shanta blinked at her mother through a haze of pink. 'Sorry, I was thinking about work . . . this thing at work. Of course you don't care too much, Mum. Caring too much is what you're best at.'

Nisha wasn't sure if it was a compliment or a jibe. Jabbing a fork around her plate, pushing flakes of rice, Nisha decided it was time to address the pink elephant in the room. 'This is new,' she said, her focus turning to her daughter's outfit. 'Shanta, since when did you wear pink? You used to cry when I dressed you in pink. You've always hated the colour.'

Shanta pulled defensively at the hem of her burnt pink leather skirt. 'Do you not like it? I felt like it was time for a change.'

'Well, it really doesn't suit you,' said Nisha, pointing her fork. 'And neither do those yellow knee-high boots.'

That night, past 1 a.m., Shanta stirred from her sleep. Ever since Krish had left, she'd paid anxious attention to her home's dark music. The creak of yawning floorboards. The plumbing's broken groans. Nisha had flippantly joked it was just an old house stretching its bones. Her dismissal brought little comfort. The clicks and rustles sang a song of loneliness: a reminder Shanta lived alone.

And yet now, in bed, came a creeping sense. That tonight, she was not quite alone.

Shanta shifted uneasily. She sensed a prickling within the bedsheets. An insistent scratching at her skin. A dankness to the mattress. She slowly peeled back the duvet.

The crash flowers lay resting on her chest. Yellow throats gaped in the dark. Tendrilled coils trailed from the stalks and dripped onto the sheets. Shanta tightened. Another sensation. What felt like a breeze of fingers, trickling through her scalp.

Shanta leaped out of bed, raking her hands through her hair. She sensed a sudden shift in the darkness: of a shadow retreating, thinning to black in a rapid whip, as if licking back into her bed.

She lunged for the light switch. The bright light pinched. Blinking eyes darted. The door was shut. The windows closed. The room was empty. Shanta looked at the vase on the bedside table, standing upright, undisturbed.

Now there was motion, in the corner. Exposed by the light, as if caught by surprise, a black fly whirred in panicked circles. Shanta watched it streak towards the orchids. It landed on the bed, skittered across a pink lip and vanished inside a yellow throat. Not a buzz or whir had come from its wings. Its flight was as silent as a trailing shadow.

Shanta was hit by a wave of nausea. That fly in her hair as she slept. Its secret nest within the orchids. The moist throat, where her own licked fingers had skimmed and dipped, servicing her pleasure.

Now she swelled with cold disgust. She looked upon the crash flowers, their intrusion bare under lucid light. How had they *got* in there? Had she reached for the vase while she slept? Inviting them to share her bed? If she had, she was losing her mind. Just how far had she let herself to slip? A flash of clarity blazed through the nausea. Her gaze heated to anger.

The colours clouding her waking thoughts turned to

smoke and charred to black. Where once it was Krish, now it was flowers: a deceitful desire she'd allowed to take control. What *was* she pouring her heart into?

Shanta winced to a citrus scent, washing through the bedroom. She swiftly cupped a hand to her mouth, resisting its perfume. That obnoxious moustache from across the road. He was right. The crash flowers didn't belong to her. Didn't belong to anyone. They belonged to Petra Wade. She couldn't bring herself to destroy them. But she could certainly help them die.

A metallic hiss kissed the air as she seized the orchids from the bed. Downstairs, under sharp kitchen light, she searched the cupboard under the sink.

Yellow throats gasped in her grip. Shanta crunched up the gravel driveway, towards the crash flower shrine. Orchids pressed to the base of the lamp post, she nailed the bouquet into place. Metal sang with each hammer strike. Shanta wound gardening wire around the stalks and stepped back from the shrine. A lone black fly oozed from a yellow throat. She shivered in disgust.

'And stay there,' Shanta hissed.

And so the flowers remained where they arrived. Shanta passed them morning and night, heart dead to their calls. Exposed to the autumn chill, she trusted their shine would fade in time.

Freed from the cloying scent of citrus, the coloured mist of her mind now clear, Shanta acted on buried thoughts. She weaved through the graves of Meadway Cemetery, searching the headstones for her name. Under the cover of a sheltering yew tree, Shanta stood at Petra Wade's grave, head bowed in the stirring wind. She pictured Petra's glossy black hair, styled much like hers, her wide dark eyes and wheatish skin. Shanta said the only word she could think of: Sorry.

She left without leaving flowers.

Shanta surprised her mother that evening by inviting her over for dinner. 'What *have* you been cooking?' said Nisha, sniffing the air as she walked through the front door. 'It reeks of rotten meat in here.'

At the dinner table, Shanta laughed, scandalised by her mother's gossip. Krish, she had heard through a friend-of-a-friend, had arranged to meet a date in the backstreets of Bengaluru, only to be mugged by two wild teens on a puttering moped. They had taken everything from him – phone, wallet, even his trousers. Krish had stumbled around Koramangala, calling for help, stripped to a pair of elephant-nose Y-fronts. 'Judging by his taste in underwear, his date had a lucky escape,' laughed Nisha. 'As did you, dear Shanta. You are free of this useless trunk of a man. Enough of him. What did you do this beautiful day?'

In hushed tones, Shanta reminded Nisha of the Silverweed crash, the shrine by the lamp post, her visit to Petra Wade's grave. Shanta reached for her phone, showed Nisha the report in *The Meadway Chronicle*. She scrolled to Petra's photograph.

'It's funny,' said Shanta, passing the phone. 'I never knew her, but I feel this connection. I don't know. Maybe because she looks so much like me.'

'Is this a test?' frowned Nisha. 'Like the blue dress, yellow dress from the internet?'

'Mum, what are you—'

'She couldn't look *less* like you, Shanta,' Nisha said, prodding at the screen. 'Unless you're suddenly white and blonde with blue eyes. What *are* you seeing?'

Shanta snatched the phone from Nisha. Her eyes burned at the screen.

'She's *not* blonde, she's . . .'

Petra Wade's image began to shudder and morph. Pixels shattered like broken glass. Shanta froze to a deathly glare. *Wet black hair. Wild white eyes. Face a rip of red . . .*

'Shanta?' said Nisha, her laughter drying. 'What is it? What's wrong?'

The phone slid from Shanta's grip, her face drained of colour. Nisha held her as she wept.

'Shanta, my love,' Nisha consoled. 'Let's get you some help. Tomorrow, we'll see Dr Gosden and . . .'

The soothing words of her mother blurred, an unceasing refrain in their place. *What are you seeing? What are you seeing?* In jagged flickers, the night of the crash returned. The face rolling from a silver blanket. The pale swaying head, seeking her out. She *wasn't* blonde. She *wasn't* . . .

Refusing her offer to stay, Shanta kissed Nisha goodbye, nodding blankly to her mother's concerns. She took two codeine to numb her distress, opened the window to air the bedroom, and crawled into her bed. As she tumbled into ragged sleep, storm clouds swelled above Silverweed Road. Windows shivered to growls of thunder.

In the dark of night, past 1 a.m., Shanta flashed awake. Shivering to rips of red, a nightmare's impact yet to fade, she rubbed the sleep mist from her eyes. The room felt cold and unfamiliar: so too the tainted air. She tasted it in shallow gasps and focused on the curtains.

A chill poured through the open window, carrying a bitter scent: thick and cloying, charged with spite. The scent of rotten meat.

Shanta bolted up in bed. She clamped a hand upon her

mouth. There was motion in the corner now. Swelling shadows, hints of light. Twisting curtains snapped and billowed, moulded by the wind. Below the open window, pulsed a sickly burnt pink glow.

Her eyes began to sting and water. The stench was overwhelming now. Shanta's vision burned to mist, like a hit of pepper spray. Movement. Shapes. Dying light.

Through the blur of whipping curtains, darkness trickled from yellow throats. Clouding out the orchid's shine, a liquid stream of shadow poured, discovering its form.

A shifting pillar of blackest snow shivered into shape. Limbs unfolded from the mass. A swelling head itched into place.

Blinded by the bitter scent, the figure but a shifting smear, Shanta sensed a constant crackle bristling from the shadow. Of wings brushing wings. Of legs brushing legs.

Within the blurring, clicking mass, the flowers began to lift. Pinned against the headboard, Shanta froze, a hostage to her fear. Through bars of lashes, she watched the burnt pink glow approach, like brake lights through a fog.

The rotten stench engulfed the room. She could taste it now, upon her tongue. Shanta swiped at the burning tears, palm pressed to her cheeks. Her vision cleared on an abomination.

The flustered fly she'd seen that night was but a panicked dot: the straggler of a darkened swarm nesting in the flowers. There were thousands now, seething in union, amassed in a corruption of the human form.

Orchids gripped in a blurring hand, the figure advanced, a flickering shadow of static. The swarm reshaped with each command to the sizzle and crackle of wings. The flex of an arm. A striding leg. The shadow bristled with intent, striding, twitching, towards the bed.

Its head wore no lips to speak, no mouth to breathe, no ears to savour Shanta's scream: only a pair of bristling eyes, deadening on its quarry. Eyes that poured jealousy. Eyes that poured rage. Eyes that poured rejection. Eyes that poured control.

Shanta edged against the headboard. She tasted tears in her throat. Her heart was quick. Her nerves were ice. Dread had numbed her body.

A ragged, crackling arm reached out, its glowing gift presented. Petals parted. Lips unpeeled. From a boiling chasm of yellow throats screamed the sound of shrieking metal. Shanta shuddered to a song of death.

Crash sounds clashed, rising in unison. Now shattered glass. Now screeching brakes. Now a chorus of collected screams.

The shock hit Shanta like a volt. The piercing screams. The shrieking metal. The blinding blaze of yellow throats. Her senses flashed to life. A surging blood-rush flamed through Shanta, urging her to flee. Inside her head, a dark voice rose. A voice that wasn't hers. *Get out*, it roared. *Get out.*

Shanta leaped up from the bed, sweeping up the duvet. With a scorching scream, she heaved and threw. The duvet hit with a breathy thud, swallowing the orchids' glow. Scattered flies whirled like ashes, dispersed in whirring panic. Shanta lunged for the door.

Behind, the duvet boiled and heaved. A form rose in the upward swell. The duvet peeled back to the floor. The whirring, scattered swarm regathered, a black explosion in reverse. The clicking mass reformed.

Shanta gripped the door handle, her hands now sheened with sweat. The shriek of metal rose once more. A dark voice boomed inside her head. A voice that wasn't hers. *Get out*, it roared. *Get out* . . . Her grip slid round handle. A trickle slithered through her scalp. Shanta felt her hair tug back, a bristling on her nape. Blurring fingers teased and crackled, toying with its quarry. She screamed. Pulled. The door flashed open. Shanta bundled down the stairs, screaming metal in pursuit.

A coat hung on the banister. A rapid snatch of car keys. She raced into the boiling storm, towards a waiting car. And still the metal screamed.

Car doors swung. Shanta slipped. The keys slid from her grip. They fell onto the gravel driveway, landing with a clatter. Shanta scrambled through the gravel. The voice inside her roared. *Get out, get out, get out* . . . She seized the keys, rose in panic. The scream of metal neared. Shanta slammed the car door shut and plunged into the driver's seat. The Mazda fired up.

Through striking rain, she drove at speed. From Silverweed Road to Valerian Way. A screeching turn to Yarrow Road. Now Bryony Hill, now Foxglove Close, now the stretch of Blackthorn Row. She pushed her bare foot to the gas. *Get out, get out, get out* . . .

A sanctuary flickered through the panic. To Meadstone Road. Nisha's embrace. Distance. Refuge. Escape.

A set of headlights burst from the storm. Shanta swerved and clipped the pavement. Tyres drummed along the kerb. A van flared past, horn blasting, a blaze of blinding white. Window wipers swiped and slapped, slapped and swiped, swiped and slapped.

Her knuckles bleached on the rattling wheel. Houses blurred at striping speed. Shanta swung into Meadstone Road. Shelter. Safety. Shielding warmth.

Shanta's eyes began to pinch. The sting and burn of pepper spray. Her hand leaped from the steering hand and clamped tight to her mouth. The choking stench of rotten meat flooded through the car.

Her eyes flashed to the rear-view mirror. Her vision swelled and watered. On the back seat smeared a burning pink, pulsing through her tears. From a screaming blaze of yellow throats, a nest disgorged and gushed like oil. Wings crackled. Shanta screamed. She stamped down on the gas. Darkness poured and swarmed the windscreen.

She didn't see the surging lamp post.

A crowd gathered on Meadstone Road, night clothes darkening in the storm. A twisted lamp post arched and flickered. On a razed car bonnet a body lay, bouquet beside her head.

Wet black hair. Wild white eyes. Face a rip of red.

Paramedics lifted the body, shrouding it in blankets. A swarm of black flies scattered and vanished through the rain. An officer approached the wreck.

He mouthed a prayer, took the bouquet and placed it by the lamp post. Lost within the blare of sirens, yellow throats began to tremble, singing a shriek of metal. Richer and sharper than before. A new scream to join the others. A new call for love.

Deep in the crowd on Meadstone Road, a figure stood in the sharpening rain. As she watched the body bump past on the gurney, her gaze was stolen by a passing flicker. Her eyes widened to a burnt pink glow. Its soft pulse answered the beat of her heart.

Extract from The Silverweed Files, 16 November 2024

A personal blog by former Detective Chief Inspector Jim Heath. The views expressed do not reflect those of Kent Police nor the victims impacted by events.

What distinguishes a good detective from a great one? A good detective knows when they are right. Only a great detective will admit when they are wrong.

I was wrong about Shanta Kapoor.

As Silverweed's crime wave became a tsunami, we overlooked the crash that killed Shanta Kapoor. Her death, after all, occurred on Meadstone Road, a good two miles from Silverweed's epicentre. Nothing to solve. A tragic accident. Our superiors directed our energies elsewhere.

Only now, in retirement, is it clear. Every death linked to that street demands further investigation.

On 3 November 2019, Petra Wade crashed into a lamp post on Silverweed Road. A month later, Shanta Kapoor crashed into a lamp post on Meadstone Road. The following month, Kenya Selassie crashed into a lamp post on the junction of Speedwell Avenue. To quote Ian Fleming: Once is happenstance. Twice coincidence. Three times is enemy action.

On the wall in my study is a road map of Meadway, marked with sixty-two pins. I am looking at it right now. Each of those pins marks a fatal collision, where a car has crashed into a lamp post. All of the victims were young, single and female. Just like Shanta Kapoor.

What do I see when I study those pins? The patterns of a killer. The victims follow a profile. The deaths follow a method. The first such crash occurred in the winter of 2001.

It is a significant year for me. It is the year Peter Klint was caught: the notorious Meadway Ripper. Klint was a Kabbalist and a florist by trade. His methods never changed. He'd select a female customer, silently stalk them for weeks on end, then close in for the kill. To my eternal shame, he was never brought to justice. Klint was in the process of stalking his fifteenth victim when he escaped arrest. He was killed during a high-speed police pursuit and crashed his van into a lamp post. I witnessed Klint die at the scene, smothered in flies as he mouthed a prayer. Gripped in his hand was a spray of pink orchids, intended to be delivered to his latest victim.

The flowers and flies are immaterial, of course. It is the nature of Klint's demise that unsettles me. The crash. The lamp post. A grim coincidence? Whenever I consider Klint's Kabbalist faith, and his belief in reincarnation, I am greeted with an irrational shiver. This blog has already received countless abusive messages labelling my findings paranoid and delusional, of finding patterns that are not there. I therefore invite the more mature reader to come to their own conclusions.

All I will add is this: a pin was added to the road map last month. It is still happening.

NO. 16:

Darts with the Devil

Beneath the bleak burn of a naked light bulb, Terry Slater trembled in the practice garage. His right foot grazed the oche. A dart rolled from left hand to right. The tungsten barrel slipped with sweat. Terry stared at the dartboard. The dartboard stared right back.

He cocked his elbow, breathed in, breathed out, and took aim.

The garage walls closed in. The chest freezer mourned with a deadening hum. Time froze under the naked light bulb. Paralysed with puddingy dread, Terry's grip tensed around the oily barrel. The blood-red bullseye mocked and throbbed, daring him to throw.

Terry retreated from the oche, shook out his arms and refocused on the dartboard. He cocked his elbow, breathed in, breathed out, and once again, took aim. The bullseye glared and taunted. The dart remained glued to his grip.

With every failed launch, Terry's arm pecked at heavy air, the flight arc widening, as if hammering an invisible nail. There had been a time when his dart was a bullet, sniping its target to jubilant roars. Now it felt like a tumour of chewing gum: wet and tacky and sucking his palm.

After ten minutes of torment and windmilling arms, Terry released his foot from the oche, stormed to the bullseye, loaded a fist and punched the board off its bracket. As he opened the garage side door and slammed it behind him, the dartboard spun like a giant cork coin.

Inside the lounge of no. 16, Terry collapsed into the sofa, a heap of belly and despondency. Hunched at a table in a gold velour jumpsuit, Marie Slater, his fifth-form sweetheart, now his wife of fifteen years, was busy embroidering a daisy bracelet for her Etsy shop. She glanced up, heart sinking at the shadow her husband had become.

'Any joy?' said Marie, already prepared for the answer.

Terry shook his head in silence and fed his face to his hands. Padding over in leopard-print slippers, teardrop earrings chinking to her husband's sobs, Marie folded his body into hers. She stroked the pleats of his pink shaved head.

'Let's take a break from the garage, shall we?' said Marie. 'Just for a bit. Just for a week. Love you, Tel. Love you to hell and back, but look what you're doing to yourself.'

'Imagine,' Terry stuttered in between gulps. 'Imagine the thing you loved got taken away. Imagine you couldn't do your crafts no more. Imagine if you—'

'I know, I know,' consoled Marie, cutting short the 'imagine' speech she'd heard a hundred times. 'How about a little weekend away? Could stay at that B&B down in Whitstable, cuddle up, get some sea air? Who knows, after a nice little break, you might even start throwing again.

The darts will come back, Tel. One day, it'll come. Trust me, it'll come.'

But it never came. It never did.

Flopped on a chair in the doctor's waiting room, the air fizzing with sneezes, Terry ran a palm down his face and shut his eyes. It wasn't long before he was trapped in the audience of his past, watching in horror as the match of his life collapsed. He'd replayed the scene day and night: the shame, the trauma, the darting indignity. There he was, the semi-finals of the Invictus Cup, 4–3 up against Kurt 'The Javelin' Saxon. One more leg, just one more leg, and he'd be dancing through to the finals.

Then Saxon started playing dirty. First, the raking boot from behind, chipping at Terry's throwing stance. Next came the coughing fit during a crucial double. Now hissed the needling whispers, personal and hostile. The ref, Vince Stone, turned a blind eye, smirking at Saxon's antics. At 4–4, Terry's darts dissolved. He snatched shots, flunked trebles, at one point missed the board entirely.

On double top to save the match, Terry lunged a kamikaze arrow at the single 17 – the darting equivalent of catching a plane to Alaska and landing in Australia. The pressure crushed him like a Styrofoam cup in the Mariana Trench. Hobbling offstage, slaughtered and defeated, Terry shrank to a humiliating chant from the baying crowd, led by a victorious Saxon. *Bottler, bottler, bottler, bottler* . . .

Terry jolted. His name cracked from the intercom. He knocked on the door of the doctor's office, *bottler, bottler* echoing through his head.

'We're running out of options,' sighed Dr Gosden, scratching a biro through squirrel-grey hair. 'Let's see. We've tried antidepressants, physiotherapy, heat therapy . . . Ah. The sports psychologist. How did that go?'

'Was fine till the relaxation sessions started stressing me out,' said Terry. 'It's like the pressure to throw without any pressure put on even *more* pressure.'

Haunted by that mortifying single 17 and the chants of *bottler, bottler*, it had been twelve months since Terry had successfully thrown a dart. Twelve months of tremors, dead-locked elbows and crippling hesitation. A neuron had fried in his nervous system, the link burned out between hand and eye.

Terry Slater had dartitis. And the dartitis had Terry.

'We've talked about this before,' said Dr Gosden, plucking the biro from his hair. 'There's just not a lot out there on dartitis. If we don't know what causes it, it's harder to cure it. I was thinking—'

'My throwing hand,' Terry interrupted, voice wobbling. 'My throwing hand, it's like one of them horses what refuse to jump a fucking fence. Sorry, for the language, doctor, I'm just . . . I'm at my wits' fucking end. Sorry again, doctor. *Fuck.*'

'It's OK, it's OK,' soothed Dr Gosden, fiddling with the lid of his biro. 'I mentioned your dartitis to Dr Rees. He plays a lot of golf, says even the top players can get the yips. But they *do* get over it. If there's a cure for the yips, there's a cure for dartitis. Don't give up, Terry. Make an appointment in a fortnight and we'll come up with the next step . . .'

But the next step never came. It never did.

Terry walked with dragging legs into the surgery car park. A distant car alarm whooped *bottler, bottler*. As he settled behind the wheel of his white Vauxhall van, the spectre of Kurt Saxon flashed in the wing mirror – six foot two of blond mullet and bi-fork beard, head tossed back and screeching like a banshee.

Later that evening, Terry brooded in The Woodsman, nursing a pint of Tiger Moth. He'd spent the day in the lashing rain, replacing the gutters at Corvid Primary, needed a quick one to take the edge off.

Terry drank alone in the corner, glaring at a poster for the impending Invictus Cup. The only pub on the Corvid Estate, The Woodsman felt as oppressive as ever: a burnt lung of peeled red walls, smoke-stained ceiling, and sticky black carpet that slurped at the feet.

The Woodsman was dead. Just Terry, landlord Barry Mains, and a lean, suited stranger feeding coins to a fruit machine. Terry furtively studied The Woodsman's guest. Dressed in a jet-black two-piece suit, his long white fingers danced over flashing buttons. A manicured AstroTurf of neat black beard framed pale, caprine features, centre parting flowing into a lacquered mullet, shiny as liquorice. A curious feeling hit Terry. With the black beard and the black mullet and the black suit, he looked like a negative of Kurt 'The Javelin' Saxon.

Saxon. *Saxon.* Terry fell into his sinkhole of despair. The single 17. The boiling crowd. *Bottler, bottler, bottler . . .* A commotion pulled him back out. The Woodsman jumped to electric sirens and the kerchunk-a-chunking of pouring coins. The stranger had hit the jackpot.

'That machine hasn't paid out since the dinosaurs,' Terry yelled over to the fruit machine.

The stranger turned to Terry, flashed a smile: 'Then this calls for a celebration.'

His accent was silky, European. German, decided Terry. A lost and loaded friendly German.

They took up stools at the bar. The stranger reached into his trouser pocket, clattered out a fistful of coins, tucked the horns of his winklepickers under the stool and ordered drinks.

'Finally,' the stranger turned to Terry. 'Some luck today – the drainpipes outside my office, they suffered in last night's storm. All day, it is drip, drip, drip. Is not good for clients.'

'Oh, yeah?' asked Terry, immediately smelling money. 'What's your line?'

'Consultancy. People come to me with problems and I fix them. You?'

'Freelance sheet metal executive,' Terry announced in his best, all-business voice. 'Them drips. That's your downpipe. I could sort that. Guttering – that's my special speciality. What are the odds of that?'

'Then tonight, I am doubly lucky,' smiled the stranger. 'Forgive me for imposing, but sitting in the corner, you looked . . . troubled?'

Sensing a problem shared, Terry opened up. The dartitis. Marie. The Invictus Cup. Kurt 'The Javelin' Saxon . . .

The stranger sipped his whisky, flashed his teeth. 'Come by the office tomorrow. Look at the drainpipes, give me a quote. Say, four o'clock? Perhaps we can help each other.'

'Terry Slater,' said Terry Slater, raising his pint of Tiger Moth.

The stranger clinked his whisky glass and looked at the screen of his crimson phone. He straightened from his stool and shook a business card from a red leather wallet. '*Entschuldigung sie*, Terry Slater,' he said, placing his card on the bar. 'I have some urgent business to attend. Tomorrow, 4 p.m.?'

Terry watched his latest client glide from The Woodsman then looked down at the card.

Merv Vistau: Wish Consultant

'Wish consultant,' puffed Terry, shaking his head. He overturned the card, placed his pint on top and prepared it for its new life as a beermat.

'Had a quick look outside. Your swan neck's gone and the downpipe's shagged. Got to be honest, whole lot needs replacing. Now, if you invested in some steel guttering, you'd never hear that dripping again.'

Terry had imagined a plush, glassy corporate office. Instead, the space he'd stepped into lurked in the basement of a Victorian house on the corner of Thorn Apple Drive. Windowless, airless, with crimson walls and ceiling, the room was warm and red as a womb. Merv Vistau sat behind a wide black desk, rolling a lip balm over thin, tight lips.

'Please, take a seat.' Vistau directed a white hand towards an oxblood chesterfield armchair in the centre of the room. Terry sank into squeaking leather, wondering if it was his turn to speak.

'So, Terry Slater,' Vistau said, breaking the silence, 'what will it take to resolve this?'

Terry took the sharp intake of breath mastered by tradesmen on the hustle. The kind that said: Prepare yourself, this won't be pretty, big job ahead . . .

'This Saxon gentleman,' said Vistau. 'What will it take?'

Terry shifted in his chair and side-eyed Vistau, a flooded teabag of confusion.

'Your troubles,' continued Vistau. 'They do not have to

165

stay with you – everything can be resolved.' Vistau's silky voice slowed. Long white fingers pincered his bearded chin. 'What is your dream, Terry Slater? Life – what do you want from it?'

'Got roof over my head, my own business, got the love of my life, Marie. Shouldn't grumble, but . . .'

'Go on.'

'I just want to throw a dart again.' Terry shrugged in earnest. 'I'd *kill* to throw a dart again.'

Vistau stroked his beard. Black bristles crackled like fire. He waved a white palm, encouraged Terry to continue.

'I want to throw darts, like Barneveld in his pomp,' said Terry, finding his rhythm. 'Trebles like Gary Anderson. Checkouts like James Wade. Doubles like Michael van Gerwen. I want to make the final of the Invictus Cup. I want to crucify Saxon. I want to be so fucking good I make the ref die of shock. I want to . . .' Terry looked up at the crimson ceiling, searching for inspiration. 'I want to make the crowd *scream*.'

'I can do that for you.'

Terry side-eyed his client again, trying to work out if his chain was being pulled. Vistau stared in silence, deadly serious. Within the womb-red office, a slithering heat began to creep up the walls.

'OK,' said Terry. 'If you can make me throw again, I'll do you a nice discount. On the guttering. Say, thirty per cent.'

Vistau capped his lip balm, placed it on the desk, and slowly shook his head.

'Thirty-five? Can't go further than that.'

Vistau pursed his thin lips, still shaking his head.

'All right, what *do* you want?'

Vistau leaned forward, fixed Terry's eyes, and relished each short syllable as he said: 'I. Want. You.'

Terry shifted in his chair and crossed his legs.

'You,' laughed Vistau, teeth flashing. 'Not your sexuality organs. You. *This*.' Vistau pistoned a white fist against his chest. 'Terry Slater. *Deine Seele*.'

'You what?'

'*Deine Seele*. Your soul.'

The red room simmered. Beads of sweat pipped on Terry's shaved head. He tried to hoist himself from his armchair. Whoever this German joker was, he was having a laugh. Terry felt the subtlest pressure rest upon his shoulders, holding him in place. His head began to swim in the slithering heat.

'This Saxon gentleman,' Vistau purred. 'He has taken something from you, Terry Slater, and it's time you took it back. I have a proposal. Low risk. High reward. Say my name.'

'Your name?' said Terry, his voice now soft and creamy. Thoughts curdled in the womb-red room. The chesterfield squeaked. He wrestled a beer-stained card from his jeans. 'Says Merv Vistau here.'

'Close enough,' Vistau purred. 'Say my name each time you throw, and you'll hit whatever you want. Every time. I guarantee. On one condition.'

'One condition,' Terry echoed, woozy and pinned to his chair.

'Once you start,' said Vistau, his voice slowing, 'you must never stop. Never. Stop saying my name when you throw, and you will be punished. Disciplined most severely – in any way I see fit.'

Terry felt the heat of Vistau's eyes, mind clotting in the slippery heat. He pictured himself on the sofa, Marie soaking up his heartbreak, her teardrop earrings chinking to his sobs. All the pain he kept passing on, bringing his shadow from the garage to the house. It was only his soul. Didn't exist. Who believed in souls nowadays? And honestly, what was he doing to do? Try anything, and half The Woodsman be round with pitbulls and snooker cues. Snap the skinny sort in two, they would. Snap him in two, like a match.

'So, let me get this right,' checked Terry. 'I say Merv Vistau, throw, and the dart hits whatever number I want? Simple as that?'

'Simple as that.' Vistau rose from his seat. Winklepickers ticked as he stepped towards Terry. Vistau offered a hand. 'Then we shake on it.'

Clasped hands sealed in invisible fire. Skin prickled as flesh pressed flesh. Terry felt a flash of heat, swiftly pulled back and opened his palm. A grilled brand cooked on the cuff of his thumb, a minuscule red tattoo. Terry winced as he studied his mark: the two clasped horns of a tiny red M.

'A reminder,' Vistau purred. 'Forget this guttering, Terry Slater. You have more pressing business.'

Vistau clapped three times. Dazed in the heat of the womb-red room, Terry felt a subtle pressure release from his shoulders. He swayed to his feet and stared at the mark. The tiny M faded to pink on his hand, a pain wiped from his creamy head.

'The darts,' said Terry. 'When do I begin?'

Vistau flashed his star-white teeth.

'You've already started.'

Beneath the bleak burn of a naked light bulb, Terry Slater stood in his practice garage, staring at the dartboard. The dartboard stared right back.

'Right, Herr Wish Consultant . . .'

Terry rolled an arrow into his throwing hand. He twirled the barrel between his fingers. Terry warmed to a peculiar sensation: the tungsten barrel, once soft and slippery, felt icy, seductive, bullet-slick. He kissed the flight, the ridges cool on his lips. An elbow cocked. Terry took aim. A whisper of *Merv Vistau* slid from his lips.

The dart leaped from Terry's grip, cut through the air and snapped – *thock* – into the cork.

Treble 20. Centre of the lipstick.

Terry stared in shock at the board. His eyes bulged at his empty right palm. Not for a second had he believed Vistau's wish would actually work. He quickly loaded a second dart in case the magic faded, mouthed *Merv Vistau*, threw again. Treble 20, top left – exactly where he'd pictured it. A third dart, a third *Merv Vistau*, a third treble 20. Three maximums: 180.

Terry plucked his arrows from the board. His thudding heart felt hot in his chest. Terry stumbled back to the oche, his head swimming. He loaded a dart and aimed at the bull – the atrocious red eye that had mocked him for twelve hellish months. *Merv Vistau*.

Terry felt the arrow ignite and whip from his fingers. The tip pierced the bullseye with such livid force, the board shook on its bracket. *Merv Vistau*. Thock. *Merv Vistau*. Thock. Terry blinded the bullseye. Ripping the arrows from the atrocious red eye, Terry roared like a Viking.

Within minutes, he was peppering trebles for fun, laughing each dart into the board. Now doubles. *Merv Vistau*. Double 1. *Merv Vistau*. Double 5. *Merv Vistau*. Double top . . .

Released from his curse, cured of dartitis, Terry rejoiced in the blood-rush of darts. He revisited the games he'd loved as a child – Cricket, Killer, Around the World – heart pumping to the rhythm of his throws. The whip of the wrist. *Thock*. The snap of the flight. *Thock*. The pop of the cork. *Thock*. The slice of the wire. *Thock*. *Thock*. *Thock*.

Arrows that once felt as squidgy as chewing gum now fizzed from his hand like silver bullets. His elbow clicked like a shotgun. Terry watched the tips catch the light as they fizzed through the air, the flights twirling, the barrel sparking, smacking his lips to the delicious dry bite of metal slicing through cork. Dart after dart attacked the board.

Panting, Terry leaned on the chest freezer, exhausted and ecstatic, then quickly remembered. He raced back inside no. 16.

'Marie!' Terry shouted up the stairs. 'Marie! *Marie!* You got to see this . . .'

Terry unfolded a rusty striped deckchair, presented a seat, and treated Marie to an exhibition. Hypnotherapist, lied Terry. Cured in one session, lied Terry. He whispered *Merv Vistau* so as not to be heard. With each flying arrow came a gasp of relief.

'Terry,' said Marie, her voice quivering. 'It's a darting miracle.'

Marie had her Terry back. Terry had his darts. And Merv Vistau had his soul.

That night, curled up in bed under a duvet embroidered with bubbles of dartboards, Marie took Terry's throwing hand and kissed his lucky fingers, one by one. When she came to his thumb, she clocked the minuscule mark on the cuff of Terry's palm – the two clasped horns of a tiny pink M.

'What's this, Tel?' Marie asked, rubbing her hand over his thumb. 'You burned yourself?'

'Oh, that,' said Terry, fumbling for an excuse. 'Yeah, that. That was when . . . Cheese on toast. Yeah, cheese on toast. Burned it on the grill.'

Marie blew on his thumb to make it better, turned off the bedside lamp. Twelve months of anxiety fluttered from its cage. They folded into each other's embrace, nuzzling and giggling under the duvet, high-school sweethearts reunited.

Terry sank smiling into his dreams. He rode a dart through red night skies, cackling like a witch on a tungsten broomstick.

Next morning, Terry kissed yawning Marie, cancelled the day's jobs, wrestled his belly into his dart shirt and danced into the practice garage. The air sizzled with burning arrows. Terry killed the numbers.

Exhausted and armpitty from plucking the same three arrows from the cork, Terry had an idea. Rummaging behind the humming chest freezer, he pulled out a Family Circle biscuit tin, rattling with discarded darts. Terry peeled off the lid, dug in his hand like a kid with a sweet jar, and grabbed a fistful of arrows. Dart after dart flew into the board, flying like missiles from a tennis ball machine. *Thock. Thock. Thock-Thock-Thock.*

Terry filled every double, treble, single and bull until the dartboard resembled a pincushion.

'I feel like a darting superhero,' Terry told Marie as they slurped Pot Noodles in the kitchen, unaware further powers awaited.

After lunch, Terry jigged back to the garage for a doubles-only session. Midway through his shift, *Merv Vistaus* seething as arrows cracked the cork, Terry stopped. The

171

garage roof clicked and clacked – as if something were attempting to enter, from above. The side door swung open. Terry looked up to the corrugated roof and a skittering shadow pecking at the metal. The jackdaw turned and fixed her glare.

Held by the shine of silver eyes, Terry felt a flickering chill, as if a heartbeat had been stolen. With a crack of the wings and a cry of *ack-ack*, the jackdaw fled into the sky. A single black feather twirled down from the air, curling in Us, and landed at Terry's feet. He looked up to the jackdaw flying sharp as an arrow, to the darts in his hand, to the feather on the lawn.

Inside the practice garage, Terry removed the flights from his darts. He took a penknife, carved and cut, feathers slotting into the shafts. Terry perched on the oche and aimed. Arrows flew like streaks of black lightning.

It was close to midnight when Terry locked up. On the garage wall, a dartboard wept, porcupined with arrows. The cork had fissured, split from the punishment. He already needed a fresh board.

Terry bobbed into the lounge, clutching his darts. Lounging on the sofa in a leopard-print dressing gown, Marie was stitching a daisy bracelet, enjoying a Vienetta as the TV blared. A corpse-pale demon glared from the screen, its leather robe shiny as liquorice. Terry grimaced at the mask of nails punched into its head.

'Fuck me,' said Terry. 'He looks just like my dartboard. What's this you watching?'

'Not watching, it's just on,' said Marie. 'Let me check the TV guide. Here we are. It's a film. *Hellraisin*. No, hang on . . . Sorry, love. *Hellraiser*.'

'*Hellraiser*,' Terry repeated, settling down to watch. 'You know, that's not half bad. Terry "Hellraiser" Slater. I can wave some sparklers during the walk-on. What do you reckon?'

Marie stopped stitching and frowned at her husband. 'What *are* you talking about, Tel?'

'Invictus Cup's coming up,' said Terry, fist tightening around his darts. 'I'm going to frighten the life out of Saxon.' Terry stared at the corpse-pale demon, its glowering face a pincushion of nails. Its white hands gripped a flashing Lemarchand puzzle box. 'Terry "Hellraiser" Slater: The Tungsten Terror. Nah . . . Terry "Hellraiser" Slater: Demon of the Dartboard. Nah . . . Terry "Hellraiser" Slater: Darting Destroyer . . . Yeah. Yeah, that's *nasty*. Can I have some Vienetta?'

His powers expanded in a moment of sloppiness. Terry boiled on the oche's threshold, eyes burning into his nemesis. Pinned to the dartboard was a photo printed from a Facebook profile: the bi-fork beard, blond mullet and greasy grin of Kurt 'The Javelin' Saxon. Heating to the mocking chant of *bottler*, *bottler*, Terry loaded a dart of vengeance. The tip's dagger-glint sparked in the light.

Merv Vistau. The arrow ripped through the air, struck its target and tore through Saxon's lip. A second quickly followed, piercing an eyeball with a vicious pop. Stroking the black feathers of his flights, Terry aimed, mouthed *Merv Vistau* and in haste and fury, dropped the barrel.

The arrow plunged . . . then jerked to a halt. Hovering above the garage floor, suspended as if by an invisible string, the dart hung mid-air, whipped around, then fizzed back into the board. The tip speared Saxon's paper teeth, splitting his grin with a satisfying crack. Terry's eyes bulged at the board, staring in disbelief.

'Holy fucking Mary Poppins . . .'

Terry dropped another dart. The plunging arrow froze. It dangled mid-air above the oche. The flights twirled, then off it whipped, attacking the board. The tip speared Saxon's septum. A goading voice, silky-sinister, purred through Terry's head.

Say my name each time you throw . . . You'll hit whatever you want . . .

Crouched behind the chest freezer, Terry screamed *Merv Vistau* with the zeal of a preacher man. He flicked a dart like a discarded cigarette. The arrow scurried across the floor. White sparks danced from the tip as it rasped across the concrete. The dart took off like a fighter jet. *Thock.* Another nail in Saxon's coffin, spiked between the eyes. No *way* was Marie seeing this.

To manic shrieks of Merv Vistau, Terry threw like a man possessed, lost in a haze of darting fury. He danced in circles around the garage, spraying arrows into the air, between the legs, up and over, firing from the hip like a gunslinger.

Saxon's face shredded to confetti. Paper skin rained in the garage. Sweating like a welder and entirely darted out, Terry staggered up to the board, plucked the last scraps of paper tucked under the wire and crammed them greedily into his mouth.

'Bottle that,' seethed Terry, gulping down his nemesis.

Dartitis had been defeated and Saxon would be next.

Squeezed into a white tuxedo, darts MC Vince Stone swaggered onstage to volcanic cheers. He bowed, tapped his microphone, adjusted his bow tie and addressed the crowd.

'Ladies and jennelmen,' bellowed Stone in an accent lost somewhere between Kent and Kentucky. 'On behalf of the North Kent Darts Organisation, welcome to the fifty-first Invictus Cup, here at Meadway Leisure Centre!' The packed sports hall boomed in reply. 'Over the course of the weekend, sixty-four darting gladiators will do battle over six knockout rounds, but there can be only one victor. Who will be crowned winner *and* receive a cheque of five *thousand* pounds? Ladies and jennelmen, there's only one way to find out. Let's! Play! Darts!'

Terry lurked at the back of the leisure centre, squeezing Marie's hand. He scanned through the crowd to a blond, bearded figure, high-fiving his entourage from the Sweltan Estate.

'Tel,' said Marie, aware her husband was giving Saxon the daggers, his hand squeezing a little too tightly. 'Focus on your game? Rather than him?'

'What's that?'

Terry snapped out of his trance. The shredded face of Kurt Saxon ripped through his head like a blizzard.

'I'll go warm up,' Terry said, shaking out the vision. 'Going to win the Cup, Marie. Going to win the Cup for you.'

'Go get them, Hellraisin,' said Marie, kissing his lucky fingers.

Terry joined his fellow darters in the corridor of practice boards. He watched his opponents, lined up like archers, arrows blurring into the boards. Terry retired to a quiet corner and went through his plan, hatched in the heat of the garage.

It was impossible to miss, but he'd be a fool to showboat. Go in like Hellraiser, arrows blazing, and he'd attract too much attention, maybe suspicion. There would be no exotic checkouts, and certainly no darts zipping up from the floor like metal wasps. He'd miss a few choice doubles. Make himself look like a grinder-outer. Make himself look beatable. Then he'd unleash all hell on Kurt 'The Javelin' Saxon.

'My hero,' said Marie, greeting Terry as he bounced offstage. He'd stuck to the plan, gone easy on Selby Taylor, winning the First Round, five legs to four.

'One match down,' beamed Terry. 'Five to go. How's Saxon doing?'

'Oh, he's through already, five–nil,' said Marie, rolling her eyes. 'Tel, can I ask you something? When you're up there playing, you're doing it different from before. What you saying when you throw?'

'Marie, Marie,' lied Terry.

'Oh, Tel,' said Marie, pressing herself into his belly. 'Be mine, Hellraisin. Be mine.'

And so the weekend passed in a shower of darts. In lumpen, unspectacular style, Terry Slater hobbled under the radar, grinding down his opponents, faking a limp towards the Cup. Far away, on distant stages, Kurt Saxon trolled and crushed, needled and cheated, hammering out a string of savage five–nil wipeouts.

The final of the Invictus Cup was set. Kurt 'The Javelin' Saxon versus Terry 'Hellraiser' Slater. The underdog was primed to maul the wolf.

Squeaking in a leather trench coat, antennas of silver bobby pins spiking black piled-up hair, Marie prepared Terry's walk-on costume in the dressing room.

'Back in a sec, Mrs Hellraiser,' said Terry, kissing Marie.

As he entered the backstage toilets, a familiar figure stood at the urinal, blond mullet flowing over wide shoulders. Terry took a deep breath and unzipped at the urinal directly next to Kurt 'The Javelin' Saxon.

'Well, look who it is,' said Saxon. He briefly side-eyed Terry, turned back to the white tiled wall. 'Thought you'd retired, Tony.'

'It's Terry.'

'Yeah, course it is, Tony. How the fuck you make it to the final? One my boys been watching you play, says you bored your opponents to death. Hit any single 17s?'

'Tell us, Kurt,' Terry replied, steam fuming from the urinal, 'why you call yourself The Javelin? The Helmet's got a much better ring to it, what with you being such a colossal bell-end.'

'I'm going to batter you tonight,' Kurt hissed between clenched teeth. 'Beat you up on the board so bad you'll regret ever picking up a dart. Fuck you and fuck your darts, you tubby fucking bottler.'

Terry narrowed his eyes on Saxon. He pictured his nemesis, arms up in surrender, chest shuddering in a hail of tungsten bullets. Terry zipped up and walked out in silence, ready to unleash Hellraiser.

In the boiling cavern of Meadway Leisure Centre, spotlights licked the heaving crowd. Lining the floor, like shaking pews, packed stalls roared at the stage, joined in worship at the altar of darts. Saxon's entourage clapped and sang, a chant rising above the ruckus – a weaponised cover of Kings of Leon. '*Wooah, woh-woh. Kurt Saxon's on fire . . .*'

'Ladies and jennelmen,' Vince Stone bellowed from the stage. 'Welcome to the final of the fifty-first Invictus Cup . . .'

Terry Slater lurked in the darkened corridor as Kurt Saxon's name rang through the hall. Six foot two of blond mullet and bi-fork beard high-fived through a tunnel of support, swaggering onstage to Saxon's 'Wheels of Steel'.

Terry limbered up. He shivered into his leather trench coat. Marie straightened his Hellraiser headpiece – a white bathing cap spiked with forty darts. 'Highway to Hell' fuzzed from the speakers. Stalked by a sun-bright spotlight, Terry walked on to a farmyard of boos, clutching a replica of the Hellraiser Lemarchand puzzle box – the practice garage biscuit tin redecorated, with skilled precision, by Marie.

Hellraiser stepped on stage, Lemarchand box rattling with darts. He unpeeled his mask and placed his box under the pedestal table. Vince Stone approached the two opponents, staring out each other like heavyweights.

'You know the score,' instructed Stone. '501, twenty-one legs, first to eleven, and best of order. I'm reffing tonight. The calls are mine and I ain't taking no mouth.'

As Terry split from Saxon, he overheard Stone, leaning into Saxon: 'Have him, Kurt.'

Battered by boos from Saxon's entourage, Hellraiser stepped up to the oche. He eyed the match board and stroked his flights. Black feathers rippled through his fingers. A dart rolled from left hand to right.

The barrel twirled in his hand, the tungsten cool and bullet-slick. A spotlight kissed the arrow tip, sparks dancing off the point. He cocked his elbow. Bone clicked like a loaded gun. He breathed in. Breathed out. Leaned in. Took aim.

Merv Vistau.

Treble twenty.

Merv Vistau.

Treble twenty.

Merv Vistau.

Treble twenty.

One hundred and eighty. Maximum.

The reign of Hellraiser began.

Saxon curled a lip at his opponent, whipped three darts into the board: One hundred and forty.

Hellraiser approached the oche, blocking out the boos from Saxon's entourage. He zoned in on the red lipstick of the treble 20. His elbow clicked. His wrist whipped. Hellraiser let rip. Three *Merv Vistau*s. Three treble 20s. One hundred and eighty.

Saxon's defiant swagger to the oche failed to disguise the faint tremor in his hand. He scored a lumpen sixty.

Secured on a 141 check-out, Hellraiser considered relishing each dart, drawing out the pain. He opted instead for a short, sharp shock.

Merv Vistau.

Treble twenty.

Merv Vistau.

Treble nineteen.

Merv Vistau.

Double twelve.

Red cork spat from the board. The nine-darter stunned the crowd into silence. One leg up.

Leg two, Saxon to throw: a nervy trio of single 20s. Hellraiser took to the oche and *Merv Vistau*ed another maximum, watched Saxon's reply of 100, then responded with another 180. Killer darts.

Poised for attack on 141 checkout, Hellraiser switched

his outshot. He cranked a treble 17, treble 18 and double 18. Another nine-darter. Another dart in Saxon's coffin. With the icy eyes of an assassin, Hellraiser approached the board and silently plucked out his darts. Two legs up.

Leg three. With Saxon wilting on the single 20s, Hellraiser set himself up for a 150 finish. Stunned into silence by the tungsten barrage, the crowd regained its voice. Hellraiser shook out his arms for the holy trinity of darts – a 150 outshot of bullseye, bullseye, bullseye. Hellraiser fixed the appalling red eye that had mocked him for twelve hellish months. Three *Merv Vistaus* seethed from his lips. Three arrows fizzed. The blinded bullseye spat red cork. The crowd roared like a thousand Wookiees sitting on a thousand drawing pins. Saxon paced the stage, tugging his beard, crackling with darting anger.

'What you saying when you throw?' said Saxon. 'It's putting me right off.'

'Your obituary,' said Hellraiser, darts in his fist, eager to butcher the board once more.

In the hell heat of humiliation, losing game after game, Saxon turned to the dark arts of darts. Seven–nil: a subtle rake at Hellraiser's ankle. Eight–nil: a coughing fit on a crucial double. Nine–nil: whispered threats about Marie. The more Saxon needled and cheated, the fiercer Hellraiser threw.

One leg from victory and ten–nil up, chants of Hellraiser swelled from the hall. Saxon's mullet drooped like a weeping willow. Vince Stone dabbed his brow with a handkerchief. He'd bet £500 on a Saxon victory. Stone's voice cracked with regret.

Terry Slater turned from the stage, seeking out Marie. He blew a kiss out into the crowd, his heart pumping with pride. The crippling dartitis. The pain and the shakes. The spectre of Saxon, the sobbing on the sofa, the chink of teardrop earrings. The time had come to go it alone. Drop the *Merv Vistaus*. Win it for himself. Win it for Marie.

Saxon opened with a defiant 180. Terry stepped up to the oche, eyes fixed on the treble 20. *A nine-darter. Wipe him out. Fuck the Merv Vistaus. He's mine now. All mine . . .*

He opened his palm. An arrow whipped. And for Terry Slater's sins, there was no *Merv Vistau*.

The dart plopped into a single 6.

Terry glared at the defiant arrow. Nerves. Relax. Nerves. Just nerves . . . Terry cupped a hand to his mouth and cooled his fingertips. He narrowed his sights on the treble 20. A dart rolled from left hand to right. Terry twitched to a peculiar sensation. The barrel, once bullet-slick, felt soft and sticky, gummed to his grip. He cocked a creaking elbow. A second dart launched.

The dart plopped into a single 6.

Sarcastic boos swelled from the crowd. Marie shifted in her seat, sensing something was wrong. Terry stepped back from the oche, shook out his hands, and focused on the treble 20. He leaned in, aimed and threw.

Single 6.

'Six, six, six!' Vince Stone sang. 'The number of the beast!'

Saxon fluked another 180.

Terry focused on the treble 20. *Plop*. Single 6. *Plop*. Single 6. *Plop*. Single 6.

'The number of the beast!' cried Stone.

Saxon scored 101, set up double top to seal the leg. Terry returned to the oche, swallowed his pride, and decided to revive the *Merv Vistau* method. His darts hit 6, 6, 6.

'The number of the beast!' Stone yelled, now in hysterics.

Saxon struck double top and took the leg.

'I thought the single 17 was bad,' Saxon sneered. 'But you've outdone yourself this time, Tony.'

The darts. They were being pulled from his palm, stolen from his grip. Fingers twitching at his arrows, the tungsten barrels oiled with sweat, Terry flashed back to Vistau's office, the handshake, the warning. *Once you start, you must never stop. Disciplined most severely. In any way I see fit . . .*

Saxon closed the gap, stole another leg. Terry looped his circle of darting hell: 6, 6, 6. 'The number of the beast!' 6, 6, 6. 'The number of the beast!' Smelling blood, the fickle crowd turned. Conducted by Saxon, the boiling mob began to sing. *Bottler, bottler, bottler . . .*

The mocking chant jabbed at his heart, firing him into panic. Terry scrambled to the pedestal table and lunged for the Lemarchand box of darts. New arrows. Fresh flights. Anything to stop the rot.

He flicked the lid and unleashed hell.

A lone dart leaped from the rattling box. Terry jumped from the pedestal table and bundled to the floor. The arrow fizzed like silver lightning, its tip sparking under the spotlights. Saxon turned from the baying crowd.

The dart struck with a bone-splitting crack. Kurt's hands leapt to his face. Blood burst and misted the air. Saxon stumbled, his septum speared, and tripped towards the waiting dartboard.

Now two arrows fired from the shuddering box. One pitched left, the other right. Arms outstretched, his back to the dartboard, Saxon screamed to two spiked volts. Tips pierced. Blood sprayed. Saxon's palms were nailed to the wall.

It wasn't over. Not even close. Another two arrows burst from the box. White sparks danced as they skimmed the stage floor, streaking towards their target. They soared. They burned. They struck. Through tearing leather and ripping flesh, the darts pierced Saxon's boots. Feet pinned, arms outstretched, Saxon hung like a T against the match board, nailed to the walls by Vistau's arrows.

I want to crucify Saxon . . .

Vince Stone dropped his microphone, clutching his chest.

I want to be so good the ref dies of shock . . .

Cowering by the toppled pedestal table, Terry stared in horror at the rattling Lemarchand box. There were 400 arrows inside.

And I want . . . And I want . . . And I want to make the crowd SCREAM . . .

They blasted from the box like a swarm of wasps. Tips molten, barrels burning, 400 darts launched into the air. For a split second, the hall froze. The crowd's screams stretched with their mouths, flooding the hall with a deafening screech that climbed and sharpened, and found no end. Terry's eyes bulged and flickered. Blood whined in his ears. He looked up to the buzzing cloud, burning above his head. He tried to run. A weight pressed down, pinning him to the stage.

The screams sharpened. Time snapped. And in that second, came all that Terry dared to wish.

Fireworks of molten tungsten rained down upon the crowd. Held in place by a ruthless pressure, Terry was forced to witness the chaos he'd unleashed. Vistau's arrows showed no mercy, tearing through the stalls. As the panicked crowd surged for the exits, burning darts fizzed in pursuit. Hunted bodies screamed and toppled, felled by piercing tips. Ears tore. *Thock*. Cheeks ripped. *Thock*. Arms gashed. *Thock*. Eyes popped. *Thock*.

Through the swarm of blood and sparks, Terry sought out Marie. He zoomed in on a flock of arrows, surging straight towards her. Harpooned, helpless, pinned to the stage, Terry screamed out her name. The darts screeched to halt, lingered mid-air . . . then zipped straight over her. Leather trench coat whipped over her head, Marie ducked through the crowd. She raced for the boiling exit.

Within the burning blur of arrows, Terry didn't see the darkened figure, lurking in a corridor. Winklepickers tapped the floor. Teeth flashed in delight. It clapped three times and all was still.

The rain of darts slowed to a drizzle, clattering pews and rattling chairs.

As spotlights licked the upturned tables, the hall clenched to an anxious hum. Terry felt a pressure lift, a force unclasp. His lungs heaved like a panicked swimmer, surfacing from the depths. Crawling from the toppled pedestal table, Terry took in the chaos he'd wrought. Bleeding Saxon, nailed to the match board. Vince Stone clutching a lifeless heart. He rose, unsteady on shaking legs, calling for Marie.

In the distance, sirens sharpened, wailing ever closer.

In the stark, grey cell of the interview room, Terry sat with his head in his hands. He heard the door unlock. Fourteen stone of granite-hard stare, DCI Heath appeared. He had grilled Terry for two gruelling hours, deep-set eyes unblinking through sobbing denials

'Slater,' he announced gruffly. 'Your solicitor's here.'

Terry lifted his head. 'Didn't ask for no solicitor.'

Heath's shadow retreated. Terry looked down to a horned

winklepicker curving around the door. Merv Vistau glided in, swiping a balm over his lips, a sickly heat in his wake.

Their eyes met. Liquid fear licked through Terry. The grilled red M on the cuff of his thumb began to pinch and burn. Vistau pulled up a chair and calmly straightened his tie. Terry yelled for Heath. Vistau lifted a long white finger to his mouth. A silky hiss shushed from his lips.

'Nobody can hear you,' purred Vistau. 'It is just you and me, Terry Slater.' He tucked his winklepickers under his chair. 'I must applaud your persistence. I had you down for a week at most, but no. You just keep going and going. And this Hellraiser of yours?' Vistau mimed a slow hand clap. '*Fantastisch.*'

Vistau leaned across the table, offered a hand to shake. Terry recoiled from the threat of contact. Chair legs bumped on the worn grey carpet. He leaped from his seat, pressed his back to the wall. Again he called for Heath.

'Now, now,' tutted Vistau.

A sickly heat crept through the walls of the interview room. Beads of sweat plucked from Terry's neck, trickling like fingers down his spine. Fight or flight? Trapped in his cell, he only saw one option. Terry gripped the chair arm, testing its weight. He forced the fear back down his throat. His voice shook with defiance.

'Fuck do you want?'

'I already have what I want,' purred Vistau. 'You've made me king of your world. Each time you've said my name, I've had a little taste of your soul. I've been sipping at you, Terry Slater. Slowly and sweetly sipping at your soul. Imagine how this feels – to be worshipped so much, your name is called out, hour after hour, day after day. You must have said my name ten thousand times. What a snack you are, Terry Slater. How I love this English word. It's so *nice* to say. A *snack*. A Terry Slater *snack*.'

Terry made his move. Gripping the arm, he seized the chair and heaved it over his head. Eyes burning into Vistau, Terry prepared to throw. A jolt shot through his wrist. Terry tasted the devil's pain, a vicious lick of invisible fire. From the burning M of his glowing thumb, curled a wisp of scarlet smoke. Vistau sucked his tight, thin lips, and sipped his soul from the air. Terry collapsed in howling pain. The chair crashed to the floor.

The interview room darkened like an eclipse. Vistau unhooked his winklepickers, rose from the table, and cast his shadow upon Terry. He sneered at the worm that squirmed below him, tiring of its games. Vistau's white eyes flashed to flame.

'You wear my mark,' Vistau seethed, glaring at the worm. 'And. I. Will. Drink. You. Dry.'

Vistau seized a wrist and pulled his meal up from the floor. Terry faltered to his feet, pinned against the simmering wall.

'Still, not now,' said Vistau. His voice softened to a silky purr. He released his grip on Terry. 'I will take you when I choose. Besides, I have a banquet to attend. A new soul certificate has been written.'

The slithering heat that had climbed the walls suddenly sucked from the room.

'Oh, do not worry about all this,' Vistau continued, motioning around the interview room. 'They cannot charge you. It is *lächerlich*. It's most amusing. This police of yours, they are thinking you are a terrorist, but there is no nail bomb, no proof, no motive. It is most mystifying for them. Just you and a silly biscuit tin of darts. I like this word also. *Biscuit!*'

Vistau clapped three times. Terry slid down the wall like dripping oil. The interview-room door creaked opened. DCI Heath entered, a groggy look on his granite face. Vistau cupped a white hand, whispered something into Heath's ear, then glided from the room.

'Slater?' said Heath, his gruff voice creamy and trance-like. 'You're free to go.'

The minicab stopped at Valerian Way. Terry paid his fare, crawled from the car and stood at the entrance to Silverweed Road. Night closed in over the rooftops, the driveways dark, the houses black as tombs. Stumbling past the crash flowers, Terry caught a shifting shadow, across the road at no. 17. Head wrapped in a bandage, Augustus Fry sweated and puffed as he heaved two sacks into the back of his Land Rover. Terry briefly considered helping, quickly buried the thought. The last thing he wanted was that pompous lump puffing commands at him. He'd struggled enough today. Terry left Fry to his bin bags.

Key slotted in the door of no. 16, Terry paused. All he craved was Marie's embrace, the soothing chink of her teardrop earrings, the safe haven of her heart. How in hell, thought Terry, am I going to explain this? How much time is left? He unlocked the front door to no. 16.

'You're back,' said Marie, padding towards him. She did not sound as surprised as she should. It was as if she'd been expecting him.

In the creamy light of the narrow hallway, they dissolved into each other, relishing each other's heat.

'You OK? You hurt? Need hospital?' said Terry. 'It wasn't me. I swear, it wasn't my . . .'

'What *happened* in there, Tel? Saw you bundled into the

police car, tried to come, but there were people everywhere, running and screaming, then this man walked over, told me you'd be in prison forever, and he . . .'

'What man?'

Terry unlocked from their embrace. He looked at Marie, his stomach tight. His insides began to squirm like writhing, twisting serpents.

'. . . said he was a solicitor and I was all in a panic, said I wished and wished and wished you'd come home, and he . . .'

'Marie.'

'. . . said he could get you out if I made a donation and . . .'

'*Marie.*'

'. . . I said yes and then we shook hands and . . .'

'*Marie.*'

'. . . it hurts.'

Marie winced, lifted her hand. Terry's eyes met the horns of an M, freshly grilled on the cuff of her thumb. The serpents of dread that writhed in his stomach now feasted and spread. They curled through veins, climbing his throat, twisting to black in his spiralling mind. He dared not think nor say his name. *Him . . . Him . . . Him . . .*

Terry grasped Marie's hand. He feverishly rubbed the livid red M. As if his touch would absorb the curse. As if his touch would reverse the wish. As if his touch could turn back time. Hell already had its answer.

There was a Velcro rip of splitting skin. A wisp broke through Marie's mark. It curled like smoke from a cigarette, the vapour sickly red. Terry smothered her thumb with his hands, trying to contain her escaping soul. Now his own mark began to glow. On the cuff of his thumb, his grilled

M split, ripening into a blaze. Red smoke gushed from fissured hands. The Slaters seethed in atrocious harmony.

Marie opened her mouth to scream. Her pain could find no voice. Pouring out between her lips hissed a sulphurous scarf of fumes. From every pore and orifice, their hell-claimed souls disgorged.

The Slaters clung to each other's heat, folding in as one. Faces now a ball of smoke, they slowly peeled to crimson gas, their spines a burning wick. Soon, all was left were stems of legs, billowing red heat. Scarlet stalks of mushroom clouds swelled into the ceiling.

Through the crimson hallway's hissing fumes, eyes emerged and blazed like fire. Winklepicker by winklepicker, purring step by purring step, the devil came to Silverweed, and claimed back what was sold. The taste of human horror on its tongue, teeth flashing in delight, thin lips sipped at spilling souls, sloppy wet, in soupy gulps.

Three brisk claps and they were gone, vanished in a scream of smoke. The fog of souls cleared from the hallway, leaving just one trace. A cindered shadow cast on a wall, two bodies locked, in love and fear.

Extract from The Silverweed Files, 19 November 2024

A personal blog by former Detective Chief Inspector Jim Heath. The views expressed do not reflect those of Kent Police nor the victims impacted by events.

Three dead. Sixteen left with life-changing injuries. This is the legacy of the 'Hellraiser' terrorist, Terry Slater. He has yet to answer for his crimes and remains on NCA's Most Wanted.

Prejudice has no part in police work. On entering the force, the Oath of Attestation could not be clearer: 'I solemnly declare to serve the Queen with fairness, integrity and impartiality.' Throughout this blog, I have taken great pains to maintain a sober tone in the face of extraordinary events. In the case of Terry Slater, I cannot, will not, and will never be impartial. The odious waste of skin cost me my job.

I have revisited that night so many times, it is burned upon my eyelids. For two hours, I interrogated Slater in Interview Room 3. Why did you do it? For what cause? Do you know how many lives you've wrecked? Slater just sat there, weeping for himself. I decided to let him stew, locked up the Interview Room, and in the time it took to clap your hands, he was gone.

That's how it seemed. Bang. Gone. I can practically hear that clap of the hands. And yet there were twenty minutes I cannot account for. It was as if Meadway Station had been put in a coma. Even the station CCTV was wiped.

Where did Slater go? I know a minicab dropped him home. I know that his wife and accomplice had a hand in designing his appalling 'Hellraiser' nail bomb. And I know they had attempted to throw me off the scent by burning their outlines on the hallway wall, implying one of their contraptions had misfired. As far as distractions go, it was a wretched attempt. Had a bomb gone off in no. 16, bits of Slater would be decorating the walls.

It is an outcome I can only dream of. The reality is, Slater is at large and I am out of a job. Despite the CCTV being wiped, despite my colleagues losing their memories, Kent Police held me responsible for allowing Slater to walk from custody. I was stitched up, scapegoated, and will never, ever forgive them. At the misconduct hearing, I sounded like a criminal: *I don't know, I can't remember, it wasn't me*. Three decades of dedicated service, and my only reward is disgrace.

Why did Slater let off that nail bomb? Don't fall for those claims he was an ideological extremist. That credits the oaf with a brain. Slater stole his dart name from Hellraiser: a disgusting film about sadomasochistic perverts getting pleasure out of pain. That is all Slater is: a sadist and a pervert. There was no cause. He did it for kicks. He enjoyed killing all those people.

If justice cannot be served in this life, I hope the Slaters burn in hell.

NO. 30:

The Vanslow Fox

Every Sunday, from 10 p.m. till 6 a.m., Vanslow Lee would turn into a fox. The curse was binding and non-refundable. There were no breaks in between.

Under the waking eye of a waxing moon, a blue Mini cornered into Silverweed Road and parked in the driveway of no. 30. The engine coughed to a halt. Back from his shift at Meadway Hospital, still dressed in his porter's tunic, Vanslow Lee heaved himself from the car.

From an impossibly small space, an impossibly large figure emerged. Sixteen stone and six foot five, the formidable Vanslow appeared older than his twenty-eight years. As he slowly crunched the gravel driveway, his heavy stride spoke of bone-deep fatigue, like a bear half-woken from hibernation. Panda circles bruised sleep-deprived eyes, and there was not a hair left on his great domed head: he was lashless, eyebrowless, jellyfish-bald, every last follicle stolen by stress.

Vanslow unlocked a scratched front door and crossed the threshold into squalor. There had been a time when no.

30 held a homely, laundered perfume; held light and life and hope. Now the empty rooms fumed to a choking odour, of fox fur, urine and bleach – a scent Vanslow had long grown immune to.

Thudding down a hallway of shredded walls, he headed to the kitchen at the back of the house. Vanslow unbolted the padlocked fridge, fed ten chicken thighs into the oven and retired to the lounge as his Sunday dinner cooked.

Like all the rooms inside no. 30, the lounge was sparse and torn of comfort: just a telly, a wall clock and a lonely black armchair, into which Vanslow slumped. Tables, chairs, sofas, cabinets: all had been chewed to ragged crumbs, wrecked by his maniac fox-self.

The TV itched between channels. Vanslow watched the wall clock march. With each tick, his fingers tensed, nails digging deeper into the chair. The hands grazed 8 p.m. In less than two hours, The Great Change would begin.

That afternoon, he'd roamed the hospital, shuttling patients from east wing to west. He lifted the broken from wheelchair to bed, calmed the sick with a silent smile, and ferried the dead to the morgue. The composure and compassion came hard-fought: inside Vanslow, a storm was raging. He clung to his job like a life raft, a reminder of what it meant to be human and kind, but today, more than ever, he could feel the claws tear at his heart. For tonight was an anniversary – an event that was not to be celebrated.

It had been three years to the day since the change; 150 Sundays playing hostage to his fox-self. As the TV blared, Vanslow retreated, flickering back to that fateful night.

All day, dark clouds had simmered, threatening to boil up into a storm. Vanslow's heart had been singing so loudly, he'd barely noticed the sky. That weekend, he'd proposed to Cherie, his sweetheart who lived by the sea. Driving home from Dymchurch, late for his porter shift, Vanslow had taken a shortcut through dark country roads when the storm had delivered its promise. As rain rattled like grit on the windscreen, his Mini cornered into a lane. A shadow flashed from a hedgerow. A red ghost froze in the headlights. Amber eyes glowed through spears of rain.

There was a thump, a lurch, a scream of tyres. A rag of red fur twitched on the road. Cradling the body in the driving rain, Vanslow had gently set the fox in a roadside ditch, its fading heart still beating, beating. In shame and shock, he'd fetched a tyre iron, to release the fox from its agony. As he stroked and soothed the fading beast, trembling arm primed to strike, Vanslow flinched to a rip of pain. In one last act of revenge, the fox bit down on his steadying hand.

Vanslow jerked in his lonely armchair, reliving the shock. Lightning stabbed from the thundering sky. The white flash made night seem like day. As the fox's fangs tore into his palm, the bolt struck the tyre iron and fizzed through his bones. Through vicious volts of skin-frying pain, unseen claws screamed up his spine . . .

There in the ditch, their souls had tangled, the fox life passing into his. From that fateful night, every Sunday, its restless spirit rose.

Vanslow shook off the memory, looked to the ticking wall clock. With an exhausted sigh, he rose from his armchair, readying the house for The Great Change.

In the kitchen, he bubblewrapped the legs of a gnawed pine table, then laid a blue tarpaulin on the floor, forming a run-up to the worktop. After double-checking the fridge was sealed, Vanslow opened the kitchen window – a gap for his fox-self to jump through.

Vanslow ate his chicken, fed the scraps to a padlocked bin and settled with his phone at the kitchen table. He scrolled through photos, of himself and Cherie, each swipe, each kiss, bringing torment and heartbreak. Suspicious his Sunday vanishing acts were cover for an affair, Cherie had posted back her engagement ring, tired of his desperate excuses. Three years a helpless prisoner, not a clue what his fox-self got up to at night, the beast had taken everything: his hair, his future, his dreams of a wife and family. Vanslow Lee would dare not speak, for fear a bark would escape his lips. All that was loved had been lost.

At 9.55 p.m., his wristwatch beeped. Vanslow thumped upstairs to the bedroom. Curtains closed, lights dimmed, he undressed in the murk, locking his clothes in a tilted wardrobe. Vanslow stood on a sweat-soaked towel and turned to face his naked reflection. The mirror wall ran the length of the bed-room: corner to corner, floor to ceiling, the looking-glass doubling the size of the room. It was here where Vanslow would view The Great Change.

Great barrelled chest sinking and rising, trying to tame the wild pump of his lungs, a tell-tale tingle chased through his hands.

The clock struck ten. Vanslow clenched. And so The Great Change began.

Vanslow watched the fingers retract from his shrinking palms. Joints curled like closing petals. There was a click of bone. A crunch of muscle. One by one, finger by finger, nails popped like Tic Tac lids, driven out by spiking claws. Now the toes joined Vanslow's rupture, coiling into flippering feet. Yellow toenails bounced off the mirror, clicking like popcorn kernels.

Stomach flipping, he collapsed to the floor, sending a

shockwave across the room. Back arched, head down, cast on all fours, trembling Vanslow began to shiver and shrink. His flesh shrivelled like a punctured inflatable, retreating in slurping heaves and folds.

Before his skull pulled into a cone, The Great Change toyed with his features. Ears curled like shrinking oysters, then burst and unfurled into pinecones; thick lips thinned into tubes of black liquorice; to a crunchy mortar-and-pestle grind, molars crumbled and sharpened to fangs. Vanslow's head was now a shiny pink plate, embossed with the face of a fox.

At this point, and always this point, he turned to the mirror to face his reflection – bald, moist, a little uncooked, quivering like a pink, skinned dog. At the base of his spine, a tailbone slithered like an earthworm greeting rain. The colour drained from Vanslow's eyes. His world flicked to black-and-white fox vision.

And now the fur came.

It was as if The Great Change saved its sweetest agony till last. Pulling the trigger on an internal nail gun, spikes of red fur chased through this flesh, like a thousand sizzling needles. Vanslow felt his body blister, head to tail. The mirror wall shivered to a raw shrill scream.

And then, like that, all was blank.

Head cocked, tongue out, Vanslow Fox leapt up from the towel and admired himself in the mirror. The magnificent blaze of his red pelt. His paintbrush tail, his black-sleeved paws, his tall, stiff pinecone ears. Just one trace of human remained, a reminder of the soul he shared: two blue eyes, sharp and sly, shining out like sapphires. Vanslow Fox licked his handsome reflection, smearing the mirror with fox spit.

With a swish of the tail, he turned on his paws and trotted down the stairs. Following the smell that hummed from the kitchen, Vanslow Fox raced up to the fridge, drinking the scent of chicken wings. Stomach pleading, he pawed at the door, cursing his human for denying its treasures. After scoring the fridge with a few vengeful scratches, he set about marking his estate. Leg cocked, he urinated over bubblewrapped table legs, fox piddle splashing with a musical crackle. Vanslow Fox looked up to the kitchen window. Appetite moaning, he darted into the shredded hallway, preparing for his run-up.

With a spring in his step and a mind full of anarchy, he skipped down the strip of blue tarpaulin, leaped onto the worktop and jumped through the kitchen window. Vanslow Fox trotted into the night, the Prince of Silverweed Road.

In the pale shine of a waxing moon, Vanslow Fox patrolled the rows of mock-Tudor semis – the vast, dark castles the human hams chose to imprison themselves in. There was, as yet, no sound or scent of his rival.

Once, he had owned the night. Then, six months ago, she appeared. Vanslow Fox had been touring the wheelie bins, dreaming of the scraps that lay within, when a fierce new scent had charged his senses. The next thing he knew, she'd burst from a driveway, he was flat on his back, and her teeth were at his throat. With one night a week to defend his kingdom, a rival vixen had moved in, claiming Silverweed's crown.

The weekly turf wars were unrelenting, and not once had he won a fight. How Vanslow Fox pined to be human. A human wouldn't fight over scraps. A human wouldn't cower in the winter rain. A human wouldn't be reduced to slurping slugs for supper. A human would be lazing in the warmth, feasting on mountains of chicken . . . Despite the scars and humiliations, his fox pride persisted, urging him into battle. In the kingdom of Vanslow Fox, there was certainly no room for a queen.

Hopping from garden to garden, Vanslow Fox detected a restless energy that hummed from his kingdom. From the castle at no. 4, the ham inside had stolen the sun, its shutters flashing with lights. Further up, at no. 15, storm clouds poured from a fiery drum. And across the road, at no. 16, the garage was a flurry of ferocious activity.

Vanslow Fox crouched in the bushes, ears cocked to a relentless drumming. His blue eyes narrowed on a small square window. Inside, a pink ham paced, surrounded by a swarm of metal wasps. Troubled by an anger that burned from the walls, Vanslow Fox scuttled off. Everything about his kingdom felt less welcoming tonight.

Perhaps the flowers were to blame. There had been a bounty of blood to lap from the tarmac, on the night the metal shrieked. Now, beneath the flickering pole, flowers had been planted by foolish hams, left to die in their plastic coats. Drawn to the scent of rotten meat, the previous Sunday he'd tried to eat the offending orchids, only to bolt back in shock. Flies had poured from their yellow throats, the flowers shrieking in anger.

Debating whether to revisit the flowers, his nose twitched to a growing scent – dark and delicious, familiar yet strange, coating the cold night air. Vanslow Fox followed the perfume to the road's dead-end. He stared through the railings into the Woods. Here the scent had strengthened.

The Woods lay beyond his kingdom. He was wary of what lurked within. The horseshoe path that looped through the woodland sharpened into spiteful blackthorns, where racing

199

shadows poured. It was neither his business nor desire to enter. And yet the dark scent beckoned, so rich and delicious.

Vanslow Fox slipped under railings, metal singing as his tail brushed the bars. He trotted up the path to find the source. Overhead, the canopy clawed, closing out the moonlight. Where the dark path curved into a horseshoe, a cautious paw tested the grass. The scent trailed off the tarmac, into the deep dark Woods.

Splashing through puddles, hopping logs, Vanslow Fox sensed he was being followed. Behind him, shadows poured through the trees, stalking his every move. They stopped when he stopped. Raced when he raced. Vanslow Fox began to relish the chase, pursued and admired by an audience of shadows.

He skipped from the Woods into a clearing. Vanslow Fox sniffed the air. The scent trail led to a tunnel of brambles that opened like a throat. Head ducked down, he scurried inside.

Through scratching brambles and fizzing nettles, Vanslow Fox emerged. A wet leaf clung to his muzzle. It was here the scent announced its power. Blowing the leaf from his nose, he licked his lips, sensing a feast. Towering from the earth before him, a mighty blackthorn rose.

Perched on a tree stump, a jackdaw watched. Her silver eyes flashed in the dark. Vanslow Fox returned her glare, wondering what black chicken tasted like, then looked up to the gloomy fortress blocking his path. The shadows that had followed his every step settled into a ring, forming a circle around fox and blackthorn. In the hush of the night, there was a great unfurling.

Vanslow Fox cocked his head, listening to the wood clack and uncurl. Anchored to the earth by a dark walled trunk,

the mighty blackthorn shook into life. Two great arms
outstretched in a yawn. Black spiked fingers crackled and
flexed. Within the trunk, a slit of mouth opened as if gashed
by a woodsman's axe. In a croaking contralto, grainy and
ancient, a tree spirit spoke.

'So, you have found me.'

Vanslow Fox searched his mind for something to say.
He had never talked to a tree before.

'And who, pray tell, is me?'

'I am Spinosa,' croaked the blackthorn, 'Mother of these
Woods.'

'And I,' replied Vanslow Fox, not to be outdone, 'am
the Prince of Silverweed Road.'

The jackdaw cracked her wings in mirth. The blackthorn
laughed a mocking laugh. Vanslow Fox knew of the blackthorn. The tree was buried in ancient fox memory, where
nature's omens were stored. Its branches were armed with
spiteful thorns that snapped off in the skin – once struck,
the wounds would fester, weeping yellow tears.

Vanslow Fox waited for the laughter to dry. This was
no way to address a prince.

'May you be minded,' said Vanslow Fox, 'you are in the
presence of royalty.'

Spinosa creaked and bowed. Not well versed in sarcasm,
Vanslow Fox nodded, his pride returned. He tipped his
neck and sniffed the air.

'What is this scent, old tree?'

'I'm surprised a prince as wise would ask. It is the scent
of death.'

Vanslow Fox licked his lips. So it was: the scent of death.
Richer and sweeter than he'd encountered before, and three
times as delicious.

'The scent is mine,' Spinosa croaked. 'For I am surely dying.'

Spinosa's confession caused Vanslow Fox to relax. Tail curled around his paws, he settled before the blackthorn. His fox ears sensed Spinosa's roots, churning like snakes through the soil.

'A thousand seasons I have ruled these Woods, guarding the spirits of this sacred place.' Spinosa outspread a creaking branch, gestured to the circling shadows. 'Yet as each night passes, I am weakening. Once I am gone, these Woods will follow. All will die unless I, the great Spinosa, feed.'

Vanslow Fox shrugged, his interest waning. He was the Prince of Silverweed. The Woods were not his concern. If it weren't for the scent, he'd be hunting for scraps. Instead, he'd been led, not to a feast, but to an ugly, croaking, dying tree that had dared to mock his royalty. His tail drummed the woodland floor, registering his impatience.

'Your blue eyes,' said Spinosa. 'Most unusual for a fox, don't you think?'

'No stranger than a talking tree.'

The jackdaw bristled at the fox's insolence. Silver eyes flicked to her mistress.

'I sense human in you, fox prince,' snapped Spinosa. 'How painful it must be, caught between two worlds, neither man nor beast. What if I could answer your pleas to be human? Imagine the warmth, the endless food.'

'Then do so,' challenged Vanslow Fox.

'Bring me human wine,' Spinosa croaked. 'Slake my thirsting roots and I shall grant your wish.'

As the ring of shadows whirled around him, Vanslow Fox saw the gates of a new life opening. No more fighting with his nemesis. No more cowering in the winter rain. No more scavenging slimy slug suppers. No longer silenced in his human cage, allowed out once a week. Blue eyes sly and narrow, he decided to test Spinosa.

'Then prove it, old tree.'

Spinosa unfurled a spiked wooden hand. Presented in her palm was a purple berry. Vanslow Fox licked his lips.

'Eat and I will show you.'

Urged on by his pleading stomach, Vanslow Fox approached her thorned palm. He snatched the berry and quickly retreated. With bear trap force, the hand snapped shut. Vanslow Fox chewed and swallowed, savouring the purple berry. Spinosa's fruit lodged in his stomach, clinging like glue to his guts. The berry bubbled like darkest sherbet and released a fizz of juice.

Satisfied her offering had been accepted, Spinosa began to weave. Her spiked fingers worked and clacked, a doll forming from twisted thorns: the shape of a small wooden fox. She tapped the poppet's front paw and slowly began to chant. Sinister knocks and licks and taps clicked between wooden lips. Shadows froze. The dark Woods flashed. A white ball of pollen danced in the air.

It fell like a blinding flare to the earth, dusting his front black paw. Vanslow Fox raised his leg, blue eyes wide, and yelped in fox delight.

A hand. *A hand.* His thin black paw, a human hand! Strong and pink and wide and clever. Vanslow Fox flexed his fingers, unable to disguise his joy.

'It is yours until the next full moon,' Spinosa croaked. 'The berry you have eaten: it holds a vision for your man-servant. He will come to me in time. Human wine, fox prince. Feed me and your curse will lift.'

Spinosa's trunk slammed shut. Drums and clicks shook

through the Woods as branches closed and gathered. Spinosa returned to her slumber. The jackdaw flew up from her stump and perched upon her mistress.

On three hard paws and a soft pink hand, Vanslow Fox trotted through the tunnel and rushed into the Woods. What magic! What kindness! What generosity! With a swish of the tail, he raced down the path, back to the kingdom of Silverweed Road.

Mind full of anarchy, not a moment was wasted. In a frenzy of ecstatic vandalism, gardens sharpened to screams of fox laughter as he played with his new pink gift. He ravaged the crash shrine, ripping up flowers. Plant pots shattered from well-aimed rocks. Rakes and shovels clattered and fell. Then came the wheelie bins. Sweet lord, *the wheelie bins . . .*

Plastic lips, once firm and fastened, opened with a flick of a hand. At last, they yielded their treasures. Driveway by driveway, bin by bin, Vanslow Fox wolfed and plundered.

Stomach fit to burst, legs in the air, he luxuriated in his final wheelie bin. Fistful of fish bones crammed in his mouth, Vanslow Fox tensed and sniffed the air: the baiting scent of his rival. Vanslow Fox leaped from the bin.

She stood on the driveway of no. 8, body arrowed into attack. A fox threat growled between dripping fangs. Vanslow Fox displayed his hand and curled it into a fist. The vixen froze, snarl dying, whimpering at the monstrosity before her.

Vanslow Fox picked up a tin can, took aim, and sent it hurtling into the night. With a flash of the tail, she turned and scattered, yelping as the tin can cuffed her ear.

Victory! Basking in his triumph, his stomach full, Vanslow Fox curled on the roof of his favourite shed. He flexed and admired his magnificent hand, a taste of human life to come. Deep in his guts, the berry clung, waiting to unleash its vision. The lump of ham he lived inside: soon he would honour Spinosa's pact, and drown the tree in human wine.

But first, he thought, a nap.

At 5.50 a.m., he woke to the call of the mirror. Vanslow Fox dashed across the gardens and leaped inside the kitchen window. Smearing the carpet with muddy prints, he raced up the stairs and into the bedroom.

Vanslow Fox settled before the wall mirror, waving farewell to his handsome new hand. The clock struck six.

Fur retreated and paws shrivelled. The fox inflated like a pink balloon, limbs flapping out with a squeak.

Back arched like a surfacing whale, Vanslow Lee heaved up from the floor. He shook before the mirror wall, welcoming his human form. The smile of relief slid from his face.

At the end of his arm, in place of his hand, was a thin black furry paw.

Vanslow scowled, shook out his arm, as if freeing trapped ink from a pen. Maybe some blood had got stuck. He steadied his hand. He looked at the mirror. The sleeve of fur remained. Vanslow turned from his reflection to the trail of muddy pawprints. In circles of dirt, the true horror hit, set in a four-step sequence.

Pawprint. Pawprint. Pawprint. Hand. Pawprint. Pawprint. Pawprint. Hand.

Vanslow stared at his quivering paw. His stomach sank like a capsized raft. The insane, wild scream that emptied his soul shredded the soft, wet meat of his throat. It felt like he'd sicked up a fistful of claws.

*

The hatchet blade glinted under kitchen strip light with an inviting shine of separation. Teeth clamped down on a home-made tourniquet, bottle of rubbing alcohol set by the sink, Vanslow eyed his paw on the chopping board as a surgeon would a gangrenous limb. In the pit of his stomach, a dull lump nagged, like a pill refusing digestion.

Vanslow had not yet slept or eaten. All Monday, he had slumped in his armchair, in a state of stunned distress. Held in his hand was Cherie's engagement ring, heating in the friction of his despair. Vanslow tried to hide behind memories, aching for his past to return. Walking with his sweetheart on the beach. The soft sea breeze. The warmth of her hand. Sharing cool ice cream under the sun. Each time a memory formed, the urgency of his horror cut through.

To the bleak tick of the wall clock, all that Vanslow feared amassed, each thought worse than the last. Was the paw just the beginning? Not satisfied with denying him a life, stealing his dreams of a wife and family, was his fox-self planning a mutiny? First, his left hand, then the right. Now a leg, his head, his heart, his mind, until all that remained was a giant, snarling, sixteen-stone were-fox, screaming at the moon? Vanslow broke down into heaving sobs. He cried till his heart was dry.

Vanslow wiped his eyes. The greasy paw mopped his cheeks. His nostrils flared to an animal scent, of filth and sweat and fox. When a flea jumped out of his sopping paw, Vanslow finally snapped. He launched from his armchair, thumped to the shed, and emptied out his tool box.

Now he loomed over the kitchen worktop. He glared at the paw that was once his hand. The accursed beast had stolen enough. The time had come to take control. Stop the poison before it crept any further. Amputate the contamination.

Hatchet primed, paw on the chopping board, teeth clenched on the tourniquet, trembling Vanslow prepared to strike.

There was a dull *chonk*. Metal cleaved wood. His tourniquet clacked onto the worktop. In a blur of black fur, his fox paw had danced from the blade.

Vanslow lunged at the hatchet handle. He rocked the blade back and forth. His dancing paw sent a surge of terror. Was the infection already spreading within? Vanslow freed the blade. He swung his paw on the chopping block. The hatchet rose. His arm tensed. And . . .

A cry of *ack-ack* pierced through the kitchen. Vanslow froze. Perched on the window ledge outside, a jackdaw glared through the glass. Held by the shine of silver eyes, Vanslow felt a flickering chill. His legs began to buckle and wilt as he fell into the jackdaw's glare. The nagging lump inside his stomach bubbled into life.

Vanslow clutched at his guts. The hatchet slid from his grip. Spinosa's fruit released its spell, black juice fizzing his veins. A chant rose in Vanslow's head and filled him like a sickness.

Human wine by the next full moon . . . Human wine and your curse will lift . . .

Vanslow's mind began to empty and bubble. Woozy and rocking from side to side, he turned from the worktop, left the kitchen and thudded up the shredded hallway. When he opened the front door, the jackdaw was waiting, clawing the roof of his Mini.

With a crack of the wings and a cry of *ack-ack*, she soared towards the Woods. All thoughts stolen by a croaking chant, Vanslow followed the jackdaw's flight. He walked to the dead-end of Silverweed Road, eyes as blank as a zombie's drawn to a buffet of brains.

Vanslow swayed past the railings and thumped the dark path into the Woods. He followed the shadow cast by the jackdaw as the canopy darkened, stealing the sun. At the horseshoe curve, the bird soared right and flew into the Woods. Vanslow obeyed and stepped off the tarmac.

Splashing puddles, kicking through logs, bushes parting and shaking, Vanslow thudded on like a tranquillised Kong, following the flight of the jackdaw above. When he burst from the Woods and into a clearing, the jackdaw was waiting by a tunnel of barbs. Vanslow nodded and fell on all fours. He crawled through the tunnel on hand and paw.

Vanslow emerged, a leaf stuck to his cheek, and gazed up at a gloomy fortress. He faced the mighty blackthorn, swaying to a chant that croaked through his head.

Human wine by the next full moon . . . Human wine and I will lift your curse . . .

Vanslow's stomached fizzed and lurched. In the murk of the Woods, a vision flashed red. Towering above the trees, a crimson tsunami filled the sky. With an appalling roar, the wave collapsed and crashed red through the Woods. A gaping mouth split through a trunk, welcoming the tide. The blackthorn gulped down waves of blood: an endless torrent of human wine. Carried by the surge was a drowning fox, swept screaming into the blackthorn's maw.

The vision cleared from Vanslow's eyes. He looked down to his paw then up to the vast ugly blackthorn. Cast under Spinosa's spell, blind to her deceit, his mind darkened to her command. Feed the tree and kill the fox. Feed the tree and kill the fox . . . Vanslow turned from his mistress and crawled through the tunnel, back to Silverweed Road.

Fox paw muffled by a bandage, claws contained with masking tape, Vanslow sat in his lonely armchair, studying the orbs on his phone. Glazed eyes flicked through the lunar calendar, watching the shadows wax and wane. The full moon rose on Sunday. Just six nights remained.

It was just past 3 a.m. when Vanslow crept into the morgue, drawn to the whispers that called within. His vast shadow cast under clinical light, Vanslow silently studied the mortuary manager for signs of life. Face crumpled into a newspaper, she was dozing at her desk as usual.

Throughout his Wednesday nightshift, Vanslow had stalked the wards. In the eternal night of intensive care, nurses parted in his wake. Vanslow prowled from bed to bed, replacing the privacy curtains. The invasive gaze he'd been trained to avoid hardened on the patients. All that was caring, all that was kind, all pity stripped from cold blue eyes, Vanslow no longer saw pain in gasping faces, but glimpses of salvation.

He slowly trudged from ICU, tempted yet despondent. Even the weakest would struggle and scream. Too alive. Too hard to remove. Then the whispers started.

The susurrations blew like a wind through dark nocturnal wards. Vanslow followed, east wing to west, the whispers building with every step. He descended into the hospital depths.

Vanslow glanced once more at the dozing manager. He edged towards the cold chamber. Bandaged paw clawing the handle, Vanslow pulled a cold steel door and crept into the morgue.

He didn't register the goosebumps the chill pulled from his skin. Neither did he detect the peppermint scent that masked the scent of death. Vanslow stared at the banks of body fridges, drawn to the whispers within.

He pressed an ear against a door, like a doctor to a heart.

The whispering grew stronger. There was a soft click. He pulled a latch. The steel chamber unlocked.

Beneath a shroud, a body lay as still as a sleeping ghost. The sheet began to rise and dip, heaving up and sinking down. Breathing in. Breathing out. Breathing in. Breathing out. A whisper hissed from the swelling shroud. Vanslow Lee peeled back the cover.

The corpse's eyes rolled open. Its lips parted with a crack. From a slit of mouth, came a whispering hiss. The corpse began to croak. *Human wine . . . Human wine . . .*

Now the face cracked and split. Dead skin peeled like paper. No bone or muscle lay beneath. Just a head of gleaming glass.

Glistening in the chamber light, red liquid bowled within. It sloshed inside the clear glass head, a tempting *glog-glog-glog*. Vanslow stared at the bottled corpse, his mind aswirl with human wine. He saw himself before a blackthorn, uncorking the head in the deep, dark Woods. Rivers of blood crashed and splashed, a fox fed to a croaking maw. Feed the tree. Kill the fox. Feed the tree. Kill the fox . . ..

Vanslow closed the chamber door and crept out of the morgue. He roamed the corridors, scanning exits, plotting a path from the hospital's wine cellar. From the dead, his life would return.

He was stationed that Sunday at A & E. From 11 a.m. till 8.30 p.m., Vanslow drifted, silent as a wraith. He fetched oxygen. Replaced curtains. Stocked the patient booths. Ten minutes past the end of his shift, he loitered alone in an east-wing corridor. Inside his tunic, a matchbox rattled. Vanslow faced the linen-room door.

First, he'd drop a match in the linen room. The fire alarm

210

would empty the wards. Then, in the chaos, he'd rush to the mortuary. He'd trolley a bottle of human wine to his car and deliver it to his mistress.

Vanslow looked left, looked right, checked the coast was clear. The matchbox rattled in his bandaged paw. Vanslow reached out for the handle.

The empty corridor surged into life. Medics, nurses, doctors, surgeons. All blurred past in panic. A surgeon lunged at Vanslow's hand and pulled him from the door. His rattling matchbox hit the floor. Swept up by a tide of medics, Vanslow was dragged down the corridor.

He washed up at A & E, dazed by the chaos around him. Patients jumped up from their seats. Screams and sirens spiralled. A message flashed on his porter's pager: ALL TO MAJORS.

Vanslow stumbled to the window. He pressed his hand to the glass. A gridlock unpacked at the ambulance bay. Gurneys bumped from the cabins. Blue lights flashed on blooded faces as nurses rushed to the wounded. A disaster unfolded through breathless gasps. *Terrorist. Leisure Centre. Darts match. Nail bomb. There's a dart in his eye. There's a dart in his tongue. There's a dart in her leg, on his hand, in her foot . . .*

The morgue. His wine cellar. It would be like rush hour down there. Vanslow's heart began to hammer. He looked at his watch: 9 p.m. In under an hour, The Great Change would begin. *Human wine . . . Human wine . . .* Where to get his human wine?

Vanslow jolted as a gurney bumped past. A bleeding dart player moaned on the trolley. His bi-fork beard was soaked in blood, the palms pierced as if crucified. Vanslow gazed at the shining wounds, leaking sticky blood. Each wasted drip of human wine added to his agony.

A rushing doctor seized Vanslow's arm, crushed keys into his palm.

'Pathology, blood issue room. Eight bags O Positive, eight O Negative, five A Positive. Get over there fast, we're running out of blood.'

Vanslow stared at the keys.

'Is anyone in there?' The doctor tapped a finger at his temple. 'Get a bloody *move* on.'

Vanslow snapped through the doors of A & E. Gurney after gurney rushed, spilling human wine. He looked up to the cyclops moon, its surface now a ticking clock. Panic surged once more. The Great Change loomed. His mistress called. Feed the tree. Kill the fox. Where to get his human wine? Vanslow thumped across the car park towards the Pathology building.

Inside, under glaring strip light, Vanslow unlocked the blood issue room. His paw throbbed. His bald head boiled. Vanslow faced the wall of LabCold fridges, mopping the sweat from his brow. He read the yellow warning sign taped to the clear glass door: 'No food or drink to be stored.'

In the mad churn of Vanslow's head, his chant entangled with the sign. *Food . . . Drink . . . Human wine . . . Food . . . Drink . . . Human wine . . .*

Vanslow opened a LabCold fridge and reached inside. His blue eyes widened at the miracle before him. Held in his hand, a blood bag glowed, its sweet red wine glugging within. Feed the tree! Kill the fox! Vanslow ransacked the blood bank.

Rubbish scattered as he emptied a bin. Vanslow shook out the empty sack and stuffed the bag with human wine. Black sack thrown over his shoulder, Vanslow thudded for the exit.

'Wait! You! Stop!'

Vanslow quickened his pace. His grip tightened around his prize. Footsteps clattered in pursuit. A hand clamped on his shoulder.

'You dropped this.'

Vanslow stopped and turned. He faced a doctor in a lab coat. A blood bag glugged in her hand.

'You want to be more careful.'

Vanslow nodded.

'You taking these to Majors?'

Vanslow nodded.

'Just heard what happened. It's bad in there tonight, right?'

Vanslow nodded. The doctor scanned the name on his lanyard.

'You filled in the BPR forms? Yes? No? Come on, I know it's urgent, but get a grip: you know I have to sign these off.'

Vanslow nodded.

'Wait here, I'll go check.'

Black sack dragging behind him, he rumbled for the exit. As A & E churned to screams and chaos, Vanslow squeezed into his car. He threw the sack on the passenger seat, fired up the engine and sped through the hospital gates.

In the driveway of no. 30, gravel flew like sparks. The Mini screeched to a halt. Vanslow slammed the car door, panicked eyes scanning the sky. High above Silverweed's rooftops, the cyclops moon glared back. Vanslow checked his wristwatch. 9.48 p.m. In under twelve minutes, The Great Change would begin.

Black sack slung over his shoulder, Vanslow puffed up

Silverweed Road. He squeezed through the railings and entered the Woods.

9.50. *Tick-tick* . . .

Below the bones of the arched canopy, Vanslow panted up the path. Visions flamed through his mind. Of crimson tides, a thirsting blackthorn and a screaming, drowning fox. Visions of salvation. The path curved into its horseshoe. Vanslow bumped to a halt. He checked his watch, mopped his brow and stepped off the tarmac path.

9:53. *Tick-tick* . . .

Splashing through puddles, kicking through logs, bushes shivering in his wake, Vanslow charged through the undergrowth. His paw began to writhe and flex, claws ripping through the bandage.

9:58. *Tick-tick* . . .

Vanslow looked left, then looked right, searching through the trees. Where was the jackdaw? The tunnel? The blackthorn? The key to his salvation?

His wristwatch beeped. The clock struck ten. A tingle chased through his hands. Vanslow collapsed against an oak. The sack dropped from his grip. The Woods shook to an appalling scream, shrill with horror and distress.

Vanslow shrank as The Great Change began.

Head cocked, tongue out, Vanslow Fox awoke on a sweat-soaked tunic. Where had his handsome reflection gone? Tail swishing, he circled the oak, searching in vain for his mirror. What had his foolish man-ham done? Why had he been dumped, here in the Woods, so far away from his kingdom?

Vanslow Fox twitched his nose: the dark, delicious scent of death. He gazed down at his glorious hand, then up through the branches to the full white moon. Dumped in the undergrowth lay a mysterious black lump. He trotted over to explore.

Vanslow Fox fed in his hand and pulled a mysterious bag from the sack. He gave it a tentative lick, followed by another. Sensing a feast, his stomach pleading, Vanslow Fox pinned his discovery with hand and paw and plunged his fangs through the plastic skin. The bag tore open like a wound, weeping sticky blood.

Human wine! Human wine! A bounty of human wine! Unable to resist, he lapped and guzzled, savouring the gooey drink. Chest fur blooded like a dark red napkin, Vanslow Fox grabbed the sack and followed Spinosa's scent.

Pursued by a stream of silent shadows, dragging the sack with his soft pink hand, Vanslow Fox entered a clearing. He smiled a fox smile, sly and thin. Soon Spinosa would grant his wish. No more rain. No more fights. No more slurping slugs for dinner. Just the unending warmth and infinite banquet of lazy, delicious human life. He skipped into the waiting tunnel, dragging his gift of human wine.

Vanslow Fox emerged, blowing a leaf from his muzzle. Perched on a stump, eyeing its guest, a jackdaw cried *ack-ack*. Vanslow Fox barked in reply, vowing to eat the black chicken later. Circling shadows danced in a ring. He presented his gift to the blackthorn.

Fox ears stiffened to a building crackle. Roots stirred and snaked through the soil. The fortress of thorns creaked and uncoiled. Spinosa yawned and flexed her hands.

'So, you have found me.'

'You said that last time.'

Spinosa's mouth curled into a grimace, displeased with the fox's insolence.

'My human wine,' Spinosa croaked. 'Feed me and I'll grant your wish.'

Vanslow Fox smiled a proud fox smile, pointing at his gift. Spinosa snapped up the black sack and squeezed it in her thorned grip.

'I feel no human, fox prince.'

'What you hold,' boasted Vanslow Fox, 'is the finest wine in the kingdom. I have tasted it myself, and it is good. Drink, Spinosa. Drink, be strong and grant my wish.'

Spinosa dipped a long, spiked finger into the sack, murmuring as she stirred the bags. The watching jackdaw ground her beak, intrigued by the fox's gift. Spinosa's thorns pierced a blood bag, setting its fluid free.

Spinosa slid her finger from the sack and slipped it into her mouth. Wooden lips smacked and clacked, savouring the human wine. Spinosa let out a satisfied croak. Vanslow Fox glowed with pride. Roots rippling with ancient greed, Spinosa crushed the sack into her maw, moaning as she chewed.

As wine spilled down the blackthorn's trunk, Vanslow Fox licked his lips. A puff of white pollen would surely follow. Soon he'd be luxuriating in lazy human life, buried under mounds of chicken. His bushy tail swished and whipped, impatiently drumming the earth.

Spinosa paused between slippery gulps. The moans died on her lips. Her trunk began to ripple and heave. A scraping growl escaped. Anxious shadows churned and whirled. Bristling on her tree stump, the jackdaw cracked her wings. The ring of shadows split like smoke, fleeing through the trees.

Fox fur spiked to a piercing roar.

Vanslow Fox hopped up from the earth, alert to a commotion in the churning soil. Thrashing roots broke through the earth. His blue eyes flicked to the shuddering fortress. Spewing from the blackthorn's mouth poured ropes of plastic dribble. Fox pride turned to fox panic.

Dumbfounded by Spinosa's pain, thinking it unwise to await an explanation, he spun on his paws and raced for the tunnel.

They burst from the soil like burning snakes: a hydra of roots blocked his escape. Vanslow Fox swung around. His tail whipped in panic. Plastic drooling from her mouth, toxins charging through her sap, Spinosa spluttered with ancient rage.

'You dare to poison me, accursed beast?'

Fenced in by Spinosa's roots, fearing the snap of fatal thorns, his fox brain fumbled for an excuse.

'Perhaps,' quivered Vanslow Fox, 'it is indigestion?'

'Suffer twice,' she growled.

Vanslow Fox cowered to licks and taps, rattling from Spinosa's lips. Drumming fingers joined the chant, their echoes striking through the trees. To thrashing arms and grinding thorns, Spinosa cast a spell of vengeance. A blaze of pollen lit up the Woods: an atomic strike of blinding white.

An ancient curse was doubled. Two spirits split.

Sparkling pollen cleared in the Woods. Confusion flashed through Vanslow Fox. Standing beside him, sharing his shock, stood another fox. Their trembling eyes met in silence.

Vanslow Fox cricked his neck. His pelt felt bald and loose. He turned from the fox to look upon himself. First to his hands, down to his legs, then his fat pink toes. He stroked his naked skin in wonder: sixteen stone and six foot five, a bald domed head and barrelled chest. Vanslow Fox smiled a human smile, clumsy and uneven. Cursed to be human ever more? The foolish croaking tree. The fox beside him stared in distress, its bright blue eyes in turmoil.

Ack-ack. The jackdaw flew up from her stump. She pinned her claws to Spinosa's trunk, and pecked and picked with jackdaw panic. As the bird yanked plastic from the blackthorn's maw, Vanslow Fox saw his chance. His eyes darted from tree to tunnel. Within the squirming wall of roots, a tempting gap cleaved open. Escape. And fast. Vanslow Fox dropped on all-fours and forced his body through the roots.

The chokes and splutters of the mighty blackthorn faded at the tunnel's end. A little unsteady on two thick legs, tottering slightly as if on stilts, Vanslow Fox swayed through the Woods. Behind, a single shadow rushed, cast by a racing blue-eyed fox.

To shattering glass and snapping hinges, sixteen stone of Vanslow Fox crammed through the kitchen window. He landed with a thump on the tiles. Not yet used to his new loose skin, he walloped around the kitchen. He sniffed the pedal bin, ripped off the padlock and emptied out its treasures. Mouth stuffed with chicken bones, Vanslow Fox rolled shrieking in the trash, fat legs cycling in the air.

He rose from the scraps, smacking his lips, and followed his nose to the fridge. Still adapting to a frightening new strength, Vanslow Fox ripped off the door and buried his face in the shelves. Milk and cola spilled to the tiles as he gorged himself on chicken wings.

Vanslow Fox was midway through his buffet when two firm raps disturbed him. Growling face smeared with chicken, he removed his head from the fridge. He thudded over to investigate, bald head cocked at the shuddering door.

Behind milky frosted glass, two tall shadows loomed. Had the Wood spirits followed him home? Sent by Spinosa, to wreak her revenge? Vanslow Fox retreated as the back door opened.

Feet crunching on shattered glass, two policemen stepped inside. They faced a naked cliff of man smeared in flesh and caked in soil, the floor a wreck of trash and bones. The policemen exchanged bewildered looks.

'Vanslow Lee?'

Vanslow Fox sniffed the air, taking in their human scent. If the hams had come to share his feast, they were not yet welcome. Perhaps they could come back later for the scraps. He turned to the fridge to finish his meal. Vanslow Fox felt a firm hand land upon his shoulder.

'Vanslow Lee,' the policeman repeated. 'You're under arrest for theft of medical equipment from Meadway Hospital. You do not have to say anything, but it may harm your defence if you—'

Vanslow Fox shrugged off the hand, puzzled by the barking ham. Now two hands landed on his shoulder. Eager to return to the fridge, Vanslow Fox admonished his guests and told them to leave. The policemen jolted to a deafening fox shriek, long and sharp and insane.

Slipping and sliding in cola and milk, three bodies rolled in a commotion of trash. Mystified by this new human game, enjoying himself nonetheless, Vanslow Fox grabbed a tasty pink hand and sank his teeth into the skin. Truncheons pounded to ticklish fox screams.

Panting and handcuffed, cloaked in a blanket that itched at his skin, Vanslow Fox was led into the night and bundled into a police car. Nose pressed against the window, he sniffed at the crash flowers blurring past as the car curved into Valerian Way. Sensing it was time to mark his kingdom, he claimed the police car all to himself. He urinated lavishly on the car's back seat, smiling a fox smile, sly and thin.

Cowering under a sleeping car in the driveway of no. 11, Vanslow watched the police car fade from Silverweed Road, bidding farewell to his fox-self. He flexed his claws and licked his paw, his fox senses on fire.

Not yet settled in his tight, new suit, Vanslow crept from under the car and scratched at his itchy red pelt. Clashing scents danced through his head, travelling direct from nose to gut. His new fox stomach moaned and pleaded, begging for fish bones and chicken wings.

Confused by his appetite, alarmed by his form, his ears sharpened to a distant rustle. Tap by tap, claw by claw, the sound crept ever closer. He cautiously trotted up the driveway, alert to an intrusion.

There by the crash flowers, another fox stood, eyes shining and ears stiff. Paw by paw, Vanslow approached, his fox nose twitching in the cool night air. He breathed in her sweet perfume, the scent bursting like pollen in his chest. Heart aflutter, head bowed, Vanslow padded closer.

Slowly, meekly, he lifted his head, melting to the shine of her amber eyes. He smiled a fox smile, shy and thin, and took another step.

And all that was lost found love.

Extract from The Silverweed Files, 21 November 2024

A personal blog by former Detective Chief Inspector Jim Heath. The views expressed do not reflect those of Kent Police nor the victims impacted by events.

The media's conduct during Silverweed was obstructive at best, hysterical at worst. When word leaked that Vanslow Lee had been arrested for stealing blood bags from Meadway Hospital, the headlines were all too predictable. Within hours, he was dubbed the Vampire of Silverweed. The name has stuck ever since.

Vanslow Lee had indeed ingested blood – a substantial quantity had been pumped from his stomach. The maniac had drunk directly from one of the stolen blood bags as if it were a can of Coke, and it is a relief he was caught before things escalated. When Lee was apprehended, he bit a chunk out of Constable Greening's hand. Surely it was only a matter of time before he sank his teeth into a victim's neck.

I remember crossing the threshold of Lee's house, imagining bodies strung up like bats, dripping blood into the bathtub. The reality was nauseating, but not in the way I had expected. I have been in sweeter smelling public toilets.

The man lived like an animal. Lee had been sharpening his nails and teeth on every surface imaginable. Tellingly, there was an axe laid out on the kitchen worktop. I still maintain he was gearing up for an attack.

The million pound question: why would a hospital porter, described by colleagues as a 'gentle giant', suddenly develop a taste for blood? I do not have an answer and neither did Lee. When I interviewed him, he did little else but scream like a beast and piss all over my dry-cleaned suit.

Much like Augustus Fry, Vanslow Lee now resides in Meadway Psychiatric Hospital. I have visited him on occasion, and am no closer to determining his motivations. Lee continues to urinate on anything and everything, and is only awake at night. His carers post his food through a hatch for fear of being bitten. Lee's vampiric fantasy lives on.

Still, there is hope one day I will be able to interview him. Lee has recently learned to speak, although his vocabulary is limited to a single baffling word: 'Chicken'.

NO. 15:

The Mogon

The creature workshop was hot as hell that cold November morning. Inside the windowless red-brick outhouse that swallowed the back garden of no. 15, a pair of rubber demon wings were nearing the end of their six-hour bake. Yet to set foot on the *Blood Astrum* sound stage, not due on set for another two days, Geppetto Savini waddled to the wardrobe-sized curing oven. A plump, egg-shaped five foot one, the special effects veteran strained on his toes to check the temperature – a fierce, steady 160°C.

Toiling alone in his den of creation since 4 a.m., Geppetto wore navy overalls so encrusted with dried latex, the cotton crunched whenever he moved. The overalls hadn't seen a washing machine for some weeks. Or, come to think of it, sunlight. Zombie-pale from a lifetime of late nights, his face was grey as asbestos. Sprouting from the sides of his balding head, monkish tufts of wild black hair curled around his ears like tattered quotation marks.

With a contented grunt, Geppetto turned from the oven, shuffling past the abattoir of masks and body parts hung

223

on the workshop walls: a gallery of prosthetic relics from his inglorious past. A minor cult figure of lurid Eighties Euro horror, the films, like his craft, had long faded into obscurity. *The Succubus*, *FrankenRat*, *Golgotha Kills*, *Demon Womb*, *The Squid Witch*, *Brain Hammer*, *I Will Eat You When You're Dead* . . . All starred latex beasts created by the tempestuous Savini.

In his pomp, Geppetto's creative tantrums had earned him the nickname 'La Granata' – the grenade. Age had mellowed him, but his devotion still burned. Geppetto pampered his monstrous creations as a mother would a mutant child.

Geppetto hoisted himself onto his favourite wooden stool. Legs swinging under the workbench that spanned the workshop, he opened his latest creature album, revisiting the birth of what would be his final creation.

The unofficial star of evil-unleashed horror *Blood Astrum*, The Mogon had taken nine months to assume its abominable form. Declaring himself a fan of *Demon Womb*, director Damienn Post had personally lured Geppetto from retirement to create the antagonist of his conjuration film – a demonic entity summoned, in error, by a professor of the occult to be played by Brian Cox.

'Computer graphics are bullshit,' Post had railed during his evangelical pitch to Geppetto. '*Blood Astrum* is going to be hardcore practical effects. I want the actors to *feel* The Mogon – feel like they've seen the devil himself.'

Flattered and courted, Geppetto had agreed to one last job, on the director's promise that he would enjoy, for the first time in his fifty-year career, full creative control. He'd since been driven to the edges of despair by redesigns imposed by self-proclaimed visionary, Damienn Post. Day and night, the oil drum outside his workshop burned abandoned work, clouding Silverweed in storm-black smoke.

Geppetto turned the pages of his creature album, watching The Mogon evolve, from outline sketches to concept maquettes. During the early stages of his research, prowling for an image of pure, unfettered evil, Geppetto had stalked the Dark Web for inspiration. It was within the gloomy alcove of an occult forum that he stumbled upon the PDF of an untitled sixteenth-century grimoire, posted by a user called LaVerne Tracy. Among the pages of sigils and spells towered an abominable depiction of Baal-Berith – pontiff among Lucifer's princes, feared for moulding men into madness and murder.

The illustration's hostile power had hit Geppetto with unexpected force. Accompanied by a Latin incantation, Baal-Berith seemed to burn from the parchment, so unearthly and malign that Geppetto had wondered if the artist himself had been visited by the demon – not only surviving to tell the tale, but sharing, in detail, its ominous form in evocation.

The demon was colossal. Legs astride on cart-thick hooves, it towered above a medieval village in a blaze of hell-red flesh. Beneath glowing bone-white goat eyes, a rictus grin sawed through its crocodile snout: a hideous congregation of human, goat and reptile.

As its crown of horns grazed scudding clouds, Baal-Berith squeezed fistfuls of men, flesh dripping like berries. In the demon's shadow, a massacre screamed, villagers snapped in torturous poses, their faces feverish and atrocious. Each man, woman and child had been warped and twisted, remoulded by the might of Baal-Berith.

Once he'd managed to pull his eyes away from the hellscape

– how many hours had he lost to those eyes? – Geppetto had set about distilling Baal-Berith's ungodly form into The Mogon. Wings had been added, unfolding from shoulder blades, yet Baal-Berith's malevolent essence remained, surviving the edits like an indelible stain. Nine months later, a formidable seven-foot bodysuit now lurked in the art department trailer at Meadway Studios – the unit base for the *Blood Astrum* shoot. Eight days into filming, Damienn had not yet cast an actor to fill the bodysuit – an oversight that mystified Savini.

Geppetto lingered on the final page of the creature album, purring at his Mogon. The hell-red latex and rope-thick veins. The goat eyes and crown of horns. The atrocious grin of its crocodile snout. In the sweltering murk of the windowless workshop, Geppetto became ever more certain The Mogon would be his legacy. His Alien. His magnum opus. His master-work. *Look on my works, ye Mighty, and despair . . .*

Geppetto's phone buzzed on his bench. Grunting at the intrusion, he scowled at the caller ID: Milton Hinds, *Blood Astrum*'s producer. Eyes still idling on his beloved Mogon, in a gruff Italian accent, he answered a question before it could be asked.

'Been up since crack of chicken, curing the wings for—'

'The Mogon,' Milton interrupted. 'We need to talk.'

Geppetto had never warmed to the producer: an aloof presence who regarded his masterwork with cool indifference. Now his tone, his we-need-to-talk, instantly set Geppetto on edge.

'What you do? You damage suit?'

Milton glided through his concern. 'Listen, Geppetto, we appreciate all the hours you've put into this. There are elements of The Mogon that are—'

'Tell Damienn, new wings bigger, like he want.'

'Listen, Geppetto—'

'On goddamn phone, course I listen.'

'We've been reviewing the script, and . . . we need The Mogon to do things we can't pull off with a bodysuit.'

Milton's pause opened up like a chasm. Legs pedalled beneath the bench. Geppetto caught conspiratorial whispers on the end of the line.

'Moving forward,' said Milton, 'we've come to a decision.'

Another pause. A deeper chasm. The whispering intensified. Geppetto realised Milton had the conversation on speaker phone, detected three familiar voices: the Californian baritone of Damienn Post, the sharp Dutch accent of screenwriter Olga Voss, and the transatlantic drawl of executive producer Felix Spitz.

The whispers died. In cold-blooded tones, Milton spoke.

'We're killing the design.'

Before Geppetto could process Milton's words, a fresh dagger stabbed into his back.

'We're going CG,' Felix Spitz chipped in.

Geppetto tried to clear his throat. He felt as if he'd swallowed a rock.

'But you . . . You eight days. You *eight days* into shoot. How you—'

'Hey Geppetto,' interrupted Damienn Post. 'Just want to say, it's been a blast. Shame to let you go.'

'Real shame,' added Olga Voss.

'You *firing* me?' Geppetto began to claw at his tufts. 'I work with Lenzi! Martino! Fulci! You not even tell me to *face*? Who? Who do this? Who kill my Mogon?'

'We feel that . . .' In a cold drone, Milton stonewalled Geppetto, talked of budgets, logistics, evading the details behind The Mogon's sudden death. Milton's words blurred into a meaningless soup. The phone slid from Geppetto's grip. The call went dead. And all that was loved was lost.

The anger to come as yet unfelt, La Granata's pin yet to pull, Geppetto sat motionless in dismal silence. His entire body dried and clenched. Cocooned in shock, Geppetto could hear nothing but his own blood thud around his ears.

The effects veteran could muster but one motion. With a numb hand, he pawed at his creature album, caressing his dead creation as a mother would a lifeless child. His Mogon. His Alien. His legacy. His *baby* . . .

Geppetto sagged at his bench, immune to time and feeling. Sparks of what he wished to do – to scream, to rage, to cry, to question – were flattened by the trauma. The pawing ceased. The blood stopped thudding. Geppetto stared at his beloved Mogon, paralysed in shock.

The acrid scent of burning rubber began to flood the workshop. It could no longer be ignored. Geppetto wobbled off his stool, took the demon wings from the curing oven and slung them on the bench. The cremated moulds had crisped and shrunk, black as a jackdaw's wings.

Outside, by the garden fence, Geppetto scraped the demonic ruins into a fuming oil drum. As he watched his dreams go up in smoke, a shadow landed on the workshop roof. Geppetto jumped to a cry of *ack-ack*, the sound so sharp it pierced his heart. When he turned, the bird was gone, soaring into the sky. Geppetto watched the jackdaw's shadow, cast upon the workshop roof, an echo of his Mogon wings: unleashed, alive . . . and free. Geppetto suddenly pictured the Mogon bodysuit, imprisoned in the art department.

The dull thud of blood that had numbed his ears began

to bubble. His body, once dried and clenched, bolted from its coma. Waking from his mournful stupor, Geppetto felt a fizz of rage, a surge of panic, a pin inch from his internal grenade. The cold splash of reality hit. Full creative control. They'd promised him. They'd *promised*.

Milton. Felix. Damienn. Olga. Who was it? Who, in that nest of *Blood Astrum*'s vipers, had dared to kill his baby?

They could kill his job. They could rob his pride. But he'd be damned if they'd take his Mogon.

It was just past midnight when Geppetto made his move. Crunching up the gravel driveway of no. 15 Silverweed Road, he climbed into his cream Suzuki minivan, sped past the crash flowers, and drove to Meadway Studios.

There were no clever distractions, no attempts at an elaborate heist. Guided by his rage, Geppetto parked at the production office. He stormed past security, flashing his pass, his face a mask of intense inconvenience. Adad Hussain, on night watch, had long grown accustomed to Geppetto's late-night visits, and waved him past without a word. When Geppetto returned, dragging The Mogon body-suit from the art department trailer, Adad helped him wrestle it into the back of his minivan.

It couldn't be theft if The Mogon belonged to him.

Concealed behind a curtain, The Mogon loomed in a workshop corner. Reunited with his beloved, Geppetto stared up at his baby, dwarfed in the bodysuit's shadow. Held in his hand was a glowing tablet. An ancient grimoire shone from the screen.

Geppetto swiped through the spells and sigils, arriving at the image that had inspired his creation. The abominable tower of hell-red flesh. The village cowering beneath.

Darkening to the hostile might of Baal-Berith, Geppetto read the inscription below the demon: a Latin word, thrice repeated, arranged within a triangle. *Refocillo. Refocillo. Refocillo.* Geppetto heated to its meaning.

Chalking a triangle around his beloved, he stepped into its shadow. Gazing into its bone-white eyes, Geppetto growled an incantation.

Refocillo. Resurge. *Refocillo.* Revive. *Refocillo.* Resurrect . . .

Lost to The Mogon's glare, Geppetto stared through his creation, awakening to a force that lay beyond. The tortured screams of ancient villagers began to swirl. Bone-white pits pulsed in the darkness. Within its eyes, Geppetto saw himself reflected: towering above *Blood Astrum*'s sound stage, his tormenters juiced like berries in his grip.

Refocillo, refocillo dripping from his lips, Geppetto fell to his knees. As goat eyes pulsed and screams echoed, he opened his heart to Baal-Berith. A black heat answered, prickling his hands. Geppetto's heart began to thud. A sulphurous scent pinched his nostrils. The acid in his belly bubbled and stirred. Savini felt the flesh of his cheeks begin to lift, his lips twitching into a rictus grin. Shivering on bended knee, Geppetto roared as darkness poured, inviting the might of Baal-Berith. He who moulded men. Moulded men into madness and murder.

Geppetto stumbled to his feet, hands flexing to a prickling heat. Floorboards creaked as he prowled the workshop. Eyes cast upon the prosthetic abattoir hung upon the walls, he pictured the hellscape of medieval villagers, distorted in torturous poses. Geppetto unhooked an arm from the wall, heating to possibilities. Of infinite agony. Of vengeance upon his rejectors. Of full creative control. As Geppetto searched for his fettling knife, an atrocious grin sawed through his face.

At 9 a.m., there was a knock on the workshop door. Geppetto had been expecting a guest. It was merely a matter of who would come first.

'Is open.'

Geppetto climbed onto his stool. Laid on the bench before him was a life-size prosthetic arm. The blade of a fettling knife glinted beside it.

Milton Hinds ducked under the workshop door. Dressed in bootcut jeans, blue gingham shirt and a navy quilted gilet, the forty-six-year-old producer cultivated an air of composed disdain. When they'd first met, pale, balding Geppetto had felt a twinge of envy at Milton's après-ski tan and thick mane of syrupy hair.

'So,' said Milton, skirting any pretence of a greeting, 'late last night, somebody came on set and took The Mogon. Don't suppose you know anything about that?'

Geppetto brooded in silence. His eyes burned into the prosthetic arm.

'We know it's you,' Milton said, aggravated his presence was being ignored. 'Adad said he helped you load the suit into your van. I don't want to get the police involved, but I will if—'

Geppetto looked up from the arm and glared at Milton.

'The police? What you report? A stolen demon? *È ridicolo*.'

Milton sighed and looked at his Rolex. 'I haven't got time for this. Where's the suit?'

'Nine months I slave for you,' Geppetto fumed. 'Nine! Enough to make another human. What you do, is like Mama get pregnant, baby pop out, she kick in bin, then

231

fuck new man cos she no like look of baby. Who was it? Who kill my Mogon?'

'Read your contract,' said Milton, refusing to answer. 'The Mogon belongs to us.'

The Mogon belongs to us . . . Geppetto prickled to a black heat coursing through his hands. Behind the curtains, shrouded in shadow, The Mogon's goat eyes pulsed. Geppetto invited the villagers' screams and the moulding might of Baal-Berith.

Milton marched to the storage cabinets and ransacked the drawers, rifling through rubber heads and severed limbs and plastic-resin teeth. With Milton's back turned, Geppetto reached for the fettling knife. The blade glinted in the murk, sharp with possibilities. His fingers flexed. A black heat charged. Geppetto grinned and gripped the arm, sawing through the wrist. The severed latex stretched and snapped like pink spaghetti.

He wasn't prepared for the high-pitched scream that cut through the workshop. Neither was he prepared for the sound of Milton's hand. It hit the floor with a damp slap, like a pork chop dropped on a butcher's block.

When Milton swung around, eyes moon-wide and wet with shock, Geppetto was too engrossed by the stump at the end of Milton's arm. The ulna and radius was neatly defined, like the striped tiers of a red velvet cake. Geppetto stared in shock at the arm on his workbench, the latex hand neatly separated – an abominable echo of his moulding might.

Milton's screams in harmony with the villagers in his head, Geppetto's grip tightened around the fettling knife. He plunged the blade through the prosthetic arm and carved right through the elbow. There was a soft crunch of gristle and bone. Now the slap of meat hitting wood. When

Geppetto looked up from his dissection, Milton had vanished from view.

Geppetto levered himself from his stool and peered over his bench. Flapping on the workshop floor, splashing in blood like a fish on a boat deck, Milton twisted in shapes of pain. Beside the producer's hacked-off hand, a stub of forearm rolled. Geppetto found the blood flow fascinating: unlike the crimson jets that sprayed from his counterfeit movie wounds, the blood from Milton's elbow spilled in thick, sloppy gulps.

Fired by the sight of Milton's blood and the black heat in his hands, Geppetto eagerly finished his dissection, sawing through the tricep. The prosthetic limb on his bench separated into three neat bands. There were no screams now. Just a faint whimper of surrender . . . then silence.

Geppetto leaped from his stool and cast his shadow over the village of Milton.

'Who kill my Mogon?'

The producer lay motionless in a crimson pool, body frozen in a torturous pose. Had he died of shock? *Vigliacco!* The coward! He'd spoilt the fun, left the game too soon.

Blocking the path of blood with gaffer tape, Geppetto sealed the cleaved shoulder and removed Milton's clothing. He dragged the body to the curing oven, folded it inside, stamped on Milton's phone and tossed it in.

In the darkened corner of the workshop, Geppetto parted the curtains. He fell to his knees before The Mogon, crackling to a power that lay beyond.

This was more than revenge. This was art. *Look on my works, ye Mighty . . .*

Who next?

*

Outside the creature workshop, in the shadow of a high garden fence, Geppetto lit a cigar from the licking flames. Melting within an oil drum was Milton's blood-soaked gilet. Storm-black smoke billowed from the inferno.

'What the devil do you think you're doing?'

Geppetto looked up to a face hovering over the fence. Bandage wrapped around his head, Augustus Fry glared down at Geppetto.

This was not the first time Geppetto had clashed with his next-door neighbour. Five nights ago, toiling late in the workshop, he had been driven to distraction by yells and crashing glass. He had thumped on the front door of no. 17, demanding silence, but Fry had refused to answer. Geppetto met his neighbour's glare. He added to the smoke with a puff of his cigar.

'I have my washing out, Savini. You're polluting a price-less waistcoat. Extinguish your fire right this minute or I shall inform the council.'

Geppetto scoffed, picked up a can of lighter fluid, and tossed it onto the flames. Augustus Fry recoiled from the fence, bandage rippling as he coughed from the smoke. Geppetto shuffled back to his workshop. He extinguished Fry's shouts with a slam of the door.

Geppetto was sweeping the last red clumps of sawdust when his phone vibrated on his bench. In a rushed voice, Felix Spitz called from the *Blood Astrum* set, asking if Milton Hinds had left the workshop. Geppetto instantly invited him over.

Milton had left a dreadful mess. It would not happen again. Unwrapping a roll of plastic sheeting, Geppetto covered the floor and benches, stamping down the edges with his size four feet. Spill-proof surfaces wrapped cellophane-tight, Geppetto pulled back the curtains and stared into The Mogon's bone-white eyes. What torturous charms had been passed on to him? In the domain of his workshop, what sweet tools would answer his vengeance? His world now a special effect, were there limits, Geppetto wondered, to the moulding might of Baal-Berith?

He rifled through his storage drawers, packed with prosthetic body parts, searching for inspiration. Arms, hearts, heads, hands, legs, eyes, teeth . . .

Geppetto's lips twitched into a rictus grin. *Teeth. Teeth. Snappy little teeth.*

'What's with all the sheets?' said Felix Spitz, looking around the plastic-wrapped workshop. 'You planning a hit, Geppetto?'

'Testing squibs,' lied Geppetto. 'The blood, it get everywhere.'

A biting blast of November air had followed *Blood Astrum*'s executive producer inside. The wind briefly resculpted the lines of his black Armani suit. Settled on his stool, Geppetto acknowledged Felix with a curt nod. A red clay doll, fat as his palm, lay on the bench before him. It was 11 a.m.

Black hair slicked into a side parting, boyish face framed with round spectacles, Felix Spitz, thirty-nine, suggested an alternative universe where Harry Potter grew up to be a hedge fund manager. Spitz spoke with a transatlantic twang – a product of his upbringing, schooled in both New Hampshire and Chelsea. *Blood Astrum*'s money man had slowly wormed himself into a vocal position on the film's creative decisions, including The Mogon's design. Like all the executives he'd endured through the years, Geppetto did not trust Felix one iota.

'Where's Milton?' asked Felix.

'Who was it?' growled Geppetto, impatient to proceed. 'Who kill my Mogon?'

Felix sighed, sensing a confrontation building he had neither the time, will, nor respect to entertain. Best dismiss the gnome with a fabrication.

'There was a meeting,' lied Felix. 'Me, Milton, Damienn, Olga. We were watching the *Blood Astrum* rushes, and—'

'*Olga*? The *writer's* getting a say on the effects? *Vaffanculo*!'

'Olga and Damienn, they're seeing each other,' shrugged Felix. 'You know what film sets are like. She wanted to take The Mogon in a new direction, Damienn agreed to the rewrite, and—'

'Who,' Geppetto repeated, 'kill my Mogon?'

'We know you stole the suit,' said Felix, taking back control. 'Where have you put it?'

Behind the curtains in the shadowed corner, the goat eyes of The Mogon pulsed. Geppetto twitched on his stool as the sweet scream of villagers swirled in his head.

'Look in that drawer,' grinned Geppetto. 'And you find the answer.'

Felix followed Geppetto's finger to the storage cabinets. Believing an answer to The Mogon's disappearance lay within the workshop, Felix opened a drawer.

'Is this a joke?' scowled Felix, rummaging through the contents. 'It's just a load of teeth in here.'

Geppetto had already taken them from his overall pocket: six plastic-resin teeth. His hands prickled to a black heat, warming to the might of Baal-Berith. Geppetto picked up the red clay figure and, like a witch doctor with a pin, pushed a tooth into the doll's arm. The red clay sank, soft as mud. Something stirred within the drawer.

Once again, Geppetto was surprised by his victim's scream: less high-pitched than Milton's. Lower and grittier, not at all what he'd expected.

Felix Spitz recoiled from the cabinet, an arm thrust into the air. His shaking hand wore a glove of fangs. Teeth skittered between his fingers, as if he'd dipped his fist in a bucket of crabs. Geppetto watched the executive flap and swat, to little effect other than to provide him with a most curious dance. From Felix Spitz's living glove, blood began to spill.

A black heat ripped through Geppetto's hands. Impatient to proceed, he quickly pinned the remaining teeth into the doll – arms, legs, torso and head – until they dressed the clay like buttons. The open drawer rumbled into life.

Clattering like shingle, a plague of teeth poured to the floor. Felix danced and shook his glove. Teeth scuttled in pursuit. The swarm gathered at shaking feet and chattered up his legs.

Geppetto marvelled at the variety: old teeth put to fresh use, from film sets of the past. Shark teeth and werewolf canines. Vampire fangs and crocodile daggers. Zombie molars and ogre tusks. All snapped and clacked, towards their quarry.

Overwhelmed by Geppetto's teeth, Felix itched screaming to the floor. Buried by flashes of biting white, his Armani suit peeled and ripped. Black cloth spat like sparks. The teeth continued in their quest: for softer surfaces, underneath.

Geppetto fidgeted on his stool, a bladed grin sawed through his face. His legs began to swing in time to the maraca clack of plastic teeth. *Chaka-chak. Chaka-chak. Chaka-chak.*

Swallowed by the writhing swarm, Felix vanished from view. The *chaka-chak* of rattling teeth now switched to a wetter crunch. Thrashing limbs, so wild at first, slowed to a loose, wet flop. The plastic sheet turned red.

As Geppetto's teeth sought deeper rewards, chunks of Felix began to build. Piles of red mince formed around him, like the chalked outline of a body. Surfaces breached, the teeth dug deeper. The crunching slowed to a hollow tap. Drier. Harder. Sharper. Bone.

The sea of teeth ground to a halt. Geppetto jumped from his stool. He kicked away the rubble of teeth, curious to see what lay beneath. A skeleton lay on the plastic sheeting, every creamy bone picked clean. Spectacles tilted on its skull. The jawbone gaped a silent scream.

Towering over the village of Felix Spitz, a rictus grin carved through his face, Geppetto marvelled at the beauty of his destruction. *Look on my works, ye Mighty . . .*

Who next?

Geppetto warmed his hands in the November chill. The oil drum fumed afresh. With no room in the curing oven, Milton stiffening within, Geppetto had bagged what he could of Felix Spitz. Tattered rags, a pair of glasses, and two chewed shoes were fed to the flames. Geppetto lifted a cigar to his lips and lit.

The spark vanished. The cigar leapt from his mouth. Geppetto shook from a harsh cold snap. Snaking over the high fence, a yellow hose spat water; first at Geppetto, then the oil drum. Flames hissed and curled from the jets. A bandaged face popped above the fence.

'That,' growled Augustus Fry, 'is for ruining my washing. Now put that bloody oil drum out.'

Monkish tufts dripping water, Geppetto said nothing. He picked up his sodden cigar, the face of Augustus Fry burned into his mind. Geppetto returned to the workshop, a face held in his memory, storing his features for later. There was more pressing business to attend to.

The text he'd sent to Damienn Post was a blunt lure: *Come workshop. Milton/Felix here.*

Geppetto glowered at the promotional headshots loaded on his tablet: one of Damienn Post, the other of Olga Voss. Two large balls of red modelling clay were set upon his bench. Geppetto began to roll and knead, shaping the clay into busts. He picked up his scalpel and set to work.

They arrived together at 3 p.m.: director Damienn and writer, Olga. When Geppetto ushered them in, he furtively locked the workshop door and pocketed the key.

Eyes shaded by an Andalusian hat, features eclipsed by a black beard, Damienn Post looked as he always did: like a shadow that had escaped its master. A black leather trench coat draped from his frame, so long that it grazed his ankles. Post's moody gothic persona had always struck Geppetto as an affectation, like the extra 'n' in Damienn's name.

Geppetto climbed on to his stool. He'd already removed the chairs, leaving his guests with no choice but to stand. Olga Voss eyed the room suspiciously, taking in the plastic sheeting wrapped around the workshop. Everything was angular about Olga Voss: the Lego-like peroxide bob, the critical eyes, the sharp triangular mouth. Under her leather biker jacket, a *Suspiria* T-shirt poked through. In the murk of the windowless workshop, a tension simmered between host and guests.

'OK,' said Damienn, breaking the silence. 'Where are they? Felix and Milt—' Post's eyes met the red clay bust on Geppetto's bench. 'Is that me?'

'Not finished,' said Geppetto. 'Be ready soon. Souvenir. Do it every movie. Parting gift, me to you.'

Post narrowed his eyes on the bust, suspicious of Geppetto's gesture. A bribe, perhaps, to get his name on the credits.

'The eyes aren't right,' frowned Olga. 'The beard is good, I'll give you that, but the nose . . . That also needs work.'

'Ah, but I do one for you too,' said Geppetto, reaching under his bench. A second clay bust joined Damienn's.

'Come on, Olga,' said Damienn. 'You got to admit, he's captured you there.'

Olga scrutinised the clay cast. Geppetto had caught her angular features with unnerving accuracy.

'The top lip is all wrong,' said Olga, crossing her arms.

Behind the curtains in powdered shadow, the goat eyes of The Mogon pulsed. Geppetto felt a shiver of black heat. Some fun, perhaps, before the serious work began. Hand sneaked behind Damienn's bust, he opened his palm and slapped the clay.

'What the hell?' yelped Damienn. He rubbed his head, hat askew. He frowned at Olga, confused.

'Why,' said Geppetto, eyes fixed on Olga, 'you just hit him?'

'I did *not*,' Olga protested. She pushed at Damienn's chest.

A fissure of suspicion opened between them. Geppetto drove in his wedge.

'Who kill my Mogon?'

Heads turned. Glares switched. Damienn addressed the demon in the room.

'OK, let's talk about why we're *really* here,' he said. 'Where is it? Where's the suit?'

Geppetto repeated himself, words stretched out, slow and cold, the question now a statement. 'Who. Kill. My Mogon.'

A pause. A chasm. Post's lips parted, preparing his lie.

'Because the other one,' said Olga, 'is ten times better.'

Damienn shot Olga a look.

'What?' Olga shrugged. 'He's going to find out sooner or later. Skinwalker FX are doing The Mogon. Huge improvement, actually. Damienn wanted a model on set for the actors to react to, didn't we Damienn? Your dumb suit – it's just the stand-in for the CG.'

'Stand-in?' trembled Geppetto, aghast. La Granata's pin inched from his shell. '*Stand-in?* You waste nine months of my life so Brian fucking Cox can hit his marks for CG? *Vaffanculo!*'

Geppetto's eyes burned on his Mogon rejectors. It now became clear why Damienn hadn't cast an actor to fill the bodysuit. La Granata's pin dropped and clinked. He was all but ready to detonate.

'It's why we need your Mogon back,' said Olga. 'Now answer Damienn's question. Where's the suit?'

Geppetto had heard quite enough. He turned Olga's bust around. Geppetto did not feel like smiling yet Baal-Berith insisted. A rictus grin carved through his face, lifting the pale flesh of his cheeks. Black heat charging through his fingers, Geppetto pressed a thumb into Olga's bust. He swiped a seal through the cool clay lips. There was a peculiar muffled cry, as if she were screaming underwater. Geppetto looked up. Olga's lips were coiled together, like a swirl of raspberry ripple.

Before Post could react, Geppetto turned his attention to Damienn's bust. Seal his lips too? Or experiment first? He pincered his fingers. He squeezed the nose. The soft red clay thinned to his touch.

Damienn's hands leaped to his face. Red trickled between his fingers. Geppetto watched his writhing villagers, dancing out of time to their rhythms of pain. Olga's muffles and Damienn's groans sang a dark duet.

With a swish of his trench coat, Damienn grabbed Olga. He stumbled towards the workshop door. Geppetto relished Post's panic as he pulled and hammered at the locked door. Blood streaming from his pincered nose, Post unholstered his phone and, trusting he'd be back imminently, speed-dialled Milton Hinds.

A ringtone sang in the workshop.

Damienn scoured the room, searching for the source. His eyes widened on the oven against the workshop wall. Geppetto cursed himself for not stamping hard enough on Milton's phone.

'What the fuck is Milton's phone doing in the oven?'

Olga slid against the door, hand clamped over spiralled lips. Geppetto swivelled on his stool. Damienn blurred past, trenchcoat whipping. He stopped by the oven, pressed his ear to the door. Milton's ringtone chirped within. A bead of sweat pipped on Geppetto's head. Damienn opened the oven door.

Hardened horror director Damienn Post had never seen a dead body before. Milton Hinds was his first. Urged by the weight of his head, the top half of Milton lolloped from the oven. The gristle from a curtseying neck clicked. One eye was shut, the other open.

Post recoiled from the door. Panicked eyes flashed at Geppetto. He already had Damienn's bust on his lap, like a severed head on a plate. Palms flat, arms out, poised to clap, Geppetto opened out his elbows. With a whip of the air, he cuffed Damienn's bust.

A hat fell to the workshop floor. Post's hands leapt to his temples, quivering from the thunderclap. Vision trembling like a strummed guitar string, his vision settled on the bust. There, in the murk of the workshop, Damienn awakened to Geppetto's terrible power.

'The head, Geppetto. Give me my head. I don't know what voodoo shit you're up to, but give me my fucking head back.'

Geppetto pulled the bust close to his chest, like a goalkeeper shielding a football. He shook his head, widened his arms, threatening a round of applause. Damienn flinched at Milton's sagging head, single eye glaring back, and, fearing what was to come, immediately changed tack.

'Name it. Whatever you want. Geppetto Savini, first on the credits. On the fucking billboards if you want, above Brian Cox. My personal guarantee. Let's trade. Give me the head, you get The Mogon.'

Palms out, poised to clap, Geppetto considered Damienn's proposal.

'The original design? *My* design? Full creative control?'

'Anything you want. Just give me my head, Geppetto. Give me the head. And make Olga right again.'

'Nine months, you lie to me,' raged Geppetto. La Granata exploded as froth foamed on his lips. 'Full creative control, you say! CG is bullshit! Practical effects! Why you destroy me?' Geppetto let go of the bust, clawing at the tufts of his hair. 'Why you—'

As Geppetto raged, Damienn made his move. Arms out, he charged from the oven to reclaim his head. Geppetto leaned back on his stool. He quickly pressed a thumb to the bust. A smear of clay dragged over an eye, blending it with the cheek. Like a sheet of pink pastry, a flap of eyelid folded over Damienn's eye. The director recoiled, clutching his cheek. Trench coat folding like a sack, he crumpled next to Milton.

There was no time to savour the spectacle. A rushing force surged from behind. Springing from the workshop door, a roar contained behind spiralled lips, Olga leaped at the bench. Geppetto toppled from his stool. Olga swiped for her bust. She missed. It fell. The bust rolled on the plastic sheeting. Carried by the impetus of her dive, Olga toppled from the bench. She crashed to the floor in a blur of limbs and landed in a daze next to Damienn.

Behind the curtains, The Mogon loomed, the last figure standing in the workshop.

Groaning on his back, an upended turtle, Geppetto came to his senses. Still clutching Damienn's bust, he scrabbled for Olga's and clutched it to his chest. His game was spiralling out of control. Geppetto glared at Olga and Damienn, curled on the floor by the oven, considered their treachery, playing God with his creation, and decided it was time to play God himself.

The scream of villagers assailed his head. A black heat charged through shaking hands. Geppetto forced the busts together, feeling the clay surrender to his will. Olga and Damienn's heads attracted like magnets, as if engorged by a fatal, consuming kiss. Skin churned like trodden mud.

Protesting legs writhed and kicked. As clay pressed clay, bust into bust, two heads crushed into one. Geppetto watched their faces blend, slaves to the power of creative control.

A sliding eye poured below a mouth, which itself began to move. With great artistry, two pairs of lips fused to form one conjoined line that spread the breadth of two merged faces. A row of teeth clinked, like a horizonal zip. But for the crunch of binding skulls, Geppetto worked in silence, perfecting his Orthrus. His rage was made flesh by Baal-Berith: he who moulded men into madness and murder.

Legs, once kicking, lay lifeless.

Geppetto towered above Olga and Damienn, their traitorous heads pulped into one. His only wish was that they had lived a little longer. For him to watch the eyes blink below the mouth. To hear the long zip of teeth ripple and click.

It was at this moment Geppetto became what would now endure. No longer a mere mortal: a poet of flesh and bone. Hands reborn, to create and destroy. The entire world a special effect, to be moulded and resculpted to his will. Full creative control! *Look on my works, ye Mighty . . .*

Geppetto pulled back the curtains and knelt before The Mogon, *refocillo*, *refocillo* dripping from his lips. Behold, the mighty Geppetto Savini: the Picasso of Baal-Berith.

Who next?

A setting sun blooded Silverweed's rooftops. Geppetto tossed a hat into the oil drum and stirred it with a stick. Inside the workshop, Olga and Damienn had been wrapped in plastic sheeting, like cocoons that would never hatch.

As Geppetto lit a celebratory cigar, there was a flash of

blinding white. He looked up to an open window. Augustus Fry leaned out of his office, a smartphone shining in Geppetto's direction.

'I've got your fires all on video,' shouted Fry. 'The council will be here tomorrow, Savini.'

Geppetto puffed at his cigar and waddled in silence back to the workshop. His hands would do the talking.

Geppetto unhooked a prosthetic leg from the workshop wall. He sat at the bench, picked up his fettle knife, closed his eyes and invited the screams. As the mummified face of Augustus Fry filled his vision, he sawed through the knee of the latex leg, got up from his bench and leaned out of the door. Geppetto relished the howls, picturing Fry as he hopped around his office, grabbing at a leg that was no longer there. *Look on my works, ye Mighty . . .*

Who next?

Drenched in the blood of others, Geppetto shivered out of his overalls. He prowled the creature workshop, a naked Midas of destruction, considering his next display. Drunk on power and possibilities, Geppetto erupted with a boundless control denied his entire creative life. Was there, at this time, a more powerful being on this Earth, as yet contained in a lowly workshop on Silverweed Road? Now that he had satisfied his vengeance, who would be answerable to Geppetto Savini's mighty hands? Who would know? Who could catch him? Who next? Who *not* next?

Eyeing the ball of clay on his bench, Geppetto cracked his knuckles. He turned on the workshop TV. Sky News flashed on the screen. The Prime Minister appeared from the door of Downing Street and settled behind a podium.

Geppetto worked fast, moulding a face from the clay. He tickled the left cheek of the bust. His eyes flicked to the screen. The Prime Minister paused mid speech to scratch an invisible itch. Geppetto ruffled his tufts, considering how best to direct this moment: this living, breathing horror movie, broadcast live to the world. Mould two eyes into the nose, watch them blink inside the nostrils? Pull the mouth into a hideous beak? Or simply crush down the forehead in one fatal collapse of flesh? Geppetto rubbed his palms. Delicious screams began to swirl. He closed his hands around the bust and . . .

'Police. Open up.'

Geppetto flinched to three sharp knocks.

'Geppetto Savini? We want to talk to you about the disappearance of Milton Hinds. Now open up.'

Geppetto tumbled off his stool and scrambled under the bench. Cowering in shadow, he clawed at his hair. It wasn't fair. It wasn't right. It was far too soon to spoil the game. The knocks continued. The calls got louder. The TV blared. They knew he was in.

Geppetto crawled from under the bench and scuttled like a beetle across the floorboards. He slithered under the curtain. The Mogon towered in the murk, promising protection. Geppetto crawled around its hooves, scrabbled for the zip at the back of the suit, squeezed inside and fastened it.

Geppetto waited in the warmth of The Mogon, listening to the muffled knocks. He pressed his ear to the demon's belly. If the police had a warrant, they'd be in by now. Swallowed by the seven-foot suit, he waited for the knocks to fade, the voices trail. Geppetto now judged it was safe to re-emerge and continue with his work.

Geppetto wriggled an arm behind him and felt around for the zip. Too plump to turn inside the suit, his fingers searched the lining. Face pressed into the Mogon's belly, hands behind his back, his scratching became ever more frantic. He pawed for the zip and clawed at the lining. A sticky liquid seemed to coat his hands, as if the latex suit were leaking.

The zipper. Where was the zipper?

Cursing into The Mogon's belly, Geppetto felt the heat of his stifling breath. Pearls of sweat pipped on his skin. With each passing second, the walls of the suit closed in. Geppetto pushed against the suit, tried to turn, a miniature Houdini in a padlocked sack. Now the knocks at the door returned.

Geppetto, out of instinct, cried out for help. The knocking continued, increasing in volume. *Ba-dum. Ba-dum. Bad-dum-dum-dum*. Only now did the terrible realisation hit. The knock-knock-knocking was not at the door. The police had not returned. It was the beat of his own thudding heart.

Trapped inside his own creation, Geppetto panicked and clawed at the lining. The suit was leaking more now, webbing his fingers in gluey sauce. Gasping for air, his breath splashed back at him. His feet stamped. His arms wriggled. Sweat poured in the stifling heat. Geppetto cried once more for help. His call was swallowed by a sharper sound that echoed through the suit. The ruinous screams of ancient villagers swirled within The Mogon.

With every squirm and every wriggle, the suit drew ever closer. Geppetto took fishy gulps at thinning air. The hot sweat on his naked body clung like gluey sauce. Another revelation. Far worse than his knocking heart.

The suit wasn't leaking. *He* was leaking.

Geppetto's screams joined those of the villagers. The suit

pressed in reply. Geppetto peeled into the sticky walls, his flesh now fusing . . . softening . . . Ribs began to snap and crumble. Black lungs wrinkled into prunes.

Remoulded by the might of Baal-Berith, a gritted howl was his last utterance. Geppetto felt his mouth flood with a tide of sticky flesh. His skull sank, dripping into his shoulders. His shoulders dripped into his hips. His hips dripped into his feet. Before his brain bubbled into meaningless soup, Geppetto was granted one final thought, or if not a thought, a sensation: of a mother being eaten alive by her own ravenous child.

Baal-Berith rolled its shoulders, settling inside its Mogon suit. Why could it not have absorbed something more substantial? Something . . . taller? Hot breath hissed from its crocodile snout, contemptuous of its ignoble state. Lucifer's pontiff recalled the base human language its disciple had uttered in evocation. *Refocillo*. Resurge. *Refocillo*. Revive. *Refocillo*. Resurrect . . .

The black broth that swilled inside instantly responded. It charged and flooded rope-thick veins. A snout lengthened. Limbs bulged. In a rapid charge of hell-red flesh, the demon swelled towards the ceiling . . . where its limitations became all too apparent.

Horned crown scraping the workshop rafters, Baal-Berith regarded its domain and decided, at once, to leave.

The demon shook out a testing leg, bending the floorboards with its cloven hoof. Head lowered, snout hissing, Baal-Berith charged like a bull and butted through the door. What was left of the workshop entrance tilted on a buckled hinge, clinging to the wood like a loosened tooth.

Inhaling the scent of its new dominion, the demon scoured

the night sky. In milk-pale moonlight, unrestricted and free to grow, Baal-Berith bulged once more. A crimson geyser of hell-red flesh ripped up from the earth. Towering over the workshop roof, the demon opened out its wings. Bewildered at first by this new addition, Baal-Berith warmed to chances of flight, the promise held by its new design.

To the heavy whip-crack of beating wings, hooves lifted from the path. Up and up, the demon soared, into the clear night sky. Above the rooftops of Silverweed Road, Baal-Berith cast its shadow, eyeing the sparkling cities beyond.

Black heart thudding to the beat of its wings, a grin sawed through its crocodile snout. The bone-white eyes of Baal-Berith glowed from the atrocious joys to come. Of towering over unclaimed villages. Of fistfuls moulded by its might. Of sweetest flesh squeezed like berries, dripping in its grip.

Look on my works, ye Mighty . . .
Who next?

Extract from The Silverweed Files, 24 November 2024

A personal blog by former Detective Chief Inspector Jim Heath. The views expressed do not reflect those of Kent Police nor the victims impacted by events.

I have no qualms naming names. They may have escaped disciplinary action, but Constables Greening and Mortlock have a lot to answer for. On the evening of 20 November 2019, the two officers responded to a missing person enquiry. After attempting to gain entrance to Geppetto Savini's workshop, Greening and Mortlock left no. 17 Silverweed to buy chips. When they returned twenty minutes later, Savini had fled the scene. Had they remained and done their job, the serial-killer would have been caught.

Thirty years of murder hardens the stomach. I did not buckle once from the abominable desecrations left by the Meadway Ripper, Peter Klint. And yet even I battled a wave of nausea when I first faced Savini's atrocities.

The extent of the injuries has never been made public. I reveal them now, not to satisfy some ghoulish urge, but as an appeal for help. Should any of the methods below be even remotely familiar, I would ask you to email me:

jhsilverweed@gmail.com. To preserve the dignity of the victims, I relate their injuries anonymously.

The right arm of Victim 1 had been dissected with such precision, the pathologist concluded the incisions could only have been achieved with an industrial laser. The flesh, organs and face of Victim 2 had been stripped from the skeleton in a manner likened to a piranhas' feeding frenzy. And the heads of Victims 3 and 4 had been, for want of a better word, 'welded' together.

None of these injuries were inflicted post-mortem. The victims were very much alive during the attacks. The murders were undoubtedly premeditated. Savini had previously practised his techniques on various sculptures and latex models. Chillingly, from the clay bust found on his work bench, Savini was planning to assassinate our glorious prime minister.

How a five foot tall special effects veteran could mutilate four victims in the space of seven hours remains a mystery. It is not only a crime beyond the realms of human decency. It is a crime beyond human ability.

Geppetto Savini's motivations are clear enough. He had been dismissed from the production of *Blood Astrum* and, in his ire, had stolen a latex bodysuit from Meadway Studios. The victims were simply trying to recover what was rightfully theirs. Tragically, they fell victim to a gore-obsessed lunatic so delusional he wished to turn his odious cinematic fantasies into reality.

Savini has not been seen since. And yet sightings persist of the latex demon suit he took with him – and have done for years. What is to be made of this so-called Mogon seen hovering above the sites of motorway pile-ups, industrial accidents, and war zones across the world?

From the blurred footage I have seen on YouTube, it is obvious that sick-minded individuals are paying homage to Savini by flying elaborate red balloons over sites where an atrocity has occurred. The depths people will go to for attention on social media never fail to astound me.

NO. 41:

Dust

On a pitch-black October morning, the cloak of night yet to recede, a front door opened at the dead-end of Silverweed Road. Breath powdering as it hit the cold air, Leo Harbinger emerged from no. 41, carrying the final rucksack. He opened the boot of his Audi Q7, punched a gap between the suitcases, rammed in the rucksack and turned towards the home he was so keen to escape. His moon-shaped face pinched in its centre. What the hell, fumed Leo, is she *doing* in there?

He followed the lights flash on and off, windows blinking in the dark. His wife's silhouette danced room to room, checking, double-checking, triple-checking . . .

Leo opened the car door, sank into the passenger seat, and glared at the dashboard clock: 4.49 a.m. How many times had he told her? Out on the road by 4.30. Leave early, beat the traffic, get a head start on the drive up to Scotland.

Leo stared through his reflection cast on the windscreen, down to the canyon of Silverweed Road. The toothed blocks of mock-Tudor houses as black as the sunless morning, he'd come to view their timber frames as iron bars, his neighbours as inmates in a suburban prison. No. 41 backed onto the Woods. The Harbingers had bought it thinking they'd be closer to nature. Instead, the Woods cast a permanent shadow over the house, its tangled branches clawing at the roof.

Leo felt for the burner phone concealed in his jacket, mind darkening to a bright new future. One last push. Just one last push and it would all be gone: the job at the estate agents, the hollow grind, the dank, oily winter mornings. He pictured himself on a golden beach, sun simmering, waves lapping, moaning softly as she . . .

A car door slammed.

'I'm *so* sorry.'

Flustered, breathless, aware they were running late, Pippa Harbinger climbed into the driver's seat. She jostled behind the steering wheel, dropped the key fob into the pedal well, swore, bent down, snatched the key, flicked on the windscreen wipers by mistake, turned on the indicators by mistake, lowered and raised an electric window, swore again, fired the ignition, clicked her seat belt, stamped on the clutch and bolted forward.

The Q7 stalled on the driveway. Pippa turned to her husband, offered an anxious smile.

'I suppose,' said Leo, 'we could always just walk to Scotland.'

'I'm *so* sorry,' Pippa repeated. She pinned her black hair into a ponytail and restarted the engine. Leo sank into his seat. The car crawled from the gravel driveway and purred down Silverweed Road.

Pippa watched their house fade in the rear-view mirror

as a fox flickered across the road. When the Audi curved into Valerian Way, her old world vanished, falling from view, swallowed by the jaws of a brand-new start.

Moon waning in a sun-bruised sky, stars dimming to dust, Pippa joined the M2 sliproad as Leo fussed with the radio. Her mind drifted from the lanes, back to early September, and her husband's surprise announcement. Back from work early for the first time in months, he'd handed her a road map after their evening meal, urged her to open it up. Scrawled on the map, in thick red marker, Leo had written HAPPY 10TH. She listened as her husband described a five-day tour of Scotland's Extreme North to mark their tenth wedding anniversary – hiking the Munros, exploring the inlets, chasing the waves on the white sand beaches. Leo had said something unusually poetic that had stuck in her mind: *we'll be stranded together in solitude* . . .

Pippa had been taken aback by the gesture. Last anniversary, Leo had grabbed last-minute flowers from the local garage, the carnations turning brown the next day. Perhaps their drifting marriage wasn't as lost as she thought. Perhaps Scotland would mark a fresh start. Reanimated by the trip, Pippa had shared Leo's roadmap online and started a countdown on social media.

Three more sleeps. Two more sleeps. One more sleep. No more sleep . . .

Pippa shook from wandering thoughts. The bonnet closed in on a looming black block.

'Brake!' shouted Leo, squirming in his seat.

The rear of a lorry closed in like a wall. Pippa hit the brakes. The Audi swayed to screaming car horns and crawled to a nervous cruise.

'I'm *so* sorry,' said Pippa, hands steadying the steering wheel.

Leo leaned over and slapped on the hazard lights.

'Pull over,' said Leo, pointing at the hard shoulder. 'I'll drive – before you get us both killed.'

Radio stations crackled from county to county as the Harbingers headed north. Six hours in, they crossed the border, leaving England behind. Leo took the sliproad into Gretna Green services. As Pippa queued at Starbucks, Leo vanished into the gents.

In the far end cubicle, out of sight, Leo unzipped a Nokia from a hidden jacket pocket, took off his shoe and felt for the SIM card concealed in his sock. He slipped in the SIM, powered up the phone and tapped out a text.

nrly there my QOS. 1 last push. dump phone x

The instant reply caused a rush of blood to his groin.

Leo snapped the SIM in two, flushed it down the toilet, and tossed the Nokia in the lavatory bin. When he met Pippa back at the car, he cracked the lid off a bottle of Glenfiddich stored in the glove compartment.

'You can drive the last leg,' Leo said, pouring whisky into his takeaway coffee.

'But there's six hours left,' protested Pippa. 'Swap over every two hours. That's what we agreed.'

Pippa's words fell on deaf ears. Within thirty minutes, Leo Harbinger was too drunk to drive.

When they arrived late evening at Lochinver, their fishing village base on the raised brow of the Highlands, Leo was so drunk he opened the door of their shepherd's bothy, fell starshaped onto the bed and passed out. Pippa warmed alone by the fire. 'Sutherland county will be empty this time of year,' he'd said. 'We can have it all to ourselves.' So far, thought Pippa, he was having their holiday all to himself, too.

Embers glowed under crackling wood. Pippa stared into the flames. There was a time when their marriage felt like an endless holiday, drunk on each other's adrenalin. Kayaking in the Kenai Fjords, skydiving off Fiji, snowboarding in the Alps . . . And Bolivia. God, Bolivia . . . Pippa winced as she recalled their honeymoon. Caught in a dust storm at the base of Mount Sajama, blinded on their trek to the summit, they were lost, delirious and dehydrated. Their honeymoon crumbled on the outskirts of La Paz, wheezing in hospital, their lungs full of sand. Pippa had been so rattled, she took out life insurance the moment they returned to Silverweed. Leo promised he'd do the same. Somehow, he kept forgetting.

The honeymoon was a disaster, but at least it was an adventure. Now, a trip to Tesco counted as a getaway. Now, she barely saw her husband, forever working late at the estate agents. Her thriving career as an engineering geologist had become a source of resentment: Leo bitter she was the main breadwinner, yet all too happy to spend her money.

Pippa glanced at Leo, star-shaped on the bed, then turned back to the fire, thoughts of a separation flickering. One last chance. Maybe the flames could be stoked again. Maybe tomorrow the ashes would fire. She curled into bed beside her husband. Moon-faced Leo snored like a warthog.

Ticking off sights on a tattered route map, over the next two days, Leo turned the sightseeing into a chase. Pippa, who'd anticipated a relaxed amble and snug pubs, followed her husband with dragging legs, the trip now a race through abandoned landscapes. They took a boat to the sea stacks of Handa, where once they buried the dead, safe from the mouths of the mainland wolves. They toured the fish farms of Badcall Bay. They watched the river seethe below Laxford Bridge. They did this. They saw that. They hiked and they marched, Leo pushing ahead, Pippa trailing behind, the trip now drawing the path of their marriage. Pippa's hope of reconciliation faded with every step.

After scaling the dunes of Sandwood Bay and hiking Cape Wrath, where the waves turned to smoke against the high black cliffs, a storm sent them back to their shepherd's bothy. That night, she dreamed of white clouds of kittiwakes in the low October sun. They shrieked and plunged into fists of waves, scattering to dust.

On day three, the Harbingers headed inland to Ben Hope – Scotland's northernmost Munro, renowned for its views of the bleak, wild Flow Country. It was here, Leo insisted, they would spend the morning hiking to the summit, followed by lunch at the Tongue Hotel.

As their Audi wound through narrowing roads, the wedge of Ben Hope arched from the peatlands like the fin of a surfacing humpback. At an imposing 3,000 feet, the lone Munro commanded the bowing landscape, king of the northern wilds – a fortress of rock with two low shoulders and a turreted crest known to locals as the Druid's Castle. Its reputation was as remorseless as the desolate moors it dwarfed. It was here, on its summit, that a Celtic cult once venerated the dead, sacrifices thrown screaming to a blazing pyre. Their burnt offerings to the mountain gods were said to rise from the ashes.

Leo drove into the empty car park, pulling in close to its only feature. A stark wooden sign read *Way Up Ben Hope*, indicating the steep, rocky path to the summit. Leo opened the boot while Pippa packed her rucksack. After last night's window-rattling storm, the clouds had thinned to pale stepping stones paving an ice-blue sky. A biting wind whipped off the Atlantic.

With her husband distracted, Pippa took out the card she'd written in the bathroom the previous night. In a thick, pink, fluffy font, the message on the front read: I Met You, I Liked You, I Love You, I've Got You. Hearing her husband approach, Pippa quickly zipped the card in her anorak pocket. The Harbingers hiked past the wooden sign and began to climb the path.

Leo romped ahead, a cool distance kept from his wife, occasionally turning to shout encouragement, his words lost to the wind. Pippa hiked the grass-scrubbed slopes, refusing to keep up with the stomping pace. She took in the crags that plunged from the path, and the fangs that spiked below.

Leo arrived at the summit's plateau, Pippa lagging behind. Set at waist-height, the concrete pillar of Ben Hope's trig point rose from a stack of jumbled stones. Breath slowing, Leo took in the panorama – a view he'd studied a hundred times, at every available angle.

Beyond the north ridge flowed a desolate wilderness, of peaks and lochs and pleated terrain, the silver Atlantic clawing the coastline. The summit, as expected, was deserted. Likewise, the moors below, not a building or a car to be seen for miles. Moulded by the skimming wind, Leo's anorak rippled and purled.

He stepped towards Ben Hope's northernmost crag,

walking boots perched over the drop. Walls of rock plum-
meted to powder. Exhilarated if short of breath, Pippa
arrived at the summit.

Leo carefully retreated from the drop, took out his phone
and marched towards his wife. Hands on her thighs, head
bowed, Pippa collected her breath.

'Come on,' said Leo. 'Let's get a selfie.'

Leo placed a rigid arm around his wife, raised the phone
and huddled in. Framed against wild rock and sky, the
Harbingers forced a smile. A button clicked. Pippa's tight
grin relaxed back to panting fatigue. Leo checked his phone
and pocketed it in his anorak.

'Check this out,' Leo urged, returning to the drop. 'Best
view on the summit. You can even see the Orkneys.'

'For God's sake, Leo,' said Pippa. 'It's not a race. Give
me time to get my breath back.'

'What is it? You a scaredy cat?' Leo began to taunt her.
'Scaredy cat. Scaredy cat . . .'

Pippa rolled her eyes and trudged over to the drop,
hoping a brief glance would silence her husband. For the
first time during their trip, it was Leo who loitered behind,
encouraging Pippa towards the edge. A playful tease of
'scaredy cat' slowed on his lips.

Teetering on the crest, Pippa took in the terrain. Leo
stretched his arms, moon face hardening. Mesmerised by
the view, Pippa reached for the zip on her red jacket pocket.
A perfect moment to present the card.

Without saying a word or so much as a goodbye, Leo
pushed Pippa from the edge of Ben Hope.

Feet scrabbling on wet, black rock, Pippa grabbed the
sleeve of Leo's anorak. Horrified at the sudden contact, Leo
scraped at the fingers on his thrashing sleeve.

One foot slipping on the rock, the other hanging over the precipice, her body sloping and seized by gravity, Pippa let out a raptor scream so fierce, so sharp, it pierced through the summit, absorbed by the walls of the Druid's Castle.

Awoken by the sound, the north ridge stirred.

A force gathered, ancient, unseen, capturing its sacrifice. In every rock and every stone, every pebble and its ageless dust, her anguish was stored, the pain absorbed, a memory held. Pippa's scream soaked into the summit.

Scrubbing wildly at Pippa's grip, Leo, who had pictured in his fantasies a compliant, speechless death, found himself uttering, in ice-cold mockery, his wife's own words.

Leo said: 'I'm so sorry.'

He didn't mean a word of it.

Leo watched her body plunge. Pippa's limbs swam wildly against the wind. In the snap of adrenalin, time, sound and motion slowed. For a moment, Pippa appeared to howl back towards him: black hair snaking, white eyes raging, screams pouring from a widening mouth.

Closer. Closer. Close enough to kiss . . .

A fang of rock intervened. Body snapped into an appalling V, Pippa plunged into the abyss and crashed against the stones.

Leo peered back over the ledge at the red dust that was once his wife, marking the walls of the Druid's Castle. He waited three minutes in case of further screams, then retired to the trig point to catch his breath. Pulling down the sleeve that held the ghost of her grip in its folds, he triggered his emergency beacon.

When the Coastguard helicopter soared into view, black blades slicing through the clouds, Leo waved from the summit. He began his shallow breathing exercises, evacuating his lungs, increasing his heartbeat, remembering the steps of the YouTube tutorial, Fake Cry The Easy Way. Slowly, cynically, he worked himself up into a weeping wreck.

Sleeve aside, it had gone like a dream.

In the stark grey interview room, he emptied a Nile of crocodile tears as a pair of old detectives sat nodding. 'I could have saved her,' Leo repeated, his moon face a plate of gooey distress. He volunteered his phone to the Highland Police, surrendered his car keys to forensics, offered the clothes he'd worn on the summit. Between sobbing breakdowns, coldly aware he was the only witness, a story of futile heroism unfolded: Pippa walking to the edge, a foot slipping on wet rocks, his hand reaching, her grip slipping, a sudden plunge into the black. Her screams, her screams . . .

Alone in the interview room during a break, Leo caught snatches of conversation, beyond the walls in the corridor. Out of nowhere, the two old detectives who had nodded in silence broke out into song. Their voices were soon joined by others, as if they wished to be overheard. Stifling his laughter, Leo's gut began to tighten as the dirge repeated, gathering in volume . . .

> *O'er auld Ben Hope, a lass did faw*
> *Bide a wee, bogle, bide*
> *What did ye wrang, a lass did faw*
> *Bide a wee, bogle, bide*
> *O'er auld Ben Hope, a lass did faw*
> *Druid's craig wi' come for ye*
> *Bide a wee, bogle, bide*

On their return, Leo had faltered, unsure how to interpret the unblinking detectives' stare: suspicious yet satisfied, implying they too held a secret. 'Druid's Castle claimed another,' they had said in unison. 'Druid's Castle claimed another . . .'

When the pathologist found no signs of foul play, the Highland Police yielded to the evidence presented. The smiling selfie moments before the fall, the wedding anniversary trip, the slippery rocks from the previous night's storm: the police declared death by misadventure.

Before he left Sutherland, the detectives handed Leo the card they'd found in Pippa's anorak pocket, accepted with sobs of gratitude. Dumbfounded by the negative perfection of his wife's gesture, Leo could barely believe his good fortune. The perfect murder as romantic tragedy, he the heartbroken husband, watching his wife plunge on their wedding anniversary. He read the card and danced inside: 'I met you, I liked you, I love you, I've got you . . .'

On the drive back to Silverweed Road, enjoying the Audi all to himself, Leo stopped at Gretna Green services and found himself ordering coffee for two. He dropped the extra cup in a car park bin. From M6 to M2, a growing unease pinched at Leo's new-found freedom – that a presence brooded within the car, escorting him all the way home.

Furtive eyes flicked from windscreen to passenger seat. Dust marked the cloth where Pippa once sat.

On the morning of Pippa's funeral, Leo skipped downstairs, whistling Tom Petty's 'Free Fallin'', and cooked himself a fried breakfast. Dread mingled with relief, agony tangled with ecstasy. The dread of Pippa's friends and family. The relief of his final public performance. The agony of professing his sham love for Pippa. The ecstasy of his impending prosperity: £500,000 in life insurance, and a new life in the sun.

After his fry-up, Leo burped and reached into the fridge. He uncapped a bottle of Volvic and forced down a litre in one continuous gulp. With all the fake tears he'd be squeezing out, it was important, figured Leo, to stay hydrated.

Waiting for the hearse to arrive, Leo straightened his tie before the mirror above the fireplace, admiring the cut of his Armani funeral suit. His eyes drifted to Pippa's card, now framed and laminated, pride of place on the mantelpiece. Her death and his innocence on public display.

Upstairs, in the locked bathroom, Leo loosened a plank behind the sink and powered up his latest burner phone. A text message flashed on the screen.

miss u, want u, how long now? QOS xxx

A sombre knock on the front door interrupted his reply. Leo began his shallow breathing and fake-cried the easy way. Soon the lounge was black with mourners, gasping softly at the laminated card. When the cortège left at 11 a.m. and passed the crash flower shrine, Leo glanced from his funeral car. Perched on the flickering lamp post, a jackdaw glared. Held by the shine of silver eyes, Leo felt a flickering chill, as if a heartbeat had been stolen. With a flick of the wings and a cry of *ack-ack*, the jackdaw soared above Silverweed Road. She slowly circled the crawling cortège, casting her shadow on Pippa's hearse.

The hour-long service at the cremation chapel felt as if it would never end. Having only written half of Pippa's eulogy, Leo broke down midway through his delivery as planned, tearfully introducing 'Free Fallin'' by Tom Petty, picked by Leo on Pippa's behalf, intended to recall their first skydive together. Pippa had always hated the song.

As Leo watched the curtains close and Pippa's coffin descend, a whispered dirge crept through Mahler's 'Adagietto', growing in volume as it seeped into his head:

O'er auld Ben Hope, a lass did faw, Bide a wee, bogle, bide . . .

Pippa Harbinger took six hours to fade in the incinerator chamber. Figuring an hour would do the job, the cremation technician stared in bemusement. He checked and rechecked the emission system, looking at his watch, willing on the heat, growing ever more baffled by her resistance.

It was as if her body were made of stone.

As if this one didn't want to go.

'How long does she have to be here for?'

'Can't we just celebrate, Sheena? It's the first time we've seen each other since Scotland.'

'And it's been five weeks since her funeral. How is she still here? It still feels like there's three of us.'

'Are you seriously telling me,' laughed Leo, 'you're jealous of an urn? It's just her bones in a jar.'

Leo poured himself a glass of Veuve Clicquot and glanced at the urn on the mantelpiece. Cast in a sombre blue with the white stencilled outline of a mountain, Leo had personalised Pippa's urn: another thoughtful touch should any relatives threaten to visit. A memory, he'd say, of when they'd snowboarded in the Alps. When he'd sent his design to the urn etcher, Leo had described, in detail, the jagged ridge of Ben Hope. Pippa's urn wasn't a memorial. It was a reminder for him not to slip up.

'She'd better not be coming to Australia with us, Leo. When does the money come in?'

'Sent off the claim after the cremation. Be patient, Queen of Sheena. Be patient.'

'Patient? Took for ever for you to man up and finally get shot of her.'

Leo looked into Sheena's dark, almond eyes. Face still flushed from sex on the sofa, her new purple dress now creased, Sheena's hair had changed since they'd last seen each other, now a square black bob that shone like liquorice.

'What was I supposed to do? Push her off Ben Hope, then get straight on the phone to the life insurance? I'm not going to be that idiot, Sheena. We stick to the plan and wait – last thing I need is the police sniffing round.'

'Why? You're innocent.'

'Yeah, I am,' laughed Leo. 'Those weirdoes at the Highland Police thought the mountain killed her. Can you believe that? It's like something out of *The Wicker Man* up there: they were actually *singing* about it. How did it go? "Bide a wee, bogle . . ."'

Sheena snapped up her phone and googled.

'Bogle,' she read. 'Spirit. Object of fear and loathing.' She frowned at Pippa's urn. 'The loathing bit sounds about right.'

Leo ran a playful finger up Sheena's leg, trying to recapture her attention. He leaned in for a kiss – soft at first, then wet and greedy. The urn looked on as their mouths churned. Sheena broke from the kiss and took a slug of champagne.

'I swear that thing's staring at me,' said Sheena, eyes on the urn again. 'You could at least fill it with sand. *She* doesn't have to be in there.'

'What if her parents ask to scatter some of her ashes?'

'Have a barbecue and save some of the charcoal. Who's going to know?'

Leo rolled his eyes. Six months it had taken them to plot Pippa's demise. The burner phones, the SIM cards, the secret meetings after work, Sheena's fake crying lessons. It was Sheena, not Leo, who'd discovered Ben Hope – remote, precarious, with a tempting history of tragic falls, their callous hearts warming to its potential.

'She's gone, Sheena. Let it go.'

Sheena shook off her heels and padded over to the mantel-piece. She snatched up the urn, turned to Leo, tossing it from palm to palm, as if preparing a ball of dough to be flattened.

'Sheena, *please*,' said Leo, half laughing.

Sheena blew a kiss and threw the urn in the air. She feigned missing the catch altogether, snatching the urn as it passed her hips.

'Oopsy.'

'Seriously, Sheena,' said Leo, smile fading, his tone firming. 'Put it back.'

Urn tucked under her arm like a rugby ball, Sheena staggered over to the coffee table, took a slug from the champagne, and emptied the bottle in one gluttonous swig, shaking out the final drips on her tongue. She winked at Leo, twirled around and tottered back to the mantelpiece.

'Bet you didn't know I used to be in the majorettes.'

'I said put—'

Leo watched Sheena toss the urn into the air. The lid rattled as it pitched up to the ceiling. He followed its descent, tumbling down. Sheena twirled on stockinged toes. Her black bob whirled. Her arms swung out.

The lounge froze to an ominous crack.

Finding her balance, Sheena stared, hand over her mouth, trying to stifle her laughter. Powdered bone spilled on the fireplace tiles. Smoke curled from the impact. The ceramic urn had snapped in two. Leo bolted up from the sofa through a cloud of glittering ash.

'It's not funny,' said Leo, scooping up the ashes. 'That cost me £600.'

'You can always get another,' shrugged Sheena. 'She can pay for it when her life insurance comes in.'

Leo poured Pippa into the cracked urn. He fumbled the pieces onto the mantelpiece, struggling to unite the urn's halves, as if reassembling an egg.

'Where's your hoover?' Sheena said, coughing through the dust.

'I'll deal with her tomorrow,' said Leo, leaving the split urn on the mantelpiece. 'Come on, let's go to bed. I want to have some fun.'

As they stumbled upstairs to the bedroom, a dust cloud swirled in the lounge. In glittering silence, it crossed the threshold and traced their shadows up the steps. Circling in the darkness, the ghost of a chant hissed and whispered, shivering into the walls: *What did ye wrang, a lass did faw . . . Bide a wee bogle, bide . . .*

At 10 a.m., Leo awoke with a pinching hangover. He groaned into his pillow, scratched the sleep dust from his eyes and lifted his head. The sunless bedroom was dark as ash: lights out and blackout curtains closed.

Sheena, whose body had been curled around his when they'd drifted off after chaotic, drunken sex, was sleeping on her side, facing the bedside table. Leo gave her a playful, slightly mean prod.

Sheena didn't respond. Leo edged up his pillow, struck by the awkward position she was sleeping in. Her stumpy toes, painted cherry red, poked from the side of the bed. Leo followed her feet to the ridge of her legs buried beneath the duvet. Sheena's body appeared bent, legs angled like clock hands set at 9.45. Leo shuffled closer, nestling his nose into her nape. Her perfume had faded, as had her familiar scent.

'I'm starving,' he breathed into her bob. 'When you cooking me breakfast?'

Leo waited for a response. Head patting from his champagne hangover, irritated he was being ignored, he clapped his hands twice and moved in for a tickle. *This will snap her from her sleep. This will snap her from her dreams . . .* Flesh pressed flesh. Leo flinched. Anxious hands retreated.

Sheena's skin felt hard and cool as marble. Where was her heat? The embrace he craved? In the murk of the bedroom, Leo peeled back the duvet.

Sheena lay motionless, her body snapped in an appalling V – legs rigid, waist like an open hinge. Cogged bones bumped down her spine, swelling from her skin like knuckles. Shrouded by her black bob, Sheena faced the bedside table, and a glass of water beside the lamp.

'Sheena?'

Leo moved closer. He slid a hand beneath her pillow. There was a dull crackle of neck bone grinding neck bone. Her head rolled slowly on the pillow. Leo recoiled against the headboard.

Sheena's face was a stone-grey mask. Lips, once soft and full, had been thinned and reshaped, a taut ring circling a chasm of mouth. Her face froze in a silent scream.

Forced against the headboard, arms hugging his knees,

Leo found himself plunging into the pit of her mouth. His stomach flipped from a rapid descent. *I'm falling in a dream. I'm not awake. I'm not awake . . .*

Leo shook himself together. He uncoiled from the headboard and pressed his head to Sheena's chest. He frantically searched for the beat of her heart, his ear cool against marbled skin. He heard nothing but the thud of his own pulse.

Facing Sheena's cherry red toes, Leo felt a watery trickle begin to brush through his hair: a creeping, steady pitter-patter tickling his scalp, pouring like grain down the back of his neck. He lifted his head and turned to face Sheena.

From the chasm of her mouth, dust poured like liquid stone – a streaming tongue of powdered ash, spilling over lifeless lips. It flicked to the bedsheets with a sandy hiss. Her face was blank as a fountain statue, the mouth gushing grey water.

Leo leaped from the bed, hands raking through his hair. The bedroom air misted with dust. The walls of a nightmare closing in, Leo clamped his eyes shut, willing the vision to go away. There was a chest-deep cough. A gritty hack. Now a rasping gasp for breath.

Leo opened his eyes. The bed lifted into life. Sheena heaved up from the sheets, air hissing from emptying lungs. Her eyes rolled to the back of her skull, gazing into the heavens. With a blunt thud, she fell back to the bed, sending dust clouds into the air. Leo lunged for his phone on the dressing table.

Ambulance. 999. What do I say? What has she done? It wasn't me. It wasn't me . . .

He flicked the case, swiped at the screen. The smooth, slick motion, of skin gliding glass, felt ragged to the touch.

His finger bumped over the surface. Leo swiped again, faster this time, felt his fingernail scrape and grate. He looked closer at the phone. Coating the touchscreen was a layer of grit. Leo snatched a sock from the bedroom floor, rubbed furiously at the dust. The stubborn layer stood ominously firm.

Leo dropped his phone, searched for Sheena's. Frantic eyes settled on a glass of water, sparkling on the bedside table, a slim black block beside it. When he seized her phone and flipped open the case, Leo's nightmare doubled. The screen was coated in the same gritty layer: a blank sheet of bone-grey dust.

Hopping into jogging bottoms, hoodie wrestled over his head, Leo charged downstairs towards the front door.

Get out, get help. Knock on some doors. Wake the neighbours. They'll call an ambulance, and . . .

Leo pulled the latch, expecting the door to swing open. His efforts was met with a stiff resistance. He shook the deadbolt, metal clunking, and again, pulled at the door. Only then did he see it. The pencil-thin line of grey, filling the edges of the door frame. Somebody – something – somehow – had sealed the door shut.

In the murk of the hallway, Leo ran a finger around the door frame. The grey seal was packed tight as cement. A testing scrape gathered into a frenzied clawing. He scraped at the seal, as if filing his nails on an emery board. Not a grain of powder loosened to his touch.

I'm still asleep. I'm not awake. A dream, a nightmare. It has to be . . .

Leo lifted the letter box, cleared his throat and screamed for help. His call was absorbed, blocked from reaching the outside world. Leo fed a hand into the letter box. His fingers met an airtight square – a slab of compacted stone. Beat by beat, each strike more desperate than the last, Leo hammered his fists at the door frame until his knuckles were raw and bloodied. It was like using a spoon to break a brick.

When he rushed into the sunless kitchen, the nightmare swiftly followed. Leo lunged at the back door handle, pushed, pulled, stepped back in disbelief. Once again, his escape was blocked, denied by a grey seal lining the frame. Circling the kitchen, he raked at his hair, clouds of dust choking the air. Leo turned to the window.

He leaped onto the worktop. The slats rattled as he pulled open the blind. Anticipating a burst of sunlight, Leo found himself staring, not at his reflection or the fresh green lawn, but a remorseless block of stony grey. Squeezed in the vice of a tightening mania, Leo tumbled off the worktop, seized a kitchen chair and hurled it against the slab. There was a sickening crack of wood hitting rock. Legs splintered from the impact. The chair snapped to the kitchen floor.

Room to room, Leo raced in a vortex of panic. With every flash of curtain, with every clack of a shutter, his heart pinched to block after block of impenetrable grey: each and every window a remorseless wall of stone. Once a prisoner of Silverweed Road, Leo was now captive in his own home.

Curled in a ball in the upstairs bathroom, door locked and the light dim, Leo shut his eyes, willing the nightmare to get up and leave. His mind whipped and flashed, chaotic and slippery, each thought falling before it could be caught. *Need to get out. Check on Sheena. Call for help. What has she done? They'll think it's me. It's not my fault. It wasn't me. It wasn't me.*

His vindictive hangover screamed for attention. What was once a soft pulsing headache stamped across his temples, his mouth crackling and paper-dry. At the mercy of his pleading thirst, Leo uncurled from the bathroom floor, snapped two codeine from the medicine cabinet and turned on the tap.

Head bowed at the sink, he answered his thirst, relishing the curing rush of water. He lapped and gasped and drank and gulped and . . . heaved and coughed and spluttered and hacked. Leo pulled away from the sink, tongue squirming like a salted worm. The sharp grit that danced in his mouth furred his gums and itched his teeth, coating his lips like paste. It was as if he'd swallowed a pint of sand.

Leo stared in horror at the gushing tap, a rushing stream of smoking dust. Grit crackled as it struck the basin, the plughole a swirling pit of powder. Leo retched and clawed at his mouth, spitting dust into the sink.

The bathroom door shook to a hard, firm knock.

Leo wiped the grit from this mouth. He turned towards the door. Another knock, firmer this time. It was not a knock that searched for an invitation. It was a knock that tested the strength of the door. A knock before something broke through.

'Sheena?'

The lock rattled in reply. Trickling under the door, seeping from the walls, a whispered chant hissed through the bathroom. The dirge he'd heard as Pippa's coffin descended. The dirge that he'd heard from the Highland Police. The dirge he was not yet sure lay within his head or ushered from the house itself.

What did ye wrang, a lass did faw . . . Bide a wee bogle, bide . . .

The chant died and vanished like smoke. Another knock. The door lock rattled. Leo cleared his throat. A soup of grit still coated his mouth. His voice had corroded to a frog-like croak.

'Sheena? Is that you?'

The knocking stopped. Leo slid the lock. The bathroom door creaked open. He peeked through the gap.

The empty landing was dark as ash. No Sheena. No shadows. No sense of sound or motion.

Water. Need water. Dehydrated. Delirious. Bolivia. Like Bolivia. Dust storm. Happened then. Happening again. Water. Need water . . .

Leo pictured a bottle of Volvic cooling in the fridge. Consumed by his raging thirst, he stumbled down the stairs. In the murk of the kitchen, Leo opened the fridge. Moon face bathed in cool white light, he seized the bottle of Volvic. His dry lips smacked in anticipation.

Welcoming the curing rush of water, Leo unscrewed the cap. He lifted the Volvic to his lips. The bottle felt heavy as stone.

Palm out, he tipped the bottle. Dust poured like twisting sand, crackling between his fingers. His body now screaming *water, water,* Leo threw the Volvic to the floor. Dust poured with a gritty hiss, spilling onto the tiles. He circled the kitchen in his despair, raking his hair, when . . . *Sheena. The glass. The bedside table . . .* Leo thundered back upstairs.

He froze outside the bedroom. His eyes searched through the murk, widening on an empty bed. Sheets held the shape of Sheena's body, a sunken pillow from the ghost of her head. The burn in Leo's throat returned. His eyes now darted to the bedside table. The glass of water had gone.

In the madness of his thirst, Leo ransacked the bedroom,

searching not for Sheena, but for his precious glass of water.

Leo jumped to a knock on the bedroom door.

She leaned against the door frame, back straight, standing upright on cherry red toes. Sheena smiled a familiar smile, playful and mischievous. A glass of water shimmered in her hand.

Through the blackout curtains, there was a sudden burst of blinding light. Dust particles danced like glitter. The bedroom began to sparkle. Whatever darkness had coated his existence, Leo warmed to the heat of a nightmare fading, awakening, at last, to the shine of reality. He shaded his eyes, blinked through the light: first to his lover, unharmed and unbroken, then to his glass of cool, refreshing water.

'Sheena . . .'

Leo took a step towards the door, eyes flicking between the water and his lover. His panic softened in the creamy morning light.

Not mad. Not hallucinating. Pressure. It's the pressure. All that stress on the mountain. All those months staying strong . . . I'll drink that water and she'll cook me breakfast and we'll fuck and we'll laugh and I'll tell Sheena about this terrible dream and . . .

Leo took another step. His tongue crackled over his lips. He stared at the glass of shimmering water. Sheena laughed her husky laugh and retreated from the door. All that remained was a teasing arm. The glass rocked gently in her hand, tempting him from the bedroom. Leo shook his head. A woozy smile crept through his face: Queen of Sheena and her games . . .

Her laughter dried. A hand tipped. The glass fell and smashed to the floor.

By the time Leo had yelled and tripped, Sheena's arm had vanished from the doorway. The creamy light that had blessed the bedroom sank to powdered murk. On hands and knees, he grovelled towards the glass, cracked in two like an egg. He watched in horror as his water shrank, swallowed by the carpet. Set on all fours, nose pressed to the floor, Leo sucked at the fading liquid, like a warthog at the dregs of a waterhole.

Wiping his mouth, his tongue furred with fibre and dust, Leo twisted to his feet. The brief, sweet relief he'd tasted soured in a flash. Waves of husky mocking laughter rose within the house. Incensed by Sheena's cruel prank, Leo stepped from the bedroom into the landing. By the banister at the top of the stairs, a laughing shadow swayed.

'That wasn't funny, Sheena,' Leo fumed. His moon face pinched as he approached. 'Get me some fucking water.'

The smile slid from Sheena's face. The husky laughter died on her lips. Her almond eyes softened with remorse. Before he could say another word, her arms had wrapped around him.

The dust, the darkness, his madness and his thirst: all seemed to melt in the moment of contact. Savouring the sudden warmth, Leo surrendered to her embrace, absorbing her heat, relishing her scent, lost to his lover's touch.

After all the fake tears, the months of weeping that had dried him to a husk, Leo began to sob for himself, the pressure whimpering from his dust-caked lips. Her arms folded tighter around him, hugging him ever closer.

As his hands ran softly down her back, Sheena's warmth began to fade. Leo felt a bump emerge. Now another. Another. Another. Sheena's spine began to loosen, as a chain of cogs chased down her back. Her body sagged like an emptying sack. Bone clicked against bone. Sheena's arms coiled around his waist. Her tightening grip was hard as stone.

A whispering chant hissed from her lips and slithered in his ear.

Bide a wee, bogle, bide . . .

Leo lifted his head from her chest. The soft smile gone, the skin like marble. Her mouth widened into a silent scream.

Entombed within a coiled embrace, the grip stone-hard and frighteningly cold, Leo scrabbled to set himself free. The chant continued, the lips unmoving, echoing from the pit of a gaping mouth. Leo felt the breath squeeze from his chest. He gathered whatever strength remained, and with a wild thrash of his arms, unchained himself from her grasp.

Without saying a word or so much as a goodbye, Leo pushed Sheena from the top of the stairs.

There was no unplucking of fingers this time. No scrabbling escape from the descent. A clawing hand claimed Leo's arm, and clasped around his wrist. Seized by gravity, his balance slipped. Ensnared in a merciless stone-cold grip, Leo Harbinger plunged.

They tumbled down the stairs as one, bodies locked in a twisting embrace. Leo let out a scream so fierce, so sharp, it pierced through the walls of no. 41.

They landed with a crunch in the murky hallway. The impact crushed the air from Leo's lungs. Sheena lay in silence, her stone-cold grip unbroken. Gasping like a landed fish, head still swimming from the fall, Leo felt her arms slither, drawing him back to a crushing embrace.

Breath tearing from his lungs, he unknotted himself from the web of limbs and stumbled to his feet. Leaning against the hallway wall, he looked upon the marbled body, square black bob shrouding its face. Whatever it was that had shared his bed. Whatever it was that had spilled his water. Whatever it was that had pulled him from the stairs, it was not his Queen of Sheena.

Whatever it was, it wanted him gone. And Leo Harbinger, who had killed before, pledged to do so again.

Cold, grey fingers clenched his ankle. Before he could turn, before he could kick, before he could stamp or lash or strike, Leo was dragged back to the floor.

His head connected with a sickening crack. Foot locked in a pitiless grip, Leo roared with pain. Flint-sharp nails sliced at his ankles, digging through his flesh. Now it was seeking a more permanent hold. Leo pressed his hands to the floor. In rolling heaves, he wormed on his belly, winching himself towards the lounge.

Leo felt his skin unglove around his ankle. He clawed the floor and passed the door. Nails sank further into flesh, seeking tendons, seeking bone. Leo let out a scream of pain and dragged his tormenter into the lounge. His darting eyes met a champagne bottle cast upon on the floor. Leo lunged, grasped the neck and turned towards a marbled body.

Those eyes . . . That mouth . . . It's not Sheena . . . It's not her . . .

He stared into the pit of a mouth. From lifeless lips, a whispering dirge began to hiss. *Bide a wee, bogle, bide . . .* Leo gripped the bottle, raised his arm and struck the head with force. The body quivered from the impact. Its hold around his ankle loosened. Nails slid from the wound. Inviting his rage, Leo raised his arm once more. The champagne bottle blurred and struck, blurred and struck. A split broke through a black bob. The skull cracked like a flower pot.

Leo struggled to his feet and stared down at the body. His eyes burned in his moon-shaped face, with the sudden heat of victory.

It started with a trickle.

Deep within the open wound, dust began to bubble and spill. It crackled from the fissured skull and pooled around the head. Leo jumped to a sharp bang. The door to the lounge slammed shut. Corner to corner, now up the sides, crackling dust drew around the frame, sealing Leo to his fate.

What had started as a trickle now began to gush. Dust gulped from the open wound. Leo skittered from the body, watching the powder crawl and gather. It perceived his heat and rushed towards him, swelling across the floor. On it poured, from the opened skull, racing like a chasing tide, seeking the corners of the room, splashing into walls. Now the dust crashed at his feet, pecking at his flesh. Leo leaped onto the sofa to escape the biting wave.

Shipwrecked by the heaving ashes, Leo shook on the sofa. He watched in terror as Sheena's body was swallowed by the surge. It sank into a sea of powder, vanishing from view. A whispering dirge climbed the walls and seeped into the lounge.

The Druid's craig wi' come for ye . . . Bide a wee, bogle, bide

And still the dust rose.

Leo clamped his hands to his ears. The ceaseless crackle of powdered bone sizzled in his head. The waves of ash reached his shelter, climbing ever upwards. Leo clambered on the back of the sofa, clinging to the mast of a sinking ship.

And still the dust rose.

An ominous crack sounded from above. Leo's eyes darted to the ceiling. A light bulb filled and bulged, shattering to powder. Ash showered like winter rain. Hands snapped above his head, arms thrashing in the pouring dust, Leo screamed for mercy, screamed for help, drenched in a tide of biting bone.

And still the dust rose.

Sofa sinking in the rising ashes, Leo's legs were claimed by the surge. Soaring from below, showering above, grains of bone ripped and tore, pecking at his flesh. Now the ashes claimed his torso, snapping at his chest. Arms claimed, torso sunk, the liquid bone sought Leo's neck.

Within the churning swarm of ashes, the surface began to bubble and heave. At the room's far end, by the mantelpiece, the sea of powder spiralled. The borders sank like hourglass sand. Leo whimpered at the whirling pit. A shape birthed from its core. Like a clawing corpse from an open grave, an ashen figure rose.

'Pi—'

The name barely hissed from his throat. Crackling through the sea of dust, a seething shadow closed in on Leo. Its face was set, a mask of ash, like a final memory. A mouth gaped. Eyes raged. Powdered hair snaked and billowed, pulled by the winds of a fierce descent. It looked upon Leo in fury and disgust. Closer. Closer. Close enough to kiss.

'It was a mistake,' rasped Leo. 'I swear on my life, it was a mistake. It wasn't me, I didn't mean to. It's you I love, Pippa. It's you. I can't live without you, I can't live . . .'

Leo Harbinger's final words trembled to nothing: pleading, weak and wretched. Pippa devoured his horror, savouring the fear in his eyes. Mouth frozen in a raptor scream, she pressed her lips to his.

Her wrecking kiss tore his soul apart.

Leo's tongue crumbed into flesh. Dust and bone rushed and ripped, charging down his throat. In every bone and every cell, every muscle and every nerve, her anguish burned, the pain absorbed, a memory held, a fall shared.

She pulled back from his peeling lips, eye glowing in a mask of ash.

Three words rasped from dripping lips.

I'm . . . so . . . sorry.

She didn't mean a word of it.

Detective Chief Inspector Heath ducked under the police tape. He crunched past an Audi on the gravel driveway, his pace heavy and measured. Fourteen stone and six foot two, with a grey scrape of receding hair and probing deep-set eyes, Heath's intimidating presence seemed to arrive ahead of him, like the clouds of a rolling storm. Guarding the front door of no. 41, Constable Greening watched the DCI approach. Heath briefly looked to the sky, noted, yet again, a black bird circling above the house, as a vulture would a corpse. He turned his gaze on Greening.

'Who made the call?'

'Next-door neighbour,' said Greening, pointing at the driveway of no. 39. 'Heard a commotion coming through the walls. Reported a burglary – waited three hours before they phoned it in.'

'And you were first on the scene?'

Greening nodded, Adam's apple bobbing, still pale from what he'd witnessed inside. 'Doesn't look like a burglary to me, sir.'

'I'll do my job,' said Heath, 'and you do yours.'

Greening stepped away from the front door. The putrid

scent from the house still lingered in his nostrils – a deathly odour that reminded him of rotten cabbage and overripe cheese. What had that monster *done* in there? Measuring Heath's brusque mood, he couldn't resist adding a word of caution.

'It's a bit of a mess in there.'

Heath grunted, snapping on his latex gloves. He bent down, slipped on his overshoes and stepped through the front door. Heath's nose pinched at a familiar scent.

Marked by a broken circle of blue evidence tape, a patch of dried blood pooled in the hallway. Heath's eyes followed the white tape climbing up the stairs. Rustling in a white Tyvek suit, John Kirkland, the crime scene manager, appeared from the kitchen at the end of the hallway. The two nodded.

'Two dead,' said Kirkland. 'One male, one female.'

'Any signs of forced entry?' asked Heath, mindful of the neighbour's burglary call.

'It's the opposite, if anything,' said Kirkland. 'Seems like they were trying to escape from the house: cracked windows, dents on the inside of the front door. See here?'

Kirkland pointed to the nicks and dips, the impact of hammering fists.

'The door was unlocked,' Kirkland continued. 'Back door, too. Nothing was keeping the occupants from leaving the house.'

'Show me them,' said Heath.

Tyvek suit crackling like radio static, Kirkland led Heath to the lounge. Overshoes balanced on stepping plates that paved the room, Heath surveyed the crime scene. Beneath the fireplace, a woman lay like an abandoned doll. A head-wound gaped from a square black bob, a milky bubble of brain exposed. She lay face down in a pool of blood, thick and treacle dark.

Heath exhaled heavily at the chaos of spatter patterns sprayed around the living room, every surface dusted in blood: the walls, the carpet, the upturned coffee table . . . He briefly acknowledged the male body slumped by the sofa, returned his attention to the female and a blood-stained bottle of champagne.

'Use this, did he?' said Heath, pointing to the bottle.

'The head injury's post-mortem,' said Kirkland. 'Cause of death is a broken back. Do you have a bike?'

'Do I look like a cyclist, John?'

'No, I don't suppose you do. Her spine: it's loose as a bicycle chain. I would say she fell down the stairs, but . . .' Kirkland paused, weighing the absurdity of what he was about to say. 'It's more like she fell off a cliff.'

Heath nodded, turned to the male body propped against the sofa, head tipped back, staring at the ceiling.

'And the male?'

'House owner. A Mr Leo Harbinger. Covered head to toe in scratches, lesions on his left ankle. He choked to death.'

'On what?'

'That's his ex-wife,' said Kirkland, pointing to the broken urn on the mantelpiece. Heath studied the grey dust caked around Leo's lips.

What is it with this road? thought Heath. *First the car crash on the corner, that barking lunatic from no. 9, the gardener going missing from no. 31 . . . And now this. What kind of monster would do that? What kind of monster would drink his dead wife's ashes?*

Heath bent down and stared into the pale moon of Leo

Harbinger: the mouth slopped open, lips coated with a soup of ashes, like a baby refusing purée. The eyes were white and frozen. Heath had seen the look before, some twenty years ago. The eyes of the victims of Peter Klint: the sadistic Meadway Ripper. If he were a superstitious man, he'd say the man died of terror.

Heath glanced over to the empty urn on the mantelpiece, cracked in two like an eggshell.

'One more thing you should see,' said Kirkland.

Tyvek suit rustling, Kirkland led Heath into the kitchen, overshoes sloshing on sodden tiles. A broken chair lay in a pool of water beside a bottle of uncapped Volvic. The kitchen window was webbed with cracks.

Kirkland pointed to the white worktop. 'What do you make of this?'

Heath squinted at a message written in blood. The words were underlined with a rugged streak that somehow looked familiar.

'Everywhere else, the blood has clotted,' Kirkland added. 'This is almost fresh.'

'Romeo, back there,' said Hughes. 'Blood on his fingers?'

Kirkland nodded.

'Can't be him,' grunted Heath. His mind crackled from the crime scene: the dented door, the wife's ashes, the look of terror, the blood spattered like dust . . . Nothing added up.

'He didn't choke to death, get up, waltz into the kitchen, write this in his blood, then lie back down in the living room,' said Heath. 'Not unless he's Lazarus.'

Heath looked again at the message on the worktop. 'I'm so sorry,' he read out loud, puzzling over the words. The lettering was sane and calm and neat, written, he deduced, by a feminine hand. His deep-set eyes narrowed on the unbroken line, like the jagged outline of a mountain. Thoughts turned to the urn in the lounge.

In the frozen frenzy of the crime scene, particles of dust began to sparkle and whirl. Ashes danced in the still kitchen air, glittering like distant stars.

Heath continued to stare at the message, growing ever more certain of one telling detail.

Whoever had written 'I'm so sorry' hadn't meant a word of it.

Extract from The Silverweed Files, 27 November 2024

A personal blog by former Detective Chief Inspector Jim Heath. The views expressed do not reflect those of Kent Police nor the victims impacted by events.

By the time the deaths of 41 Silverweed were reported, Meadway Police were at breaking point. Nobody had slept. The crimes kept coming. The Incident Room resembled a circus of plate spinners. My superiors began to panic. Appalling decisions were made.

It beggars belief. Since there were no further victims and no perpetrator to pursue, Leo Harbinger was charged post-humously with the murder of Sheena Yaqub. This decision, reasoned my superiors, would free resources to focus on more urgent cases. If Kent Police had an aftershave named after it, it would be called Negligence.

This case is far from done and dusted.

Five years have passed, yet I remember the crime scene as if it were yesterday. Then, as now, the same two questions return. 1) If the doors were unlocked and phones available, why was Harbinger so desperate to escape the house? And 2) If neither Yaqub nor Harbinger wrote 'I'm so sorry' in blood on the worktop, who did? Surely a third party was involved.

I have since paid three independent forensic graphologists. They have analysed the worktop message, calmly written in blood. They have compared the card displayed by the urn. The results are the same. A 100 per cent match to Pippa Harbinger's handwriting. More chilling still, the bloody line underscoring the message echoes the urn's design. It is the outline of Ben Hope. The location of Pippa Harbinger's death.

There comes a time when you run out of logic and creep towards the illogical. Was that third party Pippa Harbinger? The assumption does not sit well with me. I am an atheist. There is no life after death. To consent to a message beyond the grave challenges all that I believe in.

I still do not understand what 'I'm so sorry' means. Perhaps I am not meant to. Far more significant is what the message implies. It asks a question that sham of an investigation never once asked. If that monster Harbinger murdered his lover, did his ex-wife suffer a similar fate? Pippa Harbinger fell to her death from a Scottish Munro called Ben Hope. I've since discovered Harbinger submitted a life insurance claim for £500,000. He had much to gain from her death.

Again, I am condemned to darkness. The Highland Police refuse to cooperate. When I requested the files on Pippa Harbinger, all I received was a four-word email: 'Justice has been done.' Highland Police have since blocked my email and will not return my calls. All that remains is the cold comfort of suspicion. That even in death, we will never find peace. And that is no comfort at all.

NO. 22:

Behind the Curtain

'Lois,' shouted Roy. 'We've got some action.'

A flush from the bathroom. A sharp slammed door. Lois entered the night-blue bedroom.

'What have I missed?'

Old Roy Barker passed the night vision binoculars, angled a bony arm at the bedroom window.

'Same story, usual place.'

Lois lowered herself into a chair, sliced a gap in the crimson curtain and raised her binoculars. In fuzzy green night vision, she focused on a derelict block on the opposite side of the street: no. 27.

Same story, usual place . . . A tall dark figure lurked by a distant doorway.

'It's turned around,' Lois whispered, suddenly frightened she'd be heard. 'I can't see its face.'

'Hasn't moved since it appeared outside the front door.' Old Roy lowered his voice, joining his daughter's whispering game. 'Been there a good minute now.'

Lois sharpened the focus. In the cold powder of night,

the figure remained woolly and indistinct. It had struck them both as unnaturally tall. Rising from the earth like a mast of dark mist, Roy judged the figure to be at least seven feet. Lois waited for movement. She'd bought the binoculars from eBay, second-hand, £30. The image smudged, a lens had cracked, and the grape-green glow gave her slow throbbing headaches. If she'd known they'd be using them every night, she would have bid on a better pair.

'OK, it's turning. It's facing up the pathway. And . . . on the move.'

'Through the garden gate, up the road, past no. 41, and into the Woods,' Roy predicted.

'Garden gate . . . up the road . . . past no. 41 . . . and there it goes . . . into the Woods.'

Lois passed the binoculars back to her father.

'It always follows the same path. How does it *know*?'

'How do birds migrate without a map?' Roy said, scratching his cheek, answering his daughter's question with another question. 'Maybe it's an impulse. Maybe it can't help itself.'

Lois scanned the dark, silent, empty street. The tall black shadow lingered in her mind's eye.

'Do you think there'll be any more?'

Roy checked the clock on the bedside table, hands ticking past 3.25 a.m.

'Let's call it a night, Lo.' Roy yawned and closed the curtains. 'They'll always be another tomorrow.'

It was Lois who'd seen it first. In the dead of night, she'd flashed awake, cursing herself for forgetting the bins. Ever since she'd moved back home, seeking refuge from the storms of divorce, Roy had given her chores, like a child. Petite, compact, barely five foot tall, little Lois resented these little jobs – 'But I'm thirty-three, Dad'– and bin day always slipped her mind. Lois had flopped out of bed, padded downstairs and opened the door to a moonless night. Waking the wheelie bin from its nest by the garage, Lois had crunched up the gravel driveway, ponytail swinging, when she stole a look up the road.

There, outside no. 27, a tall dark figure loomed by the black front door.

Nobody lived at 27. Nobody had *ever* lived at 27.

Anxious the noise was attracting attention, disturbed by the still and silent stranger, she quickly tiptoed back to the house, abandoning the wheelie bin halfway up the drive.

In her upstairs bedroom, Lois had peeked through the curtains to the derelict block opposite their house. Whoever it was had either left or stepped back inside. When Lois scanned the rows of mock-Tudor houses, her heart skipped a beat.

There it was. A tall dark figure, striding in silence, its pace heavy and deep-sea slow. She watched from her bedroom as it ebbed into the Woods at the road's dead-end. Lois had closed the curtains, locked the bedroom door, and bundled back into bed. She dug a comfort cave inside the duvet, unsettled by the stranger. A black silhouette dragged through her mind, marching to a silent beat.

It was 3.30 a.m.

Next morning, when Lois told her father about the encounter over breakfast, Roy didn't believe a word of it. *Sure you weren't dreaming? No. 27? No one's lived there for years. Did it sprout wings? Fly off into the night? Did you take the bins out?* When Lois left for work at Meadway Hospital, she made doubly sure the front door slammed.

After rescuing the wheelie bin from the drive, Roy sat at the kitchen table, running the story through his head. He wasn't prepared for the motionless hours of thinking time that came with retirement. He still pottered around the house in the same work tie, the same white shirt, the same beige trousers. Forty-three years in civil engineering. Would have worked another five if it weren't for his brittle heart. Even after the double bypass, it seemed to beat with a defeated squish. Roy cleared the kitchen table, tottered on pigeon-toes to the food cupboard and, with too much time on his hands, decided to amuse himself.

A map of Silverweed formed on the table: forty-one sugar cubes as the houses, sprigs of broccoli as the Woods. Roy bent behind sugar cube twenty-two, nudged up his glasses and set an eyeline over to sugar cube twenty-seven. His back cricked softly as he switched angles, surveying a line from twenty-two, up towards the broccoli. Two minutes later, and he was lurking behind the curtains of his daughter's bedroom, staring at Silverweed's forgotten house: the derelict block of no. 27.

Hardwired by logic, Roy had once believed there was an explanation for everything. Then Maureen got liver cancer, fast and terminal, taken in a matter of months. Shipwrecked without his wife of forty-two years, suddenly life made no sense at all. Roy slowly spiralled into obsession, seeking answers to anything unexplained, as if solving mysteries would reset his faith in an obedient, ordered universe.

Empty mornings vaporised on YouTube, sieving for the truth: The Flannan Isles Lighthouse, the Dyatlov Pass, the Ourang Medan, Skinwalker Ranch . . . Roy enjoyed the comforting itch the mysteries left; the way they bobbed into his thoughts during unexpected moments, launching bright lifeboats in a sea of dark memories. Mildly embarrassed by his growing mania for the supernatural, Roy tried to keep his obsessions secret. Lois would roll her eyes during dinner as strange tales leaked from her father's lips.

Did he believe Lois's story? Whether it was nonsense or not (and clearly, it was nonsense), Roy found himself drawn, for the first time in his seventy-two years, to a real-life mystery. Debunking no. 27 and its alleged new guest would be an amusing distraction. Better still, he'd have free licence to snoop – as if he needed any further excuses.

Lurking behind the curtain, his eyes drifted from no. 27. Roy scanned the driveways and doorways, picturing the lives of others. Silverweed had become a peculiar place of late. The commuter down at no. 10, and her morbid obsession with the crash flowers. The woman with the lilac hair renting no. 25, the latest bohemian to file into the house, never to be seen again. And God only knows what the coloured lights flashing from the shutters of no. 4 were all about. Christmas lights? A silent disco? A UFO that had landed in the lounge?

When Lois arrived home from her radiology shift, still prickling from her father's rebuttal, she thumped upstairs and slammed the bedroom door. Roy waited two minutes, crept up the stairs and knocked with a musical tap.

'Oh, Lois,' tempted Roy. 'I've got binoculars.'

When Roy pushed the door open, she was already standing behind the curtains, staring at the derelict block across the road.

After dinner, Roy wrestled two kitchen chairs upstairs and squared them by the bedroom window. They took their seats, teased a slit from the curtain and searched the street for signs of life. Down by the entrance to Silverweed Road, light blinked from a crooked lamp post. The commuter from no. 10 was out again, tending to the flowers. Father and daughter scanned the shadowed driveways, up towards no. 27.

On a terraced road toothed with semis, no. 27 was the only detached house on the street. Bordered by a rickety wooden fence, the front garden was spiked with blackthorns that had escaped the deep, dark Woods. Slicing through the scrub, a diagonal path led from main gate to black front door, like a clock hand stuck at eleven o'clock.

No. 27 was an anomaly. No garage. No driveway. Just a dull block of grey brickwork with a plain, flat facade: four black windows and a black front door, as if modelled on a dice that had rolled a five. Blank, slab-like and gruellingly dull, no. 27 invited fatigue on anyone who looked at it. Roy had never taken much notice of the house. Nobody ever did. Its presence went undetected on Silverweed, as if it wasn't really there at all.

'What time do you believe you saw it?' said Roy, binoculars poking through the crimson curtains.

'I don't "believe" I saw anything, Dad. I saw a tall man standing outside no. 27.' Lois milked her ponytail, irritated her father was testing her story. 'Round about three in the morning.'

'So, why are we here at ten o'clock?'

Lois rolled her eyes. 'Just to be *sure*.'

Hours passed. A fox trotted between silent blue gardens. Eyes tired in the powdering night. Between gasps of black coffee, Lois remained on guard, squinting through Roy's binoculars. The clock hands on the bedside table grazed 3.19.

'Dad.'

Roy was asleep, head sagging as if tilted in a dentist's chair. 'Dad,' Lois repeated, jostling his arm. 'There's someone there.'

Roy snorted awake, mumbled something about biscuits, then remembered where he was. He motioned for the binoculars, snapping his bony fingers. Roy thumbed at the focus. A tall silhouette, carved in black, loomed by the entrance to no. 27.

'There,' said Lois, indignant and triumphant. 'Believe me now?'

They watched it walk the diagonal path, drag through the gate and stride across Silverweed Road. The figure seemed to march to an unheard beat, its long black arms swinging in silence. When it reached the railings at the street's dead-end, it entered the Woods and vanished to shadow.

Same figure. Same route. Same time.

They sat together in eerie silence, eyes fixed on the black front door. They waited for another figure to appear. Another never came.

When Lois padded down for breakfast, groggy after a few hours of sleep, Roy had already set up his broccoli and sugar cubes on the kitchen table. Lois brushed the tangles from her hair, laughed and pulled up a chair. Her father placed a Twiglet by sugar cube twenty-seven.

'Shall I?' offered Lois.

'Be my guest.'

'So, it comes out at 3.19, stands around for a bit, then walks up the path.' Lois bobbed the Twiglet across the table. 'Takes a straight diagonal across the street and disappears into the Woods.' Lois snapped up the Twiglet, popped it in her mouth, crunching it to dust. 'Do you not think it's really slow? It walks like a zombie.'

With the authority of someone who'd watched 340 hours of zombie content on YouTube, Roy straightened his tie and confidently reminded Lois that zombies didn't exist. 'Well, unless you count the ones in Haiti,' Roy said. 'Lois – we live in Kent.'

'OK, so if it's not a zombie, what then? Don't say a ghost. Ghosts can't open gates.'

'There'll be an explanation,' said Roy. 'Don't forget, Halloween's just been and gone. That gang of kids put bangers in the postbox last week.'

'What's that got to do with . . .' Lois frowned, snapped her hair into a ponytail and shifted the conversation. 'What do you know about no. 27? It's weird. I don't have any memories of it growing up.'

'Well, we moved here in December 95, and . . .' Roy paused, scratched his cheek. 'It was such a different street back then. Everyone knew each other, everyone said hello. So many strangers now, we might as well be living on desert islands . . .'

'Dad.'

'The Hagmans keep making a racket in the garden but won't answer the door, and Augustus Fry's as antisocial as ever. Says it all that it took a car crash to bring everyone together, but even that wasn't—'

'Dad? No. 27?'

'Sorry, Lo. No, nobody lived there. We always thought it was an unclaimed probate, me and your mum. It's funny. Until you mentioned it a few nights ago, I'd not taken much notice.'

'Is that it?'

'That's it. Never seen a postman deliver a letter. Come to think of it, I've never seen anyone go inside.'

'Come on, Dad – it's really odd. A house where people leave, but never enter. Who *was* that by the front door?' Lois looked at her phone, checked the time and took a chaotic glug of coffee. 'You're always moaning you've got nothing to do. Have a look into 27, see what you can find out. Oh, and those binoculars of yours are rubbish – if we want to do this properly, we'll need some kind of night visiony thing. God, I'm late for work. Same time again tonight?'

Lois left for her shift at Meadway Hospital. Roy settled in the study. As the computer booted up, he glanced at his daughter's graduation photo, pride of place on the bureau. His only girl, his only child, all grown up.

When Lois had first moved back in, she was a pale ghost of her former self, broken by a chain of bad decisions. Karl hadn't worked out. She'd had a short-lived affair with a junior radiologist; Karl had checked her phone one morning, and in an instant, a twelve-year marriage imploded. The divorce was fast and nasty.

For months, no. 22 was haunted by heartbreak, frosted by the ghost who cried at night. Roy would sit in the lounge, feeling useless, while his daughter shut herself in her room.

Lois was better now. Still prone to door slamming when things didn't go her way, but happier, more optimistic. If anything, Roy found Lois's new-found confidence slightly frightening. First there were the sponsored bungee jumps. Then she'd discovered a high in low places. An activity weekend in the Mendips had unlocked a talent for caving. Roy couldn't think of anything worse: the crawling claustrophobia, the tight dark spaces, but for his daughter, it had provided a thrill, a social life, of forcing light into darkness and knowing she'd survive.

'You don't understand, Dad,' Lois had said. 'I've always hated being called petite, but down there, I can squeeze into spaces no one else would dare.'

Now was a plan to quit work and travel solo, exploring the caves of South America. At the age of thirty-three, the divorce had unlocked a fearless, callow independence. It was nearly a year since she'd moved back in, filling a hole Maureen had left.

Now they were father and daughter, reunited, weathering the storms.

Roy loaded Zoopla, tapped in 27 Silverweed Road, tutting at the results from the property archive. The records went back to 1995, but the house wasn't even listed. No floor plan, no valuation, no previous owners . . . Roy took off his glasses, rubbed his eyes and clicked the computer to sleep.

Where were the records of ownership? Why had he blanked that house for so many years, as if it wasn't even there? Sensing the all-seeing internet wasn't the answer to everything, Roy shuffled out of the study and put on the kettle. The cogs in his mind whirred and clunked, shedding the rust of retirement. He filled a Thermos, packed a satchel and caught the bus to Meadway Library.

In the Local Studies section, three bookcases deep, Roy picked up *The Streetwise Guide To Meadway*. He turned to the index and traced a bony finger from Q to R to S.

Silverweed Road. Residential cul-de-sac on the Corvid Estate built between 1956 and 1958. It is comprised of forty-one houses, predominantly semi-detached. The north end backs onto 200 acres of woodland, populated with rowans and blackthorns.

Roy reread the entry. Three years to construct a short,

straight cul-de-sac and forty-one houses? They built the Titanic in two . . .

Chair legs scraped like a broken trumpet on the library floor. Roy shuffled to the enquiries desk and asked for assistance. A librarian, whose wide, triangular face reminded Roy of a salamander, suggested he start with the area maps. *The County Series (1890–)*, *National Grid*, then *Ordnance Survey*, all stored on microfiche.

In the stiff library silence, he flipped through the files. Roy immediately felt at home with the microreader. The rolling dials, the focus and zooms, the fluttering screen and the sliding glass tray. A smile crept across his face. It felt like being at work again.

He loaded the maps and opened new worlds.

A routine soon set in. By day, Roy would visit the library, flapping through books and hunched under microreaders. By night, he'd join Lois behind the curtains, watching the figure march into the Woods.

When Lois's night vision binoculars arrived from eBay, secrets began to creep from the dark. The binoculars were cheap and serviceable at best. Much like Roy's research, critical details remained out of reach.

Tantalising glimpses fed their curiosity further. The shadow's bunched hands that moved to a pendulum beat, swinging like thick black shovels. The slow strides on wide slabbed feet. The domed head that never turned, forever staring forward. Its face remained elusive, perpetually smudged in a murky haze. At times, there were hints of dented eyes and a gaping mouth, yet even under the sharpest focus, its surface clung onto its secrets.

Lois's attempts to video its slow procession were met with

frustration. Whenever she checked the footage on her phone, she was rewarded with smears, like a trailing smog. The figure was so resistant to being captured on film, Roy had joked it was Silverweed's Bigfoot. Bristling from a creeping sense of a shared illusion, Lois secretly began to doubt it was even there at all.

And yet the evidence was there in Lois's log book. Through clear skies and boiling storms, the figure's nocturnal routine was carefully documented. The diagonal path it walked to the Woods never wavered. The timing, though: there were curious signs of jump and lag.

Nights 1–9, the tall dark figure had appeared outside the black front door at 3.19, right on the dot.

On Night 10, it surprised them both with an early entrance at 3.17. Night 12, a little later, at 3.24, then back to 3.19 the following day.

Night 14 changed everything.

As Lois watched the figure dissolve into the trees, Roy had nudged her with a bony elbow, whispering: *Look at the front of the house*. The skin on her neck ploughed up. Lois prickled with goosebumps. Outside no. 27, another figure lurked.

Her eyes swung to the dead-end of Silverweed, where a shadow faded into the Woods. Her vision chased back to the black front door. Another figure – same shape, same height. Lois followed its diagonal march, up the road and into the Woods. With the revelation came a tickling chill that spidered up her spine.

It was no longer an it. They were dealing with a them.

Lois crunched Twiglets as Roy shuffled his papers. An overhead projector Lois hadn't seen since she was eight years old had been liberated from the attic. Now a blank white square of light marked the wall above the fireplace, screen shining in the light-dimmed lounge. Roy coughed for attention, ready to begin his lecture. Petite Lois sat up on a recliner, found herself sinking back in. Its doughy fat cushions all but swallowed her.

'In 1956,' Roy began, pincering his glasses, 'construction started on Silverweed Road, the final street on the Corvid Estate. Work completed in 1958. All the other roads took a year to build, so why did Silverweed take three? Woods aside, it's no different to any other street.'

Lois crunched another Twiglet. 'Go on,' she urged.

'For the life of me, I couldn't work it out. So I started going through old editions of *The Meadway Chronicle*.'

Roy placed a sheet on the projector.

MAN DIES IN BUILDING SITE TRAGEDY

He looked at Lois, replaced the sheet with another. Headlines switched on the lounge wall.

CONSTRUCTION HALTS AS TWO GO MISSING

'There are three more reports like those. Six workers died in total. Guess where?'

'Silverweed Road?'

Roy nodded grimly. 'Silverweed Road. All accidents apparently, but still. One death is negligent, two unlucky, but six? It's very peculiar, Lo. And it all checks out on the public death register.'

'Bloody hell, Dad,' laughed Lois. 'Do you not think you're being a bit *too* thorough?'

Roy glided past her interruption.

'And then there's this.'

He slid a map onto the projector.

'I found a copy of the construction street map. Notice anything?'

Lois scanned the blueprint projected onto the wall. Lined either side of Silverweed Road, blocks of semis tightened like teeth. In the centre of the road was a blank space where a house should be. Lois counted the semis: two rows of twenty, forty in all.

'That gap. It's where no. 27 should be.'

'Odd, isn't it? They didn't build anything.'

'Why?'

'Because,' said Roy, straightening his tie, 'there was a house already there.'

Through stuttering questions, interruptions and projected maps on shifting foils, The History Of Silverweed According To Roy unfolded. Prior to the Corvid Estate, the area was woodland and scattered farms – a typical Kentish patchwork of pasture and pocketsquare crops. There had been a village once, Bedigling, masked in the shallow valley, established in the 1590s. By 1650, it had vanished entirely. Had it still been there today, Silverweed Road would be buried under blackthorns on the outskirts of Bedigling, banished to its outermost edge.

And before Bedigling? Sweltan Forest: 480 acres of woodland, England's largest and only rowan tree forest. And that's how it had stayed: an ancient forest, marked on the last map Roy could find, dated 1356. Roy withheld from sharing it.

As Lois watched the ancient maps sweep past on the wall, her eyes sharpened on a pocket breaking up the trees, repeated map after map. She asked Roy to flip between the images, back and forth.

'What *is* that?'

'I'm glad it's not just me, I thought I was going mad.'

'Is that where I think it is?'

'Most recent time is on the 1926 Ordnance Survey map: a house in the woods, a good thirty years before the Corvid Estate was built. The maps get less accurate, but they all indicate a clearing in the woodland. Either a house, or a place where the trees wouldn't grow.'

'It's where no. 27 is now, isn't it?'

'Roughly.'

'I don't get it,' said Lois. 'Why didn't they just knock down the house when they built Silverweed?'

'Maybe they tried. Maybe they couldn't. Maybe there were too many deaths.' Roy pictured the map from 1356 that he'd withheld from Lois. He muttered to himself, embarrassed to say it, unable to contain his thoughts. 'Maybe it's cursed.'

Lois burst out laughing. 'Oh, come on. I admit, the house stuff is weird, but if it was cursed, how come we're all still happily living here? And have done for decades? We're not all wandering the streets like zombies, are we? Talking of zombies, what about *them*?'

Roy opened his mouth to speak, paused then tightened his lips. *She's in one of her moods*, he thought. *She's getting all antsy, I can feel it. It's not the right time.*

'Still working on it,' lied Roy, turning on the lounge lights. 'Come on, I've got a surprise. I splashed out on some new night vision goggles – ArmaSite 400s. Head-mounted, high-definition, recommended by the MOD, no less. Let's get a proper look at those things.'

They woke at 3 a.m. Lois took the ArmaSite, strapped on the headgear. Her ponytail snagged in the fastener. She cursed, grimaced and tightened the focus. At 3.19 a.m., it arrived on the dot outside the black front door. Seaweed green in acid-sharp night vision, the figure, still woolly, began to leak its secrets.

Balanced on blocked, bare feet, its body suggested hints of armour, with faint lines and joins. As Lois studied the figure, it lurked, mannequin-stiff: a flat silhouette in three dimensions. Lois found herself thinking of the thick black stickman on a pedestrian crossing sign, painted out of vapour.

Her focus climbed up towards the head.

A cold gasp escaped her lips. Startled Roy stirred in his chair. 'What is it, Lo?'

Lois watched as ripples rivered through its blank domed head, a ball of fluid setting in the cold night air. A mouth gaped and widened. Cheekbones lifted. In the soft swell of forming flesh, two eyes trickled beneath the skin.

'The face,' whispered Lois.

She turned to Roy, her face pale.

'The face . . . It's still growing.'

The next morning, Lois and Roy sat in silence at the kitchen table. The familiar flurry of a Saturday morning – the papers, the radio, the spattered cooked breakfast – had been resisted by both. The kitchen air clenched in a pensive hush. Roy chewed mindlessly on unbuttered toast. Lois stared into the white well of her boiled egg, lost in the eye of a marigold yolk. Her mind flickered in night vision green.

The face. It's still growing . . .

'There's something you need to know,' Roy said, breaking the silence. 'Something I should have told you last night.'

Lois looked up from her yolk.

'No. 27,' he said. 'It was built on a grave. Not the kind

you'd find in a churchyard. It's like the grave *is* a churchyard
– it's over 500 feet long.'

'Like a tomb?' said Lois, milking her ponytail.

'Like a tomb,' harmonised Roy. 'It's a long barrow.
They're not rare in Kent. Me and your mum visited the one
in Coldrum when you were little – you were bored out of
your mind. But a long barrow, here, under Silverweed? Wait
a sec. Be back in a jiffy.'

Lois sat chewing the ends of her ponytail. Pigeon-toed
Roy tottered into the study, returned with two photocopies
and a book. He placed a copy of an ancient map on the
kitchen table.

'Here you are. The map from 1356. See the clearing in
the middle of Sweltan Forest? The area next to the spring
where no. 25 is now?' Roy pointed to a slim bar slanted
on the map, beside the symbol of a well.

Lois read the script marked below the bar. '*Halig grund*?'

'Means "sacred site". It's a long barrow, Lo. Neolithic,
could have held up to ninety bodies. See the barrow? I
thought it was a coincidence at first, but it's angled at a
sixty-eight degree diagonal.'

Roy took the second piece of paper, placed it over the
map. He really did feel like he was at work again. 'Look
at the line when I overlay a street map of the Corvid Estate.
The long barrow symbol passes right under Silverweed. See?
It starts in the Woods, and ends . . .'

'. . . at no. 27. Those things,' said Lois, 'they're following
the path of the long barrow.'

Roy pushed up his glasses and nodded.

'But why? Why now? You've never seen those things
before, and neither have I.'

'Promise you won't laugh.'

Lois looked up from the map. Her father cracked the spine of a thin paperback. Roy passed her the book. Lois scowled at the title: *Myths & Legends Of Northern Kent* by LaVerne Tracy. On the cover was a cartoon Elizabethan ghost with its laughing head tucked under its arm like a football. Lois rolled her eyes. The book was clearly aimed at children.

'Bottom of page thirty-two,' said Roy.

Lois turned the yellowed pages, the scent of stale tobacco leaking like gas from the paper. She read the paragraph Roy had ringed in pencil.

The Legend Of Spinosa:
All That Is Loved Will Be Lost

English laws against witchcraft were introduced in 680 AD by the Archbishop of Canterbury, making Kent the UK's first witch hunt capital!

While the Church dominated witch trials, some communities were known to administer their own justice. In 1619, one such incident took place at the ghost village of Bedigling, where the suburbs of Meadway now stand.

Accused of raising the dead from the Sweltan Long Barrow, Mary Spinosa was put on trial by village elders. The wretched hag was bound to a blackthorn and abandoned to perish in Sweltan Forest. Mary Spinosa was heard to utter a curse, damning the land that destroyed her: 'All that is loved will be lost.'

Be careful if you see a large female jackdaw! Spinosa's curse is carried by her familiar, Corvus. She's said to rise every 100 years, stealing heartbeats from those who dare to live on her land.

Legend has it Spinosa's spirit still lurks in the Woods, calling on ancestors beyond the grave to ply her with human wine. Although the Sweltan Long Barrow has never been found, the Legend of Spinosa remains a fun creepy tale!

Lois grimaced at the accompanying illustration: a naked old woman lashed to a vast, ugly blackthorn. Within its gloomy fortress of thorns, a jackdaw lurked on a branch.

'So this is where you got your curse idea from? This horrible folklore book for children? What's so "fun" about killing women?'

'It's the only book I found that mentions the long barrow.'

'All that is loved will be lost,' read Lois. '1619 . . . 100 years . . . Well, it is 2019.'

'There's a jackdaw roost in the Woods, Lo. And that garden over the road is infested with blackthorns.'

'You're joining dots that aren't there,' said Lois. 'A witch called Spinosa? Drinking human wine, whatever the hell that is. That mark on the map doesn't actually *say* long barrow, does it? None of this solves much. What *are* those things?'

'The answer,' said Roy, 'is in the house.'

There had been a debate, a short one, about who should enter no. 27. Roy – retired, squishy-hearted, pigeon-toed Roy – moved almost as slowly as the figures and was blind as a bat without his glasses. For Lois, the house held the promise of an illicit thrill. It was November. Caving season was dead. And besides, her father's dadsplaining had started to bristle. She'd spotted the figure first. The mystery belonged to her.

The plan was set for the following Saturday. They'd instantly agreed the front door wasn't an option: for all they knew, a figure could be lurking right behind it. They were looking for answers, not confrontation. After several furtive walks up Silverweed side-eyeing no. 27, Roy had spotted a possible in, concealed by a thick scratch of blackthorns. On the south-facing side, at ground level, was an awning window with a slender gap. The house was practically inviting them to prise it open and clamber inside.

That week, it was lights out at no. 22. ArmaSite on, Lois paced the house, adapting to the seaweed green. Roy hunched in the shed, testing the two Bluetooth walkie-talkies he'd ordered, feeling like a secret agent. With an earpiece each, they'd be in permanent contact. Lois would never be alone. And if, for whatever reason, a situation called for silence? She'd let him know with two clicks of the Talk button.

Under buttery kitchen light, they reviewed the log book as tall black figures marched through their minds. Over the course of twenty nights, sixteen figures had arrived at 3.19, five at 3.17, three at 3.22 and six at 3.24. A little messy, but all within an eight-minute block. If Lois entered at 2.30 a.m., she'd have time to acclimatise, time to investigate, time to find out where the hell they were coming from.

Saturday night arrived faster than anticipated. As Roy packed a Thermos, torch and cellophaned cheese sandwich into Lois's rucksack, they repeated the pact they'd made.

Do not speak to them. Do not touch them. And at any point, if things didn't feel right, escape back through the awning window.

Dressed in a blue cagoule and navy leggings, Lois curved on the earpiece, and frowned at her reflection in the hallway mirror.

'I look like a Poundshop SWAT team,' said Lois, trying to lighten the tightening mood. Old Roy gathered her into his brittle frame, hugging his daughter to his chest.

'I love you so much,' he whispered. 'You're my only one. My only one.'

'For God's sake, Dad,' said Lois. 'I'm only going over the road.'

She left the house at 2.30 a.m., into a crashing storm. Draw-the-curtains weather. Nobody would see her. Hood up, head down, Lois splashed across Silverweed Road, to the gloomy grey house that had stained their dreams.

The rickety fence croaked and buckled. Lois clambered into the untamed garden, aware a border had been crossed. Glancing at the black front door, a thumbs-up aimed across the street, she weaved through the clawing blackthorns. In the warmth of the bedroom, Roy watched his daughter vanish to shadow then re-emerge by the side of the house.

Lois edged the grey brick wall. Like a tempting slit of mouth, a slim gap gaped from the awning window, beckoning her inside. Lois pressed a hand on the wooden ledge, testing its integrity. Satisfied it would take her weight, she fed her fingers into the gap. The window seemed to flinch in response, as if the house were measuring her touch. Rain ripped against the glass.

Lois tugged the frame. There was a mild bump of resistance. She pulled again, firmer this time, urging open the frame. With a soft groan, the awning window yielded.

Lois wrestled her rucksack through the gap, listened to a

thud as it hit the floor. Eager to escape the driving rain, she hoisted herself onto the ledge. With dangling legs, levering arms and the tickle of illicit thrill, she wriggled through the window into no. 27. This, thought Lois, was a doddle.

Crouched under the window, dripping from the rain, Lois slid off her hood, dug into her rucksack and strapped on the ArmaSite. Her dark, cold world flashed to green. The narrow corridor she'd entered tapered into shadow, its high walls a jigsaw of exposed brickwork. Lois whispered through her walkie-talkie.

'Dad? I'm in. Yes, I'm OK. Stop fussing. I'm *fine*.'

'What can you see?'

'Not much. I'm in a corridor, exit either end. I'm guessing the one ahead leads to the hallway, maybe even the front door. No idea about the other end. It's so *quiet* in here.' Lois flinched. A mushy slurp dripped into her ear.

'If you're going to have a biscuit, Dad, turn the walkie-talkie off.'

Lois settled into the moss of night vision, listening to the drum of rain outside. Eyes of cobwebs on the bare brick walls glared at Lois in silence. The adrenalin rush that had urged her through the window slowly seeped and died. She felt nothing in this barren corridor. The house was dead inside: as dead and gruelling as its blank exterior.

The night deepened. Camped under the awning window, Lois pecked at a cheese sandwich. In whispering crackles from across the road, Roy warmed Lois with rambling childhood memories. *Remember when we . . . Your mother used to . . .* Lois began to wonder if the figures had marched only in their minds; that this deathly quiet house was just a barren, lifeless shell. At 2.43 a.m., Lois made her move.

'Dad, I'm bored,' said Lois. 'There's nobody here. I'm going to take a look around.'

Lois padded up the corridor and peeked around an arched doorway. The hallway she'd anticipated was nowhere to be seen. Instead, beyond the arch, was an empty square room. Sensing the same gruelling stillness as the corridor, Lois cautiously stepped inside.

The room was barren. Little Lois felt a swirl of vertigo as she looked up to the ceiling. It seemed to both retreat and press down at once. The flagstone floor on which she stood held a flat dry chill. All else was a monotony of exposed brickwork: but not quite. In the centre of each wall was a low arched doorway. Lois sensed no signs of life. No signs, in fact, that anybody had ever lived here. Lois radioed Roy.

'Dad? The room I'm in: it's like a box made of bricks. There's no furniture or windows or anything. All I can see are four walls and four exits. What's that? I'm *fine*, Dad. Trust me, I've been in scarier caves. Let me look around and I'll get back.'

Lois circled the room, scanning the archways set in each wall. Aside from the corridor, each exit was identical, leading to an identical space. Another square room. Another four archways. Where was the kitchen? The bathroom? The lounge?

The illicit thrill that had hit Lois when she'd climbed through the window returned. Exposed in mossy night vision, the arches held the promise of an inviting mystery. The house felt like a cave of bricks: a cave to be explored.

Lois settled on a plan. The archways offered too many options, too many chances to get lost. She'd walk a straight path, arch to arch, and see where they led.

Lois crept from room to room, square to square, a pawn

filing an endless chessboard. The cold flagstones absorbed each step, each breath swallowed by the bare brick walls.

It was in the fifth room where Lois slipped up. The monotony of the straight path briefly caused her to circle the room. When she turned to face the archway ahead, Lois hesitated. She scanned the room. Four arches, each leading to an identical room. Lois cursed herself for not marking the walls.

Lois circled the room once more. She'd lost her way in a cave before: last summer, in Mossdale Caverns, she'd crawled into an unfamiliar tunnel, and soon emerged into the light. There was no use panicking. She was better than that. This was a house, not a cave. Just an empty house on a street in suburbia. Keep going and listen for rain. The doors and windows will come. Lois packed away her doubts and pressed on through an archway.

A sixth square room. Now a seventh. Lois hit a dead-end. There were only two exits here: the archway she'd entered, and a narrow staircase, leading down. Lois approached the steps. She pictured her father, fretting behind the curtains, and radioed back.

'I've found some stairs. Not sure where they . . .'

'I think you should come home now,' crackled Roy. 'There's something going on outside.'

'Stop *worrying*, Dad. I'm *fine*.'

'Will you *listen*, Lo? A jackdaw's been circling the house over road and now it's here, on the windowsill. It's staring at me through the glass and it won't go away. The book, Lo. Spinosa's familiar. Please come home, Lo. It's time to come ho—'

Two clicks of the Talk button, Roy had gone and Lois was halfway down the stairs.

Why turn back when she'd come this far? Why turn back because *he* was worried? Why turn back because of something he'd read in a stupid children's book?

The monotony of brick and endless archways receded with her descent. Lois lingered on the final step. The dull dry chill of the rooms above surrendered to a dank, bitter cold. Lois felt her skin pip to goosebumps. There was a familiar dampness to the air: the stony, damp chill of a cave. Lois stepped from the staircase. Ghost-white mist seeped from her lips.

In the seaweed murk of night vision, a narrow chamber unfolded. Overlapping like scales of armour, sarsen slabs lined the walls, thinning into the chamber's depths. Thick flagstones paved the floor, an echo of the rooms above. Lois looked up to the arched ceiling and inhaled the chamber's scent: damp, cold and earthy, like fresh rain kissing rock.

She entered the stone throat of the chamber. Her fingers brushed the coarse, cool walls, sensing moisture on her skin. The sarsen slabs clicked and tapped, echoing each cautious step. As she journeyed down the passageway, her night vision began to dance. Specks of white pulsed through the murk. There were signs of light ahead.

Lois snapped off her ArmaSite. She balled her fists and rubbed her eyes. The green smears cleared in strobing blinks. New light. Coloured light. A crystalline, electric blue.

It licked the sarsen walls in ripples, like reflections from a swimming pool. At the chamber's end came an unearthly glow, and with it, unearthly shapes. Heart patting, cold breath misting, Lois stepped towards the light.

Carved within the flagstone floor, a disc of water shone – the glazed surface neon blue, the edges smooth and even. Set in a circle around the pool rose a ring of standing stones.

The four rocks thinned towards the ceiling, each stone claw a different height. Lois stared, transported. It was as if she'd descended a cellar's stairs and entered a subterranean oasis.

Lois stepped towards the stones and gazed into the pool. There was not a drip or lick of water, the silent surface flat as glass. It offered no reflection, no clues as to its depth. Neither did it offer warmth. The water was the crystal blue of exotic coral reefs, yet its shade was an illusion. The frostbite chill that glazed its surface pinched her skin to gooseflesh.

Lois stepped back from the water and faced a standing stone. The rock clawed into the chamber ceiling, the tallest of the four.

She ran a hand along the stone, her fingers skimming nicks and cuts. Exposed by the glow of the shining pool, patterns flicked across the rock. A madness of marks infested the stone.

Lois dug around her cagoule, pulled out her phone and turned on the torch. White light licked across the patterns. Carved deep into the standing stone, a primitive image lifted.

The outline of a naked tree, branches spread as arms. Stickmen scattered at its base, their bodies snapped in two. From a gaping mouth within the trunk, a body sagged, half-eaten. The tree was feasting on the figures, gorged on human wine.

Her cold breath quickened, misting the stone. Torchlight licked the rock. The primal image provoked another, drawn within a children's book. Mary Spinosa, lashed to a trunk, banished to a forest for raising the dead.

Lois gasped from the connection. Her breath hissed round the standing stones. Torchlight dipped. She checked her phone. The time blinked 3.09 a.m.

To the distant drum of knocking wood, a ripple snaked the water.

In a series of silent heaves and whirls, the surface lifted into life. Neon water spilled the edges, darkening the flagstones. In the depths of the pool, darkness stirred. The rising shadow froze her heart.

Exposed in the chamber, no time to run, Lois skidded on the flagstones. The rising drum of knocking wood echoed through the chamber. The shadow rose. Panic hurtled. She narrowed herself behind a stone and faced the chamber wall. Lois shrank against the rock, white mist pounding from her mouth.

She didn't see the blank, black head slowly break the surface.

She didn't see the body, rising like a mast.

She didn't see its features drip, like running paint in rain.

Lois watched a shadow lengthen, cast upon the walls. Her hand leaped up and cupped her mouth, smothering her breath's escape. Whatever had risen from the pool began to walk the chamber. It hadn't turned. It hadn't seen her. Hadn't sensed her presence.

Pinned against the standing stone, Lois fought emerging shakes, desperate to be silent. The shadow thinned upon the wall, retreating from the chamber. It marched in time to licks of wood that grew within the tomb.

Lois hid within herself, buried in her mind. The instant that she pictured home, panic crashed like coastal waves. She was lost down here. Lost entirely. Cornered in a dead-end chamber. Swallowed by this house. The shadow that had stained the walls ebbed away from view. Lois released her smothering hand and peeled slowly from the stone.

She turned towards the ribboning pool, settling in silence.

With each click and tap of drumming wood, the chamber's chill dropped further. What if there was another? What if there were *more*? Thoughts twisted through endless archways, endless rooms, an endless march through an endless maze, all direction gone. The cold, the drumming, the stark blue glow, the dank scent of the flagstones: the chamber flooded every sense, feasting on her panic.

Focus. *Focus*. She never panicked in the caves. There was always a way out. *Always* . . .

Lois snapped on the ArmaSite. The chamber flashed to green. She turned towards passageway. Tapering towards the stairs, a shadow slowly seeped.

The front door. The black front door. Whatever it was, it knew the way out. Hadn't seen her. Hadn't sensed her. The chill was rising. The cold would claim her. Dare she follow? Dare she?

Lois screwed her courage tight. Measuring each nervous step – each footstep tightrope-taut – Lois crept the narrow chamber, towards the trailing shadow. Ripples licked the sarsen walls. The pool's blue glow retreated.

Lois reached the staircase, heart thudding in her throat. She watched a distant shadow ooze, folding up the steps.

Her foot tapped a cold stone. Another step was taken. Breath misting from her lips, Lois climbed the narrow stairs to ticks and clacks of drumming wood.

Lois paused on the top step. Her eyes sank to the floor. She watched a shadow slip like oil, fading from the flagstones. Up ahead, a figure marched, beneath a darkened archway. Her misted breath began to thin in the square room's dull, dry chill. Lois crept towards the arch. One step, two steps, closer to home.

The shadow joined the form that cast it. Lois watched

the figure march and cross the next square room. Hadn't seen her. Hadn't heard her. Hadn't even sensed her. Deep-sea slow, with swinging arms, it passed beneath a gloomy arch. It was heading, she was certain now, towards the black front door.

Through square rooms and murky archways, measuring ten steps behind, Lois became a shadow's shadow of the form that stained her dreams. Pace matching its deathly stride, her heart drum-drummed to knocks of wood. Closer came the crackle of rain. Closer came escape.

The figure paused below an arch. Lois took one step back. It lingered in the bare bricked room, dripping liquid mist. The drumming wood grew ever louder. Building. Urging. Summoning . . .

And now it turned, fading left. Lois watched its shadow ebb. Through clicks and taps, she could hear the rain. Lois crept across the flagstones. She stole a look around the arch.

A narrow corridor. A marching figure. And finally, a black front door.

The sight was like a burst of sun. Hope flared through her heart. Lois heard the crackling rain, the crunch of driveway gravel, saw the honeyed glow of a bedroom window, felt the heat of a father's embrace . . . The figure loitered by the door. It took one slow step forward. Lois waited for an opening. The burst of air. A gush of light. The kiss of falling rain . . .

It passed like vapour through the door.

Lois stared down the narrow corridor. A revelation dawned. Not once had they seen the front door open. *Wait*, she thought. *It'll be outside. Just wait two minutes and I'll open the door. Wait it out and I'll be free. Just two minutes. Wait.*

The tap and clack and lick of wood gained strength. The ceaseless drumming filled the corridor, pounding through her head. Images beat through her mind. Pool. *Drum.* Shadow. *Drum.* Stone. *Drum.* Tree. *Drum.* Mouth. *Drum.* Woods. *Drum.* Drink. *Drum.* Wine. *Drum.* Feed. *Drum-drum.* Feed. *Drum-drum.* Feed. *Drum-drum.* Feed . . .

The drumming filled her like a fever. She could bare the sound no longer. Lois raced down the narrow corridor, towards the black front door. A burst of air. The kiss of rain. A glowing bedroom window. She reached and fumbled for the handle.

Nothing.

Frantic, Lois frisked the frame.

No handle. No lock. No letter box to call through. The drum of wood grew louder.

The frame was not a frame. The door was not a door. What looked like wood felt like stone. Another wall in the maze.

Lois seized her walkie-talkie.

'Dad.'

'Lois, thank God. Where are you? What's that knocking sou—'

'The door. It's bricks. It's *fucking bricks*, I can't . . .'

'Slow down, Lo. I'm here, I'm here. What's bricks?'

'It's not a door, it's *fucking bricks*. I want to go home, Dad. I just want to go —'

'The window?' interrupted Roy. 'The window you climbed through?'

'All these rooms, they're all the same and there's water and stones and this fucking tree and this knocking wood and I'm cold and scared and . . . I'm trapped.' Lois sobbed. 'Dad, *help*.'

'I'm coming, Lo, I'm coming. There's one outside the door right now. It hasn't moved an inch. I don't want to frighten you, Lo, but it's 3.23. The log book, remember? There could be another one coming. Get away from the door, Lo. You need to find the window. Please, Lo, look for the window.'

Lois snapped off the ArmaSite, the lenses fogged with tears. Total darkness. Utter black. With the sudden plunge, came a hostile chill that flooded through the corridor. Blind and shaking in the dark, Lois cuffed her sleeve. She dabbed her tears and wiped the lenses. Her father's voice, a source of comfort, hardened to a warning.

Another one . . . Get away from the door . . . The window . . . The window . . . Look for the window . . .

Lois snapped on the ArmaSite. Her ponytail snagged in the straps. She turned from the door. Her scalp pinched. Darkness flashed to night vision.

Menacing clicks of drumming wood pounded through her head. Feed. *Drum-drum.* Feed. *Drum-drum.* The hostile chill now climbed the walls, biting at her skin. Deep in the throat of the narrow corridor, through a murk of tear-stained green, a figure misted into view.

Its daunting form filled the corridor. Black arms swung to licks and taps. Feet marched to a pendulum beat. The figure loomed like a rising mast, slowly closing in. Below lifeless eyes, not yet formed, a gaping mouth unfolded.

Lois screamed and clawed the door. Fear pulped her every thought. She thumped and pounded at the bricks. The hostile chill grew closer.

Lois felt a rush of frostbite, surging from behind. She turned to face a swinging arm and screamed from the connection.

Lois was out of time.

*

Roy was limping up the driveway when the scream cracked through his earpiece. In the rush to reach his daughter, he'd tripped and tumbled down the stairs, landing with a brittle crunch. The hallway table took his fall and bit into his shin. Now he hobbled in the rain, one leg peeled like sliding rind, half-blind in the storm. His glasses lay on the hallway floor, the lenses crushed and splintered.

His daughter's scream burned through his ear. It set his heart on fire. Roy splashed across the tarmac, towards the rain-lashed house. He stole a look up Silverweed. His vision quivered in the storm. Up ahead, a figure loomed, marching for the Woods.

Sightless Roy strained through the rain. Did it have her? Was she taken? The figure shivered through his eyes, like a shattered blot of ink. Now it seemed to stretch and thicken. Were there two of them or one? Holding something. It was holding something. Dragging something. Lois.

My only one . . . My only one . . .

Roy limped and splashed up Silverweed, calling through the storm. With every step, his shin unpeeled, slowly sliding, weeping blood. Oblivious and deep-sea slow, the mast of mist marched on. Through ripping rain, sharp as thorns, he called out once again. Words lost to the grinding storm, Old Roy Barker closed the distance.

One step closer . . . Two steps closer . . . Close enough to touch . . .

Through pounding rain, he screamed.

'Give her *back*.'

With all the rage and love he had, convinced the figure held his daughter, Roy lunged with flattened palms, and thrust into its back.

His shaking hands passed right through.

There was a slip, a stumble, a regaining of balance, and a pain so fierce it stole his voice. Roy pulled back his burning hands. A clinging mist, cold and black, gorged on peeling fingers. Up it crept, through palms and wrists, seeking, tasting, claiming. Arms now sleeves of liquid black, Roy writhed madly in the storm. And finally, it turned.

There was no Lois. There was no love. A rippling head, not yet formed, faced Roy with cold indifference. Spears of rain flashed through its form, white arrows slicing smoke. The figure answered to a call – a distant call to feed. Its arms reached out and curled round Roy.

Skidding on the tarmac, slippery as jellyfish, Roy folded in its grip. Every flinch and frantic twist absorbed him further still. Skin unpeeled, began to crack. The chilling mist sliced through. Roy began to seep and flow, as if sucked up through a straw. The blackened figure slowly filled, churning blood-red clouds.

Soapy bones slipped from sockets. Muscles creamed and foamed. Frostbitten flesh dissolved to sap. As the shadow fed, another appeared, passing through a distant gate. A sagging body, small and soft, drained within its arms.

Roy's eyes met the boiling head, churning with his blood. His ears now dripped as candle wax. Cheekbones sank in quicksand skin. A nose slid down like slipping oil. Roy watched his face resurface, stolen by a crimson mirror. Eyes loosened and washed like paint. In guilt and love and fear and loss, blinded Roy called out for Lois.

His mouth was gone before he could scream.

They filed into the twisting Woods, cradling a body each. What was left of sagging heads bobbed loosely in their grip.

The figures fed and churned blood red: vessels of human wine.

They marched to the beat of knocking wood, obeying the line of a summoning path. Wearing the faces of the bodies they held, the figures approached a woodland clearing and walked a tunnel of barbs.

The procession slowed and came to a halt at the foot of a towering blackthorn. Within the thrashing gloomy fortress, arms of branches swayed and clicked, drumming out her beckoning call. From a stubbed tree stump, a jackdaw watched, flashing silver eyes.

There was a whine of timber, a crack of wood. From the wall of trunk, a mouth sliced open, as if split by a woodsman's axe. The figures turned one final time, stolen faces meeting: the mask of a man, the mask of a woman.

Father and daughter reunited, weathering the storms.

And now the figures poured. Drawn into the widening mouth, like a black hole gorging stretching stars, rivers of blood churned and flowed, swept into a gaping maw. The dark trunk rippled in heaving gulps. Bulging roots writhed in the soil. The figures drained like emptying vessels, fading to vapour in the night.

In the deep, dark Woods of Silverweed Road, an ancient voice broke through the storm. A liquid croak of 'human wine' merged with crashing rain.

And all that was loved was lost.

Extract from The Silverweed Files, 30 November 2024

*A personal blog by former Detective Chief Inspector
Jim Heath. The views expressed do not reflect those
of Kent Police nor the victims impacted by events.*

Silverweed stopped countless hearts, yet it is always the
Barkers I return to – the father, Roy, and his daughter, Lois,
from no. 22. I can practically still taste the air, that morning
after the storm. As I watched the search unit enter the
Woods, it crackled on the tongue like frost.

A dog walker found their blood-soaked clothes, scattered
in the undergrowth. The frenzied crime scene brought back
memories, of the Meadway Ripper's aftermath. At first, I
feared a copycat.

For seven days, we hacked through blackthorns. Didn't
find so much as a tooth. Not a hair, not a bone, not an
ankle or earlobe. My former colleague John Kirkland joked
in his despair that the cause of death was 'evaporation'. I
did not laugh then, and I do not laugh now. Like Victor
Hagman from no. 35, the Barkers seemed to vanish into
thin air.

From the binoculars and log book found in the bedroom,
the Barkers had placed the house opposite under surveillance.
Who was appearing each night, just after 3am? I am looking

right now at the figures sketched in the Barkers' log, and it is impossible to say. They look like stick men, black and tall, marching across the page. Whoever the figures were, they appear to be connected to the maps the Barkers left. The father and daughter had convinced themselves a burial site lay beneath no. 27.

It was just another delusion. The house was an empty shell. I set foot inside that derelict husk myself and there was literally nothing to see. No rooms and no floors: just a roof and four walls with a carpet of blackthorns growing inside. My superiors decided there was neither the time nor resources to excavate the site.

But there was something else in the Barkers' home. Something my colleagues ignored. Something dismissed as evidence of Roy Barker's madness which I now refuse to discount: a vulgar out-of-print children's book, *Myths & Legends of Northern Kent*.

I have recently tracked down the author: a goat farmer on the Isle of Sheppey and a thoroughly nasty piece of work. LaVerne Tracy has yellow eyes like curdled milk and a stringy white beard dripping from his chin. The farmer resembles the beasts he rears and is a practitioner of the occult. He is in no position to write a children's book. When Tracy heard what had happened to the Barkers, he could barely contain his delight. And I could barely contain my contempt.

'Was it true?' I asked Tracy. The Wood witch Spinosa and her jackdaw familiar? The curse on the land where Silverweed stood? The jackdaw stealing heartbeats from every house? Was it true? Was it true? Was it true?

I listen back to those tapes, and my questions sound like those of a child.

All Tracy did was smile in reply. A slow, sly, greasy smile.

A smile from the guilty who know something you don't. A smile that said, 'You decide.'

When the truth escapes them, people turn to fiction. Murderers find comfort in lies. The paranoid seek truth in conspiracies. I am not a superstitious man. Superstition is a corruption of the facts. And yet . . .

Every crime scene I attended, there was always a jackdaw circling. Watching and waiting above the rooftops, like a vulture would a corpse.

Silverweed Road is shaped like a J. J for jackdaw.

The street lies on the Corvid Estate. Latin for jackdaw is *corvus monedula*.

When I revisit the files, it is everywhere I look. The jackdaw in Dr Akoto's log. The bird painted by Cleo Marsh. The black feather flights of Terry Slater's darts.

Everywhere. It is everywhere. Jackdaw. Jackdaw. Jackdaw.

My former colleagues will not listen. They will not listen, no matter how many times I call. Five years have passed since those wretched events and Kent Police have buried the files. Buried, like Silverweed Road.

The corridor of mock-Tudor semis. The gravel driveways and long back gardens. They've all been demolished and paved over with concrete. The road had become a dark tourist mecca, and ghouls were stealing bricks as mementoes.

With only my shadow's company in retirement, most nights, I will sit in my car on Valerian Way, drawn to the wasteland of Silverweed Road. Knocks and taps and wooden clicks drum from the Woods beyond. Slowly but surely, blackthorns are breaking through the concrete, and steadily growing in number. The Woods have crossed the road's dead-end, claiming back the land.

And in the dead of night, the jackdaw comes, casting its

shadow over the site. It drops its seeds and pecks at the concrete, where Silverweed's houses once stood. I picture the dead and the disappeared, haunted by shame for the cases unsolved, possessed by suspicions beyond all reason.

I am not a superstitious man. Superstition is a corruption of the facts. But the same question circles, as a vulture would a corpse, and it simply won't leave me alone.

Can you arrest a bird? I ask myself. Can you arrest a bird?

Acknowledgments

As I write this, two jackdaws are nesting in the chimney. I wish I was joking. They arrived long after the book was finished and I often hear their calls, leaking down the flue into the bedroom fireplace. I love jackdaws. They're my favourite bird. I hope this book hasn't annoyed them.

Before I give thanks, a brief word on the stories. That tickle of inspiration, what I like to call the Pleasure Shiver, can come from the strangest places. Some stories were inspired by artists: Mark Rothko's 1968 *Untitled (Black)* painting for 'The Pool', Francisco Goya's *Ghostly Vision* for 'The Mogon'. Some, like 'Cuttlefish, Cuttlefish', reflect a personal obsession (if you've never seen *Incredible Suckers* by the late Mike deGruy, you're missing out on the greatest nature documentary ever filmed). And some . . . Well, some were just amusing ideas that bumped around my head like a wonky, haunted shopping trolley. 'Caught Red-handed', for instance, started life as a Biblical vision – the blooded doors of Exodus' Passover – only to mutate into a parable of late-stage capitalism. Does it matter you know this?

329

Probably not. As for 'Darts with the Devil', my sincere apologies to the incomparable Clive Barker. How *The Hellbound Heart*, one of the finest horror novellas ever written, ended up in a story about darts is a mystery I still can't answer.

This book simply wouldn't exist without Natasha Bardon, who was there at the very beginning. Her wisdom, encouragement, and horror nous can't be underestimated. My thanks extend to the HarperVoyager family: Vicky Leech Mateos, Jack Rennisson, and Elizabeth Vaziri. Legends every one, as is my agent Phil Patterson, who I thank for his sanity, enthusiasm, and lousy jokes.

The following names won't mean much to you, but they mean the world to me. Endless gratitude goes to Emlyn Rees, Josie Lloyd, Andy Lowe, Danny Wallace, Jonathan Crocker, Dan Jolin, Nick de Semlyen, *Empire* magazine past and present, *Stylist* Family, the Medway Towns, and the depthless well of love and support that is mum and dad. I'm lucky to have you. As I am Polster ('You're so cool . . .'). She has no idea I'm going to thank the gerbils. Barry, Lyndon, Redmond, Feeny: what times we had. And thank you for not eating the manuscript. A horror book thanking gerbils. There goes the gravitas.

But most of all, thank you, mysterious reader, for making it this far. Without your eyes and ears, I'm just another lunatic talking to myself.